Dan & Nancy—
My daddy's favorite
Eastern friends. Lots
of love & blessings!
♡ Jen
[illegible]

Knowing Amelia

Jen Atkinson

Ink & Quill Publishers
Henderson, NV
2016

Line/Content Editor: Denice Whirmore
Interior Design & Formatting: Jo Wilkins
Cover: Amber Schmidt of Announcing You

ISBN: 978-1-941271-12-4/Paperback
ISBN: 978-1-941271-17-9/E-Book

1. Fiction/Romance/Contemporary
2. Fiction/Romance/Family Life
3. Fiction/Romance/General

www.iqpublishers.com
Published and Printed in the United States

For my momma
Kay Bell

My Doris Day, Julia Roberts, Meg Ryan,
chick-flick partner in crime.
I miss your beautiful face every minute of every day.
You would have liked this one.

Acknowledgements

I started writing this book in the early part of 2009; at the end of that year it was half done. But also at the end of that year my mother passed away. My heart was broken and every time I sat down to write, I couldn't. I'd force myself to sit in front of the computer and then the only thing that would flow were my tears. Several months later I started up again, but it was difficult, harder than it had ever been before and I didn't finish until sometime in 2011. It felt different. It felt as if I'd woven a piece of my heart into the pages of this book. So, first I thank my mom who loved me, her little girl, so fiercely. My life will be forever blessed.

I need to thank Great Grandma Minnie, whom I never met, but whose own journal sparked the idea for this novel. I don't know enough about Minnie to know if she and Amelia are anything alike, but I do know she had some passion written in the few journal entries I read. And she's got a pretty wonderful great grandson whom I happen to be in love with.

Thank you to the readers who bought, read, and loved *LIKE HOME*. You have made my first experience as an author seriously awesome—with beautiful reviews and so much support. I wish I could thank you all individually.

To my ARC readers- Thank you for your time, effort, and reviews! It's not an easy task, but one I greatly appreciate.

Thank you to my beta readers of this book, Amy, Samantha, and Heidi. You serve me so much. Your love and help make me want to sit down and pump out another chapter just to hear your reaction. I need to give a special thanks to Heidi who might actually love this book as much as I do. You've probably read it almost as many times as I have too. Thank you for your time and expertise and for shutting down my doubt whenever it tried to take over.

To Denice, my editor. I love you! We are like friends who need to come face to face one day. Thank you for being blunt! Thank you for challenging me and making what I do and what I love that much better. To Jo, my publisher, thank you for making this all possible and for doing it with kindness. To Amber, who created my cover. I had a vision and you made it a hundred times better! Thank you!!

Huge, giant, gazillion thanks to my family. To my dad for being so proud of me and bragging about me every chance you get. To my sisters, Kris and Beck—you are too good to me and I am so thankful and blessed to be your baby sister. And to my other sisters, Amy, Kristi, and Jodi—thank you for your support and love. It means so much! Thank you to my brother, Greg—you wrote me that fake acceptance letter from some made up publisher back in 1991 and I was too excited to realize it was all a joke. One day I'll forgive you ...but really, you're the best brother a girl could ask for and I'm so grateful for your example and love. To Ron and Kathy- thank you for loving me and being proud of me, for reading what I've written and asking others to do the same. I'm forever grateful we're family.

To my own precious little family, Jeff—my favorite person on the planet, thank you for loving me, for inspiring me, for supporting me, for being the man you are. Tim, Landon, Seth, and Sydney—my other favorite people. You are my precious angels who make my days worthwhile. Tim- you amaze me on a regular basis. You are kind and loving and forgiving and an example to your mom. Landon- I don't know anyone like you, my boy. You have such a beautiful, giving soul. You're someone I could write a book about—you are a star! To Seth, my baby boy- when you took my book, *LIKE HOME,* to your third grade class as your reading material I wanted to cry. You are the sweetest kid I know. Thank you, darling, for being you. To my Sydney- what would I do without you? You keep me smiling and on my toes at all times! You make sure life is always good and always a surprise. I am certain your Grandma Kay sent you down to me and that is a gift I will never be able to repay.

Lastly, I would be nothing without my loving Heavenly Father. For all that I am, for all that I expressed gratitude for in this note, and for all that I love, He has given me.

Knowing Amelia

Chapter 1

Blinking awake, my eleven-year old head pounded like my baby sister had taken a hammer to it. *Oh yeah. They abandoned me.* How could Dad do that?

'Olivia, I'm sorry, you'll have to stay here with your grandmother,' Dad had said. How could he leave me here with his grouchy old mom, just because I'd gotten sick? Why were they out exploring anyway? Weren't we here for Grandpa's funeral? Grandma hadn't even cried. Weren't wives supposed to cry when their husbands died? She had one layer—grouchy.

At least I didn't have to *see* grumpy Amelia. I'd been napping in this dusty old bedroom all morning.

Climbing out of Amelia's spare bed, I crept over to the bedroom window. I stared up at the big elm in her yard—tall, beautiful, and never grouchy. Down on the ground, I spotted a curly haired boy on the grass. He dribbled a soccer ball between his feet, right next to the elm. He laughed, and I smiled down at him. He kicked his ball, flinging it high into the air. Jumping, he hit the black and white ball with his head, smacking it into the side of Amelia's house.

"Logan Heyborn!" Grandma yelled. Grandma was grumpy—always, always grumpy—but I'd never heard her yell before.

With both of my palms against the cold windowpane, two stories off the ground, I stared at the laughing boy. "Run!" I whispered, knowing he couldn't hear me. "Run, boy!" What would she do to him?

Walking out into the yard, Amelia stood beside the lovely elm tree. Her folded arms didn't look right there, much too unpleasant for such a pretty tree. Her salt and pepper hair curled under at her neck and her head tilted toward the boy, who now stood out of my view. Watching the top of her head, I couldn't read her face. Maybe he *had* gotten away…

"Logan," I could just hear her voice through the glass—as if my head were dunked under water. "When did you get home?"

The boy spoke to her, but I couldn't make out what he said. Pressing my nose to the glass, I gasped. Grandma wrapped her arms around him, his dark curls just under her chin. The hug didn't last long, but it sent my heart racing just the same. Jumping away from the window, I lay my body flat against the wall—out of sight. But I had to look back, like when my brother Jared squishes a spider—I have to look, I have to see, is it really dead? Was Amelia really hugging some boy?

Their hug over, Amelia kicked the soccer ball back to Logan. Picking it up, he waved and disappeared into the house next door.

Running as fast as I could back to my bed, a shiver crawled down my back. What had I just witnessed? And why had it frightened me? I'd never seen Amelia hug anyone before.

Covering my aching head with Amelia's old quilt, I listened to my heavy breaths, in and out. It seemed no time had passed when I woke from another nap. Afternoon had come. My head still whirled with the curly haired boy. Had it really happened? Yawning, I rolled back toward the door. There beside the bed sat one of Amelia's kitchen chairs and on top of it a tray of food, a peanut butter sandwich, an apple, and a cup of orange juice. Maybe this wouldn't be so terrible. It didn't look as if I'd even have to speak to Amelia.

Sitting up, I felt like a queen, eating my meal in bed. All I needed now were my—oh, no! My books were all downstairs. I couldn't sit in this bed doing nothing all day, and I didn't have a servant—like a queen should, to order the promptness of my novels. If I kept quiet, maybe she wouldn't notice me. Maybe I could sneak downstairs and be back to the safety of my room without one grouchy glance from Grandma.

The creaking of the bedroom door screamed through Dad's old room. "Shh!" I glared at it. I tiptoed down the wooden staircase without much noise. Creeping over to the living room, I saw my things lying on Amelia's old square coffee table.

And then I heard it.

The horrible blubber came from Amelia's dining room. Jerking my head upright, I held my breath. What is it? *Who* is it?

Again, I heard a weak moan, this time followed by a cry. "Oh, Seth."

My racing heart pumped blood through my veins. My eyes widened as the cries grew louder. Each sob, just out of my view, as if it were right next to me. I took one step. *Just turn around.* Another step. *Just walk away.* One more—closer. *Just get out!* But—I had to see.

Knuckles white, I clutched my book to my chest, my heart thumping against the hard cover of *Romeo and Juliet*.

Peeking around the wall separating the two rooms, my eyes focused on the figure before me. Amelia—down on her knees in the dining area. She had moved the table and pulled up one of the wooden floorboards, leaning it against the wall, revealing a hole in the floor. A small wooden box sat beside her, its contents a mystery.

Sucking in a quiet breath, I let it go—she couldn't see me. Thank goodness her back faced me. Amelia didn't know I was there. Her body rocked back and forth with her sobs. "Seth," she said through another sob. "My Seth."

Grandma sat there crying. Her husband of more than fifty years had died and *finally*—finally she had decided to cry. Even grumpy people should cry when their husbands die.

Only my grandfather's name wasn't Seth.

Chapter 2

Eleven Years Later

Belting an old Celine Dion song to ease my nerves, I drove down the interstate. Had Benjamin really expected me to skip my last final of the year—my favorite class? *Humph! Some boyfriend.* Who cares if Dad didn't want me taking Classic Literature? It was my own little high each day and I wouldn't miss it. It's a good thing I had to go back for my suitcase of books Benjamin *forgot* to grab. We'd be together all summer long… Ben, Dad, and me. The thought made sweat pool in each of my pores. Yep, I needed my books, and ten minutes behind him—to cool off.

At least I would see my mother soon. That thought alone sweetened my sour mood.

Walking into my parent's tri-level home, I waited for the stampede—Mom, Baby, Dad. Jared might even have come home to see me.

Nothing.

"Hellooo?" I dropped my bag in the entryway.

Nothing.

Following the murmurings into my parent's kitchen, I stopped in the doorway. Dad and Benjamin sat at the table, Dad's pale arm draped around Ben's shoulders. From the back, the two looked as if they could be related—tall, thin and fair. From the front… not so much. Ben looked as if heaven couldn't be better with Jonathon Benson—of Benson and Clyde, snuggling up to him.

Mom stood at the stove, her crisp apron covering her clothes, cooking Ben a toasted cheese sandwich. Baby Katie, fifteen and not much of a baby anymore, slouched next to Dad—staring at her smartphone. Her auburn hair, just like Mom's, pinned up on her head. Her green eyes locked on the screen. No Jared.

"Hello," I said again, this time unable to keep the annoyance from my voice.

"Livy!" Dropping her phone and jumping to her feet, my baby sister ran into my arms. *At least someone's glad to see me.*

"Hello, dear," Mom said, waving her spatula at me. "Come here, come here! I'm just making Ben a snack. Do you want anything?" She flipped the sandwich in her pan and buttered another slice of bread.

Sighing, I gave my mother a side squeeze.

"It's so good to see you, Liv." She squeezed me back with her free hand.

"I can tell." I glared at Benjamin and Dad. Dad shrugged and spread his arms, no doubt telling Ben about some crazy case he'd been working on and Ben eating up every bit of it.

"Jonathon, your daughter is home." Mom tapped her foot, giving Dad her stare down.

Stopping mid-story, Dad glanced over, a huge smile on his face. "I can see that," he said, leaving poor Ben alone. "Hello, darling." Dad wrapped his arms around me.

"Hi, Daddy. It's good to see you." I melted into his warm embrace—like I was eight years old again and nothing could go wrong.

"You'll be seeing a lot of me. Eh? Eh?" He nudged my side, referring to the jobs he'd gotten for Ben and me this summer. "Ben told me about Ofero's class—"

"Oh, I know. I heard." I resisted the urge to roll my eyes. That's all Ben talked about—Dad's old law Professor—Ofero. "Hey, Mom, where do you want Ben? I'm gonna bring in the bags." I needed some air and we had two cars packed to the rim.

"Jared's old room."

"I'll help, babe," Benjamin said, getting up.

"Wait until you see my brother's room." I glanced at Ben

and laughed. "Everything is alphabetized, even his little league trophies."

Pointing a finger at me, Dad winked. "Now wait a minute. He learned that from me, and it can be very useful."

Benjamin tucked his long fingers into the pockets of his trousers. "I was just thinking that actually sounds like an ingenious idea," he said, as if alphabetizing was a novel concept.

"Oh, Livy." Mom's voice strained and stopped us from leaving the room. "Katie started cheerleading..."

"Yes." I furrowed my brow. "I know. So?"

Mom stood next to Dad, looking so petite next to him. "She's got all this extra stuff around the house." The spatula in mom's hand flailed about as she spoke.

"Pom poms," Katie said, from the table, her face pale instead of its usual pink.

"Yes." Mom pointed at Katie. "And uniforms, and... Well, honey, once Jared moved out, it seemed a little silly to have these three extra rooms and Katie in the smallest, so we—"

"You gave Katie my room?" I suppose it made sense. And I shouldn't care—but, I did. "So, I'm in her room then? Her old room, I mean." I turned toward the hall. "Okay, come on Benjamin." My voice sounded wrong, the pitch too high and fake happy.

Grabbing a couple bags, each from our own cars, we headed back into the house. Leading Ben down the hall of bedrooms, I nodded toward the first door. "This'll be my room. The next right is yours."

I'm not exactly sure what I expected when I opened Katie's door. My stuff set up in her room—just as it had been in mine—seemed deserving at least. The bed had been made with Katie's old quilt tucked in tight—like at a hotel, but the rest—blank purple walls and boxes. It looked like a storage compartment.

I turned to Ben, unable to hide the disappointment on my face.

Peeking his head inside, Benjamin looked the room over. "Homey."

Dropping my bags to the ground, I opened one of the boxes. Inside sat my drama and speech trophies. Folding the box closed,

I walked out of the moving-van-like space and opened Jared's bedroom door. It sat just as he had left it—untouched. Staring across the hall to my real room, I frowned. My *real* room, with its built in bookshelves and pretty green paint. Those shelves had been filled with my love—with my books, dozens of authors and titles that were now sitting in dark cardboard boxes. I wrinkled my forehead and pouted, realizing that those shelves would be covered in things like pom poms and dance shoes now. How awful.

Leaving Ben to unpack, I opened up my old bedroom door. I gasped at the bright pink covering my pale green. Tears welled in my eyes. No pompoms covered my built in bookshelves, they had been ripped out. They didn't even exist anymore. I gaped at my reflection in the floor to ceiling mirror and the vanity centered in front of it.

"Wow, bright." Ben surprised me. "This doesn't look like you."

Knocking the door with my fist, it bumped into him. "Don't you remember my room? This isn't how it looked at all. It was green and there was a—" I choked on my words. "A bookshelf built into the back wall."

"That's right, it looked like a library." He shrugged his shoulders. "I guess I forgot."

"Prrph!" I stomped past him into my storage-bedroom, throwing a little twenty-two year old tantrum.

Grabbing my arm, Ben stopped me. "Sweetie, it's just a room. I'm sorry I didn't remember it. Besides, why should you care? Isn't your real room back in Los Angeles?" Ben's thin lips pouted outward.

Sometimes Benjamin made complete sense. I am a grown up girl. I have my own apartment. He was right—he was good at being right. "Yes, yes it is," I said, my tone even and believable.

I ignored the whisper of my name over and over. I was home, in my bed, and the comfort of it wasn't worth disturbing. My shoulders shook. Benjamin repeated my name, interrupting my rest. "Olivia. Livy, wake up. Olivia."

Blinking in the dark room, my eyes adjusted to the dark. I was home. I was in *my* bed, *my* room, but it was wrong. The brightness of Katie's pink illuminated the darkness. That's right. It wasn't my room anymore. Beside me lay Katie, under her new comforter, her auburn hair strewn across her face, sound asleep. We talked and giggled until late—until we both fell asleep.

Stifling a yawn, I whispered, "What time is it?"

Pulling at my arms, Ben stood me up. "Nearly two a.m."

"Two a.m.?" And he was still awake? Benjamin was an early to bed, early to rise kind of a guy. "What have you been doing?"

His fine blonde hair roostered up in the back. "Dad and I were talking. You never said goodnight, so I came looking for you."

I hated when he referred to my father as "Dad", but I was too tired to make a fuss. "I must have fallen asleep while talking to Katie."

Guiding me down the hallway and into my room, Benjamin pulled back the blanket on my bed.

"Thank you, Benjamin." He was good to me. I shouldn't be so hard on him. "I need to change out of my clothes though."

"Okay, sure." But he didn't leave. He stepped in closer and sat next to me. Putting a hand on the back of my neck, he leaned down, his lips engrossing mine, soft and gentle. Parting my mouth, he kissed my bottom lip, his free hand falling about my waist. I moved my hands up to his face and held him there, connected to me. The shrill ring of a phone startled me and I loosened my grip around his neck. Pulling back, he smiled, beaming down at me, and I grinned back.

This is when I loved Benjamin the most, when he put his heart out there. When he showed me how much he cared. This is when I could imagine our future together.

Ben's hand ran the length of my long strawberry-blonde hair and over to my cheek. "We're going to have an amazing summer here."

Nodding, I closed my eyes and leaned into his touch.

"Your dad is… is… amazing."

And the moment vanished. Not exactly what a girl expects after a kiss like that. "He is." I studied Ben. I loved our moments.

I felt our moments—but did he?

I had read Jane Austen's *Pride and Prejudice* a hundred times. Had memorized the first line by the time I was twelve. Staring at the man before me, it popped into my head. *It is a truth universally acknowledged, that a single man in possession of a good fortune, must be in want of a wife.* But what constituted wealth? Did a successful father count?

"Benjamin, did you know in the 1800's women and men were often sought after, married even, solely for their fortunes. Isn't that… sad? I'm sure it still happens today."

Cocking his head, he squinted at me. "You are a funny girl, Olivia Benson." Laughing, he leaned in, placing a quick peck on my mouth. "Night, hon."

"Good night, Benjamin." I watched him leave, repressing thoughts of being sought after for the good fortune of having been born Jonathon Benson's daughter. I knew better. Right? He was in this—committed, just like me.

Sighing and running my hands over my tired eyes, I glanced at the alarm clock I'd plugged in, 2:12 a.m. The humming of my parent's voices reached my room. Who would call at this hour? Thinking of my brother living away from home, I jumped out of bed. He would arrive later in the week. Had something happened to Jared?

I hurried out into the living room, but didn't interrupt the ongoing conversation between my parents.

"I don't know, Shelly. I have four new people coming in tomorrow, including Benjamin and Olivia."

"Jonathon, you have to go. You aren't seriously considering *not* going. Work can wait."

Facing each other, neither Mom nor Dad noticed my presence. Dad said nothing in reply to Mom. What were they talking about? It couldn't be Jared, my mother would be panicked, and my father would be in motion—acting, ready to fix the problem. So, what *was* the problem?

"She's your mother, Jonathon!"

Amelia? We hadn't seen my estranged Wyomingite grandmother in years. I couldn't imagine *Amelia* causing this much stress.

"I know, damn it! I don't need *you* to make me feel guilty. The absent years are doing that already." Dad rarely raised his voice and he never swore. He was a lawyer for heaven's sake. He had his own special dictionary when it came to confrontation. He had no use for words like damn.

I'd never seen my parents argue, let alone fight. I couldn't sit there quiet any longer. "What's going on?"

Dad's head snapped around and then right back to Mom. He'd always leaned on her gentle ways to talk to us kids.

Pinching her lips together, Mom stared back at him.

The air grew thick with their silent tension. "It's Amelia," he said, not calling her mother or grandma, like a son should. "She's dead."

Chapter 3

Emotions are a strange thing. No one cried. Dad was upset, but not for the right reasons. It took me back almost a dozen years to when Burt, Grandpa Benson, died. I knew then no one had expressed the right feelings. Now it happened all over, but that was somehow normal when it came to Dad's family.

But the craziest thing of all? *Me.* My throat swelled and my eyes stung, threatening tears. My body worked its hardest to fall apart. Fighting the oncoming blink, I refused to let a tear fall. This is ridiculous. I'd look absurd if I broke down over *Amelia*. I hadn't seen the woman in eleven years. I never went back to that little Wyoming town again. Why on earth should I be grieving?

When I graduated from high school, I sent her an announcement. Dad had said it wasn't necessary, but I wanted to. For some bizarre reason I needed to. I never heard from her though. Not one word. No card. Not even a phone call. Nothing. So, why did I have to turn to wipe away a betraying tear?

Ignoring me, Mom and Dad returned to their ongoing discussion. Pushing my emotions to the side, I took a deep breath. I turned toward them again just in time to hear Dad say, "It's bad timing. I can't leave."

"Wait." I held up my hands. "What are you talking about?"

Jumping, he turned to me, blowing out a puff of air. "The funeral, it's in three days."

"Jonathon— " Mom's protest came out weak.

"Stop." Flailing my hands about, I shook my strawberry

hair—a combination of Dad's blonde and Mom's red. "Are you trying to decide whether or not you're going?" I already knew the answer. My eyes pricked with moisture again, and my face burned.

"Well..." Dad's stare didn't waver from mine. "Yes."

Jutting my head back, I gawked at him like I never had before. What was he saying? Shaking my head, disgusted at his words, I turned my stare to the ground, not wanting to meet his eyes.

"It's the *office,* Olivia." His arms crossed over his chest. "Not only do I have four new employees, but I've got a big case that would be nearly impossible to leave behind."

Unable to bring my head up, I let one tear fall and then another. So what if they both thought I was crazy. I was certain in that moment he *was* crazy. Looking him in the eye, I whispered, "Three employees."

Cocking his head, Dad blinked half a dozen times. "What do you mean, three?"

"I'll be going to my grandmother's funeral." My voice rang cold in the air. I was exhausted—from the time of night, from trying to please my father my entire life, from the news just given—and I didn't care if my actions disappointed him. "So, you'll only have three employees to train."

"Olivia Jane Benson." He said through gritted teeth.

I could not believe *he* was scolding *me*. "I'm not five years old."

"You don't understand. You're not living in the real world yet. I have responsibilities."

"The real world? What world am I living in then?" I had never disrespected him, but I couldn't leave this alone.

His pale face grew red to the tips of his ears. His eyes squinted together, he took a step closer to me and glared down at my frozen face. "When you pay your own car insurance, you can declare yourself living in the real world!"

"I never asked—"

"No, you didn't." His arms tightened in their hold and his red face turned a purple eggplant shade. "And you didn't ask for your college fund either, but your mother and I provided that too."

"I'm not ungrateful, but I'm not naïve either. I know you've provided well for us. I know you have to work. But Amelia was your *mother*. Doesn't that mean anything?" He acted as though she were a mere acquaintance, and maybe on some level she was, but she raised him, gave birth to him.

His face softened and loosening the knot he had tied his arms into, he put a gentle hand on my shoulder. "Of course honey, but this is an insane season at work right now."

Again my irritation boiled over into fury. I shrugged out of his caress—feeling no warmth in it now. "Of course. How thoughtless of Amelia to die during your busy time of year. Maybe you'll make it to her *next* funeral." With that I stomped off to my room—substitute room, and slammed the door behind me, reassuring my parents of my complete and total immaturity.

Lying on my bed, I shut my eyes and saw her there. Amelia, kneeling upon the ground, weeping over a secret treasure box from beneath a missing floorboard in her dining room. She turned to me, screaming. "Discover the real world!"

Panting, I woke, wet strands of hair sticking to my sweaty forehead. I sat up in Katie's old room. My hands went to work searching the dark for the lamp I'd propped onto a moving box beside the bed. I found my green bag—my book bag. Fingering through each book I found it, Jane Austen's *Pride and Prejudice.* Rummaging through my bag once more, I found a pen and opened to the back of the book. The blank back cover. And then I filled it—with everything I could remember of Amelia, of the day I found her. The box. The floorboards. The weeping. Logan, the curly haired boy. Seth? And when she turned—she saw me, without a doubt she saw me. I ran, as fast as my eleven-year-old legs would carry me. I ran to my room and hid under the quilt. She never came for me though. She never yelled.

Later, when my family came back, I set the dinner table. We were alone in the dining room, and I was more afraid of her than ever, but then she asked about one of my books, *Pride and Prejudice.*

I told her yes, I was reading it. She gave me the smallest of smiles. It wasn't the smile I imagine she gave to the curly haired boy, but still her mouth peeked. She told me it was her favorite book. That was it, the last—really the only conversation we ever had.

And maybe, it's the reason I never told anyone her secret.

Chapter 4

Rushing into the great room, I wasn't sure of my plan. Would I drive the twenty hours to Wyoming alone? Would Katie and Jared want to come? Should I apologize to my father or see if he'd change his mind? I didn't know, but with Amelia's funeral just three days away—maybe two now, I didn't have time for an elite plan. I needed to act.

Mom sat at the kitchen bar, her short legs crossed. "Hi, sweetie." She stayed neutral last night. Crossing my arms, I glared at her. I knew she agreed with me.

"Mom." Nodding, I tried to keep the irritation out of my voice. "Where is everyone?"

"Katie's at school, Dad and Benjamin went in to work."

"Work!" Shoving my fist into my mouth to stop from cursing in front of her, my short lived annoyance with Mom all but left. I had forgotten about work. "With Amelia… I totally spaced…"

"Don't worry about it. You told your father to plan on only three employees, remember?" Breathing out, Mom clasped her hands together, giving me her do-I-need-to-say-it-out-loud face.

"Yeah, I remember." Bowing my head, I rolled my eyes.

"Well, didn't you mean it?"

"… Yeah, I did. I just…"

"You just what?" She raised her eyebrows and smiled. "Said what you thought and now you're regretting it? Don't. You were right. Well, you were mostly right. 'Maybe you can go to her next funeral,' was a little overboard."

I scrunched my face and put a hand over my eyes. "I didn't

mean to get so irate. I just don't understand him. How can he not go?"

"Oh, I'm pretty sure you changed his mind. He was up half the night. He's making the arrangements, for both of you, as we speak." Mom scooped her auburn hair behind an ear and took my hands in hers. "What I really don't understand, is why *you* want to go. Don't get me wrong, Liv, I'm glad you do. I'm glad you persuaded your dad when I couldn't, but you barely knew her, honey. You were afraid of her. Why is this so important to you?"

"I don't know." I shook my head at her question. "I can't explain. It just is."

"Fair enough." Smiling, she gave my hands a pat. "You better go pack. You'll be leaving in an hour or so."

"Ben—"

"He'll be fine. He's made himself right at home, and he was thrilled to go to work this morning."

I nodded, she was right. He'd been waiting for this opportunity forever. "So, just the two of us then?" I blew out a sigh. This would be interesting.

I threw my large over-stuffed backpack into the rear seat of Dad's Cadillac, holding my cell between my cheek and shoulder. "I know, Benjamin, I'm sorry. It's just—"

"And you're taking Dad to this woman's funeral because..."

"Because this *woman* was his mother."

"And Mom said—"

It was a good thing this was a phone conversation, I may have decked him. I squeezed the receiver, my face burning up. "Well, *Mom* and *Dad* realize that marriage and life are about compromise. Maybe that's something we need to learn."

"Marriage?" Ben's laugh boomed through the receiver. "Livy, are you telling me you want to get married?"

"Me?" I gripped the phone until my knuckles hurt. "Well, no. I mean, not right—"

"Of course not. Neither do I. We aren't our parents."

That was news to me. I was pretty sure he was trying his best to replicate my father.

"We are today's generation, a modern generation, aren't we? Marriage!" He chuckled again. "Like we'd enter into a contract people like us are born to break."

The dead silence between Dad and me during our travel made hours feel more like days. He said all of five words to me on the flight and in the airport. From Billings, we had a two-hour drive into Rendezvous—two hours that could easily make this day the longest of my life.

About to drown in the awkward silence, I cleared my throat. "Where are we staying?" *Where were we staying?* If we stayed at Amelia's, would I get the chance to look under her floorboards? Not with Dad, I'd have to figure out how to get him out of the house.

Dad's eyes didn't waver from the road. "There's one motel in town, I guess we'll stay there."

Squished between my knees, I pinched my hands together. "What about… Amelia's?"

"What about it?"

"Why not stay there?"

"Because, we're not." His answer was what he'd give to a pesky six-year-old who wouldn't stop asking questions. When had I regressed in age?

"Will Uncle Red and Uncle Earl be there?" I'd met my dad's younger brothers as many times as Amelia, twice. The two looked just alike, inches shorter than Dad, dark and bald on top.

"I'm sure Earl will be. He's the one who called. Red's off adventuring again." He had both hands on the wheel, ten and two, never deviating from that position.

"Does it make you sad?" When he didn't answer right away I continued, "To think of her… gone?"

He sighed, and I couldn't tell if it was sadness or annoyance at my questions. "Yes, Olivia, it makes me sad. I'm not as heartless as you think."

The inches of space between us seemed more like miles. I stared at this man I thought I knew so well. I knew his features, his long, lean body and handsome face, his fair, full hair. I knew him, yet I didn't. "I know you aren't heartless, that's why I'm confused. You don't seem upset." I repressed the urge to bring up the fact that I had guilted him into going to his mom's funeral.

"I loved my mother. However, we had a difficult relationship. My relationship with Burt, my dad, was even more complicated, and it fed the complexity between Amelia and me." He glanced at me and then back to the road. "She told me over and over again that I didn't belong in Rendezvous—that I needed to venture out. She never said that to my brothers, Olivia. It was like she built a wedge between me and the rest of them. I didn't ask for it to be that way." His eyes narrowed and he stared ahead. "So, I left. And eventually, I saw my parents less and less. The less I saw of them the easier it seemed to be—on all of us. I knew one day I'd get this phone call. It was inevitable. Am I sad? Sure, but you can't miss what you don't have. And I haven't had a mother for a very long time."

I didn't know what to say. I almost felt bad for him. He was good at arguing, good at justifying his absence in her life. He was good at Benson and Clyde-ing it.

Dad took an in-the-middle-of-nowhere exit, that after a while fused into Rendezvous, Wyoming. Things sat just where my eleven-year-old memory had left them. We drove down one of the two paved roads. I remembered the one store in town, Farmer's. Dirt roads stretched off the main one, lined with little homes the way I remembered Amelia's. Some had grassy yards, some just dirt, and trees were very rare. A mountain sat behind the town, layered in three colors, brown bottom, green speckled middle, and white snowy top.

"Where to first?" I asked, my mind still digging up floorboards. How could I get alone time in that house?

"Earl asked me to go by her workplace. Pick up her things. Then we're driving into Cody to see her lawyer." He cleared his throat. "Ironic, isn't it. Her son's a partner in one of Southern California's most successful firms, and she hires some small town attorney from Wyoming to handle her affairs."

I pressed my lips together, locking my thoughts inside before they could burst out. He wouldn't like my thoughts. It was rare for me to vocally disagree with him. Still, I couldn't imagine Dad coming to this little town to handle a will and testament. Nope. Not in a million years.

"Where did Amelia work?"

"The high school."

That quiet, ill-tempered woman worked with... *kids*? "What did she do?"

Chuckling at my tone of voice, Dad didn't defend her profession. Amelia working with kids must not seem right to him either. After all, he knew her better than I did. Didn't he?

"I think she worked in the office," he said. "I know she didn't have a teaching degree."

Pulling into the small parking lot, Dad took one of two available spaces. There was one lot, but two buildings, one to the left and one to the right of the parking area. "Do you know where we're going?"

"I did go to school here, Olivia."

"Oh. That's right." I never pictured him anywhere but California. He never talked about Rendezvous.

"That's the high school." He pointed to the building at our left, the smaller of the two.

"They aren't both the high school?" The two buildings could fit inside my high school two and half times.

Dad shook his head. "No. That one's the elementary, K through eight."

"You're kidding?"

"There's only three hundred people in the entire town, Olivia. You're graduating class had more than that."

Stepping out of the car, I looked down at my clothes and squirmed. Dad wore his suit everywhere, but with the flight and the drive, I opted for cut off sweats and a T-shirt. Pulling at the ends of my faded, oversized, Big Mac T-shirt, I attempted to flatten the wrinkles. Splitting my ponytail in two, I yanked at the ends to tighten my sloppy do. "Uhh, maybe I should change. I didn't know we'd be going to her workplace."

"What did you think we were going to do here?"

"Well, I figured we'd be taking care of a few things." I flailed my hands about following him to the front of the school. "I assumed we'd be helping at her house." At least I hoped. I needed to see under those boards and inside that box. I needed to know who *Seth* was.

With a wave of his hand he dismissed my worries. "It's not as if you'll see any of these people again."

"I know, but they knew Amelia. They'll soon know I'm her granddaughter."

"Olivia, please."

"Fine!" Forcing my way in front of him I opened the double doors. A soft bell gonged throughout the building. There was no hustling or bustling of students in the hallways though. A handful of students exited the two doors in my view and shuffled off.

Dad walked past me and I followed after him when a boy from the drinking fountain cut me off. His eyebrows rose much too high on his head as he looked me over. "You *must* be new."

Did he think I was still in high school?

His eyes roved up and then down.

Clasping my hands together, I attempted to cover the giant hamburger on my chest. "No, I'm not. I'm much older than you."

"I'm guessing not." He laughed and stuck out his hand. "I'm Roy. What's your name?"

Staring at his outstretched hand, I pushed passed him. "Excuse me, *Roy*." Apparently RHS didn't get many visitors. I must be the new item on Rendezvous' menu. Ignoring his stare burning into my backside, I scurried after Dad to the main office.

A small, older, unnaturally blonde woman sat at one of the two desks. Her table lay covered with little pug figurines, half a dozen picture frames and a plate reading *Rachel Lemonade*. Her mouth turned down in a frown, despite all the laugh lines framing it.

The desk next to her held a stack of books, a mug with the Rendezvous High logo on the front and a nameplate with Amelia's name printed on it but zero personal items. *Lucky guess, Dad.*

The woman didn't look up from her paperwork. "What can I

do ya for?"

"I'm Jonathon—"

"Benson!" Her head shot up. Standing, she held her arms out as if Dad would fall into them and hug her. "Oh, Jonathon, well you've made me the mixer in the kitchen—"

"The mixer?" My eyes darted to Dad and back to the woman.

"The happiest of all the kitchen appliances." She nodded and kept right on talking. "Earl called, said you'd be coming. Oh, Jonathon, I am so happy to see you." Her laugh lines creased. "I can't say how sorry I am about your momma." She sighed, her head turning to me. "And you've brought with you..."

"My daughter, Olivia." Dad set a hand on my back and I crossed my arms to hide the giant hamburger covering my front.

"Hmm..." Her lips pursed together, she hadn't heard of me. "Pleased as apple pie to meet you. I'm Rachel, Rachel Lemonade, but then Jonathon knows that."

Dad's eyes widened just a touch. He *didn't* know that.

"Your grandmother will be greatly missed." She sniffled, taking a tissue from her pocket. "This was her desk." Rachel's voice cracked. "We've got an empty box here for you." She pointed to the ground. "We didn't want to disturb anything though. Thought family should be doing that."

Dad went to work, and I stood feeling Rachel Lemonade's eyes on me. I cleared my throat, trying to think of small talk to make with Rachel when Dad covered the box with its lid. "Thank you for your help, Misses Lemonade."

Her hands twisted at her chest. "We'll see you tomorrow."

"You're coming to the funeral then?" I asked.

With a loud hiccup Rachel said, "Of course I am. We all are. School's been canceled for the day so we can all pay our respects."

We left Rachel Lemonade and walked toward the school's exit. *They canceled school? Wow.* "Do you think the whole school will really be there tomorrow?"

"I'm sure they will. It's only around thirty-five students and a few staff members. A town this size, everyone knows everyone and no one has any secrets."

Putting my hand on the front door, I stopped. "I wonder if

that's true."

"What?" He pushed the door open for me.

"The no secrets part."

Dad laughed, but I didn't. My mind flashed to Amelia on her knees crying for a person named Seth.

"Livy?" Dad waved his hand in front of my eyes. "What's with you?"

"Sorry." I shook my head.

Shrugging, he trudged his way through the door, stopped just outside, and tossed Amelia's shoebox into the nearby garbage can.

Reaching for the box, I pulled it from the metal can. "Dad!" This wasn't him. He was so uncaring and mean when it came to his home, to his family. He never acted like that with us kids. If anything, he cared too much.

"Olivia, do you know what's in there?"

"N-no." I hugged the box to my chest. "But does that matter? It was hers, we came here to *collect* her things, not *toss* her things. Misses Lemonade could have done that."

"She could have, but she wouldn't. I'll tell you what's in there, an RHS mug and some number two pencils." Huffing, he pushed his car door open. "What is this fixation you suddenly have with your grandmother?"

"I don't have a fixation with her." I glared at him. "I just think someone should care about her and her things, and… her life."

He stared at me like I spoke a foreign language he didn't understand. We climbed into the rental car, Dad's face still scrunched in annoyance and me still clinging to Amelia's box of nothing.

Chapter 5

Dad's chuckles filled the car as I gaped out the window. This tourist town had much more going on than Rendezvous. The streets were lined with interesting shops and different places to eat. I had zero memory of the place, not having been here in eighteen years. The beauty of the aged brick, peeling paint and architecture of each building entranced me. It was as if we'd stepped back in time.

Coming to a stop in front of a large building at the corner, I angled my neck to take in the place of business. The faded brown brick ran along each side of the block, the entrance at the corner. A picket fence—or so it seemed—ran along the top, and at the corner in peach colored letters it read, *The IRMA*. Another sign hung from the lower section of the building, *IRMA Buffalo Bill's Original Hotel in the Rockies*. Near it, a smaller sign painted in red letters read, *IRMA Grill*.

My stomach roared with glee. "When are we meeting her attorney?"

"We've got about fifteen minutes before he shows up." Giving me the once over, Dad scratched his head. "Hmm, maybe you *should* change."

Already reaching for my bag in the back seat, I hurried through the doors of the IRMA. Taking in the spacious room, I said its name to myself, "Irma."

"It's named for Buffalo Bill's daughter, Irma Louise."

"Huh." *How did he know that?* The deep cherry wood bar ran down the length of the wall. Walking past the vintage cash register, its digits like old typewriter keys, I made my way to the bathroom near the back. I rummaged through the few things I'd brought. *What does one wear when meeting their deceased, estranged, country grandmother's lawyer?* I decided on jeans and my turquoise blouse with the ruffles down the front. It could go dressy or casual and it never looked messy, due to the wrinkled material. I took out my rubber band and ran a brush through my red tangles, but the ponytail bump persisted. Swooping it back up, I pulled my hair into a cleaner looking do.

Like a new woman, I emerged from the bathroom—it's amazing what brushed teeth and a clean shirt will do.

Dad wasn't alone at our table. The heavy, balding man to his left didn't look much like dad, but I recognized my Uncle Earl. The third man was older than Dad, his western shirt snapped to the throat, and his full head of hair an unmanageable salt and pepper, Amelia's lawyer.

With a wave, Dad motioned for me to sit. "Mr. Marx, this is my daughter, Olivia Benson."

"I see." Mr. Marx pushed his round, black rimmed glasses up on the bridge of his nose. "Glad you could make it, Miss Benson."

"Thank you." I took a seat next to Dad and leaned over whispering, "Hello, Earl."

Uncle Earl gave a small grin. He never was much of a talker—that I remember, anyway.

"May we just get right down to it?" Dad knew the drill—no sense wasting time.

Mr. Marx took a swig of his beer which meant I'd missed the waitress. *Dang it!* Dad and Earl had drinks in front of them as well. My stomach growled, reminding me, in case I'd forgotten—I was starving. I hadn't planned on paying too much attention to the legal mumbo jumbo—that was Dad's job. I wanted to eat!

Mr. Marx passed out paper work to Earl, Dad, and me. Dad scanned over the first page. Leaning over to him, I whispered, "Is the waitress coming back? I wanted to order."

Giving me a short glance, he said, "I got you a drink." He slid the water glass in front of him over to me. Ignoring my grimace, he looked up from his paperwork. "Is this figure correct? It says here this will was prepared only four years ago." Squinting, he adjusted the paper in front of him, his brows furrowing.

"Yes, everything's correct and up to date." Mr. Marx gulped down another swallow. "Now, Amelia was fairly specific about all of her assets. If something seems to be unassigned, she'd like Earl to decide where it goes, be her executor."

Dad sighed, and I could hear his complaints in my head. What did she have to give? Who would want her other meaningless shoebox items?

"First to her children: to her eldest, Jonathon, she's left her lucky silver dollar." Mr. Marx took another gulp from his drink.

Looking neither pleased nor disappointed, Dad nodded. I sat up, ignoring my empty stomach, and listened. This must have been important to her, or why would she have taken the time and paid the money to make it law.

"To her second son, Earl," Mr. Marx nodded toward Uncle Earl. "Is given her full savings and checking—at least what's left after her funeral expenses, and the family photo albums, there are four total."

"From what these figures offer, there should be a fair amount of money left over." Dad ran his finger down the length of the numbers on his current page.

Earl sniffed, but didn't show much emotion.

I flipped through the booklet not having followed along well enough to know where we were.

"Should be," Mr. Marx said. "For the youngest son, Red, Amelia's assigned her 1983 Camaro."

"Of course." A muffled laugh escaped Uncle Earl's lips.

"Yep, I was waiting for that." Dad glanced at Earl and smiled.

I never heard about a Camaro that made Dad smile like a little boy. A *good* memory? I'd have to ask him later.

"May I?" Mr. Marx eyed the two over top of his glasses.

Swallowing the rest of their laughter, Dad and Earl clammed up like school kids in trouble.

"All righty then. The title to her home and everything within it belongs to a Miss..." He adjusted his glasses and flipped to the next page of Amelia's will. "Ah-hah." Mr. Marx made eye contact with me. "A Miss Olivia Benson."

The truth of his words lay in print on the page in front of me. I bounced back, knocking my knees into the table and rattling everyone's drinks.

Saving his last drop of beer, Mr. Marx snatched his mug with both hands.

"Me?" My head whipped from Dad to Earl and back again.

Dad grimaced, Earl smiled, and Mr. Marx lapped up the remainder of his drink.

Setting his mug down with an empty clang, Mr. Marx said, "Yes, Miss, you."

"This is a mistake," Dad said through gritted teeth. Mr. Marx shook his head and half a second later, Dad jumped to his feet, bent over with his fists planted on the tabletop. "It has to be. My mother hardly knew Olivia." He snatched the form from Mr. Marx—the same pages that sat in front of him, and scanned them over. "This is ridiculous."

Staring until my eyes watered, my name came in and out of focus. "Why would she leave me so much?" I couldn't imagine I'd meant anything to her. Yet, she had left me almost all of her possessions.

Quiet, Earl smiled at me. "Don't know."

"Ridiculous... Preposterous... Completely and totally ludicrous." Dad mumbled to himself all the way out to the car. "Why on earth my mother would leave you... Ahh! Ridiculous."

Shuffling after him, I pinched my lips closed, keeping my silence.

Still ranting to himself he crawled into the rental car.

Breathing deep—and away from his rants inside the car, I tried to make sense of it all. Amelia wanted me to have her home...*Why on earth?* My father hated the idea...*Ugh!* What's wrong with him?

Leaning across my seat, Dad opened the passenger door. "Olivia," he said with a gruff voice. "Get in."

Afraid to test his mood, I sat. My father's face had turned beet red. Every wrinkle assaulting his face had creased to the core. With both hands wringing the wheel, he stared out the front windshield. "Why didn't she give the old shack to Earl's kids? Why my daughter? Why!" Biting his lip, he slammed his hands against the steering wheel.

Turning in my seat, I stared at him. "What is wrong with you?" Shaking my head, I faced front again. I was as confused as him, but also touched. Why was he so angry?

"What's wrong with *me,* Olivia?" He didn't look like himself. "I had to totally rearrange my schedule to come here—for two days. If you are the rightful owner to that hovel, then we're in charge of what's inside. Not to mention power bills, gas bills.... Understand now?"

I couldn't speak. He was ruining this moment for me.

"We'll have to hire someone to clear out the place, get rid of all the junk inside, find a realtor and someone crazy enough to buy it. She gave Earl all her money, this *gift* is going to cost me a plethora. A plethora!"

My face grew warm. He had not only ruined the moment, he had destroyed the whole sentiment. "That *hovel* is mine!" I clenched my fists until I thought the skin on my knuckles would split open. "It'll cost you nothing."

"Right." Dad laughed and sped down the highway. "You're acting like a child. You, Olivia. And you didn't act like a child even when you were one. You read books beyond your years, understood things you shouldn't as a youth. So, why can't you see that this is not a gift?"

Crossing my arms, I said nothing. I had to compose myself. If I spoke now, I'd be jumbled, flustered, and easy to dispute.

The ride sped by—quicker than it had on the way over. My mind raced with what to say. I couldn't let this go—this was a crossroad and I needed to go the right way. With my voice calm and collected, I stared out the front windshield. "Take me to Amelia's, please."

"Excuse me?" His hands gripped the wheel tighter, turning his knuckles an unnatural white.

Without deviating from my focal point, I held my arms

tighter to my chest. *I am an adult. I am an adult.* "I'll be staying there tonight." Adding force to my tone I said, "Alone."

His lip snarled upward. "Impossible."

Holding up the key Mr. Marx had given to me, I faced him. "*Please.*" It was a polite demand. "I *am* an adult, Dad. And very much the legal owner of 32 Meeteese Road."

"Fine." His face changed from red to a purplish color I'd never seen before.

Stopping the car in front of Amelia's little brown house, he stared ahead. I stepped out and looked up at the big elm tree separating Amelia's house from her neighbors. Opening the back passenger door, I snatched up my bag. "I'll see you in the morning." I shut the car door. I didn't care what he thought of me.

I stepped up to Amelia's front door, ready to be alone with Amelia's floorboards.

Chapter 6

"Carpet?" I scanned the ground where Amelia's hardwood floors had once been. Sometime, in the past eleven years, they had been replaced with... carpet. Dropping my bag to the ground, I looked about the living room—same corduroy couch, same lace curtains, same eye sore coffee table. Everything sat just where it had so many years ago. Nothing had changed except the carpet. Walking into the dining room—*no!* More beige carpet. Slumping to the floor, I crossed my legs and covered my face with my hands. "Carpet." Bowing my head, I let my eyes swell. Tear after tear fell onto the new flooring.

Dad *could* be right. He often is. Something must be wrong with me. Obsessed... Crazed... All for Amelia? This whole thing was getting in my head. Amelia's in my head. I could call him, have him come and get me, return to the comfort of our uncomfortable silence.

Laying my head back against the wall, I mulled over what I should do. Stop being insane and call my father or—*Bzzz!* Digging into my purse, I found my cell. Benjamin's face smiled on the small screen. I tapped the speaker phone button. "Hello?"

"Honey, what is going on with you?" His tone didn't sound concerned, more like, *I just talked to your dad.*

Staring at his toothy grin on my smartphone, I wished he were standing right next to me—then I could punch him. Taking a deep breath, I forced back my anger. "Nothing." *That's right—calm. Be rational.*

"Why aren't you with Jonathon?"

"Benjamin, I'm going to pretend you haven't talked to my father and let you in on my good news. Amelia left me something. You'll never guess what—"

"Olivia—"

"A house! I know, I was shocked too, but it's exciting and mysterious. I have no idea why she picked me. What do you think?" My hand tightened into a fist. Sarcasm rang in my voice along with feigned excitement.

"Livy, may I speak now?" he said like a teacher to a student. "I'm just asking if something is wrong. This isn't like you. You usually heed Jonathon's advice. Are you all right?"

Biting my balled fist, I squeezed my eyes shut. *Rational. Calm.* "Benjamin, did you know, it's usually smart to take the side of the woman you love, *not* her father's?" I punched the stupid carpet beneath me.

"I'm not taking sides. But to be fair, I do feel like Jonathon has reasonable grievances." He sounded like a lawyer not a boyfriend. "However, my prime objective is to make sure you're well."

"I. Am. Quite. Well." I jerked a fuzzy pinch-full of beige polyester free from the carpet.

"Good. Now, I would just like to say I think it imperative we regard all Dad has to say concerning this house subject. Don't you agree? We need to think about this from every angle. I mean, Livy, what are you going to do with the place while you're at school? What will we use it for, a summer home?"

A growl escaped my throat. "I'm going now."

"Olivia, I'm just looking out for you."

"Right." I seethed through gritted teeth, staring at Ben's picture.

"Honey, I'm going to have to—

Click. I couldn't listen anymore. I dropped my phone to the ground and let my scream fill Amelia's empty house. "Arghh!"

Alone in Amelia's house, the space around me seemed enormous. The kitchen just off the dining room had the same old linoleum squares I remembered, large, hideous orange blossoms with yellow ribbons tied in bows. Walking upstairs, I peered into the one bathroom and Dad's old room.

So, nothing had changed in Dad's old room, still I took a closer look. It meant more now. Now, it was *mine*. I opened the miniscule closet, running my fingers over the men's shirts and shoeboxes. With my hands on the cold pane, I stared out the window, up at the elm tree. I glanced to the side where Amelia had hugged the curly haired boy and the house next door where he must have lived.

Moving down the hall, I opened *her* bedroom door. I stood frozen on the threshold, peering around the room. I had never been in this room—not even a look inside. It was tidy and dusty, with two windows viewing the opposite side of the house. My gaze stopped at the stack of books on the floor beside her bed. My chest tightened at the sight. *Amelia liked to read.* And it appeared to be more than just a little. Thirteen books piled up, almost like an end table. I bit my lip through a grin I couldn't stop at the only visible title, *Wuthering Heights*.

Breathing in, my hands resting on each side of the door frame, I scanned the room a second time. *Amelia.*

Taking my bulky suitcase back into Dad's room—my room, I pulled out my funeral clothes and hung them in the bathroom. I hoped the steam from my morning shower would loosen the wrinkles. Changing into my sweats, I lay on the old bed, but my eyes refused to close. My head filed through a million different memories—reasons—realities. Breathing through my nose, I exhaled through my mouth. *I'm here. Really here.*

The growl in my stomach reminded me I'd missed a meal—my head wouldn't quiet as long as I was starving.

Creeping down the stairs, quiet enough to go undetected, my mind flashed to that day all those years ago. I flipped on the kitchen light and opened every single cupboard. Amelia didn't exactly stock up. I grabbed a bottle of water and a box of vegetable crackers and pushed myself up onto the countertop. Engulfed in silence, I ate every crumb in the box.

Drowning in the quiet and darkness, I raced around Amelia's house, turning on every single light I could find. Killing the darkness brought the gaping, empty space back to its normal size. "Hey, is that..." I spoke aloud, needing the noise. "Yep! Photo albums." Four brown photo albums sat side by side on a shelf below Amelia's petite television—the ones she left to Earl. I wrangled all four at one time and carried them to the confines of my room.

I flipped through the first, not recognizing a soul. The faded black and white photos seemed as if from another time. Even before Amelia's time. The second held much the same as the first. The third, I opened and though the photos were still black and white, they seemed newer. I scanned each picture, until I came to one of three boys . One toehead and two dark headed boys. *Dad, Earl, and Red.* It had to be! Sliding the picture from its sleeve, I held it close. Dad stood apart from his brothers, his smile nothing like theirs. I couldn't help but think of what he'd told me—that his mother had separated him from his family, from his brothers. Why would she do that?

Cur-plunk! Whipping my head up at the sudden noise in Amelia's quiet house, my heart leapt into sprint mode. The rattling came from downstairs, as if dishes had just clanked together. This time, the unknown noise couldn't be my grandmother—and I didn't have my eleven-year-old courage anymore. Regretting every word I'd said to my father, I prayed he'd come back and rescue me.

Closing my eyes, I forced my adult logic to kick in. *Get your head out of a story*. Dad's words rang in my head. I'm in a foreign home, with foreign sounds. It was just the house settling, or something else perfectly logical. With my cell phone clutched in my hand, I crept to the door.

I stood at the top of the stairs. Thankful I'd left all the lights on, I strained my ears, waiting for something—anything to happen. When nothing did, I compelled my feet down one step and then another. Reaching the bottom of the stairway, I walked to the entrance of the dining room. Everything sat just as I'd left it. I brushed my hands over my head and through my hair. "Whew." Yes, the house had settled, and I overreacted. I pulled another bottle of water from the fridge and took a long swig.

"Ah-hem."

Whirling around, I splashed the water in a spatter on the floor. "Bwaa!"

A grown man, arms crossed and scowling face stood before me.

I shot backwards, my waist hitting the edge of the countertop. Searching the kitchen, I snatched up the only weapon I could muster, a paring knife from the sink. I held it outward, and the man took a step back. "Who are you?" I tightened my grip on my pitiful weapon. Why didn't I yell at him to get out?

He didn't look afraid, which frightened me even more. "Who are *you*?"

I didn't answer, but shook my knife at him. His folded arms tightened across his stretched black T-shirt. The shirt may have hid the matching grease stains that smeared over his jeans, but its clinginess didn't leave much to the imagination. His tousled, dark brown hair matched the dark whiskers brushing across his chin and face. He stood there, waiting for my answer.

Fumbling with the knife, I held up my cell. Finding Dad's name on speed dial, I glance down at the number and back at the intruder. My thumb hovered over the touch screen. Did I really want to call him? "Get out!" I held the phone out. "Or I will call the authorities." Authorities—yeah, that sounded better than tattling to my dad.

"You do that. Tell Sheriff Lane I said hi." He sighed. "Then let him know you're trespassing. Put down the knife, little girl."

Little girl? He wasn't much older than me—I was sure. Still, my racing heart slowed to a gallop. He was threatening *me* with the cops? "This is *my* house." The truth came out easier than I thought it would.

"Ha, ha!" He faked a laugh and stepped closer.

I held up my hands, the knife in one and my phone in the other, he stopped. With a little less shake in my voice I spoke, "Hold on there. This *is* my house. My name is Olivia Benson and I recently inherited it from my grandmother."

"Really?" For the first time he sounded unsure of himself. "It must have been quite recent." His face softened.

"Yes, Mr. Marx handed me the keys just today." My confidence grew with each word. I *was* right—and maybe—it would seem, he wasn't here to murder me. I threw my hands out into the air and placed them, fisted and full, on my hips—finding even more courage. "Who, may I ask, are you?"

His forehead wrinkled beneath his dark hair. "Mr. Marx? Oh. Ahh—I'm sorry, Miss. I'm Amelia's—I mean your grandmother's neighbor. I saw the light on, and I thought some kids were fooling around in here. I didn't recognize you—I should have realized then..." His arms uncrossed and he looked boyish standing there apologizing. He raked a hand through his dark curly hair before holding it out to me. "I'm Logan."

"Logan!" I jumped at the sound of his name. It couldn't be. The boy I remembered from all those years ago? Standing before me? The dark curls were proof enough. His hand still held out in front of me. Looking up to meet his eyes, I set my knife and phone down and shook his calloused hand.

His brows furrowed. "Have we met?"

"Oh, no. No. Nope." I shook my head, reiterating more ridiculous no's than anyone ever should. "I... I'm... I am just Olivia."

"Yeah, you mentioned that." He smiled, and a dimple pressed into his cheek.

I had a perfect image of Logan in my head—well, a two-stories-up, top-of-the-head image. "Right." My mouth went dry, making it hard to speak. Can you be star struck with someone who isn't a movie-star? Apparently *I* can. This wasn't going to bode well for my *I'm a mature, non-crazy person* attitude.

Brushing his hands down the sides of his jeans, he gave me a sheepish look. "I'm sorry to have startled you."

"It's all right." I meant it. *It's Logan* – the *Logan.*

"So, Amelia left you her place?"

"Yeah." *And apparently my childhood memory of a neighbor.*

"I didn't even know she had a granddaughter."

"Thanks. I didn't know she had an overprotective neighbor." No one knew about me. It was getting old. Why would she leave me her house when no one even knew I existed? Didn't she mention me to anyone? Was my name on that will as an afterthought or an impulse?

"I didn't mean to insult you." He gave a short chuckle and then his eyes narrowed in on me. "You two must have been close."

He may as well have rubbed salt into my already stinging wound. I decided to avoid that topic. "She has three granddaughters actually."

"Really?" He sounded surprised.

"And a couple of grandsons."

"I knew she had sons. Red and another—"

"Two more, Earl, and my dad, Jonathon. She didn't talk about us much then, huh?"

Hesitating, he rubbed his hand across his chin. "Well, no, not at all."

I could tell he knew her better than I ever would and all at once, *I* felt like the intruder. Biting my lip, I crossed my arms, afraid to look in his eyes—for fear he'd discover the fraud that I am. Letting my gaze drop down, I met his stomach. Not wanting to gawk at his well-built abs, I shifted my eyes down again. Like a fire, heat spread to my cheeks. Had I really just checked him out? Speeding past Logan, my eyes focused on the living room entrance. I avoided his face. What must he think of me? "I'm sure you have something to get back to," I said, my voice much too loud. My nerves made me sound obnoxious.

"Yes, I do. It was nice to meet you, Olivia."

Forcing my gaze up to meet his, his face softened, his hand outstretched. I cleared my throat and shook it.

He peered around the front room. "This place hasn't changed in probably fifty years," he said, more to himself than to me. His voice had a sadness to it. He missed her. His eyes seemed to linger on the chair where she always sat. Her crossword still lay on the armrest.

Keeping my hands busy, I rubbed them together—it seemed better than my crazy urge to console him. "Well, except for the carpet." The beige rug still offended me.

"Yeah, that's right. She put that in..." He ran a hand through his dark curls thinking. "Gosh, probably five…six years ago."

He did know her. Why didn't she leave her house to him? My tired eyes shut at the thought. "Ghaa! Why?"

"Sorry?"

"Oh…" I tucked my hair behind my ears and bit my lip. "I mean, I wonder why? I loved her hardwood floors, they were beautiful." I didn't remember the condition they were in or even what shade of wood they were. I remember they were *hard* and uncomfortable to sleep on, the hole in the floor, my lone attraction.

Nodding, he smiled his dimpled grin again. "Well, neighbor, if you need something, let me know."

"Thanks." I clasped my hands together. "I won't be living here though. Truthfully, I don't know what I'm going to do with the place."

He nodded like he understood. "See you."

"Yeah, see you." My stomach punched with guilt. I didn't want him to leave. It was *Logan*. I'd thought about the curly haired boy more than a few times in the last dozen years. I shouldn't have—not with Benjamin waiting for me at home.

Chapter 7

Funeral day. I woke early. With no viewing planned, the funeral would begin at eleven, somewhere...I knew by the name it wasn't a church. Amelia wasn't a religious woman. Still, *The Meeting Hall* didn't sound right for a funeral.

I brought my only suit, rolled up and shoved into my large backpack. The shower had relieved it of its few wrinkles. A black jacket and pencil skirt that stopped at my knees, I loved how it hung on me. It was my interview outfit, though it didn't get a lot of use, still being a student and all.

I'd just finished straight ironing my hair when Dad knocked on the door. His old home and he still wouldn't just walk in. I didn't mind. I felt a bit protective of the place. I touched up my lip gloss, making him wait thirty seconds longer, he was early anyway. I flounced down the stairs to open the door.

Quite the opposite of my father stood before me. Logan. This time clean-shaven and dressed substantially better—a white dress shirt and black slacks. His dark hair was still messy, but in a more purposeful way.

"Logan," I said, trying to keep my grin from taking over my face. "What brings you here?"

"I've been feeling guilty all night. Not only did I about scare you to death last night, but I never offered my condolences. How *are* you holding up?" he said, his hands in his pant pockets. "Can I do anything? Your grandmother was a dear friend to me, I feel horrible I was so atrocious to her granddaughter."

"You weren't atrocious." I waved away his comment. "You

were making sure her home was secure. I'm sure she would have appreciated it. I'm okay, by the way, thank you—from her and me."

His face melted into a smile. "You're sure I can't do anything to make up for it?"

From the other side of the room, Ben's ring-tone sang out. "Ah, one minute. Can you wait just one minute? It's my boyfriend, I should answer it."

"Go ahead."

I motioned to Amelia's corduroy couch, and Logan took a seat. Shuffling into the adjoining room I answered. "Hello?"

"When are you coming home to me?"

"Hey, Ben." I held in the impatient, audible sigh threatening to leave me.

"I'm serious, how soon until you leave?"

"Aren't you basking in the bliss of work?"

"Actually, I am," he said, losing the whine from his voice.

I laughed. "Or, slacking off with the boss gone?"

"I'm on break, honey. You know I don't slack."

"Oh, I know!" I peeked around the corner at the model, I mean man, sitting on Amelia's couch.

"So?"

Distracted for a second, I jumped at the sound of Ben's voice. "So, what?"

"So, when will you be home?"

"Oh," I said, unable to keep in my sigh. My chest ached at the thought of leaving. There was still so much I wanted to investigate. "I'm not sure, Benjamin. The funeral isn't until eleven. We may not even leave until tomorrow."

"Tomorrow? Jonathon said you'd be on the road by one."

A groan sounding more like a growl left my throat. "Did he? Then why bother asking me?"

"Come on, Liv, I tried you first, but I got your voicemail. You must have been in the shower."

"Hmph! I should go, Benjamin."

"Olivia, don't go like that. Sweetheart?"

"What?"

"I love you." He sang the words in my ear.

"I know, Ben, and I love you." Tromping back into the living room, my face burned. *Why can't he understand this is important to me?*

Logan stood upon seeing me. "Is something wrong?"

Blinking slow and long, I shook my head. "No, Benjamin, my boyfriend, he…" But I stopped, not wanting to share our troubles with a stranger.

Logan waited for me to continue, his brown eyes wide with anticipation.

"Never mind." I blew out the air I hadn't realized I'd been holding. "It's nothing."

"This must be a hard day for you. Can I ask why you're alone? Where's your dad, or Benjamin?"

"Ben had to work," I said. "And my dad, he stayed at a hotel."

"Hmm…" His forehead wrinkled. "You're sure you're all right?"

"Yes." I attempted a smile for him. "Thank you, Logan, you're very kind."

"Okay then. I should probably…" He walked over to door.

"Yeah." I understood his unvoiced thought. I opened the door and Dad's car pulled up out front. I followed Logan outside.

"Good morning, Olivia," Dad said, climbing out of the running rental car.

"Dad, this is Logan Heyborn, Amelia's neighbor."

"Good to meet you," he said, his voice hurried. Taking Logan's hand, he gave it a quick shake.

"You too, sir. Your mother was a good woman. I'm sorry for your loss."

"Thank you, Logan." Dad only bothered a glance Logan's way. "Olivia, are you ready to go?"

"Yes, let me grab my purse." Running back inside, I snatched my bag.

Logan still stood next to Dad. "I'll see you there," he said to me.

"Okay." I turned for the car, but his rough hand caught my wrist, sending ticklish pins up my arm.

"Oh, I wanted to tell you. I know you loved those hardwood floors, most likely they're under the carpet. Next time you visit, I could help you pull it up."

Speechless, I grinned back. *The next time I visit...* Would there ever be a next time? And the hardwood—there might be a chance it was still there...Amelia's secret could be there too.

"Come on, Livy. Let's go."

I nodded for Dad's sake, but kept my eyes on Logan's dimple. I slid my wrist from his grasp and shook his hand, giving it a squeeze. More tingling pins ran through my body. "Ahh—thank you, Logan."

Chapter 8

Amelia's house grew smaller in the passenger door mirror. Would I ever get a chance to pull up those floorboards? I couldn't see how that would be possible. It's not as if Dad would give me an extra day in Rendezvous.

"I'm surprised the Heyborns still live here," Dad said, interrupting my thoughts. "Or at least that their son hasn't fled."

I whipped around to face him. "Wait, you already knew Logan?"

"No." He laughed at the absurdity. "He's barely older than you, Olivia. I knew his parents. I went to school with both of them. His mother grew up in the house, right beside your grandmother's. They were married before high-school graduation! It didn't surprise me they both ended up in Rendezvous, but I heard their only son was bright, graduated with honors. I am bewildered he's still here."

I had to admit, it surprised me too, to find Logan still in this little town. What did it have to offer him? "Did he go to college?"

"I don't know." He shrugged. "What I know, I've told you. I'm not really sure why I know that much. Amelia must have mentioned it. She was always fond of the kid."

"She talked about him?"

"Once or twice."

My throat tightened and my eyes stung with threatening tears. She'd spoken of Logan, but never me. It's not as if I were bragging about my Wyoming grandmother to my friends. Giving my head a small shake, I pushed the sting out of my mind. "When did you speak to her? I mean, the last time?" *Did she* ever *mention me? Or Jared – or Katie? Were any of us worth mentioning?*

A shameful pink spread across his cheeks and his brows creased. I hadn't heard the answer yet, but I already regretted asking. "Two years ago, my birthday."

I didn't risk speaking again. Yesterday's rocky events weren't mentioned. Dad looked all business in his navy suit, his pale hair slicked back. I studied him as we drove. He was a good man. I knew that, he'd raised me after all—but I didn't always understand him, now more than ever.

Dad drove to the top of a hill and pulled into a dirt parking lot, next to a large barn-type building. This couldn't be the right place. But then others appeared, dressed in their grieving clothes. Nothing fancy, but solemn strides and clean, neat, dark attire. The sign on the side of the brown barn read, *Meeting Place of Chiefs*. This was it. Dirty and rustic, it seemed to me the oddest place for a funeral. Inside, the air turned floral. I closed my eyes and inhaled the scent. Flower arrangements of all sizes and colors lined the room. The chairs aligned in neat rows with a white ribbon running down several in the center, creating an aisle. *Perfect.* Who had done it all?

The sight of Rachel Lemonade answered my unspoken question. She pointed and directed a couple of teenagers, their arms full of flowers. She scanned the large room, stopping as my eyes caught hers.

Her short, platinum curls bounced as her petite frame rushed over to us. "Jonathon! Jonathon!" she called out, waving her hands.

The few stares and whispers coming our way doubled at Rachel's display. The entire town had shown up and everyone knew everyone—except for us of course. Rachel was the only one who knew who we were.

"Hello, Mrs. Lemonade. Everything looks lovely," Dad said, seeming to know she'd been in charge. Perhaps another good guess?

"Thank you." Rachel's wrinkles creased with her grin. Her eyes sparkled from lingering tears, but she held herself together.

"I've got spaces for you, Earl, and Olivia right up here." Rachel led the way to our assigned seats.

"So, Red's not coming then?" I turned to Dad. Rachel had only saved three seats for us.

Dad didn't look back at me. "No."

"Strange," I whispered to myself. Who skipped out on their mother's funeral? Dad almost had. If Grandma Isle had passed, Dad would have rearranged everything to be there. But Amelia, his own mother—I'd never known him to be like this with anyone.

Dad stopped next to our reserved folding chairs and looked at me. "Sure you don't want to switch majors? Go into law rather than medicine?"

I furrowed my brow, puzzled.

"You're judging again. I can see it on your face."

"I am," I said. "I just don't understand it."

"Red's not exactly known for his planning expertise. He's always in and out of different jobs. He earned enough money to get to Argentina, but not enough to get back."

"But you would have—"

"Helped him? Maybe, if he'd asked. Although, I'd feel as if I were aiding his handicap. Anyhow, he didn't ask."

My ivory cheeks burned pink. Where was his kindness? This raw, harsh man didn't raise me. "I need a drink," I said, leaving him.

Certain I'd seen a drinking fountain when we first walked in, I hurried to the back of the building, ignoring the curious stares. Reaching the fountain, I wet my palms and moving my long hair out of the way, rubbed the back of my neck. How did I get so far out of my comfort zone? Every other minute disagreeing with my father and call me crazy—or maybe vain, but every single eye in the place seemed to linger far too long on me.

"We meet again." The voice came from above me as I gulped down the cold water.

Sucking in a breath, I pulled up. "Roy?" I cringed at his gawking face.

"You remembered." The boy from Amelia's school looked delighted. His long hair was pulled back out of his eyes, and he gave me an awkward wink. "Not that I'm surprised. I mean, I get like, etched in one's mind."

A smile pulled at my lips, this kid had seen too many movies.

"Down boy."

Both Roy and I scanned upward to meet Logan's face.

"Hey, Logan, figures you'd show up. Have you met my new friend?" Roy straightened his posture, and puffed out his chest.

Logan grinned, his dimple creasing.

Coughing out a laugh, I held my hand toward Logan and he took it, staring at Roy, waiting for introductions. Of course he didn't know my name. I hadn't offered it to the pushy high schooler.

Roy's mouth dropped, a sound like an engine dying escaping him.

Releasing my hand, Logan motioned to Roy. "Roy Cox, meet Olivia Benson."

Roy's rumbling turned into a whistle with his cheeks shading to a deep red. His mouth closed into an angry O and he refused to look back at Logan.

"Hi," I said, offering Roy a curt wave. He marched off, still whistling and rumbling with no real words leaving his lips.

"He's really harmless," Logan said.

"I'm sure."

We grinned at one another for a moment. Tearing my eyes from his, I scanned the room. Seats were filling up. "It looks really nice, doesn't it?"

"Yeah, Rachel did a good job," he said.

My emotions caught in my throat. "I hardly knew her," I said to him, needing to be honest with the boy I'd remembered all these years.

Logan's eyes were gentle—not surprised, as if he'd suspected as much. "I'm sorry," he said. "She was a wonderful person."

"I'm sorry too, more than anyone realizes. I can't explain it, and my dad thinks I'm having some type of breakdown, but I just wish..." I hung my head. I wiped at my eyes, shooing the unexplainable tears.

Reaching out, his hand clasped about my arm, his thumb

rubbing back and forth, consoling me.

"I'm sorry." I sniffled and looked around. Had anyone noticed my momentary madness? But we *were* at a funeral. There weren't any more stares than before.

"You can still know her. Maybe that's why she left you her home. Maybe she felt the same regret."

"I wouldn't know how to do that. I'm in school, it's summer break, but I have a job. How will that happen? I can only go through so much before my dad sells it."

"It's your house, Olivia," his tone serious, he furrowed his brows, "only you can sell it."

He should be right of course, but I knew better. It wouldn't work out that way. "We should take our seats." I needed space in case my stupid water works turned on again.

Turning away, I took two steps when Logan stopped me. "There's a job opening here."

"What?" I asked, turning back.

"You said one problem was your job. You're working. You could always work here."

It was the most absurd thing I'd ever heard—even more than Amelia giving me her house. I stared at him. Why would he even suggest such a thing?

"She was worth knowing," he said, answering my unasked question.

The funeral didn't last long. The speaker, Principal Levitz, spoke very little of her family, he mentioned her husband and three children. He described her as *esteemed by all who knew her*. She loved her job as a school secretary and she also worked as a part time teacher's aide. In the summers she continued her work through a short semester of summer extracurricular classes. She won a peach pie contest last year at the town fair, and her house was never missed on Halloween. She made caramel popcorn balls for every child in town.

We drove with the rest of the town to the graveyard where they lowered her coffin into the ground. Uncle Earl wept like a child, while Dad stayed dry eyed as ever. Standing close to Earl, his blubbering diverted from my own quiet sobs.

Once the final words were spoken, Dad leaned down, and without looking at me whispered, "Ready to go, honey?"

My sigh gave him confirmation. He started ahead of me, saying polite goodbyes to those we passed. Following after him in silence, I stared at the passing shoes. I looked up long enough to catch Logan, watching me. I needed to at least say goodbye to *him*.

"Just let me say goodbye to Logan." The memory of the little boy next door meant something to me. I couldn't explain why, but *Logan* meant something to me. I wouldn't leave without a word—not when it came to Logan.

Dad caught my wrist. "Livy, let's go."

"I'm just going to say goodbye." What did he care? Why couldn't he stand to be in this place? Maybe all this was harder on him than he led me to believe—then again, maybe it wasn't.

He looked over to Logan, who didn't shy away from staring at me. "No, Livy. You're practically a fiancé, this isn't appropriate."

I sighed and freed myself from his grasp. "Benjamin is not my fiancé!" It didn't look as if he ever would be. He made that clear to me before I left California. "And telling someone goodbye is not inappropriate behavior."

Leaving Dad protesting, my heels sunk into the dirt beneath the long grass. Logan's eyes sparkled as I approached him, waiting for me to cross the yard to meet him.

"I wondered if you'd say goodbye."

I grinned. "Of course. I guess we're in a hurry, but I wanted to tell you how happy I am to have met you." Logan. The boy next door. He was special to me—even if he didn't know it.

I should have left, but I didn't. We'd said our so-longs, but my feet refused to move. "Uh, Logan. I want to tell you something. I know it's a little strange, but..." I stared at him, seeing the memory of a loving, affectionate Amelia in my mind—something up until that point, I didn't know existed.

He tilted his head to the side and smiled. "Ah, okay."

"I saw you. When you were a little boy, I was staying with my grandmother, and I saw you outside her house." The words seemed to come out faster than the thoughts in my head. "I heard her yell your name and well, I was afraid for you."

"Afraid?"

"Yes, she was always so cold with me and my siblings. I watched as she hugged you, and it frightened me."

He was silent, his eyes meeting mine.

"She never once hugged me. I-I don't know the woman you knew. I don't know why it was that way with my dad, with my family, but I wish I had known her like you did." A tear rolled down my cheek. I reached up to swat it away, but Logan reached over and smoothed my cheek with his thumb.

From the corner of my eye I saw Dad striding over to stop my spectacle. I stepped away from Logan's touch. "I have to go."

Once again, I trailed after my father for the exit. Like a weight in my chest, my heart dragged me down. And Logan—my one true link to Amelia grew smaller in the distance behind me.

Dad's bolt for the car would have taken all of twenty-three seconds if Rachel Lemonade hadn't jumped in front of him. "Nails, bells! You're not leaving, are ya?"

"We must," Dad said, not bothering to fake politeness.

"We were hoping you might stay a few days with Miss Olivia being the new owner of Amelia's house and all."

Wow, news spreads fast.

"No." Dad pushed past her.

"Wait." I stopped again. "Where's Uncle Earl? We didn't say goodbye to him."

Slapping his hand to his forehead, he shook his head at me. "Earl's already finished off a six pack, he won't remember you saying goodbye by the night's end."

"I just..."

"What, Livy? What?"

I wish he could understand. I wish he could feel what I do. I wish I could talk to him like... like normal! "I just don't feel ready."

"Then stay," I heard his low voice behind me. Logan had followed us out.

Turning a horrible beet color, Dad stared at Logan, laughing a sarcastic laugh.

Glancing at Logan, for a moment, I considered it.

"Olivia, your responsibilities, your life, are a thousand miles away. Now, get in the car." Dad's arguments made sense and slapped me back into reality. He was right. I did as he asked.

"I need my things." My hands knotted in my lap and I stared at my whitish-pink fists squeezing together.

"I don't understand you, Olivia." Dad sighed, impatient, but started for Amelia's. "You need to get your head out of a book." I sniffled and he softened his tone. "Honey, you're my little girl. I'm trying to help you, protect you, like always. Amelia is not a fairytale character that's going to—"

"You need to quit treating me like a child." I was more aware than ever that my life was no fairytale. "I'm not a little girl anymore." Thankful for the sight of Meeteese Road, I slammed the door behind me and marched inside Amelia's house—my house.

Closing the door to my room, I pulled out my cell to call Benjamin.

"Hey, sweetie pie, how far along are you?"

"Benjamin..."

"Honey? What is it? What's wrong?"

"I did just come from a funeral." Could he not allow me to grieve?

"For a woman you didn't know." He was right. I didn't know Amelia.

I took a deep breath. "That's what I'm struggling with. She's still my grandmother, and I need to know her."

"Livy," he said, using the same tone my father just had. "Be realistic. This is somewhat ridiculous, surely you can see that?"

Tears drowned my face at his reprimand. What was I doing with my life? Is this really where I was headed? Reprimand after reprimand? I covered my mouth, holding in a sob. I couldn't possibly reevaluate my entire life all because Amelia Benson died and left me a house.

"Honey," he said. "One second."

I found my voice, choking back the cry. "Tell me you're not

answering call waiting. Benjamin—"

"Sweetheart, it's your dad, I'm sure he's worried, just let me reassure him."

"Benjamin, he is standing right outside my door. Don't—" But he was gone. Gone. Gone. My face went hot, and my heart fell to pieces.

Holding my thumb to the red stop signal on my screen, I ended the call. In that moment of heart crushing insanity, I broke. I lost it. Sliding my finger to the side, I held down the button and turned off the device. Tossing the thing into the trash can next to the bedside table, I let out a shaky breath.

With my face flaming, I left the room. Seeing Dad's expression, I was certain I looked crazed.

"I'm done," I whispered.

Hesitant and quiet, Dad said, "You're ready now?"

Rigid, I nodded.

Walking down the stairs together, just before we got to the door, I spoke, "I'm done."

He opened the door and stepped out, waiting for me to follow with raised eyebrows.

"I won't argue with you anymore, I won't. I'm not going home. I'm staying here, at least for a few days." His mouth opened to speak, but I cut him off. "I'll find a way home. I've made up my mind." I shut the door, locking it behind me. Locking my dad outside, out of *my* decision for once in my life.

A weight lifted from my shoulders. I could breathe again. Letting out a small squeal, I jumped in place. My phone didn't sing—it couldn't. The door didn't open—he didn't have a key, and he was much too proud to knock after I'd shut it in his face. For the moment, I was free.

Chapter 9

I wasted no time. I knew exactly what to do with my first moment of freedom. But how should I go about ripping out carpet? It's not as if I could pull it up with my bare hands. *First things first.* That's just what Dad would have said. The man taught me plenty of good things, no sense in wasting them. So, first, I had to get out of these dress clothes.

Options were sparse. I opted for jeans and my Big Mac T from the day before. Had it really only been one day since I inherited Amelia's house? I shook my head.

Next on the list—tools. I searched the porch and backyard for a tool shed, a toolbox... something that would hold some kind of metal, sharp, manly object. I found where she kept her *vacuum* but no tools. Not a one.

Walking in from the porch, I stomped my foot. Didn't the woman need a screwdriver every now and then? But then I spotted Amelia's *Sharp Style Cutlery* sitting atop her counter. *Yes!* I grabbed the largest knife, the butcher knife, and, remembering back to that night so long ago, retraced my steps. Starting in the living room, I rounded the corner to see the dining area, like I had all those years ago. My eyes closed, I envisioned Amelia there on the floor, down on her knees, her body rocking. Opening them, I stared almost dead center at the odious carpet.

Pushing the little table and chairs out of the way, I knelt onto the rug. Raising the knife into the air, I stabbed the center of Amelia's beige carpet. Back and forth, I sawed, but it was far more difficult to cut up than I thought it would be. If only I could get more than just the tip of the giant knife into the rug. Ten minutes of work and all I had to show for it was a two-inch hole.

Maybe scissors would work better. Now that I had the hole, maybe I could cut the carpet. I searched a couple of drawers and found a pair. Forcing half the wedge into my pathetic hole, I attempted to cut the carpet. It didn't even make a mark.

The dumb carpet was taunting me—making fun of me! I stabbed it again.

I needed a break. My stomach growled. Dinnertime had come and gone. I already knew Amelia had no food in the house. Rendezvous didn't have a drive-thru—not that I had a car.

To appease my grumpy stomach, I opened the refrigerator again. Still bare—except for a half gallon of expired milk, a couple of eggs and a few condiments. I supposed scrambled eggs would have to do for dinner, but—sure, I could *shop*. Why not? I wasn't totally helpless! And I did plan on staying a few days. Yes, I needed to shop, and I needed to eat. The carpet would have to wait until morning, or at least until after food. I ran upstairs and grabbed my purse. I only had a small amount of cash, but my checkbook was somewhat stocked.

Opening the front door, I found Logan, his hand up ready to knock.

"Logan," I said, not bothering to hide my surprise.

"I saw your light on." He grinned down at me. "You stayed."

"Yeah." I beamed back. "I couldn't go yet."

"So, are you hungry?" He held up the foil wrapped plate in his hand.

My new neighbor was a mind reader.

Heading back to the dining area, Logan set the plate on the pushed-aside table.

I followed after him, mumbling as I went. "It was so kind of you to bring me something. I—"

"Wow." Turning around, his eyebrows rose over his wide eyes. He gave a low chuckle. "This carpet really has offended you, hasn't it?"

"Oh, um…" I twisted my hands together.

Logan stared at my "tools" in the middle of the floor, along with the second-rate hole.

"I was ah... just taking your suggestion, you know. I want to get the carpet out, so I thought—"

"That you'd kill it?"

"No," I said, my voice much too high. He must think I'm ridiculous. *I do!* Obsessed, ridiculous... it's all blending together now.

"Yeah," He eyed my pathetic hole. "Looks more like torture, or maybe you were just threatening it."

"Ha, ha." I bent over to pick up the butcher knife and flimsy kitchen scissors. "I guess you could say I'm not exactly sure how to go about it."

He laughed again, but it wasn't mocking. My eyes glued to his lips as he said, "Come on. Let's eat, and then I'll help you."

"You don't have to do that." I twisted my hands together. I had pictured making my discovery alone. If there was nothing under the carpet, I didn't think I'd be able to keep myself together, and I didn't want to make a spectacle in front of my new friend.

"Well, I can't sit around next door waiting for you to slice your hand or even murder perfectly good carpet. Believe me, there's a much easier way."

"Well, maybe a little help getting started wouldn't hurt." I did need a new idea. I was fresh out.

He laughed again, shaking his head at me. "Good."

Sitting down at the table, Logan removed the foil and pulled another paper plate from beneath the first. Getting up, he went to the kitchen and opened a drawer. "Do you mind?"

"Ah, no, no, go ahead." He knew this place better than I did, that was clear.

He retrieved a couple of forks and came back to the small rectangular wooden table. Scooping half the delicious smelling pasta up, he laid it on the plate in front of me.

My eyes stayed glued to the bicep that popped with his movement. Clearing my throat, I forced my stare down to my plate. "Thanks." I would need to learn how not to stare... or drool this weekend. Embarrassed, I stood from the table. "Water! Do you want some?"

"Yeah, thanks."

Rushing over to the sink, I pulled a couple of glasses from the third cupboard I tried and filled my head with thoughts of Benjamin. I was still upset with Ben, so it didn't do much good. Instead, I filled our cups with water and took a deep breath. I loved Ben. At the moment, it was difficult to convince myself.

I set a glass in front of him, forcing my eyes to stay on my plate. "This is delicious. Did you make it?"

"Who else?"

"You don't live with anyone else?" When did I get so nosy? The question left my mouth before I really thought about what I was saying.

"No, it's just been me for years."

"You live in your grandparent's house, right?"

"Yes." He leaned a couple inches closer to me.

"Oh, ah... my dad, he mentioned your mother grew up in the house next door. They went to school together. Did you know?"

Setting his fork down, he said, "No, I didn't. Anyhow, it's my home now. I gained it very much the same way you did this one."

"Your grandparents left it to you?"

"They left it to my parents. My parents left it to me."

"Oh." It occurred to me what that might mean. "Umm... Where do they live now?" I didn't like to pry but really, I was just hoping. He was too young, he couldn't have lost his parents. Not both. Not yet.

"No, they didn't move, they've passed," he said, his voice reverent.

Somehow I'd known before he said it. Was I being cruel, making him affirm it aloud? Sometimes I hated my inquisitiveness.

"I'm sorry." How long had he been alone? "They must have been young." Dad was only fifty-something. He only had a speck of gray hair, he golfed, he skied, and I couldn't imagine him as anything but active and healthy. My heart broke for Logan.

"They were."

My curiosity won again over good manners. "How old were you?"

"Seventeen."

"What happened? If you don't mind me asking?"

He shook his head. "I don't mind. I'd rather you ask than assume." He said it as though things *had* been assumed concerning them. I thought of Dad and his judgments. "Six years ago they were driving home from Cody when a storm hit. They weren't drinking, no one fell asleep. They had misfortune, in horrible weather."

It was awful, but I didn't understand. "Why would someone assume they'd been drinking?"

"My parents married young, not because they *had* to, but because they loved each other. They stayed in this town because it made them happy, not because they weren't intelligent enough to escape. People who don't really know them have always assumed they made poor choices, all the way down to their death."

Did he mean Dad? Or maybe just every other person they'd gone to school with? I reached across the table and put my hand over his. I didn't know what to say, the whole thing made my heart hurt. I couldn't imagine how it must make *him* feel every day of his life.

He smiled at me and it wasn't sad, but kind. "It's okay."

"Have you been here ever since?" I asked, taking my hand from his. I felt like a vacuum. I needed to suck up all the Logan-knowledge I could before I left for home.

"No," he said, looking at me. It was just polite eye contact, but it made my heart rate speed up. "I went to school in Alaska for a couple years."

"What brought you back?"

"I missed home. So, I came back and took over my dad's business."

"What's that?"

"Mechanics. My dad taught me. I've actually never been formally educated as a mechanic, but I know what I'm doing."

I wondered about Logan's dad. Was he like Logan? "Did your father push you in *his* direction? I mean, is it really what you want to do? What did you go to school for?" I couldn't imagine

Logan being coerced into *anything*. He was strong, body and mind. While I've let the two most dominant men in my life assure me that *my* educational choices were wise—and that my present choices were at best, ridiculous.

His answer interrupted my thoughts. "My dad taught me to be happy. So no, Olivia, he never pushed me one way or another. Mechanics was my decision. And I studied art in school. I still do, just not in a classroom."

"Art, huh?" I'd be lying if I said it didn't surprise me. Though, really, it's not as if I knew Logan well. My subconscious seemed to think we'd been friends since we were kids, since that day I first saw him. I did feel comfortable with him—as long as I could keep my eyes off his abs.

"It's always been a love of mine, but it's more of a hobby. I'm happy with my career. I like being handy," he said, and I made sure to focus on his face and not the tight T-shirt he wore. "What about you, Livy, what do you love doing?"

My instincts said *reading*, but my trained self answered him. "I'm going into medicine. I'm not sure which field yet. I've just been getting my generals done. I'm still figuring out what I'll focus on."

"So, you love helping people. That's nice."

"Um, sure, I don't dislike helping people. I hadn't really thought about it that way." The minute the words escaped my mouth, I knew they were nonsensical.

He gave a small laugh before saying, "You're going into a medical profession, and you're not sure you love helping people?"

"No, I mean, I do, I do like to help people."

"You're sure?" He widened his eyes, teasing me.

"Well, sort of."

"What does that mean?"

"That means I didn't want to be a lawyer." I had never said those words out loud in my life. Never. Not once. I'd thought them a few times, on rougher days, but never aloud. Not to Benjamin, not to Mom, not even to my cynical roommate, Rose.

"I'm lost. What does that have to do with anything?"

I crossed my arms, my defenses up. There was a reason I

didn't talk about this with people, it didn't make me look good, at best weak and unintelligent. So, why I felt like sharing with the supreme being across from me, I'll never know. "That means I was given two choices: law or medicine. And I wasn't about to follow in my dad's footsteps."

He studied me for a moment with a confused expression.

"My dad is a good man, but he isn't like yours. He has specific expectations for me. I was given two options, law or medicine."

I couldn't tell if he believed me. And then he tilted his head to the side and said, "There is a third option."

It was my turn to stare at him confused.

"Do what *you* want to."

"I don't think you understand. It's…it's different. I can't do that." I didn't even know what that was.

"Sure you can," he said, shoving his last bite into his mouth.

"What makes you so sure?" My cheeks burned up in irritation. He knew as much about me as I did about him. How could he know my situation?

"Because you're here."

The angry burning in my cheeks cooled, and I laughed. He was right. I was here. "That reminds me, are you ready to rip out some carpet?"

Chapter 10

"Hopefully you have a better tool." I held up the butcher knife and dull scissors. "This is all I've got."

"No, no, no." Logan pushed my hands down. "We don't need those."

"But—"

"Trust me. I can get the carpet up without killing it." His eyebrows bounced with his grin and at once I believed him. "All you need is a little muscle."

My eyes darted to his abs at the word muscle. I covered my face with my hands. I needed to find some self-control. This was not like me, and I wasn't about to jeopardize my new found friendship because I couldn't stop gawking.

"Ah... you okay?"

"Yes." I rubbed my eyeballs over and over again. "There's something in... uh... my eye. Excuse me." Like a robot I walked back to the kitchen. There I continued to rub away. Talk about idiotic! Had it been Rose, I would have just told her—*I'm checking out your fabulous abs.* But I couldn't say that to Logan.

I hadn't heard him coming, but all at once I felt his palms on the sides of my face. He pulled my hands down. "Don't rub them."

Startling at his touch, my long hair flopped across his arms. The strawberry strands stood out against his tan skin.

Tipping my head up, he peered into my eyes, searching for the non-existent foreign item. "I don't see anything." He concentrated on the whites of my eyes. He stood so close, his clean soapy scent filled my head.

Benjamin! Benjamin. Blinking, I stepped away from him. "Yeah, yep, hm-mm, it's gone. Thanks."

"You're okay?" He waited for my nod. "Then let's get to work."

Pulling my hair back, I tied it into a knot. "How long do you think this will take?" I forced my focus to the carpet.

"Not too long. What's your plan for now? Do you want to take it all up tonight or just see if the hardwood is underneath? I can pull it up and roll it, but it might take a few guys to get it out of here."

"Huh…" I hadn't thought of any of those things. I just had to see what lay beneath the floor boards. The hour was getting late, and I wanted to be alone for my discovery. "How about we see what's under it tonight. Tomorrow I'll make a plan."

Logan went to the corner of the room and knelt on the floor, with his fingers he picked at the edge of the carpet.

"You sure you don't want the knife?" I stood on my toes behind him peering over his shoulder.

"I'm sure," he said, and I thought he might laugh.

The small corner of the rug came loose. Working a couple of fingers beneath it, he jerked. More of the beige mess wrenched up. "Stand back." He stood and yanked at the carpet. It ripped up around the walls edge, half-way around the room.

Gasping, I covered my mouth, my heart racing. My cheeks burned, like someone had cranked the heater.

Flipping the rug over, like a burrito, he did the same with the carpet pad.

And then I saw it. My trembling fingers shook over top my lips. Staring at Amelia's hardwood floor, my eyes pricked with tears.

Giving me a weak grin, he yanked back, revealing more of the floor. My tears spilled over as he uncovered almost the entire dining area. "It needs work," he said in a soft voice.

I nodded in agreement. The boards did need refurbishing. But I wasn't really seeing the floor. I saw Amelia, and her secrets.

"Are you okay?" he asked.

I was more than okay, but I couldn't speak. I couldn't explain. I nodded again.

"I can help you with this tomorrow."

"Sure. Thank you," I said, finding my voice.

Letting go of the carpet pad, he walked toward me, his dimple indented. "Anything for Amelia Benson's granddaughter."

My heart jumped and at once my skin pricked, anxious. I wasn't sure what to say to that. So, I ignored the smell of his faint cologne and the way the muscle in his arm popped out when he brushed his hair back. Instead, I stared at the wooden floor before me.

"I'm gonna go."

"Thanks again for dinner." I walked him out. "And for your help. You're the perfect neighbor." My nerves came out in laughter. "Can you keep it up for another day?"

He just smiled, not answering my silly question.

Breathing in the air so clean and crisp, I peered over to the elm tree, my favorite part of Amelia's house. It happened to be the only thing separating her house from Logan's. I shuffled my feet and looked down at the dirt. The little homes around us were quiet—Rendezvous was quiet. There was something beautiful in the silence.

He didn't get too far before I asked, "So, how far is Farmer's?"

"How far?"

"Well, before you came, I was planning on walking there to get a few things. I was just wondering how far I'd be juggling groceries." It was lame. As much as I wanted to rip up those floorboards, I wasn't exactly ready to say goodbye to the boy next door. So I asked a question I already knew the answer to.

"You're going to walk? Your dad left, right? How are you planning on getting home?"

Kicking the dirt again, I said, "The bus." I wasn't ready to think about home just yet. "A bus comes through, right? Greyhound?"

Logan chuckled. "Uhh, no."

My eyes widened in slow motion. *Crap.* Maybe I hadn't thought this out so well.

"Cody does though."

"Taxi?"

Shaking his head, he laughed again. "Nope. I guess you're stuck here." Narrowing his eyes at me, he teased. "I can give you a ride."

Pinching my bottom lip between my teeth, I let out a squeak. "Home?" I could only imagine Dad and Ben's reaction—*I'm home! And I've brought a man with me.*

"No." He chortled. "To Cody. And to the store."

"Ohh—right." Of course. "Thank you, Logan." He was too thoughtful. Were normal people this thoughtful?

Backing up to Amelia's small porch, I watched him cross the yard to his little yellow house. I stayed there for a few chilly minutes. A breeze kicked up, and I shivered. It reminded me what waited inside. Hurrying back in, I breathed in Amelia—a mixture of dust and cinnamon.

Logan had folded the carpet back down. It was so simple. And I had attempted butchering the poor thing.

Walking over to the corner of the rug, I jumped when a shrill old-fashioned phone rang. It wasn't my phone. That one was dead in the trash can. I listened, confused, and then realized it was Amelia's home phone. Dad's flight would have just landed in California—it wouldn't be him.

I followed the old sounding ring into the kitchen. I hadn't noticed the green, rotary phone sitting at the back of the counter.

My hand hovered over the receiver... "Hello?"

"Livy? What's wrong with your cell?"

"Ben." Of course. "Hi, Ben."

"Hi? That's it. I've been worried." I couldn't imagine him fretting over me with Benson and Clyde at his fingertips.

"I'm sorry." I rolled my eyes. "My phone... must be dead." Hey, it was half-true, my cell had to be dead by now.

"I'll come get you this weekend, when my schedule allows it."

"Oh. Well, I can find—"

"You're falling behind at work, you know."

"I know, Benjamin. I just, I need—" He wasn't going to understand my need to be here, and I couldn't tell him about

Amelia's secret box—I hadn't told anyone. "You don't need to leave work to come get me. I'll take the bus."

"Honey," he said, his tone turning sugary. "I'd love to come get you. Besides, I wouldn't mind seeing your little place there."

"Really?" He wanted to see Amelia's house? Maybe he *was* worried. I never gave him enough credit.

"Yes, really."

I jumped up onto the counter, leaning my back against the cupboards and twirled my fingers through green phone cord. "I'd like that, Benjamin." With a promise from Ben to call later, I hung up. It was Thursday night. I wanted time with Amelia's secret box before Benjamin arrived.

Back in the dining area, I pulled at the carpet. It was heavy, but easy enough to lift now that Logan had unstuck it. I pulled until it fell back on its own, revealing half the wooden floorboards. I sat and admired them for a second. How was I supposed to go about this? I couldn't rely on Logan this time. I didn't even have Google to help me. Amelia had no computer and even if I were willing to dig my phone out of the garbage, I doubt Rendezvous provided enough service to use the internet.

On my knees, I pushed down on the ends of each floorboard, hoping one would pop up out of place. None of them did. I was hesitant to go for the butcher knife again, but I needed a lever—it was the best option I could see. Poking it into every crack I could, I pried at the boards. I'd meddled with a quarter of them when one of them wiggled. Yes! Yes, this was it. It had to be. My heart couldn't take it if I found nothing. Forcing the knife in further, I pushed and pried as hard as I could. As certain as I'd been that it had to come up, it was an utter surprise when it actually did.

My hands were cold and each one of my breaths echoed in my ears. My heart threatened to jump out of my chest. The darkness beneath the floor blinded me to what might be there. I pulled at the adjoining board, and it came out easily. I still couldn't see a thing. It would take too long to search for a flashlight. Shaking, I reached a hand inside the black hole, groping around. The crisp air in the ground crept onto my already cool hand and brought a chill up my arm and throughout my body. I touched the dirt floor below, feeling around, patting the ground and searching with my fingers. My hand crept in a circular motion and stopped as it hit something. The object felt rectangular, about three inches tall. Eager, I put my other hand into the hole and pulled out what I hoped were Amelia's secrets.

The brown wooden box was old and dirty, I brushed the sand and filth from the top. Breathing heavy, tunnel vision had kicked in. I had one objective. Leaving the dining room in disarray, I took the box and headed back up to my room. Setting it on my bed, I changed clothes, keeping an eye on the box—afraid it might disappear. Next to the window, I glanced out at the pretty elm tree, high above the house.

Breathing in, I stared at the elm, trying to calm my tension. What if I'd made more of it all than it really was? What if I opened the box and it didn't explain a thing, or worse, it was empty? Would it tell me who Seth was? Would it tell me who *Amelia* was?

Letting out a shaky breath, I went back to the bed. I sat cross-legged, gazing at the box. Timid, I lifted the lid. The hinges attached at the back keeping the lid upright and in place. The inside, lined in dark velvet, made the outside look more aged and faded than before. The first thing I saw—of course being me, was the *book*. The tattered leather journal bulged from its aged and wrinkled pages. I pulled it out carefully and set it aside. Beneath it lie photos. I picked up all three. The top black and white photo showed a small group of people around my age. It had to have been taken fifty or sixty years ago. The sharp crease in the photograph showed where it had been bent, separating the group. I flipped to the second picture, a man alone, broad and fair, in casual clothes. I didn't know his face. The last was a close-up of a pretty, young woman and the same man from the picture before, big smiles on their faces. I didn't recognize the woman either. I set the photos next to the journal. Picking up the thin gold band, I twirled it between my fingers. Examining the band, it wasn't anything special or expensive. Last, a letter, still in its envelope, with Amelia's name scripted on the front. I left the pages inside, unsure about opening it.

Filing through the pictures once more, I set them back inside and found the journal again. Opening the cover, I read her name. Amelia Wall. Her maiden name. Biting my thumbnail under a grin—I remembered—her maiden name, I remembered it.

Should I read her journal? It was so obviously hidden. What if she never meant for this book to be found? But then, why write one? Why write something you didn't plan to have read one day. I hope my granddaughter will read what I've written. But Amelia was different, she didn't feel like my grandmother, nor did she ever treat me like her granddaughter.

I set the book in my lap and ran my fingers over the soft cover. Glancing to the alarm clock, one a.m. Maybe I should wait until morning to see how I felt about it all. "Hmph." I hung my head, tired. "This is emotionally exhausting." I tossed two of the pictures back inside the box, keeping out the one of the man and woman, side by side. I looked at them... his fair hair, her eyes—something did feel familiar... sort of. Anything could become familiar after staring at it for twenty minutes, I supposed.

With a yawn, I tossed it in the box as well. It flipped in the air, landing on its front, backside facing up, and that's when I saw the scrawl marks on its back. I retrieved it and read the messy script. *Seth and me 1956.* "Huhh!" Seth! Seth! This was proof that I wasn't a crazed child, hearing things all those years ago. "Seth." I said aloud—unable to help myself. I turned it back around and looked at the man for a moment. I ran my fingers along the side of his face. Seth. I'd found him, but I still didn't know him—or Amelia. I set my reservations aside and put the picture down. Picking the journal back up, I opened the cover and read.

Chapter 11

June 1, 1956

I can't believe I'm stuck in Ganesworth all summer. What does Dad think I'll get out of this? I'm lonely. I'm so lonely. I've been here one week and decided I'd absolutely die if I couldn't spill my feelings somewhere – thus the diary.

Penny's at home and Gladdy got married two weeks ago. At least Daddy let me go to the wedding before he sent me off to this dejected place. I don't understand how working at Uncle Herb's store will help me forget about college. It's not as if he doesn't have the money to send me! I'm so lonely! Penny's cousin went to college. Oh, it sounded wonderful. Culture and science and the literature! Oh, the reading I could accomplish there. But Daddy says – the only women who go to college are the ones planning on ending up old maids. Who can think of men when there are books to be read?

I'm sure I'll have nothing to write of – nothing happens in Ganesworth!

Amelia

"Who can think of men when there are books to be read?" I laughed. I'd never seen even a fraction of the passion Amelia portrayed by her hand sixty-some years ago. She thought this town, this Ganesworth, was lonely—how on earth did she survive Rendezvous?

I picked up the picture of Seth and the woman—I was sure

now, this had to be Amelia. She was quite pretty. I would never have guessed it was her. I felt bad for that, but the face I'd known had always been wrinkled and cross.

I retrieved one of the albums belonging to Earl and plopped it on top of the bed. A photograph of Amelia, sitting in a rocker, holding Dad. He was an infant, and his name was scrawled underneath. She looked at least ten years older in this photo, her coldness ever present. Wait… Dad was born in 1957.

"No, that can't be." I turned the picture over and read Amelia's handwritten information once more: *Seth and me 1956.* A year later? That's it? How could she have gained so many years, so much hardness, in just one short year? The passion I read in that first journal entry didn't exist in this photo of her with my infant father.

Yawning, I stood up and stretched my legs. I couldn't get over Amelia's first journal entry. The Amelia I knew in person couldn't be the same as this woman from so long ago. Placing the brown journal back in the box, I tucked it in the guest room closet under the shoeboxes already there. I shook my head. Why I felt the need to continue hiding her secrets…I didn't know.

Stopping at the bedroom window, I heaved it up until it opened. Without a screen, I was free to poke my head outside and get a better view of my elm. It stretched high in the black, night sky, its bark arms pointing upward in a scrawly, crooked way. The starry background made a lovely canvas. I took a deep breath, the air so smooth—like a cold glass of water. And quiet… nothing, no cars, no people, only crickets singing.

"Hello, Liv."

I shot up, surprised, whacking my head on the window. Logan's head poked out his own window. "Hey. You startled me."

"Sorry about that." He looked up at the view. "Pretty night, isn't it?"

"It is." I followed his gaze and rubbed the lump on my head. "Is is always like this?"

"Pretty much. In the winter the ground is white and the birds don't chirp."

"Ooo, I bet that tree is lovely with a blanket of snow."

He smiled back at me. His wet hair looked black and curlier than before. A shower was something I should consider. It had been a long day.

"So, is that tree mine or yours?" I asked, ignoring the flirtatious tone in my voice.

"I guess it's half and half."

"Don't ever decide to cut down your half, okay? I'll sue, I know a fabulous lawyer."

"Don't worry." His laugh faded into the stillness, the quiet of the night returning.

Before the silence could last too long I said, "I should go, to bed I mean. It's been a long day."

"Yeah, it has. I'll bring breakfast by around eight."

"What? No, no, Logan, you don't need to do that."

"Sure I do. I've got an old Chevy coming in at eight-thirty, so I'll see you at eight." He flashed me another fantastic grin, and then ducked back into his house, a grey curtain falling behind him.

"Breakfast," I mumbled to myself. "Eight o' clock." I yawned again. My shower would have to wait until morning. I was much too tired and it was far too late.

I had planned to wake up bright and early, shower and look half way decent before Logan arrived. I did wake up fairly early. I decided I had time to read another entry from Amelia.

June 6, 1956

I figured out Daddy's design in sending me here. He wanted me to meet Philip Harlem. I'm certain of it. Two nights ago Phil's father invited me to dinner in their home. He's an old friend of Dad's. I had heard of the Harlem's and their fortune from Dad and then half the town has something named after a Harlem. Phil may be in charge of the family business, but he's boring. He smiled and cooed at me half the night, but said nothing of interest. How could one go through life with conversations like that? I should be happy to have the company, but he was so unbelievably dull.

Uncle Herb's store is so tiresome. I had three patrons today. No wonder he has a second job. No one in this little town wants to buy art. And the three who did come in used it like a museum. Why couldn't he have invested all of his money into a book store? Then at least I'd have something to read while I sit here five hours a day, five days a week. I'm so forlorn, I could cry.

I got a letter from Penny today. She's a carhop again. She loves it. That has to be more exciting than my job. Myron Lewis asked her to the Summer Moon Dance. I love that dance, the first one of every summer. I've only been twice. How depressing is that?

Amelia

June 8, 1956

Philip Harlem asked me to a dance. It's called Under the Stars. It's outside, the whole town's invited. I said I'd go. Phil's horridly boring, but being out under the stars and getting dressed up—I couldn't resist. It has to be better than sitting at the store or in Uncle Herb's house all day. Uncle Herb doesn't even have a television.

Amelia

Sitting in my pajamas, I laughed as I read two more journal entries when—*rap rap rap!*

"No. No, no, no. It can't be eight o' clock already." Another knock told me it was. "Crap. Crap." I looked down at myself—PAJAMAS! I couldn't leave him outside knocking though. Despite my wardrobe, I ran down to Amelia's front door.

"Hi," I said with a nervous laugh.

"Good morning." Logan stood tall in his dark jeans and fitted T-shirt.

Moving aside, I said, "Come in."

"Thanks." He carried a box of cereal in one hand, a gallon of milk hung from the other.

"You brought cereal?" I laughed—*wait, was that rude?*

Breaking into a grin, Logan said, "Yeah, well, it's better than nothing."

"I'm sure I could have found…" Yeah, there was nothing to eat in this house.

"Exactly." He crossed the threshold.

I followed after him, his upper arms were so thick—swinging back and forth with the milk jug. And his back—*Ugh!* Shooting my eyes to the ground, I kept walking. What was it about this man that made me want to examine him? Crossing into the dining area—*whomp!* Logan had stopped short, and I ran right into the back of him.

"Oh!" My hands flattened on his back. Unable to stop the momentum, my face smashed into him as well. "Sorry," I muffled into his shirt.

He turned, unjostled, his face giving away that something else was on his mind, something other than my clumsiness. Turning around, his eyes narrowed on me. "What have you been doing in here?"

Peeking around him I saw the mess in the dining room, the mess I had been too busy to clean up last night. "Oh, shoot," I whispered. "I… uh, I… I was just checking out the floor."

"By disfiguring it? You have a vendetta against this flooring, don't you?"

"No, I didn't hurt it. See, it's fine. It's totally fine." I ran around him and picked up one of the pieces of hardwood lying cockeyed. Kneeling down, I shoved and pushed, trying to force it back into its hole.

Walking over, Logan set the cereal and milk aside and then knelt next to me. So near, I breathed him in. Putting his hand on top of mine, he stopped my frantic motion. With gentle fingers, he removed the piece from my hands. He turned it around like a puzzle piece facing the wrong direction and easily slid the section back into place.

"Um, thank you." I rocked back, sitting upright.

He stood, his hand extended toward me. I took it, and he brought me to my feet.

With the food and bowls at the table, Logan poured some chocolaty puffs into each of our bowls.

"So, do you wanna tell me what that was all about?" He glanced to the side where the hole had been.

I wasn't sure what to say. I didn't have it in me to lie to him. But the truth…I couldn't share that either. Instead, I stuffed a spoonful of cereal into my mouth.

He chortled. "You don't have to tell me, but for a person so in love with the wooden floors here, you were sure quick to dismantle them."

I tried to laugh through my giant-sized-chocolaty bite.

"It's your house." But the way he said it, I didn't believe him. "But, it was hers." He was right. What he didn't realize was he wasn't the only one protecting Amelia here. I had kept her secret eleven years. I didn't see how I could betray her now.

"How well did you know Amelia?" I asked.

"I'd say pretty well, we were neighbors for a long time."

"Do you think she was happy here?"

"Yeah, I do."

"How private was she?"

"What do you mean?" He'd put his spoon down, staring at me.

"Just what I said. Do you know? Was she private?" I put down my spoon too and locked my nervous fingers together.

He leaned back in his chair and crossed his arms across his chest. "Will you answer *my* question?"

Eyeing him, I knew what was coming.

"What were you doing to that floor?"

I cleared my throat and avoided his question. "You loved her, right?"

His black brows scrunched together. "I did."

I couldn't answer his question. I couldn't bring myself to say something I'd made sure stayed silent for so long. Even if he loved her, even if he knew her better than me.

He waited, watching me. The house was quiet, too quiet. A horn honked outside, breaking through the silence. "That's my eight-thirty."

I nodded. "Thanks for breakfast."

"Anytime." He smiled, and I was surprised his tone wasn't angry. I hadn't answered him in the least. "I'm going in to the market later, if you want to join me."

"Uh- yeah. That'd be great. Thank you."

"Eleven o' clock?"

"Sure."

I walked Logan to the door and out into the sunshine. Shielding my eyes with one hand, I waved with the other. "See you—"

Laughter interrupted my goodbye. A hearty, loud sound that came from neither Logan nor myself. Turning to the left, I saw a middle-aged man with a big smile on his lips, leaning against an old Chevrolet in Logan's driveway. Logan's eight-thirty found something to be quite humorous.

"Don't mind me!" He hollered. "I didn't mean to interrupt."

Aware of my pajamas, I tugged on my shirt, making sure my stomach wasn't bare. Still, I watched the man rather than retreat into the house. He was dirty, not from work as Logan had been the first time I met him, but from not showering in who knows how long. His greasy, dark blonde hair lay in no particular direction. His dirty jeans were torn at the pockets and his tan flannel shirt looked as though it had never seen the inside of a washing machine.

Logan didn't address him. "See you at eleven," Logan said to me and headed over toward his house.

"Yeah, see you then," I said, but my eyes were locked on the filthy chuckling man behind him.

"Not even gonna kiss her goodbye, Logan?"

Taking a step forward, I thought about answering him—Logan hadn't and I didn't like the man's implications.

"You're not much of a date, are you? Who is she anyway? I never seen her before."

I wanted to correct his English as much as I wanted to deny his assumptions. But not exactly wanting an introduction, I waited for Logan to put it right.

"That's Olivia," Logan said to the man. "Amelia's granddaughter. She owns the place now. You would have met her

Hank, if you'd shown up to the funeral." Where was the—*it's not like that* modification. He was letting this man believe whatever he wanted. Why didn't he correct him?

"Funerals ain't my thing," Hank looked past Logan to me. "Pretty girl though."

"That she is," Logan said, glancing back at me.

My cheeks burned pink. What did he just say to the dirty man? Turning on my heels, I hurried through the door, slamming it behind me.

I ran up to the bathroom and showered, clearing my head. I slipped into my skinny jeans and turquoise ruffled blouse. Taking my time to get ready, I applied my granite eye shadow—it always made my blue eyes pop and curled my long, strawberry hair into waves. I still had time before the grocery store, but at least I was calm and collected—and maybe more deserving of the word pretty.

Coming out of the bathroom, I walked to Amelia's bedroom door and peeked inside again. Her dusty cinnamon scent was strong inside the door. I still hadn't gone all the way in. I considered taking a step when Amelia's phone rang. She only had the one, so I raced down the stairs and into the kitchen. She didn't have an answering machine—nothing to stop the racket. I reached my hand for the receiver but stopped it mid air. I knew who it was. I couldn't listen to another lecture though, not now. The ringing stopped and a rap on the door turned my head. *Logan.*

Another rap.

"Come in!" I hollered, jutting up the stairs to fetch my purse. On the way down the ringing began again.

"Hey, Liv," Logan called. "Do you want me to get that?"

"No!" I ran down and into the kitchen, grabbing his reaching wrist. "No! Sorry, it's just there's no caller ID, and I just don't want to hear it."

His eyebrows furrowed with sympathy. "They want you to come home?"

"Yeah."

"Pretty persistent, aren't they?"

"It's my dad. Benjamin's fine, I'm certain. He's all about work right now, anyway. But my dad… I think he's talking Benjamin into badgering me. And it's driving me crazy."

He slid the hand of the wrist I still held down until his fingers met mine. "That doesn't make sense to me."

"Wh—What do you mean?" Amelia's house needed an air conditioner.

"I would think *you* being gone would drive Ben crazy."

My hand tingled where he touched. Needles in every one of my fingers made it difficult to think straight. I pulled my hand from his. "Benjamin… is… really focused right now."

"So focused it doesn't matter to him that you're not there?"

I started out the door, ignoring his question. Walking toward his place, his long legs caught up with me easily. I'd never really noticed the old beat up truck sitting outside his house. The greenish-brown color kind of blended in with the background. He opened the passenger door for me, and I hopped inside.

Folding my arms, I stared out the passenger window. "Neither of them understands my side of this. You know? They can't even pretend to. I just wish they would *try*."

"I thought the silence meant we weren't talking about this," he said, both of his hands on the wheel.

"No." I rolled my eyes. "We're not… I'm just so frustrated."

"Livy," he said, turning to me. "If you need to talk, you can, but I won't be able to stay silent. If you talk, I'll voice my honest opinion. You may not like it."

I suppose I had been warned.

"Go ahead, tell me about the puppy, I mean Ben."

My arms flew out of their fold and I whipped my head, staring at him. "Did you just—"

"Call your boyfriend a puppy. Yeah, I did. Talk all you want, Liv. However, you take the chance of me insulting your boyfriend again."

"Okay," I said, shaking my head. "I'm done. We're not talking about this." I held my hands in my lap and stopped myself from twisting them together. "But why would you—"

"He follows your dad around like a—"

"Okay." I held up my hands to stop him. "Got it."

"So, how long do *you* think you'll stay?"

My head found my hands again. "I don't know. I don't know! I just wish what I *want* to do and what I *should* do could be the same—for once!" And then, Ben is *supposed* to come get me this weekend.

"Wha—?"

"I want to stay, I can see myself staying here...a while. But my responsibilities, Ben, my family...I should go home and work."

He started the truck and pulled out before talking again. "Why is it wrong for you to stay here? Why *should* you go home?"

"That's what I've committed to do."

"Yeah, but things change. Your grandmother died, you inherited a house. Your situation has changed. You have two choices: stay or go. Neither of them is a bad choice, or a wrong choice. If you *want* to stay, then maybe that's the right choice for you. No one can tell you that but yourself. Not even dear old Dad."

How did his brain work? How did he make sense out of my chaos? "You're an interesting person, Logan."

He burst out in a laugh. "Thanks. I think."

Chapter 12

"I normally go into Cody once a month," Logan said, as I reread the price of eggs three times. "Really, Farmer's isn't bad. Joe, the owner, he's got to make a living too. And he's real good about taking people's tabs down and billing them later."

"Hmmm, well, not knowing how long I'll be here does make it more difficult." Still staring at the eggs before me, I finally said, "Why don't you grab your things and I'll get mine. I'll meet you at the front?"

"Sure." He snatched the carton I had been staring at.

I skipped the overpriced eggs and went on to the staples, like Captain Crunch, wheat bread, and milk. But Farmer's didn't carry Captain Crunch. The cereal aisle wasn't really even an aisle. It was more of a stand in the middle of an aisle. I settled on the chocolaty goodness Logan had brought me that morning. I moved on to peanut butter and choked back my curse word at the price. I decided strawberry jam ought to wrap things up. This would do for another day or two. At least Logan wouldn't have to provide every meal for me. I could live on PB&J's until Ben came for me.

There was one other woman in the store. She was pretty and looked to be in her mid forty's. She watched me as I strolled about each aisle. Whenever I made eye contact, she'd smile and quickly look away. Had I been wearing a dress, I would have checked to make sure the skirt wasn't tucked in my underwear, showing myself to the world. Something was up. I made my way over to

Logan examining the cold lunchmeats.

"Hey!" I whispered.

He glanced over to me. "Are you ready to go?"

"See that lady?" I gave a slight jerk of my head in her direction.

He tilted his head to the side. "Marlene?" He questioned, making eye contact with her and then giving her a short wave hello. Without making direct eye contact, I saw her erratic wave in return.

"What are you doing?" I did my best exacerbated whisper.

"What?" He asked, looking down at me. "I'm waving to Marlene."

I grabbed his gesturing hand and held it to his side. "Why is *Marlene* staring at me?"

"Oh, that. Livy, you're new. This isn't a big city or even some smaller town of twelve thousand. This is Rendezvous, population, three-hundred thirty-two. You stick out like a sore thumb. She's probably trying to be friendly, figuring out how to approach you."

Before I could protest, I realized Marlene had inched her way over to us. She was eyeing us and then she spoke. "Hi there, Logan."

"How are you, Marlene?"

"Very well. Thank you. I didn't get a chance to meet your friend yesterday." She glanced my direction.

"Oh, this is Olivia Benson." He pulled his hand from the pin I held it in at his side. "Olivia, this is Marlene Jacobs."

"You two seem to know each other well," she said, her mouth still wearing a Joker size grin.

"We're neighbors now," Logan said.

"That's nice." Marlene smiled again and with a wave she was off and done gawking my way.

"Why didn't you say that earlier?" I asked.

"Uh, when?"

"With that guy at your house who was all, 'Ooo! You're not a good date.'" I cleared my throat. "You know, that guy."

"Hank? It doesn't matter what you tell Hank, he'll believe whatever he wants to."

"Still, you didn't even..." I threw my hands up, not sure what I wanted to say.

"Olivia, I didn't mean to upset you. I know Hank, it wouldn't have helped."

I had no reason not to believe him. Then again, did I have any reasons, other than my childish intuition and yes...infatuation, to *believe* him? "I'm ready. I'm gonna go pay."

"Okay, I'll be right there."

I worried the man with the bright orange hunting vest at the one checkout lane wouldn't take my debit card. The register looked about a hundred years old.

"Hello, there," he said as if we were old friends. "How's it going today?"

I read his nametag. Joe. I couldn't remember a Joe from the funeral, but then that didn't mean much. "Oh, good. I'm good."

"That's great. So, Olivia, are ya getting all settled?"

"Ah..." Crap. We had met. "Sure..."

He chuckled. "We met at the funeral, miss."

"Oh, yes, that's right." I had zero recollection of the cheerful older man. "So, Joe, do you take debit cards?"

"We sure do." He pulled a black card machine from under the counter and set in on display for me.

Logan stood in line behind me, a smile playing at his lips. Placing his things on the counter next to mine, he leaned close and whispered, "He had the card terminal installed a month ago."

My ear tingled and I swayed an inch away. "Lucky me."

Joe shook open a brown paper bag and placed my items inside.

"Is that all you got?" Logan asked.

"Well, yes. I'll be leaving in a day or two, so I just got the essentials."

"Leaving so soon?" Joe asked.

I didn't look at Joe but kept my eyes on his working hands. "Most likely. It doesn't look like I'll be able to stay."

"That's too darn bad, Miss Olivia. We were looking forward to getting to know ya."

Looking up to meet his kind eyes, I gave the man a small courtesy smile. Maybe it would be better to leave sooner rather than later. The longer I stayed, the more people I met, the more explanations I needed to give. Really, would any of them care once I'd gone? Rachel? Marlene? Joe?

"You're not alone there, Joe," Logan said.

Logan?

Chapter 13

"How about lunch?"

"Okay." I studied the passing town from the cab of Logan's truck.

Riding down one of the roads I recognized, Logan turned where Dad had, two days previous, into the school parking lot.

"What are we doing here?" I asked.

"Lunch." He opened his door, not offering any more explanation and got out of the truck.

Following after him, I asked, "Here?"

"I thought we'd go to Amelia's favorite place to eat."

I couldn't help but laugh. The high school was Amelia's lunch spot. I guess it made some sense. "Okay," I said, "but next time lets go somewhere around town. I've never been anywhere... but Farmer's."

He stopped before we reached the front doors, a small smile playing at his lips. "Will there be a next time?"

Not meeting his eyes, I shifted my feet. Maybe I shouldn't have said that. "Sure." I really didn't know.

"You're still leaving though?"

"I am." I looked up to see his reaction, but couldn't read his face.

"You think you'll ever come back?" he asked.

"Sure," I said again, as convincing as the first time around.

His brows rose with doubt, but I wasn't sure why he cared. He loved my grandmother. Why he cared if *I* stayed or went was a mystery. His eyes peered into mine and then he scooped a hand through his dark locks and looked away.

"Shall we?" I opened the door. I didn't like being uncomfortable with Logan. He was like a long lost relative or an old friend. We always seemed to pick up where we left off with good conversation. Feeling awkward with him made my skin tighten and my head ache.

Walking in ahead of him into the quiet building, I followed the same path as before, just down the hallway to the office. We arrived without seeing another soul—the only sound was our footsteps.

Amelia's seat sat empty, like the last time. It had only been two days—I had to keep reminding myself.

I didn't see her get up, but all at once, Rachel Lemonade took up my entire view. She must have been on her tiptoes, her five foot two inches only coming up to my nose. She lunged at me, grasping both of my shoulders and pulling me into a tight hug. I patted her yellow and green pug covered sweatshirt on the back.

"Hello, Rachel." I managed to get out through the strangulation.

"It warms my heart to see you." Rachel pulled back to look up at my face.

"How are you, Rach?" Logan asked.

"Me?" she said, at last releasing me all together. "I'm fine as China. Not surprised to see *you*." Rachel's quirky remarks always caught me off guard. I stifled a giggle.

"Oh?"

"Hank came by this morning. Sierra forgot her algebra book—again."

My eyes went wide, and the threat of giggling left at the mention of that dirty, pretentious man, who Logan made no explanation too. Apparently he didn't just believe things that weren't true—he liked to talk too!

My mouth opened, but only a squeak escaped.

Logan rolled his eyes and said, "Ah, Rach, you know Hank. He's a good old guy, but how often can you count on what comes out of his mouth?"

"Well, that's true, he's ten times worse than any gossiping

goose!" Rachel wagged her finger at Logan.

Heat settled in my cheeks and wouldn't budge. I wasn't all that sure what a *gossiping goose* was, but I knew it wasn't making me look good. Rachel gave me a grin that had my guilt level rising—when I'd done nothing to feel guilty about. Hmm, if this is how it was going to be, I could probably skip lunch. Amelia's journal was waiting for me, anyway.

"So, how's work going?" Logan asked, changing the subject.

"Oh my, oh my indeed." Rachel shook her head. "It's rough. I depended on Amelia, as she did me. Now she's gone and my behind work is taller than a never ending stack of hotcakes." Rachel sniffed. Snatching a tissue, she dabbed at each of her eyes.

"Too bad there's no one here to hire to help out." Logan put an arm around Rachel and she turned, crying into his stomach.

"I know Callie'd do it in a heartbeat," Rachel said, looking up at Logan. "But she's got three classes this semester, as well as a pregnant belly bigger than a hot air balloon. I just can't do that do her."

"What does she teach?" I asked, watching the pair.

Rachel's head swooped around toward me, her hands out like a traffic controller. "Olivia Benson!"

Confused, I looked from Logan back to Rachel. "Yes?"

"Olivia Benson." She took two steps towards me, her finger pointing outward. "You're staying here? Aren't you? Your father's gone home and you own Amelia's house." She glanced to Logan and raised her eyebrows as if he were another, silent reason. Her tapered jeans made her baggy sweatshirt look too large for her petite frame, her platinum hair curled to perfection. She may have been somebody's grandmother, but at the moment, her small eyes boring into mine terrified me.

"No, no..." I waved a hand at her. "No, I'm leaving. I—I have a boyfriend and he's picking me up."

"The job's yours. All you have to do is say the word and it's yours."

"Rachel, did you hear me? I'm...I'm going. I can't stay."

Pinned against her desk, she stood close, just inches separating us. "You call me when you change your mind. Okay?" She smothered me into another squeeze. "All righty, I better get back to work."

"Rachel, I…" Guilt settled in, but I didn't know how to end that sentence. What could I say that wouldn't upset her?

Logan winked at me as if to convince me I didn't need to say anything. Leaning down, he kissed her on the cheek. "We're going to lunch. Can we bring you back anything?"

Rachel smiled at his gesture. "Nah. I'll be down in a bit."

Walking down the empty hallway, I looked back at Rachel. "I do wish I could help. I feel bad. She's got so much extra work."

"She misses her friend more than anything," he said.

The lunchroom was small but full and for the first time since entering Rendezvous High, it seemed like a normal high school. The room bubbled with chatter with what looked like thirty to forty teenagers doing what they do best, eating and gabbing. A few kids waved to Logan and stared at me… again the only person in the room whom they didn't know. We got in a short line behind five or six students.

"So, what's on the menu?" I asked Logan, picking up my empty tray.

"Looks like saucy meatball sandwiches today. You're not a vegetarian are you?"

I laughed. "No, but if I were—"

"Logan!" called the older woman behind the lunch counter. Her eyes grazed at me for half a second, before turning back to the man beside me. "What are you doing here?"

"Hi, Lucille. I'm taking Olivia out to lunch." Logan motioned to me. "Did you get to meet Amelia's granddaughter?"

"No, I did not," she said glancing my way again. Before I could respond to her curt greeting, she said, "Speaking of granddaughters—my Sadie will be in town next month."

Clearing his throat, Logan nodded, giving Lucille a small smile.

Lucille's grin back showed a full set of teeth. Waving a marinara covered spoon in the air, she sang out, "She's still single."

Unable to stop my grin, I watched Logan in his awkward state.

Lucille plopped an extra meatball onto his plate and handed him the tray. He offered it to me and gave Lucille another empty tray. With narrowed eyes, Lucille looked to me. I smiled at the large woman, her graying hair covered with a net. Her blue uniform bulged around her large bust, her pale white face pulsing at my very presence.

Filling the second plate, she watched me. "How long do you plan to stay in town *Miss* Benson?"

"Not long."

Her expression smug, she said, "That's too bad."

"It is," Logan agreed not seeming to notice her insolence. "Ben's coming soon, right?"

"Ah, yes, yes he is," I answered, though I didn't need to—he already knew that.

"Ben?" Lucille echoed.

"Her boyfriend."

"Ah, I see." The older lunch lady gave me a pouty lip and then a toothy grin covered her face. "Well, honey, it's just too darn bad you couldn't stay a little longer." She pointed her marinara spoon at me, her tone sugary now. "This town could use a young sweet thing like you. Logan here's just about the only twenty-something we've got."

Looking up at him, I wondered if what she said was true. I followed him down the counter edge, food in hand. He stopped at the end and paid the student aide.

Sitting at a half empty table, we were swarmed by students. I recognized Roy. He sat too close to me. Logan sat across from us, a couple of kids on each side of him.

"Logan, could you fix a '54 Ford? It needs a new engine and... probably other stuff."

"Other stuff, huh?" Logan stabbed a meatball. "I already told your dad to bring it by."

"Cool," said the boy next to him.

"Hey, guys." Roy inched closer to me. "This is Olivia."

The blonde boy shook my hand and the other said nothing, simply smiled in my direction. Since Roy didn't try, Logan made further introductions. "And this is Ken," he said pointing to the blonde and then to the quiet boy, "and Andrew."

"It's Friday, you got any plans tonight?" Roy's voice came out low.

Again, I inched away. "Yes. I do." I lied.

Roy smiled baring his white teeth. "Saturday?"

"Saturday my *boyfriend* Benjamin will be here." Or Sunday… but when it came to Roy…

"Looks like she's all booked up, Roy." Logan reached across the table to slap Roy's shoulder.

Rocking to the side, Roy rubbed his shoulder. "That doesn't seem to bother you." Andrew and Ken's eyes widened bouncing between the two. "Come on Roy, let's go," Ken said, tugging on Roy's shirt. Roy stood, and Ken waved. "See ya, Logan."

Andrew's face was indifferent as he gave a wave our direction.

"Bye." Logan called after them. "Go finish your homework!"

"You know, Roy's actually not much younger than me." Logan's reaction to Roy's endeavors surprised me. "Besides, you said he was harmless."

"I've been wrong before. Besides, it isn't his age. As if *you'd* be with someone so pompous. The most important person to Roy is Roy."

"He's what, eighteen? That doesn't surprise me." I thought for a moment. "So, are you really the only twenty-something in this town?"

Again his dimple hollowed. "The only single one, yes."

"Wow." I shifted in my seat. "That's… weird."

"It's just normal here."

"Yeah, but how do you meet people?"

"I guess I get lucky every once in a while. I met you, didn't I?"

The nervous inflection in my laugh annoyed me. "That's not exactly what I meant."

"That's what you asked."

June 26, 1956

Philip Harlem is not only boring, but he can't even dance a simple stroll.

Daddy was thrilled when Uncle Herb told him the news. He

even sent over a new dress for my date with Phil. I asked Mother to send one of my books too, but I guess Dad wouldn't let her. At least, there wasn't one to be found in the package. Thankfully, Uncle Herb isn't opposed to me going to the local library. It isn't much, this is Ganesworth after all. Still, it's better than nothing.

Back to the dance. Philip's father let him take his new Chevrolet. He came with the top down. It changed my mind about the night. Maybe it would be magical, worth writing about. We arrived a half hour late. I was surprised to see the parking lot of Ganesworth School almost full of people. The air was warm and the stars were out. My silvery-blue dress sparkled in the moonlight. I could hardly wait to get on the dance floor. It truly started out peachy.

However, the minute we arrived Philip paraded me around to his little friends. I spent the first hour watching other people dance while Phil talked about himself and his future. He didn't even speak to me once, but to everyone else around me. I was just his ornament. When he was finally quiet for two seconds I asked him, "How do you like dancing? The Madison is one of my favorites." I thought since that dance had just started it would be a good hint that I was ready to dance! All Philip Harlem said was, "I'm not a lover of dancing." I wanted to scream, 'THEN WHY ON EARTH DID YOU BRING ME TO A DANCE?' I'm a lady, so of course I did not. The cad finally asked me if I wanted a drink. When I answered yes, that I did indeed, he called over another boy to get it for him! Apparently, I didn't hold back the glare I gave him. To which he responded, "What? Seth works for my father." And Seth may indeed work for Mr. Harlem, but there were no waiters or servers of any kind at this event. The poor boy was just there as a guest, like we were. I've never been on such a horrid date in my life.

So, when Seth came back with my drink and Phil was gabbing with someone once more, I decided to completely ignore the meathead. When Mr. Harlem's employee brought me back my drink, I truly looked at him for the first time. He was dressed plainly, nothing fancy like Phil. He's tall and blonde and honestly nothing eyeballing special, but his smile was nice, kind.

So, I turned a full 180 away from Phil – who seemed opposite of this boy in every way. And who didn't even notice, by the way, and I smiled flirtatiously at Seth. I thanked him and engaged him in conversation. He was eager to talk back. He must not have had a date. It was the best thirty minutes of my evening. Probably of my entire arrival to Ganesworth. At last, not caring one bit for Philip Harlem, or for what he thought of me, I said to Seth, "Do you care for dancing?" To my utter horror and humiliation, he kindly answered that he didn't know how to dance. And with that, the only good piece of conversation I'd had all night, walked off, red in the face too.

On top of it all, Philip had the nerve to make advances on Uncle Herb's doorstep. I quickly told him I was tired after the long night and escaped through the door.

What a night! What a ridiculous, embarrassing, appalling night. If I see Philip Harlem in the next life it'll be all too soon.

Amelia

Chapter 14

The picture of Amelia dancing never entered my craziest of scenarios. This couldn't be the same woman. I fell backwards onto the bed and stared at the ceiling. This whole thing seemed surreal. I had been waiting for Seth's name and then BAM! When it showed up, I wasn't prepared. I stayed up until one o'clock in the morning reading her next three entries. He wasn't mentioned again. Maybe he wasn't the same person. The bumpy popcorn ceiling turned 3D as my eyes bore into it. I'd read about her loneliness, her hopes, Philip Harlem asking her out again and Uncle Herb blowing a gasket when she declined, but no Seth—at least not again. How could that be?

Sitting up, I thumbed through the one entry that *did* mention Seth's name. I jumped when the doorbell rang. Picturing Logan with a breakfast tray in hand, I raced down the stairs. The soft bell rang once more.

"I'm coming, Logan," I called. Opening the door I teased him. "You better have more than cereal to—"

Benjamin's tall frame hovered in the doorway. Smoothing his already perfect hair, he cocked his head to the side. "Cereal?"

"Benjamin!" Sucking in my breath, I started to cough. "What are you doing here?" Giving myself a mental slap, I reached up to hug him.

Giving my back a pat, he pulled back. "I told you…"

"I know. I know. Sorry. It's just—it's nine in the morning. How'd you get here so quickly?"

"I started yesterday." Raising his eyebrows, he tapped his

foot. "Are you going to let me in?"

"Oh!" I jumped out of the way. "Yes, of course. Come in. Come in."

Setting his overnight bag inside the door, he bent and kissed me quick on the lips. He scanned the front room without changing expressions and walked without a guide into the dining area.

Chasing after him, I said, "Hey, let me give you a tour."

He smiled, but it was too polite, forced.

If only I could read minds. On second thought, I didn't want to know what he was thinking.

"So." I ignored his long, breathy sigh. "This is the dining room, obviously. And the kitchen." I waved my hand, motioning to the small area off the dining room. "What's with the floor?" He pointed to a corner of the carpet that had flapped up.

"Oh that! When I used to come here Amelia had these old hardwood floors, I was hoping she still did. So, the neighbor helped me pull up the carpet to see and they're still here. I'm thinking about refinishing them." The half-truth ran from my mouth fast and easy.

His lips sprouted to a frown. "Huh?"

I flipped the rug up to show him the floorboards.

"Hmm."

Again, I disregarded his grunts. "Come upstairs, I'll show you my room."

Ben followed me up, listening to my small facts here and there. I didn't know much.

"There's just the one bath. It's small, but not terrible." We walked past the bathroom without going inside. "Here's my room." We entered the small space. I'd forgotten about her journal atop my bed. I picked it up along with the brown box and set them inside the closet. "Just a few of her things." I shut the door tight. He didn't ask about it and I blew out a sigh. I would have lied to him. I would have looked him in the eye—and lied.

Opening the window, I hung my head out. "And my favorite part... Come here."

"Livy—"

"Come on."

Ben's heavy steps trudged my way and he too poked his head out the windowpane. He gazed up at the tree. "Pretty."

"It is, huh? This was always my favorite part of Grandma's house."

Bringing his head back inside, he stood straight. "Grandma?"

"Amelia." I said, back in the room. I was happy to share this with Benjamin, but he wasn't proving the process easy.

Arms crossed, he said. "You don't normally call her that."

"So?"

"I'm just saying..."

"You're saying what? That's what she is, my grandmother."

"In theory."

Shaking my head, my fingers gripped my hips. "In reality, Ben! I haven't forgotten the past or my life, but I own this house now, and for me that changes things."

Rolling his eyes, unimpressed with my speech, he turned away, and for a minute examined the opposite side of the room before walking out.

Starting for Amelia's open bedroom door, I dashed in front of him, blocking his entry. "What—what are you doing?"

"I haven't seen this room." He took a step forward running into me.

"Oh." I didn't budge from my blockade in the doorframe.

"Livy," he said using his sugary tone. "Why won't you show me this room?"

"It's not that I don't want to show you this room, it's just, it's hers. Her own private space and *I* haven't gone in yet."

"What?" He chuckled. "You can be so silly." He touched the tip of my nose with his finger and bent down to kiss my cheek. With his hands under my arms, he moved me out of the way like a pesky three year old. He flipped the light switch on and walked inside.

"Ben!" But he ignored me.

Sitting on her bed, her quilted comforter wrinkled under his weight. Then he picked up three of the books lying in a stack on the ground. Turning them on their sides, he read aloud. "*Mansfield Park, The Scarlet Pimpernel, Sense and Sensibility.*"

I listened from the doorway.

"Livy, come in here. She's not waiting to haunt you."

"I know that." My head burned with annoyance. "I just feel intrusive… I guess." Even as I said the words I entered the room. Crossing the threshold, I glared at him—in her room, sitting on her bed, when I had not. He patted the bed next to him.

Shoulders slumping I obeyed, sitting beside him.

He handed me the three books, ten more still lay piled on the floor. "Seems like you two had the same taste."

"Yeah." My burning anger simmered. "Strange, huh? I hardly knew her and yet we have more than one thing like that in common."

Benjamin's eyebrows rose unconvinced. He shrugged. "A lot of people like these books, Liv, they're classics."

Standing, I turned my head away from him before rolling my eyes. "I know that." I walked over to her long dresser. Knick-knacks and pictures covered the wooden surface. In fact, it was the one place in her whole house where she displayed photographs. Ben was right. I'd been silly about this room. In wooden frames, pictures of each of her sons smiled up at me. Then one of Amelia and Burt, young, standing side by side. The rings already rimmed her eyes. I couldn't help but compare the picture of her with Seth to this photograph of my grandparents. She couldn't be, yet she looked so much older in the one with Burt. I picked up the only family picture sitting on her dresser. The color photograph was light and faded. The boys were young, Red just a baby. Amelia's face held a small grin while Burt sat listless, neither frowning nor smiling.

"Is that Dad?" Ben stood next to me pointing to the twelve-year-old boy in the photograph.

"Yeah." I smiled.

"He's tall."

I laughed. "Yeah. He always has been."

Benjamin took the picture from my hand and examined it closer.

Gazing another lap about the room, I scanned her space more in depth now. The rest of her house had always been tidy and uncluttered. Here in her room she had books and pictures and little figurines that must have meant something to her. A rocking chair sat in a far corner that I hadn't seen from the doorway. An afghan lay sprawled over it. I crossed the carpet and opened the door to her petite closet. Her few clothes fit tight inside and at each end hung male, flannel, button up shirts, no doubt Burt's. They'd been taking up space in her tiny closet for the past dozen years.

"You should change," Ben said, interrupting my exploring.

I looked down at my nightclothes. "Oh, right. I really should do some laundry though. My supplies are limited."

"Oh, I brought you a bag. Your mom packed you some clean clothes."

My head perked up. "Thank you, Mother!" I kissed Ben hard on the lips.

"I'm anxious to tell you about the office. We've got a long trip back for that though."

I nodded, not looking forward to the trip home. "I'm gonna grab the bag." Leaving Amelia's room, I started down the stairs.

Following behind me, Ben said, "Good. We need to make it back to Montana by six."

Did he just..."Huh?" I stopped halfway down the flight of stairs.

"Montana—"

"I heard you. I thought you said you wanted to spend some time with me here. See my new house?"

"Liv, I've seen it. It's not *that* grand of a tour." He checked his watch, which fired my irritation more.

Was this his idea of spending time here? An hour or two? My insides boiled. "In a hurry?"

"Well, we—"

"Knock. Knock," sang a women's voice I didn't recognize. She opened my front door and walked right inside.

Startled, I whipped around.

"Hello? Excuse me? Who are you?" I tugged at my Big Mac T, forcing it to stretch farther over my body.

Twirling, her eyes scanned every corner of the living room.

Was this normal for Rendezvous? Was she some crazy neighbor? Why hadn't Logan warned me about this?

"You must be Olivia," the strange woman said. Her red tattered suit matched her red out-of-date heels perfectly.

"Who are you?" I asked again. "What are you doing in my house?" I couldn't deal with crazies at the moment. I needed to deal with my joy-killing boyfriend.

"You mean Amelia's house," Ben said, a lack of concern in his voice.

Why did he seem so calm? Was it not obvious that this odd woman who'd just broken and entered was not someone I knew? Why was he not sprinting over to save me from the psycho in the 1980's suit? Sure, she wasn't muscular or big, but she could have a weapon!

"Janie Forester," she said in a high singsong tone, extending her hand. "Jonathon said you'd be expecting me."

My mouth fell opened.

"We were." Ben shook her waiting hand.

I peered up at him, my heart sinking. Change joy-killing to betraying boyfriend. I wished Rachel Lemonade were here, she'd have a perfect word for *what* Ben was.

"Well, I'm your—" But I knew what *she* was, even before she said it. "I'm with North West Reality. Will you be clearing out the house?" Janie's head bobbed from Benjamin to me.

"No." The impossible words came from Ben's lips. "We're hiring out."

"Great." Janie clapped her hands together. Twirling on her heels once more, she gaped at *my* house.

I wished she were an intruder holding a weapon. That way I could attack her and it would all be justifiable.

"Here, babe." Ben reached down for the duffle next to the doorway. He held the bag toward me and had the gall to smile.

Unable to reach for the bag, I stood frozen. My insides ached like I had the flu. Blinking with the ring of the doorbell, an angry, hot tear ran down my cheek.

Dropping the duffle, Ben opened the door to meet eye to eye with Logan.

"You must be Benjamin." Logan's dimple creased. He held his hand out to Ben, waiting.

Narrowing his eyes, Ben stepped back, his mouth in a flat line. Looking down at Logan's hand, he grasped it, his knuckles turning white. "Yes. You?"

My vision blurred with the oncoming tears that had yet to fall.

"I'm Liv's neighbor—"

Wiping at the moisture on my cheeks, a shaky breath fell from my chest. Forcing my feet to move, I made my way over to the door. "Logan."

Shifting away from Ben, his brow furrowed, a vertical worry line forming between his eyes. "Liv, are you okay?"

Rubbing my wet face again, I said, "Yeah." *Nope. Not one bit.* "What are you doing here?"

"I came to see if you needed help with your carpet."

Ben put his arm around my shoulders, marking his territory. "She doesn't."

"Sorry, Logan, I—"

"We're selling." Ben tightened his grip on me.

"You're selling?" Logan asked his eyes on me. I could see the surprise in them, or maybe it was disbelief.

"She's selling!" Janie Forester sang from the dining area.

The room spun around me. Benjamin, Logan, Janie. Around and around. The dizziness increased. Benjamin, Logan, Ja—I couldn't do this. I couldn't lose control. "Benjamin," I said, ignoring the fact we weren't even close to alone. "I need to speak with you." I closed my eyes, trying to ground my spinning head.

"We'll have time," he said, not understanding me.

I pulled back and opened my eyes to glare at him. "Now."

"Babe..."

"Don't mind me." Janie twirled into the room. "I'm just going to check out the upstairs."

My world crumbled. I lost any chance of control. Amelia gave me a gift. Was I going to lose it in less than a week? Betrayal, hurt, physical-pinching pain filled me like an overflowing fountain. And I knew in that minute, I did *not* want to sell Amelia's house. I pulled myself up from my puddle of weakness and shouted.

"Stop!" I pointed in Janie's direction.

Confused, she gaped at me, frozen on the fourth step.

I pushed myself away from Ben. "Stop it." I glowered up at him.

"I need to check out the upper floor to fully—"

"Don't take another step." My jaw clenched, I peered over to the stairs.

Janie's face went white and she slinked down the few stairs she'd climbed.

"Olivia—"

"Don't!" I jabbed my finger into Ben's chest. I turned back to the middle-aged realtor, who, to my satisfaction, looked to be afraid of me. "Let me clarify a few things. This house is *not* for sale."

Gaining back some courage, Janie said, "Miss, your father made his position clear."

"I don't care what they've told you, Miss Forester. They have no right! I own this house, not my father or Benjamin. And it's not for sale."

Ben's face turned a red I'd never seen before. "Olivia—"

"How dare you? You knew about this and you said nothing! So, don't look at me like I'm the bad guy."

He opened his mouth, but I couldn't listen anymore. I couldn't hear his voice without wanting to vomit. "Get...out," I said through gritted teeth. It was the cruelest I'd ever been to Ben but I wouldn't stand here and let him tell me what was best for me. Of all the things he'd done to anger me, this one I hadn't seen coming. This one I didn't know if I'd ever recover from and I didn't care what daggers left my mouth.

"Livy—" Ben's lips pouted out.

"You heard me. Get out. You," I turned to Janie whose eyes popped at my pointing finger, "and you." I jabbed his chest once more then backed a good arm's length away from him.

He stepped toward me, his face soft and sorry. I'd forgiven his thoughtless selfishness time and time again, but if he thought this would be the same, he was wrong.

Janie squeezed through the door, but Benjamin continued to

inch toward me. "Olivia." His gentle tone didn't fool me.

He would not take me seriously—no matter how I growled at him. My first night in this house popped into my memory. It seemed so long ago. Logan had threatened me. My mouth opened and I spoke his words without another thought. "You are trespassing and I won't hesitate to call Sheriff Lane."

"What?" Ben's lips parted almost into a grin.

Logan had remained quiet, shrinking out of sight, but I knew he still stood in the doorway. "Logan, will you please call Sheriff Lane?"

Logan walked past us, hitting his shoulder against Ben's. Amelia's old rotary nosily circulated as he dialed.

"What do you plan on doing, Livy?" The kindness and repentance left Benjamin's voice. "Sit around the old lady's house all day and try to figure out why she never contacted you? She isn't worth this." He backed up toward the door. "Jonathon won't support this."

He still didn't get it. "I don't care."

"No, I mean, he'll cut you off, he won't provide for you while you take time exploring here."

Did he believe I wanted Dad to pay for a little Wyoming get away for myself? He stepped out the door and I followed onto the cement porch for a moment. "Don't worry about it, Ben. I've got a job here. I guess I'll see you when I see you." Stepping back inside, I slammed the door.

Chapter 15

Shouldn't I be crying? Regretting everything that just left my mouth? Possibly hyperventilating? I *was* breathing heavy, but with excitement, not self-reproach.

Rounding the corner, Logan shoved his hands in his pockets. "So, you're staying? You okay?" His arms had stains from work and his plain navy T-shirt didn't hide the oil like his black one had. His brows furrowed and his eyes narrowed in on me—waiting for me to break, I guess.

Releasing the breath I didn't know I'd been holding, I sighed. "Yeah, I'm staying. And, well…I'm *good*."

Nodding, he kept his gaze on me. "Good. I'm glad." Sliding his hands from his pockets, he motioned toward me. "I'll let you give Rachel the good news," he said, referring to the job I told Ben I already had.

Following him into the kitchen, I made the call. I held the receiver away from my ear as Rachel rejoiced. "I'll see you Monday morning."

Logan had busied himself with the floor while I spoke to Rachel. He lifted the carpet and ran a hand along the hardwoods.

Leaning against the table, I watched him. "Does she really have the authority to hire me?"

"Technically? No." He looked up from the floor. "But if Rachel says you're hired, then you're hired."

"Really? That's interesting." Rachel Lemonade had some power.

"That's just the way it is. Besides, Principal Levitz really appreciated Amelia, and Rachel will end up making him think it was his idea all along." He stood, brushing his hands off on his jeans. "I should go. I have a Volvo coming in any minute now."

"Thanks for your help."

"I didn't do anything," he said. "I'm proud of you, Liv. Are you sure you're okay?" Rubbing a hand over his neck, he said, "I mean, you just broke up with your boyfriend."

I guess I had. It sounded odd hearing it said out loud. I'd been with Ben so long, I didn't picture him really gone—but then I didn't want him here. It was all so confusing. "Uh...I'm fine."

"I'm glad. I couldn't stand to see you with a 'Roy'."

"Roy?" My brows scrunched together, confused. What did he mean? "Are you really placing Benjamin and Roy in the same category? Benjamin is a genius."

"Clearly." He slapped his hands at his sides, his forehead wrinkled. "Ben may be a *genius,* but he's also pompous and self-absorbed. He has no idea how to treat another person."

"You've known him five minutes!"

"He helped your dad hire a realtor and told you nothing of it. You're going to argue with me about this?"

Why was I arguing? Maybe it had become habit to defend Ben. Maybe I was defending my own pride—after all, I'd chosen to be with Ben.

"I just can't believe of all the men out there, you'd pick *him.*"

"Okay," I said, finding my voice and pointing a finger at his chest. "That's stepping over the line. You don't know Ben, you barely know me. Benjamin can be a good person. He works hard and he's very passionate."

This behavior was strange for Logan. He'd even given Roy a break. What was with the meanness?

He passed me for the door, but turned back, folding his warm hand inside mine. I didn't pull away. His calloused hand was tender and kind. For a moment I forgot my anger. His chocolate-brown eyes locked with mine and he gave my fingers a light squeeze. "For such a good person, he's horrible at showing you he loves you." Letting go, he left.

My hand felt strange with his gone. His grasp was so different than Ben's. His hands coarse and firm, rather than soft and supple. I squeezed my hand to a tight fist—he'd left something there. I held up the little business card and read the pink words: Janie Forester *I'll stamp it sold!* A headshot of the blond sat in the left-hand corner of the card.

My eyes swelled with tears again. My excitement and energy gone, I slogged up the stairs. I retrieved Amelia's book from the closet and collapsed on the bed.

June 30, 1956

Four days. It's been four days since that dumb dance. Philip has called three times. Two days ago I pretended to be in the bathroom when Uncle Herb called for me. Then I "forgot" to call him back. Then yesterday he showed up at Uncle Herb's store! There's no way Philip Harlem cares about art. How could he possibly think I'd be interested in him after the other night? I've already declined a second date. Apparently the girls around here swoon at the sight of him. Who cares that he's dull and completely in love with his rich self?

So, it's been an uneventful, somewhat annoying few days, normal for Ganesworth, until today. Today was interesting. Seth, the man from the dance, the one I spoke with, came into the gallery today. Seth Garrison, I learned is his full name. He seemed just as surprised to see me as I was to see him. He looked at a few local, unframed, pieces and then he came to the counter to ask a question. I asked him if he remembered me and he did. We spoke mostly about art. He's an artist, he only works for Philip's dad to pay his bills. He was nice. I'm surprised at myself for calling him plain before. He has a nice face, pretty blue-green eyes. I like him. I hope he stops by again. It would be nice to have a friend.

Amelia

I couldn't stop my storybook mind as I read this entry. She thought him plain and then suddenly she didn't. Of course it made me think of Mr. Darcy. He'd found Elizabeth plain before he loved her. I still struggled with my image of Amelia matching up with this girl who wrote so fervently. They didn't add up. I wondered if they ever would.

I didn't see Logan the rest of the weekend. Two days dragged by. I'd grown accustomed to him being around often, and it was strange being here in Rendezvous and not seeing him. Once we passed by our parallel windows at the same time, but I didn't want to appear needy—or stalkerish.

No phone calls, no going out, no Logan. So, I spent time in Amelia's room. I went through everything. Now that I had ventured in, I decided it was time to clean house. There wasn't anything out of the ordinary, a few knick-knacks, pictures—just the usual. Her books were the best, to see which she loved the most, just by the pages and bend in the bindings. I flipped through *Pride and Prejudice,* its pages worn the most. The ending page flopped quick into position as I flipped. It was no wonder. It was heavier than the other pages. She had taped at the end of the book a silver dollar. Her lucky silver dollar, I wondered? The one she left to Dad? She hadn't mentioned where we'd find it. Did Dad know where? Did he care?

I boxed up a few of her things, but mostly just gave the room a good cleaning and then left it hers.

I had a running list of things to purchase for my new home. Number one, caller ID. How had the generations before us lived so long without it? I often pictured myself back in Elizabeth Bennet's time, and then one little piece of technology would set me straight. Two days without phone calls. That didn't mean my phone hadn't rung. I just refused to answer it, knowing that the minute Benjamin spoke with my father I'd be hearing about it.

Monday morning I woke early. Rachel had said I should be to the school by nine, and since I didn't have a car, I'd be walking. I was grateful for two things. Amelia only lived about a mile from the school, and the weather was nice. I hadn't been to Rendezvous in the winter, but Dad had told me about the feet of snow and the bitter cold. I borrowed some black slacks from Amelia and paired my turquoise blouse with a black jacket that seemed too stylish for her. I straightened my long, strawberry hair and decided to leave it down. I gazed at myself in Amelia's full-length mirror, turning to the side. My heels had me a few inches taller than my five feet seven inches. I bit my lip through a grin. I could do this—a new adventure! Then I remembered my new occupation, temporary high school secretary assistant. I couldn't really call myself *the* secretary. There were only four weeks of school left. I'd be assisting Rachel in her work and that was about it. Not exactly high-adventure, but something new—something different.

By 8:15 I sat down to my bowl of cereal. Giving the box a shake, it sounded almost empty and I was grateful. It had gotten old serving as both breakfast and lunch.

Stirring the still full bowl of chocolate puffs, I ran Amelia's last journal entry through my head. Could the Seth she cried for from my childhood be the same one she spoke of in her journal? How could he not be? Yet, at the same time how could he be? He had been in her life so many years ago.

My thoughts were interrupted by a tap on the front door. It had to be Logan. Ben wouldn't miss a day of work to talk me out of my insanity, and who else did I know? Solitude exhausted me. I was so over it. Anxious, I opened the door and my heart quickened at the sight of him.

"Good morning, Livy." His eyes glistened.

"Hi, Logan."

Shoving his hands into his pockets, Logan rocked on the balls of his feet. "I'm sorry if I was rude the other day. I didn't mean to be unkind to you."

"Thank you." I didn't want him to leave, not just yet. "Would you like to come in? I just started on the last of my cereal. It's a good thing too—It's going to be a month before I'll be able to eat chocolate puffs again!"

"Actually, I was wondering if I could take you to breakfast and then to work."

"Yes!" I agreed—too readily. Not having to walk to work in my stilettos would be wonderful, something other than cereal to eat would be fantastic, and spending the morning with Logan...

"I'd love that."

Rendezvous had one sit down restaurant. La Familia. In any other town it would have been considered small or fast food, not the swanky sit down joint. One of the few Hispanic families in town owned it, but they served more than Mexican. The menu held a combination of both Mexican and American dishes. The only other place to eat out was at Mel's, the one and only gas station. Like any convenience store, Mel's sold microwavable burritos and fat hot dogs. Logan had mentioned something about an infamous "Mel Dog".

La Familia—the old house had been gutted out to one large room. A dozen booths surrounded the teal walls and they were all full. I had never seen so many people in Rendezvous in one room before—besides Amelia's funeral.

"Gabe has a great breakfast menu." Logan leaned against the wall, waiting for a seat.

"Loga-an!" called an older Hispanic woman with dark hair and full hips. She waved from across the room and her lips spread into a grin.

Logan waved back to her. "Maria Mata," he whispered, leaning down to my ear. "You met her at the funeral."

"I have your seat!" she said with a slight accent, pointing at a booth by a window.

Every seat beckoned a 'hello' as Logan passed, and each had lingering eyes for me. Would I ever get used to being news? I hoped Rendezvous would just get used to me and I wouldn't have to.

"I know you're in a hurry," Maria said as we approached. "So I kept a booth open for you."

"Thank you, Maria," Logan said. "You're too good to me."

Reaching her hands around Logan's neck, Maria pulled him down and left a large red lipstick mark on his cheek. "Only for you!"

Logan was like everyone's favorite nephew. Rendezvous loved him. I watched as another Rendezvous-ite loved on Logan and then Maria turned to me. "*Hola*, Olivia. How are you?" With a hand on each side of my face she leaned in, kissing my cheek as well.

Laughing a breathy, nervous laugh, I said, "I'm good. Thank you, Maria." But most of my thanks went to Logan—I hadn't remembered meeting the woman.

"Ahh," Maria said, patting my cheek. "Such a nice girl."

We sat and she left us to read our menus. "I probably met every person in this place," I whispered, holding the menu up to hide most of my face from the ogling eyes.

Wiping at his lipstick mark with his white linen napkin, Logan glanced around the room. "Yeah, looks like it."

A bead of sweat slid from my forehead to my ear. My cheeks burned to what could have been called *Olivia's uncomfortable pink.* If the day continued this way, I'd soak through my blouse by lunchtime.

Logan handed me his napkin and reminded me of my own kiss mark from Maria. "Don't worry. They're good people. Just assure them you know you've met—but that you've forgotten their name. They don't all expect you to remember who they are."

"You're sure of that?" I lay my menu down and forced a smile for a tall man in a Stetson waving to me.

Soon Maria brought out Logan's biscuits and gravy and my stack of blueberry pancakes. I dug into my cereal-free meal.

"So, when do you want to work on the hardwoods?"

"Oh, ah..." I hadn't thought much about the flooring since I'd found Amelia's secret box. "I'm not sure. I might give it a year. You know, think about it, see how much it'll cost."

"Really?"

"Yeah, now that I'm living here and I'm getting paid...what, minimum wage. I think maybe I should hold off on the flooring." I shoved another bite in—the food was either divine, or I really had eaten too much chocolate puff cereal.

"Olivia." Putting down his fork, Logan narrowed his eyes. "Am I missing something?"

"What do you mean?" I said, through a half-eaten bite of blueberriness. Why did I feel so guilty?

He grinned, but it didn't reach his dimple. "You're not telling me something. Days ago you were ready to rip out that carpet as if it infringed on you personally somehow. You stabbed it, as I recall."

I nodded. What else could I do? He had me there, and I didn't trust my words.

"Liv." And just like that it appeared, his dimple.

Across from me sat a person who genuinely loved Amelia, who knew her better than I did, maybe even better than Dad. And in that moment I decided. "I have a small secret." Even though it had been a consious choice, I slapped my hand over my mouth.

"Okay…"

I leaned in to the table. "I haven't told another soul."

Reaching until his forehead almost touched mine, his soft musk scent filled my lungs. "Does this secret have anything to do with Amelia's floors?"

"Yes." I whispered the word through my covered lips.

"Are you going to tell me?" His whisper mocked my own.

"Not here." Setting my hands flat on the table top, I glanced over my shoulder.

"Oh, no, it isn't safe here," he said teasing me.

Rolling my eyes, I sat back against my seat once more. "I'd just feel more comfortable doing this in private."

"Livy, you don't have to do *this* at all. I was just confused about the carpet."

"I know." He wasn't going to pressure or force me. "Well, I think I'd still like to tell you… if you want to hear." And I *did* want to tell him. After years of keeping Amelia's secret, I was ready to leak, but not to Dad or Ben or even Mom. I was ready to tell *Logan*.

"Sure, okay." He pointed his fork at me. "Dinner?"

"It's a date."

Chapter 16

"Assisting" Rachel in her work turned out to be a bit of an understatement. Rendezvous hadn't enticed a counselor to accept a job in over two years—so Rachel and Amelia were two people doing the work of four. We had our secretarial duties as well as filling in for the counselors. The senior class this year had eight graduating students. The counselor should have been helping them fill out college applications and scholarship forms. May wasn't really the time to start thinking about college, so most of these had already been done, but there were still two students who needed assistance. Also, it was the end of the year, each student needed to have their yearly progress interview and underclassmen had to pick their electives for the next school year.

Rachel put me to work as if I'd been doing this job my whole life and somehow I wasn't drowning. Diving in was probably the best way for me to learn my way around things. Nearing the end of my first day, I found myself in an empty corner with a red head I recognized. "You're Roy's friend, right?"

He nodded.

Yeah, the quiet friend. "I've met so many people. I've misplaced your name."

He smiled a little broader and then in a raspy voice said, "Andrew."

"Andrew, that's right." I flipped through my eight files of student grades. "Andrew Peterman, here you are." This was my fourth progress report interview, first for college assistance. Still,

I was finding my comfort zone. "You're a senior, but you haven't filled out any applications for college or scholarships."

Peeking at me over his eye lashes, his hands held in his lap, he shook his head.

"Okay. Well, Andrew, I'm confused, I have your grades right here. You're a good student. You don't want to attend college?" If I had reading glasses, a bun on top of my head and a few wrinkles, then I'd look like the older authority this job had turned me into. In reality there were what, maybe four years separating me and this boy I counseled.

"Miss Benson—"

"Please, Livy, call me Livy." Did he *think* I was twenty years older than him?

His thin lips parted into a grin once more. "Livy. It's just I want to be a welder, like my dad. He can teach me what I need to know."

"Ah..." I knew nothing about welding. "Well, don't you think an education is important? I promise you, you'll be more successful in whatever profession you choose if you have an education, I don't care what you do, an education *will* help you."

Andrew stayed quiet.

"And you would easily qualify for the... the..." I flipped through another stack of paper work.

"Hathaway," Andrew said.

"Yes, the Hathaway." What right did I have counseling this kid? I couldn't even figure out my own life. "Andrew, what does your dad think? About college I mean."

"He's fine with whatever I decide."

"Okay." *Lucky him.* "Well, I want you to take this application. Fill it out. If you end up not using the scholarship, that's fine, but will you fill it out for me?"

Quiet, he nodded.

"One more thing," I said as he stood to leave. "Would you mind coming back in tomorrow morning?"

Nodding again, he stood, shoving his hands into his pockets and examining the office carpet.

Logan's house...I couldn't imagine it. Maybe bachelor stuff? But, non-Benjamin-type-bachelor stuff. Still, pizza boxes and video games weren't right either. Maybe tools and tight T-shirts...

Not knowing what to expect, I crossed the threshold of Logan's clean, simple home. A shelf cluttered with piles of books and magazines sat in the corner. His couch was as aged as Amelia's. The front room held no television, only a couch and a coffee table facing the front window. The opposite walls were a dark cocoa color with two framed pieces of artwork. A chalked hillside scene with no real detail, but the hill and the starry night blended in a unique way—no way I'd know the artist. The other seemed to be a field with a home in the distance. Again the details were smudged together with the black chalk. They had to be the same creator, but I knew authors, not artists.

"I'm sorry, I didn't have anything to bring," I said still looking around the room. "I guess I could have brought cereal."

"Don't worry about it." He motioned toward the kitchen. "Dinner's ready."

The spicy, sweet aroma grew stronger as we headed into the kitchen. With his dining area right inside his kitchen it was different from Amelia's, but cozy. Walking over to the stove, Logan stirred the sauce on top and then peeked inside the oven. His damp hair was curly as ever and a sprig fell across his forehead.

Shutting the oven, he turned back at me. "I'm going to Cody tomorrow if you'd like to join me. You could get some grocery shopping done."

"That would be great, thank you." I ran my hand through my hair, hoping he truly didn't mind me tagging along. "You're such a good neighbor, Logan, no wonder Amelia loved you."

"Amelia and I were friends." He leaned against the counter, watching me.

"Right. Yes." I pulled out a chair and sat down, staring at my fidgeting hands. My mouth just kept right on rambling. "I know. That's what I meant, you're a good friend."

He peered at me as if he were figuring out what language I

spoke.

"That's why, you know." I flung my hands as I spoke. "I feel like I can talk to you."

"Right. Your secret." Crossing his arms over his chest, a grin played at his lips.

"Yes, my secret." My cheeks burned and my skin pricked. Could I really tell him? What if he laughed at me?

Serving dishes in hand, he sat across from me.

Sliding off Amelia's black jacket, I hung it on the back of my chair.

Logan dished two plates of the Spicy Chinese Chicken over a bed of white rice and passed one over to me. "How was your first day of work?"

"It was good. I actually enjoyed myself. Rachel is good company, and I like helping the kids." I stopped, my filled fork halfway to my mouth. "In fact, that reminds me. Do you have the internet?"

"Yeah, you need to use it?"

"Yes, if you don't mind. Later, after dinner. There's this boy, well you know him, Andrew Peterman. He's one of two seniors not signed up for college. He says he wants to go into welding and so he's not going to college, just learning the trade from his dad. I want to give him some information, show him that college can help him." It occurred to me in that second, Logan had learned mechanics from his father and that's what successfully employed him today.

"That's a good idea. Andrew's a bright kid."

"Yes. Well... that's what I was thinking." I watched him, my fork hovering, waiting for him to find offense at my words.

He nodded. "That's really great of you to help him out."

I wasn't thinking about Andrew though. Why did I have this incessant need to know more about Logan? "Did you ever think about going back to college?"

"Sure. The two years I spent in Alaska were great, but in the end my place was here. I learned a lot, but I knew this is where I'd end up, this is what I'd be doing."

"How? How do you know? I *still* don't know!" I asked without trepidation, someone needed to share with me the secret formula for figuring such things out!

"Sure you do. You just let other voices get in your head."

Glaring at him, I set my fork down. "I wish I could argue with that."

He laughed at my stare down. "But you can't. My point is what's right for one person isn't right for another. I knew this is where I needed to be, so here I am."

"So, maybe I shouldn't bug Andrew with college info?"

"That's not what I'm saying. We all need guidance at times, but when it comes down to it, we have to follow what we feel inside—what we know is right for us individually. You're giving him options and that's great. Education is priceless, I hope he goes."

"Did your parents go to school?"

"No, they graduated from high school, but never left Rendezvous."

"You said they married young. How young is young?" I knew Logan well enough now to know he wouldn't mind answering questions about his parents. "What were their names? You've never mentioned them."

"Laurie and Joseph." Looking past me, his demeanor changed. He seemed to leave this space and time and go somewhere else. His chair squeaked along the kitchen tile as he pushed it out to stand. Walking into the hall, he pulled a picture from the wall and handed it to me. "They both had a semester of high school left when they decided to marry. My dad's family was moving. He couldn't stand the thought of leaving Mom."

"So, they got married?" I blurted the words. The picture was dated, but there stood Laurie Heyborn in a cream-colored church dress with the biggest smile I'd ever seen on anyone's face. Next to her in a white shirt and brown tie was Joseph, so happy, a dimple very much like his son's indented in his right cheek. They were a handsome couple and looked like they belonged together.

"They knew they would one day anyway."

"Are all you Heyborns so certain of the choices you make?"

"I guess it's in our blood." He took the picture from my hands, looked it over once more and replaced it on the wall.

"How soon after did you come along?"

"Thirteen years."

Jerking, the rice I'd scooped fell off my fork. I suppose people often marry young because they feel they have too.

"They weren't ready to be parents, so they took their time. Mom used to say all she wanted in this life was to walk hand in hand through the park with Dad until they were ninety—that and me of course." He stared at his plate, lost in his own thoughts. "All she ever wanted was time."

"To ask for so little and to be denied it, it's cruel."

"She's still with *him,* and she was the best mother. Cruel would have been leaving her here, without him."

I didn't have a reply to that. I didn't understand that kind of love. I supposed it was a love made over time, but I only knew it from books. Instead, I placed the last bite from my plate into my mouth. Quiet settled over us for a moment.

Taking my plate, Logan headed over to the sink and filled the basin with suds.

"I'll wash." I bumped him out of the way with my hip.

"Okay." He opened a drawer and pulled out a clean dishcloth and waited for a clean dish to dry.

"So, you said you'd make dinner and you did."

Smirking, he concentrated on the plate he wiped dry.

"I said I'd share my secret, but I asked you a million questions instead."

"I thought maybe you changed your mind."

"No," I said. "I haven't." If anything, I was more certain now.

He waited, patient. So different from Benjamin.

Breathing in the suds with Logan so close, I collected my thoughts. "The last time I saw Amelia I was eleven years old. The same trip when I first saw you. Burt, my grandpa, had died. I expected her to be sad and upset, but she never showed much emotion around us." I cleared my throat, handing Logan the last of the dishes.

Putting the last clean dish back into the cupboard, he motioned for me to follow him. "Come sit down." We walked back into his warm living area and sat on the couch. The curtains were drawn and the room was dim with the lone standing lamp. The quiet, the dark—it was the perfect place to share a secret.

Folding my legs beneath me, I made myself comfortable beside him. Telling him my secret might not be as difficult as I thought it would be.

"The day before the funeral my parents went to Cody. My siblings went with them, but I was sick. So, I stayed behind. Amelia had offered to take care of me. I was terrified. She frightened me a little."

He listened without interruption, but I could see at his furrowed brow, my words confused him. He didn't know the cold, intimidating Amelia I did.

"I slept most of the day in her spare bedroom, but when I couldn't sleep anymore I decided to go after my book. I'd left it in her living room. I snuck down the stairs, not wanting to see her. That's when I heard her. She was crying. So I crept up on her in the dining area. She was there, on her knees with a floorboard popped out of place. A box sat next to her. Then she cried out the name…Seth." The words flooded from my mouth. Relief washing over me as I shared Amelia's secret after eleven long years.

"Seth?" Logan said the name aloud, speaking for the first time.

"Yes, I'm certain of what I heard, she repeated it. *Seth.* I was so confused, I knew Grandpa had died, I knew she should be crying, but Grandpa was *Burt.*"

"So, your fascination with the flooring—"

"Yes!" In my excitement, I inched closer to him. "I had to know what was in that floor. My imagination has run wild for eleven long years, without discussing it with anyone."

"You haven't told *anyone*?"

"No. It was her secret, not mine. I couldn't, but now she's gone and she gave me her house, knowing I'd seen her and her hiding place."

"Wait, she saw you?" His words were urgent and my heart drummed faster.

"Yes!" I inched ever closer.

"She never explained?" He shook his head as if the idea of Amelia having hidden secrets was absurd.

"No—really, she didn't. I was afraid she'd be angry with me, I just ran from the room, but later that night when I saw her again, she never spoke of it."

"You were a child. Didn't you want to tell anyone? That's amazing in and of itself." He gazed out into space, still pondering my story.

"It is strange, but I just couldn't tattle on her. Later that evening we had a small moment together. I was setting the table, no one else was around, and she asked me about my books. She was different, and I don't know...we sort of connected in those few minutes. Although, even before that, I knew I wouldn't say anything."

"And now?" His eyebrows sunk low, just above his big brown eyes. He was worrying for her again.

"And now, I don't know. I've told only *you*." I motioned toward him. "Her friend. Someone she trusted. And someone I trust. I don't know that I'll tell anyone else. I guess it all depends in the end."

"On what?"

"Well, when I opened the floor boards I found her things."

His eyes widened.

"The box, with pictures, and a journal from 1956. I've started reading her journal. It's fascinating and sweet. It's an Amelia I never knew."

"Has she mentioned Seth?" This time, he inched closer to me. He waited for me to answer, his breathing matching mine.

"Yes." I fed off his elation. "She has. And there's a picture of him." I couldn't talk fast enough now.

"Wow." Whispering, he rubbed the whiskers on his chin. His face scrunched in confusion again. As if he weren't sure he believed me or not. "That doesn't seem like the Amelia I know either."

"Doesn't it? You only knew about one of her sons, yet she had three as well as five grandchildren. She was private, you must've noticed that."

"She *was* private, but still honest and kind...hardly secretive.

She was part of this community. We *all* loved her."

He looked sad in that moment, which is probably what possessed me to reach for his falling face. I put a hand on his cheek and pressed against the stubble of his five o' clock shadow. "I loved her too. I didn't know her well, but she's my family. And I want to know her."

Logan's calloused hand covered mine. "You're like her, you know?"

My head tipped in question. I stared into his dark eyes.

"She was kind and genuine. Forgiving."

I had inched so close to him and with his melancholy face in my hold, it seemed so natural, so right, to comfort him with a kiss. With my empty hand I touched the opposite side of his face, closing my eyes. Little by little, I brought my mouth to his. His soft, warm lips responded to my touch. My fingers tangled in his curly hair and he pressed his mouth more urgent to mine.

Coming back to my senses, I released him. My head spun full of drunk, uncoordinated thoughts. I had done something wrong. But what?

Biting my lip, just inches from his, I said, "Ah... sorry."

His dark eyes peered into mine. "Don't say that. Not unless you mean it." The pressure of his hands tightened on my waist.

"Ah..." I wasn't sure what to say. I wasn't sorry. I'd sort of, maybe been wanting that for a while. I couldn't lie to Logan, but I couldn't confess to him either. "Can I still use your computer?"

Sitting back against the couch, he sighed and rubbed his hands over his face. Letting his hands fall, he pressed his lips together. "Yes. You may use my computer."

I worked alone in Logan's upper spare room, only coming out to ask him if I could print my document.

"So," I said over the hum of the printer. "I guess I should go now. It's late." And it was, it was past eleven, and I wasn't sure where in the world the time had gone.

"Okay." Logan shoved his hands into his pockets and blew a puff of air through his lips. "I'll walk you home."

I laughed at his serious comment. "I don't want to put you out."

"I think I can make it."

Following me down the stairway, he picked up my black jacket and helped me slide back into it. His warm hands lingered on mine. Releasing me, he opened the front door and waited for me to step outside.

Despite it being spring, I shivered in the crisp air. I folded my arms as we walked side by side to Amelia's front door.

"So, are you answering your phone yet?" he asked, once on Amelia's porch.

"Wha— You did call me!" I said, wishing all too late that I'd hid how pleased I sounded.

Logan chuckled. "Yeah, I called you. I figured you were still angry with me."

"Believe me, it's not you I'm avoiding. I need to invest in caller ID. I can't handle a conversation with my father or Benjamin right now." I laughed, but then my face fell. It spread all through my body, like a ton of guilt-filled-bricks smacking me in the face. "Benjamin," I said, my lip snarling upward in annoyance. I hadn't thought of him all night long, certainly not while I kissed Logan. What was I thinking?

"Can I remind you of something?" Logan lifted my face with his hand. "Without you getting angry with me again? You broke up with Benjamin, I was there." He stepped forward and wrapped a hand around my back. Pulling me to him, he placed a soft kiss on my lips. And with that it was easy to believe all he said. I melted into to him, forgetting everything in the world but Logan Heyborn.

Logan shifted his head to meet my eyes and then he kissed me again, convincing me this time. Pulling back, his breath warmed my cheek. "Good night, Olivia."

Chapter 17

I couldn't sleep. I had to work early and my eyes refused to shut. My heart thudded as if Logan were lying next to me rather than an entire house away. I rolled onto my side and took a deep breath, smelling Amelia. Her cinnamon and musky scent still lingered despite my thorough cleaning. It had grown on me though.

Amelia. There was still so much I didn't know. So much I didn't understand.

July 3, 1956

I've decided Dad sent me here as punishment. What I've done wrong exactly I'm not sure. I haven't spoken to another soul except for Uncle Herb and Aunt Lila in three days. I may die of loneliness or possibly boredom.

A strange thing happened yesterday. I was helping Aunt Lila in the garden. She grows everything! It's quite beautiful. Anyway, I was assisting her in the garden, we were weeding. I told her how I visited with Seth Garrison at the store. She didn't say anything. She usually acknowledges me when I'm talking at least. Then, when I asked her if she knew him she said, "Of course I know him, this is Ganesworth." She sounded ornery and I couldn't understand why. I was helping her on my one day off! Why would I be irritating her? However, I decided to continue and that's when Aunt Lila became extremely strange. I said, "I like him. He's nice, much better than Phillip Harlem!" She stopped her work and looked me in the eye. She said, "You'd be wise to stay clear of Seth Garrison." Yet, when I asked her what she meant she refused to talk again. After my third plea for some type of explanation she left. She just tossed down her hoe and went inside leaving me to care for the rest of her massive garden myself!

So, before I keel over from this insipid town, I'm going to find Seth Garrison and make him explain to me exactly what Aunt Lila meant. If anything, it's something to do. He signed the guest book at the gallery. I'm going to see if he recorded his address. If so, I think I'll pay him a visit tomorrow.

Amelia

"So, what did Amelia say today?" Logan sat beside me in the cab of his truck.

I'd already explained to him about her staying with her uncle as well as how she met Seth. Licking my lips, my heart thumped in my chest. Could he be as obsessed with *this* Amelia as I was? "She said at the end of her entry that she was going to find Seth, ask him why her aunt warned her about him."

"So, did she?"

"I don't know."

"You didn't keep reading?" His lips parted to a grin, and I recalled how well they blended with mine the night before.

Shaking my head, I concentrated forward on the blank road in front of us. I cleared my throat. "No, I'm pacing myself. If I didn't, I'd be done by now. I'm enjoying this way too much to have it done and over with."

He laughed, pulling up in front of the school.

"You think I'm ridiculous."

"No. I don't." His hands fell from the wheel and he turned his head to me. "I'll pick you up at three."

"You okay, honey?" Rachel interrupted my confused thoughts of Logan.

"Oh! Yes, yes, I'm fine."

"You sure? Your face is the darkest shade of guilt I've seen in a long ol' time." Rachel's smile froze on her face, waiting for the latest buzz. "This wouldn't have anything to do with a few little rumors I've been hearing about a certain somebody's next door neighbor—"

"Rachel!"

Rachel stood from her desk, walked the two steps and sat on the edge of my desk facing me. In two days I already had the desk more decorative than Amelia had over years. I'd set out her mug and filled it with newly sharpened pencils. I used one of her frames, placing a wallet sized picture of my family inside. I set out a couple of her knick-knacks too—little tea cups, they weren't really my thing, but they brightened up my desk and made me think of Amelia.

"Right, of course not, because you have a boyfriend." Rachel crossed her arms, watching for my response.

"Ahh—" The sound hummed from my mouth for far too long. "Well, I did, yes." I couldn't meet her eyes.

"Did?"

Crumbling my face into my desk, I covered my head with my forearms. "I sort of broke up with him."

Rachel reached out and nudged my shoulder. "Dish, girl!"

Looking up to her eager face, I said, "Excuse me?"

"Dish, I said. What happened?" Rachel stood and danced from one foot to the other. "Your grandmother and I never kept secrets from each other, now don't you start."

Did that mean Rachel knew who Seth was? And about the box under the floor? Or just that she *thought* she knew Amelia through and through.

"So…What happened?"

"Well," I said, feeling this strange obligation to Rachel. Like the youngest child, I couldn't deny her. "We had a fight. Benjamin came, and he brought a realtor with him."

Rachel gasped and slumped back on the corner of the desk.

"I'm not ready to sell. It sounds kind of silly, but it was the last straw."

"It could have been the one and only straw!" Rachel's face burned red, validating my own feelings. "That's as awful as spoiled prune juice."

This only encouraged me. I must have been in need of some girl talk without realizing it. I thought of my roommate Rose. I'm sure I had two hundred text messages from her, too bad my phone sat in a dumpster somewhere. I nodded at Rachel. "Yes!"

"Lover boy bringing in a realtor, talk about betrayal." She inched her face closer to mine. Her lavender scent and gray roots filled my senses.

"Pretty bad, huh? So, I shouldn't talk to him? Or even consider—" What I *always* did—forgive and forget. It was more of habit than anything. Even as I hinted at it to Rachel, bitterness filled my mouth.

"What you ought to consider is an old fashioned tar and feathering of his a—Ah, good morning Mr. Levitz." Our boss exited his office. She stood and beckoned Mr. Levitz as if we'd been discussing grades.

"Rachel. Olivia, how's Rachel breaking you in?"

"Oh, good. She's really got me going."

"Great. I'll see you girls around." Mr. Levitz patted his round belly. "I'm going to see if Lucille saved me a cinnamon roll."

Rachel waved dramatically. Talk about looking guilty. Then she was back on my desk, in my face waiting for more.

"What?" I asked.

"What about Logan?"

"What about Logan?" When had she switched gears on me?

"You've got chemistry." Her shoulders rolled up and then down. "Not to mention the whole town's seen you two together at one point or another."

"Friends, Rachel. What, people can't just be friends here?"

"Of course they can, honey, but have you taken a look at Logan?" She winked, conjuring images of biceps and abs in my mind. "Not to mention yourself. Chem-is-try." She drawled out.

I couldn't help the laugh that escaped my lips. "Rachel, stop it!"

"I knew it," she said, taking my response as confirmation.

I ignored her accusations the rest of the day, but I can't say it helped much when Logan walked in at three o' clock. My eyes roved over him. Different than any man I'd seen before, he was sure of himself, but humble, so deliciously humble. He thought the best of everyone and followed his heart. He stood there, his well-built, laid back self, in jeans clear of stains and a button up shirt opened at the top. His clean-shaven jaw was all too appetizing. He smiled at Rachel.

"Well, Logan Heyborn, imagine seeing you here," Rachel said, hands on her hips.

"Hi, Rachel. How's Leo?"

"Sweet as ever." With all Rachel had gabbed, I didn't know who Leo was. "He is so funny. He spun circles yesterday all for a milk bone."

"I'd like to see that." Logan laughed with her.

Dang it! He was kind, too. That was possibly the sexiest thing about him.

"Hey," he said to me. "Ready?"

"Yep." I picked up my keys and flung my purse over my shoulder. We needed to get on the road before Rachel started talking *chemistry* with Logan.

Rachel's brows rose up and down when I waved goodbye. Turning away from her, I pulled on Logan's shirtsleeve, forcing him to follow after me.

"How was work?" he asked.

"I gave Andrew the school information. He said he'd look it over."

"Good." He grinned.

Curse that dimple. Trying to talk myself out of being attracted to Logan wasn't going over well. "I have a proposition for you," I said inside Logan's truck.

Glancing away from the road, he looked at me for a brief moment. "Okay."

"I'll give you something if you take me to more than just the grocery store."

"Where else do you need to go?"

"I really need a clothing store, my supply is limited. I can fit into a few of Amelia's things. Still, my options, especially for work, are this…" I motioned down, "…and what I wore yesterday. Also, someplace to get a caller ID box, I *need* caller ID, and a few other essentials, like shampoo." I held up a few strands of my hair, examining the ends.

"You know I'd take you to those places without anything in return."

I controlled my focus to stay on the road. "I know. Still, I'd like to give you this."

"What is it?"

"Not much really." I pulled Amelia's brown backed journal from my purse. "I thought we could read an entry or two on the way there." I waited for him to laugh at me. When he didn't, I risked asking, "Would you like that?" I couldn't help but look at him now. I had to see his reaction.

Glancing over at me in the cab, his eyes darted down to the book in my hands. "I would."

> *July 4, 1956*
>
> *It's midnight. Aunt Lila calls this the devil's hour. I know I should be in bed, but I can't sleep.*
>
> *What a day! What a non-boring day and in Ganesworth! I went to work this morning on a secret mission. My stomach was jumping inside. I was so anxious and nervous when Aunt Lila asked me if I wanted eggs this morning, I practically yelled, "No!" at her. I couldn't help it. I felt like she could see right through me. As if she knew I was up to something.*
>
> *The minute I set foot in the gallery I ran to the welcome book. I found Seth's name easily and his address was recorded below. It wasn't far from the gallery. I knew it wasn't exactly appropriate to go see him without being invited, but my curious mind was already forming a plan. With my nerves as jumpy as ever I also knew I wouldn't be able to wait until after work. The three hours it took until lunch were agonizing enough. Two people had come into the gallery. Two! Could this place be duller? Anyway, I waited until lunch time. I gave myself a full hour today, knowing that Uncle Herb wouldn't find out and the chances of someone coming into the store weren't likely. I walked the five blocks to Seth's house. The outdoors seemed*

to ease my anxiousness. I felt brave knocking on a stranger's door. But then his mother answered and I wanted to hide under a rock. She must think I'm completely unladylike. I shouldn't have called on Seth at home. Still, I convinced myself in that minute that I wasn't there to get her approval, but to find out this mystery from Seth himself. So, I forced a smile and said to the woman, "May I see Seth?" Without any emotion on her face to hint what she might be thinking, she told me he was working. I only said, "I see." I'm sure my disappointment was evident. She offered no return time and so I left. What else could I do? I'm not completely inept.

Walking back to the store, utterly disappointed, I saw him! I felt just like Nancy Drew – from my old kid's books, I was on the trail! I crossed to the other side of the road and quickened my pace. When he looked up and saw me I waved – dumbly. Still, he waved back. When we reached one another I decided I was down to 45 minutes of my hour lunch and honesty would be best. I told him, "I just came from your house." He was shocked. I wish I could have photographed his face. He was pleased, too, I could see. I told him I needed to ask him a question, and he offered to accompany me back to the store. So, on the way I asked him just why my Aunt would tell me to stay clear of him. Had he done something awful? Was he in trouble with the law? He just didn't seem that way. When he didn't answer at first I couldn't help myself, and I asked him if he was at all dangerous. A small part of me hoped he'd say yes. That may sound like a child or maybe even crazy, but that's why I record these things in my journal rather than telling real people. I've never had a conversation with a precarious person before. He laughed at me. Okay, so he wasn't so dangerous. Once back at the gallery, I asked again. We sat in the back room and he told me that several years ago his grandfather and my grandfather worked together. They had some sort of falling out. My Grandpa Wells apparently cost his grandfather's company the entire business. Our families haven't been friendly since. He didn't know much more than that. I've never even heard of this feud.

"It's like Romeo and Juliet," I said, looking up from the book.

"What is?" Logan asked.

I'd almost forgotten he was there, sitting in the driver's seat. My habit of reading alone had me caught off guard. I flushed a little, embarrassed. "The feud between the two families. You know, Romeo and Juliet, forbidden love."

"Did you ever think that's what made Juliet so enticing to Romeo? She was forbidden."

"No," I snapped. "That wasn't it. Have you ever even read Romeo and Juliet?"

"Of course I have. Junior year, English class."

I rolled my eyes. "Yeah, well, that's not *why* he loved her, but it did make for a fantastic story."

"I guess."

"You don't like Shakespeare?"

"He's not my favorite, too tragic. I like a happy ending."

I laughed. He had me there. Shakespeare didn't exactly end things happily. Still, I fell in love with Romeo too many years ago to deny I loved him now.

"Besides," Logan said. "You've already got Amelia and Seth *together*. If that's true, then how is it she ended up with Burt? Maybe they just became good friends."

My story-book head did already have them together and in love, forbidden love, but I wasn't willing to admit that. "May I?" I asked, motioning to Amelia's book.

"By all means."

Seth stayed my entire lunch hour. He's so easy to talk to. He asked if he could see me tonight.

I wanted to shout HA! But I refrained. Besides, I suppose it still didn't prove they were together. One thing I can usually tell is a good story and a good story always has tragedy and love. And this was a good story.

I probably should have said no, knowing how my aunt and uncle feel about him, but I couldn't. He's the only interesting person I've met in Ganesworth. He's the only person I care to see. Luckily for me, my aunt and uncle aren't the type of people to really celebrate. That fact has always bothered me until today. Today is Independence Day. Of course they had no plans to watch fireworks or have a dinner party. I knew I could slip away without anyone caring.

And it was easy. I had to lie, but I'm not so opposed to that, not when it means saving myself from a slow tedious death. I met Seth just outside of The Coachman. I asked him if he thought it was safe there. Again, he laughed at me. Apparently the feud is a quiet one. The entire town isn't involved or knowing all about it. Seth bought me dinner and talked my ear off about art. I never knew art could be so interesting. Not just a painting or a drawing on the wall, but a scene, a memory, a theory. By the end of dinner, I was totally enthralled with this stranger.

Later, he drove me to the top of a hill. It was deserted, with no one else nearby. We could still see the small town fireworks, not much of a display if you ask me. However, small as they were from that pretty hill it all seemed wonderful to me. And there on that hill under the stars and fireworks, Seth kissed me.

"Ha!" I couldn't contain myself this time. I didn't wait for Logan's response, just turned the page to finish the entry.

I snuck home not long ago and here I am. Until tomorrow then, actually excited for what's to come, in Ganesworth no less!

Amelia

I shut the book, breathing out a heavy contented sigh.

"Ha?" Logan said, raising his eyebrows, teasing me.

Twisting my hands together, I flushed. "Yeah, sorry about that. I'm not always a gracious winner."

Minutes later we pulled into Cody. Stopping at the Supercenter, I got groceries for my month's menu, as well as a few odds and ends. I spent a large amount of money and was thankful I'd always been a saver and my check-book sat full.

We filled Logan's coolers with our cold items and then drove downtown, where Logan said I'd find a clothing store or two. I had plans for three to four new blouses and a new pair of jeans. At home my closet was spilling with clothing, but I didn't dare ask Mom or Dad to mail me anything.

Bags in hand, we exited the clothing shop. Across the street, a bicycle shop caught my eye. The sign in the window bragged, *New and Used Bikes!*

"Do you mind if we stop in one more place?"

"Where to?"

"Let's check out the bike store."

"Do you enjoy riding?"

"Well, sure. I did when I was ten. I haven't in probably eight years, but it would be a way around town. I like the idea of not having to walk or bum a ride all the time."

We walked into the shop. Empty, besides the one clerk, he sat behind a counter with a bicycle upside down and his hands greased up. "Hi there."He looked in his mid-forties, but his salt and pepper mustache must have been from civil war times.

"Hi," Logan and I said together.

"What can I do ya for?" He wiped his hands clean.

"I think we're looking for a bike," Logan said, turning to me.

"Uh, yes. I'm thinking about purchasing a *used* bike. Just something to get me from here to there."

"Oh, I've got just the thing. It just came in last week." He pulled out a purple mountain bike from the back. "Hop on."

"Hop on?"

"Sure, try her out." He motioned to the empty space in the large shop.

So I did. I hopped on. The seat didn't even need adjusting. I looped the large store as best I could.

"How much?" I asked, feeling like that ten-year-old girl.

"Two-fifty."

"Two hundred and fifty dollars?" I got off the bike and held it at arm's length. "Isn't this a used bike?"

"Yes, it's a Gary Fisher in prime condition and new sells for more than seven hundred and fifty dollars."

"Would you take a hundred?" I asked.

"No."

"One-twenty-five?" I pleaded with my eyes.

His mustache twitched and he removed his hat to rub a balding head. "I'm already giving you a deal."

"We'll take it." Logan handed me a folded bill. "Call it a house warming gift."

"No, no, I'll keep looking."

The man rolled his eyes, as if I hadn't a clue.

"It's a Gary Fisher," Logan said to me, a playful smile at his lips. "She'll take it."

I had fallen half way in love with the Gary Fisher, even though I'd spent a total of ten minutes with it. "Well, then—I guess I'm taking it." I placed my hand in his and squeezed. "Thank you."

"You're welcome."

Logan loaded my bike into the back of his truck and I stared out the back window at it, somewhat elated.

Pulling away from the downtown curb, Logan said, "It's almost seven, want to grab some dinner?"

My stomach growled, but the sit down restaurant Logan pulled into had my nerves up. It wasn't about being alone with Logan or the chem-is-try (as Rachel put it) between us, or getting home late. It was silly, but "What about Gary?"

Logan's eyes narrowed a bit and he tried not to laugh at me. "I don't think he's hungry."

"No. He's just in the back, without a cover or a lock."

"We'll get a seat by the window. *Gary* will be fine." He was already around the truck opening my door. He took my hand and pulled me from the cab. "We're in Wyoming. People don't steal other people's bicycles here." Intertwining my fingers with his, he dragged me along behind him.

"Is that true?"

"Mostly," He chuckled. "Trust me, your bicycle's safe."

Peering out the window we sat next to, I checked on Gary every few seconds. I sucked in a breath as a boy stopped next to Logan's truck to take a better look.

"He's nine, maybe ten," Logan said, reaching across the table to unclench my fist. "Besides, I thought you didn't love biking."

"I don't, I mean I didn't. I don't know." I watched the boy until he left my view.

Our food was long gone before we left the café. There'd been ample time for someone to steal Gary. However, Logan was right. He was safe.

"I guess you were right," I said.

"That's one for you, one for me," he said.

"Huh?"

"You were right, about Amelia and Seth."

"Oh, yes, I was." I contorted my face, trying not to smirk.

Laughing at my effort, he took my hand and we strolled toward his truck.

"Logan." I stopped, looking at our knotted hands and then up to him. My head still full of questions. "I just—"

"Liv, I like you," he said. "And I'm pretty sure you like me."

"I just, I don't know. I was with Benjamin a long time. It's awfully soon, don't you think?" I held our clasped hands into the air.

He didn't answer me or let go of my hand. He walked me to the passenger side of his truck and opened the door for me. Helping me in, he shut the door.

We started for home in silence. *Home.* Home to Amelia's house. My house. How much my life had shifted in such a short time.

"So," I said, lifting the silence. "You're an artist and a mechanic."

"No." Somehow I expected irritation to fill his voice, but it didn't. "I said I studied art. I'm not an artist."

"Oh," I said. "So, the chalk work in your house, you didn't do that?" I kind of assumed after he'd told me he studied art.

"Nope."

"It's just I didn't see a name or a signature and I thought..."

"You thought they were mine?"

"Yeah."

"Amelia gave me those," he said.

I turned in the cab, my whole body facing him. "Amelia?"

"Yeah. They were hers. She called them a graduation gift. She knew I planned to study art in Alaska."

I couldn't stop the green monster inside of me. I was jealous! Jealous of a silly gift, given years ago. Jealous after she'd given me a *house*. Facing forward, I crossed my arms, my entire posture rigid.

"What is it?" He glanced away from the road for only a second.

"Nothing." I lied.

He drove me home and pulled Gary out of the back for me, leaning him against the house. "It'll be safe here." It was the first thing either of us had muttered since my shortness. Then he pulled the coolers out and set the one he'd brought for me on Amelia's porch. Together, we retrieved my bags and brought them into the house. Logan left to get the cooler from the porch, and I began putting my groceries away. He set it down and turned for the door.

"Logan, wait," I said, coming to my senses.

He stopped and turned to face me.

"I'm sorry. I was rude. She never gave me a gift. Birthdays, graduation—nothing. And…it's stupid, but I was jealous."

"I'm sorry."

Shaking my head, I said, "Please, don't be. I'm glad she had you. I just—I've never understood her. I don't get why she wouldn't want to know me, or give *me* a graduation gift. I was the only one of my siblings to invite her to graduation, you know? My dad said why bother, but I insisted. I wanted her to know. I wanted her to come or send a card, a note, anything. But she didn't. Stupid."

"No, it's not." His arms wrapped around me, comforting *me*. I'd been childish, rude, and *he* was comforting *me*.

"I guess that's two for you, one for me," I said.

"Huh?"

"You're right, Logan. I do like you."

Chapter 18

July 5, 1956

I feel like a woman today. Not a girl or a daughter, a sister, or a niece, but a woman. I feel like I could do anything. It's all because of Seth. I love him. I know it sounds hasty and crazy, but I do. I love him. We shared one evening, one kiss. My first kiss. Still, I can see myself at his side the rest of my life.

Amelia

"How could she say that?"

"That's how she feels," Logan said, listening to my gripes over dinner.

"I just don't understand, she barely knows him, how can she say she's in love with him?" I pointed my fork at him.

"I don't know. It must have been one heck of a day."

Slamming my fork down, I stared at him. "How did she get here?"

"Keep reading."

Logan cleared away our plates and I stood up to help him, prattling on about my day. Once we finished washing the dishes, I checked my watch. "I'm gonna have to go, Rachel sent me home with work."

"All right." He followed me back into the living room.

Slipping into my jacket, I stopped to stare at the chalked hillside scene. One of the two that Amelia had given to Logan.

"I'll walk you over."

"Thanks." We stepped outside. "Thank you again for dinner. I'll cook tomorrow and the next day. I owe you."

He smiled.

"Only if you want to, I didn't mean to imply you had to or—"

His laughter warmed me from the outdoor chill. "Liv, I want to."

"Okay then. Goodnight."

"Goodnight, Olivia."

Heart pounding, I walked through Amelia's front door. The answering machine I bought to accompany my caller ID blinked its red light on and off. I hit the button and listened to the electronic woman. "You have three messages. Message number one."

"Liv, could you possibly pick up the phone? I've tried your cell two hundred times. Then, I get a call from good ol' Ben asking if I've heard from you. He gave me this number. Which, by the way, you never answer either! So, you're kick'n it in Wyoming? Why haven't you called me? I'm pissed and you're in trouble. Eddie says, 'hey'."

Rose. I should have called her.

"Message number two."

"Hi, honey, it's Mom. I'm worried about you. Dad and I keep calling. Please call us back, sweetie. I love you."

Mom. Guilt. *Ugh.* So, not answering Dad's calls was one thing, but I'd been ignoring my mother in the process. Of course she was worried about me. I hadn't talked to Mom or Katie, or even Jared.

"Message number three."

"Hey, babe, I'm sorry things got out of hand, but not speaking to me won't fix this. I wish you were here, working beside me. This experience is incredible and you're missing it."

Benjamin. I didn't feel the floodgates of guilt like I had with Mom. My skin prickled with annoyance, and brief second thoughts. His voice sounded too chipper to be mourning the loss of our relationship, either he didn't believe it was over, or he didn't care. He was in love with work, so it could easily be the latter!

Rose was easy, so I picked up the phone and dialed her number. After being yelled at for not answering her calls, I started from the beginning, leaving out only Amelia's secrets and the part where I sort of attacked Logan with my lips.

After a few curses of disgust for Benjamin and a few complimentary cursings at my description of Logan, she became quiet.

"What? What do you think? Am I crazy, Rose?"

"Olivia." She hadn't called me by my full first name in I don't know how long. "This is the sanest thing you've ever done. It's about time you made some choices for yourself."

That cut to the core a bit. "I make my own choices, Rose. I just respect my dad."

"I'm talking about Ben. I'm glad to see him squirming. He doesn't deserve you. He's always right there telling you which way to turn instead of respecting what you want. Medicine? Bah!"

Had it really been that bad? And how had I been so blind? The whole thing was mind boggling, it hurt my head. I picked up my escape and began to read.

July 13, 1956

I've hardly had time to write. And I don't really have time now. Seth will be here any minute to pick me up. I told Aunt and Uncle that I was going to the movies with Cheryl Hull. Cheryl Hull would never take me to the movies with her and her clique. But they don't know that. Really, I came to the store, the same thing I've done every night this week. I normally sneak out of the house around 9pm and meet Seth at the gallery. Today's my day off, so we're getting an early start. I'm not sure where we're going, it's a surprise.

I can hardly believe I've lived my life this long without Seth. He's the best man I know.

Amelia

I rode Gary to work the next morning, thinking about Seth, Amelia, and Logan somehow all at the same time.

I ate with Rachel in the lunchroom. I always brought my own meal, which irked Lucille the lunch lady. She'd heard rumors of Logan and me and that didn't sit well either, seeing how she planned for Logan to fall madly in love with her granddaughter. This annoyed me more than it should, which was another reason I chose to bring my own lunch. A few teachers sat with us and chatted about the school's end events, they were more like town events, everyone seemed to get involved. I had gotten to know the teachers at Rendezvous High. Three of the five sat with us.

"Where's Callie?" I took a bite of my sandwich. Callie McMurphy was the part-time, pregnant gym teacher. Her baby seemed to be a celebration for the entire town.

"She called in sick." Hannah Jackson turned to me. Hannah, always the serious one taught History, Government and Social Studies. Even her short, simple, dark hair said *serious*.

"Poor thing, she's nearing the end." Denise Black shook her head, her long gray hair swaying. In charge of Art, Denise was clueless to the smudge of paint smeared across her forehead. The older woman was close to Hannah's opposite. She had to be nearing retirement, but the students loved her and wouldn't allow it.

Marty Mickelson—Science and Math instructor, sat silent, eating away and ignoring our girly chatter.

"Oh, that's right." Rachel jumped in. "Olivia, I'll need you to substitute for Callie."

"Excuse me?" I said, through the bite of turkey sandwich still in my mouth.

"Fill in, for Callie." She stared at me expectantly.

"Rachel, I don't have a subbing license."

"Well, that's something you have in common with the rest of the town." Her head bobbed side to side and she laughed.

Denise joined in like the two were sharing some old joke. She pointed at Rachel, her body shaking with her giggle. "Wait, Mr. Barns?"

"Yes," Rachel said, her silly grin leaving her, "but Mr. Barns stopped subbing after his last stroke. He hasn't worked in three months."

Denise's body froze and her mouth formed a frown. "Oh, that's right."

They conducted their own little conversation while I choked on my lunch. Rachel slapped my back, never taking her eyes from Denise.

"You're serious?" I coughed out.

"Quite." Rachel nodded as if it were a done deal—and I remember Logan saying *if Rachel says you're hired, you're hired*—Rachel Lemonade had a way of getting what she wanted. "Callie only works a half day anymore anyway, so you'll only have three classes. Play dodge ball."

"What? No lesson plans?" My hands flattened on the tabletop in front of me, panic rising in my chest.

"It's gym, Livy, there was no reason for Callie to stress out making *lesson plans*." She mimicked my pained voice. "She's expecting you know."

"I'm not a teacher, Rachel." I wished I had a paper bag to breathe in. "I don't think I can do this. "

"It's gym." She gave me a pat on the leg. "You'll be fine."

Laying my head on the lunchroom table, I took slow deep breaths.

"So, how's Logan?" Rachel nudged me with her elbow.

My head popped up at her question and the chatter among the other woman stopped. Marty continued to eat, but looked at us. His interest in my love life null though.

"Fine, I think. How would I know?" I shrugged my shoulders and shook my head—the double action too much to plead innocent.

Logan hadn't kissed me since I'd admitted to having feelings for him. Which was weird—right? I admit I like the guy and he *stops* the kissing? I should be grateful—I attempted relief—not well, but attempted. I needed time, didn't I? I'd only had a week and a half without Ben.

Denise smiled at me.

Hannah stared.

Lucille from the kitchen let out an indiscernible holler. Had she heard Rachel from all the way back there?

I cleared my throat. "Uh…how, how is Harold, Hannah?"

"Same as ever." She spoke about her husband with little to no emotion.

"That's wonderful, really great. Okay, I'm done, I think I'll go get ready for… class?" I tossed three-quarters of my lunch into the trash can and pretended not to notice them staring.

Escaping to the back office for the rest of the lunch period, I picked up the phone and dialed.

"Logan!" I sounded panicked. I *was* panicked.

"Liv? Are you okay?"

"Yes. No. I mean, yes."

"Ah…okay."

Winding the phone cord around my wrist I watched my fingers turn a light shade of purple. "I have to substitute today! For gym!"

"Oh, and that's bad?"

"Logan! I'm not a teacher, and if I were, Physical Education class is the last thing I'd teach. I'm a bookworm. Gary has brought out enough athleticism to last me for years."

He laughed. He actually laughed. Here I hid, petrified of the next three hours yet to come and he found it all humorous. I could have revoked his perfect neighbor status.

"Olivia." He was all business now. "You will be fine. Just pass out a few basketballs and call it free time."

"Free time, right. I can do *free time*. I think."

"You can." His voice encouraged me. It might just be possible that I would climb Mount Everest if Logan told me I could.

"Okay, I have to go." I let out a heavy sigh. "Logan, thanks."

"You're welcome, silly girl."

He found me silly, I found him sexy. That didn't say much for me. Still, he admitted he liked me.

My thoughts were far away when Rachel's head popped in. "Livy, honey, your first class starts in five minutes. I suggest you get your tail over to the gymnasium."

My first class had eight kids total. I did as Logan had suggested.

I pulled out the basketballs and told them they had a free hour. I was tempted to give them a choice between that and dodge ball, but I was afraid of them turning on me. I didn't want to become a dodge ball target. The hour with the freshman and sophomores went by fast.

The second hour had seven students, mostly juniors, and a couple of seniors. I did the exact same thing I had the first hour. Again the hour flew by without any trouble. I gained confidence by the minute.

My third hour contained a combination of all grades and a total of nine students. Nine, that's not even half what my P.E. class had back home, but the combination of the grades or the kids in this particular class wanted to overrun me, I could feel it. My false confidence vanished. I had stayed quiet and out of the way until now.

Roy. It had to be Roy. He bounced his basketball off a lower classman's head—waiting for me to test his non-existent authority.

"Roy!" I called across the gym, sounding very much like a mother at the playground. The twerp pretended not to hear me. "Roy," I said again, advancing on him.

He turned his head just a bit to smile my direction and then bounced the ball off the smaller boy again.

"Do it again and you'll be in Mr. Levitz's office."

The younger boy, Mason, hid his face despite my warning.

"Mason? You okay?" I put a hand on his shoulder.

"Yes." The freshman squeaked, looking more embarrassed that I asked than getting beaten with a ball.

I took the ball from Roy's hands. "What's your problem?"

"You think you're so tough, Roy." Mason had more bravery, now that the ball lay safe in my hands. "Like you're Casanova."

I looked at the fifteen-year-old, my brows furrowed. *What?*

Roy puffed out his chest more.

"Casanova would have been when he attempted to hit on me, Mason, not when he acts tougher than he really is."

"You hit on Miss Benson?" Mason gaped at Roy with a mix of disbelief and awe.

Roy laughed like I'd cracked a hilarious joke.

Putting my hands on my hips, solely for effect, the ball stuffed under one arm, I said, "Just lay off. All right, Roy?"

"Whatever." He grouched and stalked off.

I wasn't sure I'd ever understand the male species, teenage boys in particular.

"Miss Benson?"

I turned at my name. A junior girl, whose named I couldn't remember, stood before me. "Livy, please. Yes?"

"Livy." She grinned, her dark hair falling to her shoulders. "Who *was* Casanova?"

"Oh." The tension went out of my shoulders. That I could answer in my sleep. *Where did basketball get started* would have baffled me. "Well, he was a famous womanizer."

"He's a real guy?"

"Oh yeah. He was from Venice. He wrote an autobiography all about his life and many loves. He's known as the *world's greatest lover*." I spouted off in my element.

Her face lit up. "Wow. Where'd you learn that?"

"I read," I said.

She giggled. "I'd read about *him,* too." Then she ambled off with the other students.

I laughed. I actually enjoyed the moment. Talking with the students, even helping Mason hadn't been terrible.

Roy kept his eye on me in the corner with his posse. He would be off to college in the fall. I helped him with his paperwork. That would be the best thing for him. Soon, the big wide world would humble him. There it was again. Blah. The longer I worked here, the more I sounded like a protective, reproving mother.

Back in the office, Rachel worked at her desk. "How'd it go?" She looked up at me.

"Actually, okay, it wasn't awful after all."

"Good." She looked back to her computer screen. "Mr. Ice needs you to substitute for him all day Monday and Tuesday."

"What? Rachel. That's—that's too much. I don't know how to teach."

"You're subbing. You'll be fine. Jamie—I mean, Mister Ice—

will have lesson plans for you. Get here half an hour before school starts so you can look things over. And it's extra pay, lucky girl."

"Lucky? Rachel—"

"Oh, and Logan called. He wanted to know how class went."

I pressed my lips together. What could I say? Rachel giggled and I stopped myself from smacking her shoulder. Crossing my arms, I glared at her.

"You called him about substituting. It's sweet."

"No, I—"

"Well, I certainly didn't call him. So you—"

"Yes, Rachel, I called him. Are you happy?" I crossed my arms over my chest.

Holding her hands at her heart, Rachel sighed. "Immensely. I love that boy. He comes from good genes."

My arms fell to my sides. "You knew his parents then? I guess that makes sense. How were they? I mean, were they like him? Was it weird when they got married?"

"They were the best people. Joseph was a decent man. He wanted Laurie and so he married her, not weird, just a high moral standard. Logan has that too."

"I guess it's just strange in this world we live in today."

"I guess so," she agreed. "It was a little strange then. People thought all kinds of wicked thoughts about the Heyborns, but they were just happy, hard working, regular people. They never let it bother 'em. And it didn't take long before people stopped talking about it. No one really brought it up again until that sad day when they both passed."

"Did Amelia talk about them?"

"Oh, sure, they lived right next door for so many years. She'd give a mouthful to anyone who spoke badly about those kids. Young love isn't a crime or a sin and she'd let them know it. She just adored all three of them. Most of all Logan, though. She'd be thrilled to see the two of you hitting it off so well."

My cheeks flushed. "Yes, well, sadly I would never have met him if she hadn't died."

Rachel peered at me. She opened her mouth to speak, but must have thought better of it, because she didn't.

Gathering my things, I waved goodbye to my little blonde friend. I hopped onto Gary, my backpack strapped on. I decided I must be better at biking than most people since I could ride so well in my four inch heels.

My sweet tooth had devoured all of the ice cream I bought in Cody, so instead of home I rode to Farmer's. I could afford to pay eight bucks for ice cream with my new job and free home. I locked Gary up at the small bike rack in front of Farmer's. I could hear Logan laughing at me in my head. Still, I wasn't about to risk it. Gary was the best thing I ever bought myself.

"Hello there, Olivia."

"Hey, Joe. I'm looking for Ben and Jerry's."

The older man behind the counter smiled at me. "Very back, at the right."

"Thank you." I trotted to the back of the market and found the carton I needed. *Chunky Monkey.* I stopped myself from going down the candy aisle. Rachel had me a little stressed out with my new substituting chore. It enhanced my need for sugar.

Pulling up to my house, I walked Gary onto the porch. Taking the two pints out of my backpack, I ran inside for a spoon and to store one away. Back outside, I dipped into the creamy goodness, walking over to Logan's. His garage was open, and a country tune blared from inside.

He was under an old-fashioned car, only his filthy jeans sticking out. The garage was stocked with all sorts of tools and gadgets that didn't mean a thing to me. I tilted my head as he bent a knee in and readjusted his position under the vehicle. "You really like this old twangy stuff?"

His movements stopped. He slid out from under the car, his back against the down dolly. Smiling, he stood and wiped his greasy hands on a rag tucked in the front of his jeans.

"Sure, I like George Jones. You're telling me you don't?"

"Hmm, I can't say I'm a fan."

"Maybe you just don't appreciate *old* country music."

I laughed. "That must be it." I held out my carton to him. "Chunky Monkey?"

"Is that supposed to be ice cream?"

"What do you mean?" I pulled it away, clutching it to my chest. *Chunky Monkey* had been my favorite—forever.

He peered into the carton of Ben and Jerry's. "They add so much, you lose the ice cream. I'd rather just have a plain old chocolate cone."

"Try it." I held my spoon out to him. "If you don't like it I'll go buy you a chocolate cone."

He didn't look convinced, but took the spoon. "It's like cold chocolate and bananas, with a few walnuts. Not a lot of ice cream. It's good, but it's not ice cream."

"Yes it is." I snatched back my spoon. Leaning back against the car, I hummed along to a new twangy artist on the radio.

Crossing his arms over his chest, he stood next to me. "So, you survived today?"

"Yes, I did. I got to yell at Roy and everything, so it was... almost fun." I shoved another bite of chunky goodness into my mouth.

"Roy? Did the kid ask you out again?"

"Oh, no, he's far over asking me out. He's just annoying me now." I shook my head digging through the pint. "Here's my real problem, Logan, Rachel has me set up to sub again. Monday and Tuesday."

He waited for more, not comprehending my worry.

"I am *not* a teacher. Three hours of free time in P.E. is one thing, but I can't teach English. And I know about as much Spanish as the students do."

"Come on," he said. "Let's talk inside." He reached out to take my hand, but when I stretched to give it to him, he seized the *Chunky Monkey* from my hold and drove another spoonful into his mouth.

"Hey!" I laughed, thankful for the second carton safe inside my freezer.

"You wanted me to like it," he said through a mouthful.

Following Logan into his kitchen, I slumped into a chair. Opening a drawer, he retrieved another spoon and handed it to me. I took it but didn't dig into the carton he set on the table between us. "I don't know how to do this, Logan." I looked down at my hands, shifting the spoon from one fist to the next.

"Hey." He pulled me to my feet. "You just need to relax." Staring down at me, he wrapped his arms around me, circling his hand on my back. I settled with his touch. One of his hands cupped the back of my neck and I rested against it, looking up at him. Closing my eyes, I waited for his lips to meet mine.

They didn't.

"I know what you need," he said, after a minute.

"You do?" *Then why aren't you kissing me?*

"You need to relax. Let go. Have a little fun. Do you have plans tonight?"

I almost laughed. *Dinner with you, duh.* "No, why?"

"Good. After dinner, we're going out. Get you loosened up. Have you been to *Ruthie's*?"

"Seriously? Logan, if you haven't taken me there, I haven't been."

His smile reached his dimple.

"So, what is Ruthie's? How do you plan to *loosen me up*?" I wasn't sure I liked the sound of that.

A devilish look crossed his face. "Karaoke."

Chapter 19

"Yes. Mom, he should absolutely know that I broke up with him." I shifted my new cordless phone to the other ear.

"He doesn't. I'm certain. He's the same old Ben, happy as a clam, joining your father every day." She sounded worried. "Livy, isn't this hasty? I'm fine with you being in Rendezvous. I think it's wonderful Amelia would give you such a gift, but Olivia, breaking up with Benjamin? He's all you wanted for so long."

"Is he really?" I asked more myself than Mom.

"You're not happy?"

"Well, I am now. I thought I was before, but now I'm not so sure. I feel like I was settling to make everyone around me happy." Not to mention, I had no idea how often things in that relationship agitated me until I came to Rendezvous.

"Oh, honey, I don't know what to tell you. I wish I had more answers."

"I think I have to figure this out for myself. I don't think you're supposed to have the answer, Mom." If anything—Rendezvous had taught me that.

In my entire life, I had never had the desire to sing karaoke. I can sing just about as well as I play sports—not so hot. Logan was right about one thing, karaoke took my mind off substituting. I should have told him no, but then he asked me, officially, like a date and well, I couldn't say no. We hadn't been on a legitimate date yet.

Logan and I lived in the land of *non-complicated.* So, I didn't stress or fret or freak out when I knocked on his front door.

He'd showered and changed from his work clothes into clean jeans and a plain, black, button up shirt. The smell of strawberry shampoo from his curly, wet hair wafted over me.

"Is that what you're wearing?" I said, standing in his doorway.

"Ahh—yeah." He moved to the side, letting me in.

"Okay, I'm gonna go get dressed now." I turned for the door, still figuring out my wardrobe.

He shook off my nonsense—at least I'm sure it made little sense to him. "Wait, Liv." Taking my wrist with one hand, he closed the door with the other. "Did you get to talk to your mom?"

"I did." I turned back to him. "I'm glad I called. She's been worried."

"Did you talk to anyone else?"

I'm guessing he implied Dad, but I had purposely called when Dad and Ben would still be at work. "Katie." I rolled my eyes. "Ugh. I think she's mad at me, too."

"Yeah?"

"Yes. I abandoned her and left her with my daddy-obsessed boyfriend—who apparently drives her crazy."

"Ex-boyfriend."

"Right." I pointed a finger at him—exactly! "That ticked her off too, that I hadn't told her I'd broken up with him."

Picking up my hand, he said, "So, are you okay?"

"Yeah, actually, I'm great. It's only home that stresses me out." Logan at times made me light-headed, but never stressed.

"What about subbing?"

"Oh, yeah, that too." I nudged his side. "Thanks. Aren't you supposed to be distracting me?"

"Oh, right." He thought for a moment. "Have you picked up the journal today?"

"Yes." I bit my lip. "Her entries are so short now. I cheated, I read four today."

Logan laughed and then reached over and tucked a stray hair behind my ear. "It's not cheating. You're the one who made up the rules, you can change them. So, what'd she say?"

I couldn't stop my smile. I loved a good love story. A content sigh left my chest, and I was certain I seemed *silly* to him again. "Same as her last six entries. She's in love, happy, still hiding it from her family, but oh so happy and in love."

"So, do I have to follow your rules? The curiosity is killing me."

"Yes, you do." I pulled at his collar. "Well, dinner isn't going to cook itself. See you soon?"

"Yes." He slid his palm into mine, his fingers closing around my hand.

He opened the door, and I pulled him until he stepped in closer to me. "Good." Tired of waiting, I reached up on my toes, and kissed the side of his jaw.

Bringing his free hand up to my neck, he drew my face to his, depleting any space between us. He lay a soft kiss on my lips. My body warmed and tingled like a furnace.

"Goodbye," he said, pulling away.

I had the strangest desire to drag him home with me. He'd be over in a half an hour, but that wasn't soon enough.

The pretty elm separating our houses seemed to say *home* to me. Looking up at it as I passed by, I felt home, body and mind. Half that tree was now mine, and I was happy to share it with Logan. Walking into Amelia's house, I saw her things mingled with mine. This was *my* house. And I already loved it here.

I changed, deciding on a casual skirt I found in Amelia's closet. It stopped mid-knee and was just retro enough to be back in style. I had just enough time to curl the ends of my hair when Logan knocked at the door. I gave one last glance in the mirror before skipping down the stairs to greet him.

"Come in," I said, a little breathless. His smile made my knees weak. He clutched a frame in his hands. "What's this?"

"I thought you'd like to have this." He flipped the frame around to show me the hillside chalking Amelia had given him.

"Logan, I can't take this." I stared at the pretty picture. "She gave this to *you*."

"She did, but I think she regretted not knowing you, too. I think she'd like for you to have it. I want you to." He handed me the picture. Filled with guilt, I took it. He wouldn't have given it to me if I hadn't been so emotional about the gift in the first place.

I set the artwork on my coffee table and followed him into the kitchen. Placing my hand on his upper arm, I marveled at the muscle there. "Thank you. That's very sweet."

He sat, and I handed him Amelia's journal. I had a marker holding my page. "I'm almost ready. You read, I'll cook."

August 24, 1956

I snuck out to meet Seth at midnight, once I knew my aunt and uncle were sleeping. My life is a million times better, now that I have Seth.

This morning though, I was terrified. Aunt came into my room, I'm certain before dawn, and turned on the bedroom lights. She threw off my quilt and told me to get up. I had no clue what was happening. She took me by the arm and once we were outside she handed me a rag and a bucket and told me to start with the front walk. My aunt's never been the friendliest woman, but never ever cruel.

"They know," I said, interrupting Logan. This was another lifetime. This had all happened…years ago. And yet my hands sat frozen, afraid for Amelia. Afraid for Grandma. Afraid for what was over and done with. Afraid for something no one and nothing could change.

I washed the whole walk, confused and scared when she came back out. Dragging me up by the arm once more she took me to the back walk and drive and told me to get working. I begged to know what was happening and that's when she said, 'I told you to stay away from Seth Garrison.' She knows. I was certain my uncle knew, too. But then she said, 'This is your warning. You see him again, and I'll tell your father and Herb.' I started to sob, I begged her not to say anything and she promised as long as I never see Seth again.

That isn't an option. I'd been up for hours by the time I got to the store. Seth came to me at my lunch hour. I was frightened for him. What would she or Herb do if they found us together? So I rushed him to the back office where I was certain he wouldn't be seen through the front windows. I explained everything, and he was so angry. I think he would have harmed Aunt Lila if I hadn't protested.

Then the most unexpected and amazing thing happened. Seth pulled a ring from his pocket and told me he hadn't planned to wait too long so he might as well ask me now. The ring was his grandmother's. There's no diamond and it's nothing glittery, still it's the most beautiful thing I've ever seen. It fits perfectly. We can't tell anyone, yet. If my aunt and uncle knew, they'd tell Dad and ruin everything. So, he's keeping the ring for now. Seth has a plan and knows a preacher who will marry us secretly. At least he hopes he will.

Soon I will be Mrs. Seth Garrison, and then everyone can know and no one will be able to separate us.

Amelia

"You were right." Logan closed the book. "They know."

My heart beat as if Amelia's scene were playing out right in front of me. Yet, it was over. Everything was over. My heart broke for poor Amelia. She hadn't married Seth, but Burt, hundreds of miles away. And clearly she never got over it. My childhood eyes were a witness to that.

"Something bad has to happen to her, and soon." I gave up on cooking and sat down by Logan.

"How do you know?"

"Because," I said. "Because my dad is born only a year after all of this started."

"Do you want me to go on?" He picked up the book again.

"Um... no." The whole thing was unsettling. "Not tonight." Her words were still so full of life and love and hope. But I knew the end. I knew she didn't end up that way. She didn't end up with Seth. The man she cried for at the time of Burt's death. She still loved Seth.

I turned in my seat, hiding the sudden tears filling my eyes.

And then Logan was up, finishing my chopping at the counter. "What should I do with these?"

Wiping my face, I stood and walked over to him. Spouting instructions, the two of us finished making my stir-fry.

We sat down at the table. I couldn't seem to find my voice.

Devouring half his meal, Logan asked, "Are you okay? You're quiet."

Looking up from the food I'd pecked at, I offered a false smile. "I'm fine. Honest." I stirred the vegetables and rice in my bowl. "I'm just confused. She ended up so different, so unhappy."

His brow creased. "Liv, she *was* happy. I don't mean to argue or make you feel bad, but I knew her," he looked almost repentant when he said, "and well. She may not have been this spontaneous, vigorous Amelia from her youth, but she *was* happy."

I guess I would have to take his word for it. He did know her, and I, well, I didn't. I'd be lying if I said *the facts* didn't pinch though.

He gave me a soft smile. "Are you ready to forget your worries?"

"You mean switch what I'm worried about, right? I'm not a singer."

"You don't have to be. It's karaoke, not American Idol." His grin widened. "We don't have to go, you know."

"I know." I couldn't resist that dimple. "But we're going."

He reached across the table and took my hand. His touch, still so new, electrified me. My skin reacted a bit like a live wire with him around. He intertwined my fingers with his.

"You're a cute silly girl." He rubbed his thumb back and forth along my hand.

Silly? The word turned me into a little girl. A-house-playing little girl. And that's not who I wanted to be as I sat next to this guy who was very much a man. A little girl wasn't the woman he made me want to be. How had I fallen so fast and hard? Despite my falling heart, I conjured up the best glare I could.

"What?"

"*Silly girl*? How many times are you going to call me that?"

"How many more times do you plan to be silly?"

I didn't allow his rugged grin to overwhelm me. "Do you really find me that childish? You don't think I'm able to make my own choices—like Benjamin?" It slipped out of my mouth before I could stop it. My over-sensitive self took over in that oh-so-attractive moment.

His face fell, and for the first time he looked at me annoyed. He released his hold on me and stepped away from the table. "Why would you do that?" His muscles popped out with the tightness of his crossed arms.

"What?" I asked, not-so-innocent, but still frustrated.

"Compare me to *Benjamin.*" He said his name with such disdain.

"I didn't mean it like that. I don't compare you to Benjamin…I don't think about Ben." I sighed. This wasn't at all how I wanted this night to go. I was hoping for maybe a little more kissing and a little less arguing. "I'm sorry." And I was.

Running impatient hands once over his head, he squeezed his eyes shut. "You are silly because you lack so much confidence, Olivia. You don't realize you're capable of doing anything."

Tears sprung to my eyes. I'd never had anyone declare so much faith in me. He meant the opposite of how I had interpreted it. And I repaid him with insults. I turned away from him and jolted up the stairway, into my bathroom. Holding a tissue up to my nose and eyes, I let out a soft sob, overwhelmed. Concentrating and attempting to control my breathing, I wiped at my wet face. I peeked at myself in the mirror. My cheeks were blotched with redness and the whites of my eyes bloodshot. Mascara running, I pulled out my makeup and reapplied just about everything.

Not wanting to keep Logan waiting long, I trotted down the stairs.

Waiting at the bottom, he watched for me. His forehead wrinkled in worry and his whole facade appeared miserable.

I stopped with two stairs to go, meeting him eye level. "No one's ever showed that kind of conviction in me before. I'm sorry I jumped to conclusions. I didn't mean to offend you." I didn't want to lose his confidence, and I never wanted him to look at me with those worry wrinkles again. "When you said that…"

I shook my head at how ridiculous it sounded now. I'd been so rash and so hasty at his playful words. "When you called me *silly*, I thought you were judging me. I'm sorry. I should have known better. I just…" I blew out a puff of air. "I like you, Logan. And—"

His lips curved upward—just slightly and the sadness left his eyes. "It's okay."

I wrapped my hands around his neck, letting my fingers play with the curls at the back of his head. Leaning in, I kissed him. His lips moved with mine as his arms slid about my waist.

Pulling away, his eyes met mine. "I need to grab my wallet. Okay?"

"Mm-hmm."

He turned to leave and I rocked his way, as if a magnet pulled me in his direction. And then I knew for myself how Amelia could fall in love after such a short amount of time.

Switching into some high heels, I slid into my jacket. Logan's musky scent lingered on me and in the house, but was so much more pungent when he walked back in, not bothering to knock.

"Ready?"

"Ready," I said, pressing my lips together.

Ruthie's wasn't clumped with the other few businesses in town. After a five or six minute drive, we pulled up to an old brown house—a single house, no others around. A dozen other cars filled the parking spaces.

"Ruthie's is an old place that a couple of families purchased years ago. They turned it into a bar," Logan said, turning off his truck. "One Friday a month, they have karaoke and let anybody come. There's no alcohol, so families and teenagers come out."

"You're kidding?" I said, not hiding my horror.

"What?"

"You're saying you expect me to get up and make a fool of myself with half the students I work with watching? How could you possibly think that would relax me?" Wouldn't that just give them ammo for Monday morning?

"Livy, you don't *have* to sing."

"Oh." I bit my lip. I didn't? I let out the breath I'd been holding.

Whew.

"Better?" He cupped his warm hand on my cheek.

Okay, so I would relax by watching other people make fools of themselves. I could do that. I nodded into his hold.

I had never been to karaoke night, anywhere, but I was pretty sure as I entered Ruthie's hand in hand with Logan, that this wasn't really your average karaoke night. The outside was clear that the establishment had once been someone's home, but inside the majority of the interior walls had been torn down with only supporting beams here and there, where walls once stood. Round tables sat scattered throughout the large room and a portable stage had been placed at the front. There were two microphones on stage as well as a home-owned karaoke machine. Two huge speakers faced outward. They were the kind of speakers my dad probably once used—in high school.

The speakers boomed with semi-on key notes. I recognized the man singing on stage at once. "Joe!" I said aloud through a spurt of laughter.

"Joe never misses karaoke night," Logan said in my ear. I clasped to his hand with both of mine as he led me through the group to an empty table in the middle. Everyone we passed said hello, and others in front turned at their welcome and waved a greeting to us. I recognized probably half of the people there and they *all* recognized me of course.

We sat in the wooden chairs and listened to Joe belt the rest of *Only the Good Die Young*. The older man had a strong voice, the crowd loving his version of the Billy Joel song.

When Joe finished, Logan leaned across the table. "I'll grab a couple drinks, you can stay and watch."

"Okay."

He stood and walked to the back of the room where the bar sat. The eyes that roved my way were ten times worse with Logan gone. I was still a newcomer, a foreigner to Rendezvous.

With a tap on my shoulder, I turned to see the junior girl who'd asked me about Casanova. She stood with Sierra Henderson, whose grin ran from ear to ear. Grateful I had learned her name since gym class, I said, "Hi, Amy, Sierra."

"Miss Benson! Hi!" Amy's teeth glinted in her wide-mouthed grin and she glanced to the bar where Logan stood.

I didn't follow their gaze. "It's good to see you. Please, call me Livy."

"Right," Amy said.

Another songster headed up on stage, a high school student this time, Ken, Roy's friend. He chuckled into the mic before starting into *Like a Virgin*.

Sierra rolled her eyes at the boy and Amy took Logan's seat next to me. She scooted her chair an inch closer and raised her voice over the noise. "So, Livy." She emphasized my name. "You're on a date?"

"Um..." I gaped over to the bar, hoping Logan was on his way to rescue me. Sierra bent down, better to hear my answer. "I guess...I am." I said each word as if it were my last. Every minute I was more certain of Logan, it was the entire town being involved that gave me misgivings.

Sierra snagged a free chair from the table next to us and sat at my opposite side. "I thought you had a boyfriend."

I cleared my throat. "I did. However, I no longer do." Why was I explaining myself to teenagers?

"I wouldn't either, if Logan were showing an ounce of interest." Sierra raised her eyebrows across the table at Amy.

"It's not like that." I grew more uncomfortable by the second. "Logan isn't the reason I—"

"Is this your first date?"

Okay, this had to stop. Miss Benson needed to find her big girl voice and stop this. Now. "Girls, let me save you some time. This business isn't yours. And I'm really not comfortable talking to you about this." And...I wasn't sure of the answer to that question. Did dinner together every night in the privacy of our homes count?

"Come on, Livy. We've been drooling over Logan since we were twelve years old." Amy's arm flew out in the direction of Logan at the bar. "And *you* just walked in holding his hand." They looked to one another and let out a quiet, but high pitch squeal.

I didn't offer up anymore. Miss Benson had spoken. Still... how long did it take to buy a drink? Where was Logan to save me from this? They'd stop their giddiness once he returned—wouldn't they?

Ignoring me Sierra turned to Amy. "Do you think she's ever—"

"Hi, ladies." Logan. Hallelujah.

"Hi," the girls said together through a jumble of giggles.

"Come on, Sierra." Amy dragged her friend away.

"Is Coke okay?" Logan set the bubbly glass of soda on the table in front of me.

"Thank heavens you're back." I pulled him into his seat.

Grunting, he hit the chair. "Miss me?"

"Logan! People are asking me about us."

"Oh." His eyes went to the girls still watching us. "They're harmless."

"Isn't that what you said about Roy?"

He cracked a grin. "Yeah, probably. He is though. So are they. Please don't worry about it." He picked up my hand from the table.

"I just don't know how to respond, I guess. The stares, the talking, it's just so far out of my comfort zone. In L.A. everyone ignores everyone else." At this point, it wouldn't surprise me to have my relationship broadcast in the *Rendezvous Times*.

He nodded. "I get that. I do. *However*, I'm pretty fond of you." He brought my hand up to his lips. "And I'm not going to hide that because people here tend to watch rather than ignore."

My heart fluttered and my cheeks burned.

"Is that okay with you?"

I might agree to anything if it came out of his mouth. I nodded, putty in his hands.

Ken's horrible rendition of Madonna ended, through loud background music the karaoke host said, "Who's up next folks? Hmm?"

I stared at Logan across from me, as if I were watching someone else's life. Leaning his head toward mine, he connected our lips, placing a small peck and leaving me spinning.

"Miss Benson!" I heard Amy's excited shout above all the

background noise.

Another call came from the crowd, "Yeah! Miss Benson!" I didn't spot the boy who yelled my name. My eyes were on the host, who knew exactly who I was.

"All right then!" he called into his microphone. "Miss Benson, get on up here!"

Widening my eyes, I begged Logan for help. He laughed and winked at me but didn't offer a rescue. How could he not save me from such an impossible situation? Releasing my hand, he waved me on. I narrowed my eyes at him. I would kill him later—less witnesses.

The host pressed his lips to the microphone. "Come on up here, Olivia!" And the crowd gave a shout of approval.

Taking a quick swig of Coke, I somehow stood and started toward the stage. I looked around at the dozens of eyes watching me and by some means continued to move forward.

"What'll it be, *Miss* Benson?"

"Uh... Got any Loretta Lyn?" I said it sarcastically and to myself. It wasn't my actual answer. I'd seen *Coal Miner's Daughter* with Grandma Isle at least five times. It was one of her favorites. Maybe it was being here in Rendezvous, but it was the first thing to come to mind. Within seconds I heard the twangy western tune begin and the words to *Coal Minor's Daughter* strung across the small T.V. screen.

"Wait!" I followed the host to the edge of the stage. "Joe got Billy Joel, Ken sang Madonna! Wait, I was kidding."

But he'd already taken a seat, waiting with all the others for my show.

I started slow, the first line stringing out over the television screen and nothing coming out of my mouth. But then Logan hooted, cheering me on and I found him in the crowd. I didn't need the screen—thanks to Grandma Isle. I sang. I sang my heart out and added every twang I possibly could.

Chapter 20

"Thank you." I handed Logan a glass of lemonade. The lamp light in Amelia's house gave off a quiet, dim environment. "It *really* was fun, and it did get my mind off of things."

"That's funny. You think I asked you out for *you*. I'll just let you keep thinking that." He smiled, and my heart jumped in my chest.

Rolling my eyes at his comment, I sat beside him at my little kitchen table.

"Seriously, your nerves were just an excuse."

"Like you need an excuse," I said, unable to reduce my blaring grin.

His eyes lingered on mine and then wavered to the side. "Looks like you have a message."

Looking behind me, the little red light blinked in the distance. "Oh." With our moment gone, I walked to the counter and hit the button.

Livy, it's Mom. Please call me honey, I'll make sure I answer and no one else. Love you.

Before I could even consider calling her though, the phone rang. Checking the caller ID, it was my California home. "Hello?"

"Liv? Honey, where've you been?" Mom sounded anxious.

"Hi, Mom." I leaned against the counter. "I was actually on a date." I peeked over at Logan who stared back at me. Getting up, he walked into the living room, giving me privacy.

"A date? Livy!"

"Mom, what's wrong with that? I happen to like Logan very much. And Benjamin and I have—"

"Olivia, he's bought a ring. I shouldn't be telling you this, but I couldn't let him shock you."

"A ring?" I coughed out. "He doesn't even believe in marriage. He told me so."

"Well, looks like you've changed his mind. You, my dear, really need to think about this. He loves you and you loved him for a long time. He's made mistakes, but we all have."

Words didn't come in my shock.

"I am on your side, Olivia. That's why I'm calling you. That's why I'm advising you to give this careful thought. We will support you no matter what, but think things through, honey. A month ago you loved Ben. A month ago you wanted this."

A month ago Benjamin hadn't told me his marriage theory or tried to sell my property out from under me. A month ago, I didn't know Logan. "I have thought about it. I need it to be over. I've never been happier than I am right now."

She sighed again. "He's planning on coming next weekend. Just think about it. Be ready when he comes."

Stomping into the living room, I had almost forgotten about Logan—sitting on my couch, one of my Jane Austen's in his hands, his feet crossed on top of the coffee table.

He looked up and the bridge between his eyes wrinkled. He set the book down and sat up straight. "What's wrong?"

"Nothing." I lied, but he didn't believe me.

"No, really." He walked over and wiped at the moisture on my cheek.

My anger had turned to weeping. Shaking my head, defeated, I said, "Mom was calling about Benjamin."

"Oh." He dropped his hand from my face. He liked the topic of Ben as much as I did.

"It's just tricky for my family. I was with Ben a while. Confusing, you know?"

Giving me a single nod, he said, "Are you confused?"

"Well, no. I mean sort of, it's just—"

"It's just, what?" He picked up his jacket. "Maybe I should go while you figure things out."

"Will you let me finish?" I grabbed his arm and he came to a halt. "I know what I want. I don't know how to get my family or Ben to accept my decisions."

His face softened, and I put my hand up to his rough cheek. "Logan. Don't go." He cupped my jaw line with his hand and I shut my eyes at his touch. *I need you, Logan.* And it was true. In the short time of my self-governing, I'd become dependent. I wanted it. I allowed it. Now I *needed* just one thing. Logan.

I hadn't yet opened my eyes. The soft peck of his lips brushed mine.

"You can't leave me now." I spoke between kisses. "I can't do this on my own. Not with Benjamin coming next weekend."

"Why would ol' Benny do something like that?" His lips pressed to mine once more.

"He's crazy. He's bought an engagement ring—or something." I half puckered my lips. "I can't imagine why. He doesn't even believe in the institution of marriage."

My lips were still puckered. When no kisses came, I opened my eyes.

"What?" Logan stood frozen in front of me. "Why would he do that?"

Pressing my lips together, I crossed my arms. "Mom said he didn't really believe I'd broken up with him and well, he's bought a ring."

"I can't believe this." He snatched his coat back up and started for the door. "I can't sit here and kiss you and act like everything's okay. As far as Ben's concerned, you two are still together. He's about to propose!"

"But, we're not together. Logan, you were here, you heard me."

"I know!" He shook his head. "But obviously he didn't. Maybe if you'd talked to him when he called— I'm sorry, but I can't do this." He pushed through the door. He left. He walked away.

How could he do that? This wasn't my fault! *Stupid, moral Logan.* Why did I like him so much anyway? Oh, yeah, his morals. He wouldn't cheat someone else, he had faith in others, he gave people the benefit of the doubt, and he wouldn't make a fool of Ben—not on purpose, no matter how much he disliked him.

I needed to talk to another girl. I needed *womanly* advice. I found myself wishing I could speak with Amelia. Amelia of all people! *Strange*. I went to the next best thing.

August 29, 1956

I was married today.

It was my day off. Seth called in sick. Aunt was watching me closely. She told me I wasn't allowed to spend the day with Cheryl Hull as I'd asked. She's suspicious. As she should be, but I'd hoped my lie had convinced her. I've never been so deceitful, but Seth was waiting for me, so I gave her a glass of iced tea with one of Uncle Herb's barbiturate's crushed up inside. I still can't believe what I'm capable of. Aunt was asleep within the hour. I told Uncle she was sick and had given me permission to visit Cheryl. It was easy, and Uncle didn't even think to ask why I went out in my best dress.

I met Seth at the store and then we drove to the church. I'd never seen it before. A Methodist church, just outside of town. Seth's cousin is the Pastor there. I swear it's the prettiest little church I've ever seen. I don't ever want to forget. It's all natural, almost like a little cabin except for the stained glass windows. There's three of them, one on the door and two above the doorway. The one on the door is sky blue with a white dove in the center. The two above it look like ocean waves with a floating boat filled with men and Jesus walking on the water. The building sat amongst a field of wild flowers with only a small dirt parking lot to one side of it. I picked a few of the wild flowers for a bouquet. The whole scene took my breath away. I couldn't think of a better place to marry my Seth.

Arnold isn't any older than Seth, but he's the one running the little church. I, of course, called him Pastor, but Seth referred to him as Arnie. They joked for only a minute as old friends or, in this case, cousins might and then he turned to introduce me. I swear he beamed as he did so. No one's ever looked at me like Seth does. Arnold was kind, Seth had told him of our situation and although he wouldn't normally agree to marry a couple without consent from their parents, he agreed for Seth's sake. What a blessing. What a miracle. God must be on our side. I'm seriously considering joining the Methodist church.

The ceremony didn't take long. Though Arnie made sure it was sweet. One of his priests stood in as a witness. Seth put his grandmother's gold band on my finger, and I made a promise to always wear it. So, I suppose for a little while I'll have to wear it on my right hand. We left the church within half an hour of arriving. Then we spent the next several hours on the hillside where we first kissed.

My husband and I talked about our future. We decided the best plan was to continue to hide our relationship until Seth's next pay-day. That will be in a week and a half. We're going to move, Seth has other job options and could find a position easily in Forester, which is a hundred miles away. Then, I'll call Mother and Daddy and tell them my happy news. I'm hoping before my aunt gets the chance. Hopefully we'll be settled and then they can fume all they want. Mother won't stand for nonsense once a grandchild is on the way.

I am just about the most content woman alive. The only thing that would make this better is if I weren't alone in this room right now. If only I could have a true honeymoon with my husband. Soon enough, as Seth says. We'll be together always, soon enough.

Aunt is still asleep. Uncle hasn't any idea. I am certainly ~~lucky~~ blessed.

Cheers to a week and a half from now!

Mrs. Seth Garrison

Finishing the entry, I sat there panting. She did it. She married him. Amelia married someone else before my grandfather. I couldn't see how that was possible, but here the proof sat in her own handwriting.

The clock neared midnight but I could hardly stand it. I swallowed whatever pride I should have and picked up the phone to call Logan. What if he didn't answer? My head ran through a dozen excuses he could use. So, instead, I walked the few feet to his home, Amelia's journal in hand. I knocked, just loud enough that he couldn't ignore it.

Opening the door, his bare chest, pajama pants, and squinting made my insides boil. How rude. He'd been sleeping. His black curls all disarrayed made that clear. We had fought and he went to *bed*. How could he sleep?

"Liv?"

"Yes, it's me." I poked him in the chest. "Can I come in?"

He sighed. "Uhh, sure."

"You were sleeping?" I needed him to say it. Confess.

"Yeah." He rubbed a hand over his tousled hair.

"Hmph." I pushed past him. "I couldn't sleep." In fact, I hadn't even changed out of my karaoke clothes.

"I'm sorry." His eyes glanced to the bulging book in my hands.

Oh, yeah! I held it up. "Logan," I said, forgetting my resentment. "She did it! She got *married*."

His eyes widened. "She did?"

Standing in his living room, I opened mid journal and read him the wedding day passage.

"Amazing." He yawned, and I repressed smacking him. "It makes me all the more curious though."

"Me too." How on earth did she get here? With Burt? Silence filled the room as our thoughts wandered. I let the silence be, thankful we weren't arguing or discussing Benjamin.

"Ahh!" Logan gasped. "No way," he said in a hushed tone.

"What?"

"Liv, look at this." I followed him to the back of the room, the long brown wall, with the two—now one chalking Amelia had given him.

"What?"

Taking the picture off the wall, he turned it around to face me. The house on the hill. Only, now that I looked closer, it wasn't a house exactly. A church with a small steeple at the top, next to a hillside covered in flowers. The small windows of the church weren't detailed, but a dove could be made out in the round window upon the door. And the two above the doorway held what I could now see were ocean waves.

Logan went to his room, slipped on a shirt and shoes and seconds later we were back at Amelia's examining the other chalking, the one Logan gave me. I'd mounted it on the wall in the dining area. We sat at the table and looked at the hillside scene. The black and white picture showed a hill with a dark starry night beyond it, two tiny figures sat in the distance.

Logan let out a small laugh. "This is where he took her on their first date, where he kissed her, where they went after their ceremony."

"Seth drew these for her." I looked at him. "And she gave them to you."

His eyes wide, he shrugged his shoulders, as confused as me.

"She must have loved you very much." My storybook head reeled. "Did she give them to you in these exact frames?"

"Yeah, I haven't altered them."

Turning the frame over, I unlatched the backing. With care, I peeled away the cardboard. On the back of the parchment, an unknown handwriting scrawled: *Amelia, All my love, Seth.*

Logan had his picture in hand. He followed my lead and pulled at the back of the frame.

My heart knocked with the thrill. The same foreign script, with one word: *Amelia.*

Logan adjusted the frame and the parchment slid part way out of its spot. Yet, the glass wasn't uncovered. He looked at me and shrugged again. How could that be?—a second parchment! There were two pictures in this frame. Logan pulled the hidden one all the way out. Another chalking and *Amelia* was scribbled on the back because it *was* Amelia, a side-view headshot. A younger, happier, beautiful Amelia. The Amelia Seth knew and loved.

My tears leaked out before I could stop them. I couldn't help it. I knew how this story ended.

Logan examined the Amelia picture.

The lines of the folded notebook paper were faded and almost blended into the parchment. I just saw it through my watery vision, taped to the back of the church chalking. The one that had hid the picture of Amelia. Detaching the document, I read Seth's script on the opposite side: *To My Love, Always, Seth.* I let out a stifled breath.

"What is that?" Logan asked, looking at the extra paper in my hand.

I raised my brows—I didn't know for sure. I unfolded the paper. "It's a letter."My eyes flickered up to his. "From Seth."

"You should change." He glanced down at my skirt. "Get a little more comfortable. We could read it together."

Nodding, I hurried to the stairs. My insides jumped, nervous, like the letter was for me instead of Amelia decades ago.

Changing into my favorite grey sweats and one of Amelia's plain T-shirts, I thought of snuggling on the couch with a cup of hot cocoa while Logan sat next to me reading Seth's letter. *Perfect.* Glancing in the bathroom mirror, I ran a brush through my hair. It looked more red than normal in the dim light. I pulled it back into a ponytail.

Barefoot, I skipped down the stairs and went right to the kitchen to heat some water. It was easy to forget my worries and focus on the task at hand—the man and letter waiting for me. I hoped and prayed Logan had forgotten our troubles as well, at least for the night.

Handing Logan a mug, I said, "Careful. It's hot." It was so late and the house was quiet. It almost didn't feel right breaking the silence.

"Thanks."

Taking a brief sip of the hot liquid, we both set them on Amelia's tattered coffee table. I'd come accustomed to it, the old table that I'd disliked so much before was an antique to me now, bringing character to *my* living room.

Grabbing the afghan that lay across the back of the couch, I sat at the opposite end from Logan. Spreading my legs out, I settled my feet in his lap and covered myself with the blanket. "All right, I'm ready. Go ahead."

Holding the letter up in his one hand, the other fell across my covered legs. It was as if Logan and I had been together our whole lives. No angry dads, no confusing exes, no worried moms. Just me. Just him. The way it should be. It was easy to believe it. At least while the real world sat quiet.

Picking up my sweltering mug, I warmed my hands and waited for Logan to read.

Amelia- my love,

These drawings are my wedding gift to you. I would give you the stars from heaven if possible. You deserve them. You made my world come to life and there's no turning back.

Thank you, my darling, for taking a chance on me. I know our road will be rocky, but I promise you it will be worth it. I will do whatever needed to make sure you're happy. Nothing can be too awful or too difficult, as long as we're together.

I already have a home secured in Forester. Our life begins there. We'll fill it with laughter, love, and children. Soon enough, we'll be there, together. I promise.

All my love,
Seth

Reverently, Logan folded the letter at its crease and set it upon the table.

I wanted to hide my face. The tears streamed down. This was my grandmother. Her life, before Rendezvous. Her life before Burt. Somehow, it fell apart. And yet if it weren't for Rendezvous, for Burt, there'd be no Dad, no me.

Taking my hand, Logan squeezed my fingers, warming me more than the coffee mug could.

"It's silly," I said through more tears. "It happened so long ago. I don't know what's wrong with me—"

"It's okay." His thumb caressed the back of my hand.

Clutching to his hand, I leaned back against the couch. Closing my eyes, I sighed. "He's going to die," I said through more tears.

"Liv—"

"The man who wrote that letter wouldn't have left her. She was willing to give up her family, all she knew to be with him. I just don't see anything short of death separating them."

I woke early, the crick in my neck not allowing me to sleep any longer. Yawning, I blinked, and then gasped at the man beside me. Logan hadn't moved, his hand still tucked inside mine. The sun rose through Amelia's window. He stayed all night. His feet were stretched out on the table and his head lolled off to one side, his eyes still shut.

Sitting up, I let Logan's hand fall free and straightened my tired arms. Taking my legs from his lap in a slow, careful motion, I sat next to him. Moving closer to his side, I looked at his eyes, his nose, his mouth. Inching closer, and trying not to breathe, I leaned in, kissing the side of his full lips.

He didn't move.

Pressing my lips together, I suppressed my grin. Lifting my hand and with soft fingers, I caressed his cheek.

Again he didn't budge.

I laughed inside, keeping quiet. Covering my mouth—even though no sound had escaped, I dropped my gaze to the table. Seth's letter wasn't there. It was in Logan's hand. Sometime in the night, after I'd fallen asleep, he had picked it up and read it again, but he hadn't left me.

"I think I might love you," I said, whispering the words. I waited for any change, any notion that he was waking, but there wasn't any. Closing my eyes, I sighed. *Amelia's not the only one with secrets.*

Chapter 21

Amelia's journal sat untouched. Not many things could tear me away from such an exciting and mysterious time of her life, but substituting creeped up on me. The weekend was half over and I had laundry and housework done, as well as a call to my brother. I called Mr. Ice about his class.

"Worksheets for Spanish and reading for English," he said.

"Reading. Okay, anything else? If I know the novels—"

"You want to do more?" he asked, an amusing pitch to his voice. "If you know the novels, Miss Benson, you could conduct a discussion. That would be more productive."

Jamie sounded pleased I wanted to help more. And I was a bit giddy myself when he told me the novels, *Wuthering Heights* for the ninth and tenth graders and *Jane Eyre* for the upperclassmen. I knew both books well. Maybe this wouldn't be a nightmare after all. I could talk books with anyone.

After my conversation with Mr. Ice, I jotted down a few key notes from memory for a literary discussion. I needed a refresher though—to truly be productive. I needed to read.

Did Rendezvous even have a library? I knew who to ask. I hadn't talked to Logan since he left my house after spending the night. All through laundry—all through housework—I'd been talking myself out of my insane, strong feelings for the man. But at the thought of calling him, those crazy emotions came rushing back. Maybe I wasn't crazy. Amelia knew. After one date with Seth, she knew she loved him. Then again, maybe crazy just ran in the family.

Too weak to stay away from him, I picked up the phone.

"Hello?" he said.

At the same time someone knocked on my door.

Holding the phone to my ear with my shoulder, I opened the door. It was him. Of course it was him. "Hi." Why my sudden shyness? I hadn't actually confessed to a conscious Logan that I loved him. *Normal. Be normal.*

"Hey." He hit end on his phone. "What's up?"

"I just had a quick question." I held my hands up in surrender. "I didn't mean to interrupt your day."

"Liv." Taking my hands and forcing them back down. He sighed. It wasn't impatient, more like, I should know better.

I forced out a laugh. "Yeah. Okay. Um, come in."

Sitting on the couch together, he scooted an inch closer to me. "I'm going to call Benjamin, Logan. Tell him not to come. Remind him what I said when he was here."

Picking up my hand, he said, "Yeah. Okay."

I pressed his calloused hand to mine. How strange that a month ago I'd never touched him—I couldn't imagine being without this hand now. Our interlaced fingers must have meant I'd assured him with my promise. Maybe he had a hard time staying away from me as well.

Remembering the actual reason I had called, I held up my free hand. "Does Rendezvous have a library?"

"Sure." He played with my fingers. "The school, it isn't open today, though."

"That's the only one?" I pictured a back room at Joe's or an old lady's house trailer, but the school? That wouldn't help me now.

"Yeah. Why?"

"I called Jamie Ice about his class. I've read the books we'll be discussing, but it's been a while since I've read *Jane Eyre*. I was hoping to borrow it and brush up real quick."

"I'm sure Amelia has a copy. She loved to read."

"That, I actually knew. She told me that *Pride and Prejudice* was her favorite book. It was the evening of the day I saw her crying. I was so afraid, but she was...*nice.* It was the only real moment we ever had together." I sighed. "I already looked for *Jane Eyre* though, it's not here."

Sitting up straighter, he said, "I wonder if that's why she left you her home. You said you didn't spend much time with her. But maybe when you did, you reminded her of herself?"

"I don't know. Feels like a long shot. She hardly knew me." Still..."I do have a theory though."

"Really?" His eyes roved over my face, waiting for more. He waited, for *my* thoughts, *my* theories. That burning in my heart started again. "Olivia?"

"Oh, yeah. Sorry." I shook out of my tunnel vision. Facing him, I squeezed his fingers. "I think I'm the only person to know she had this secret. I think she wanted me to find it."

"I think you're right. I think I am, too, though," he said, smiling. "You remind *me* of her."

I had learned to take that as a compliment. The Amelia I knew growing up was not someone I ever wanted to be like, but Logan and I didn't know the same person. And the woman from the journal was a stranger to us both.

Sitting my back against the couch once more, I looked up to the ceiling. "So, no library. No Jamie—"

"I wonder if Callie would have a copy."

I didn't know much about the pregnant P.E. teacher, but I couldn't picture my high school gym teacher reading anything other than *Sports Illustrated*.

"Cal's a reader. She likes the classics, too. Paul asked me to check in on her today anyway, want to come?"

"Where's Paul?" I had never met Callie's husband.

"He's working construction near Cody. The baby will be coming soon and he's a little anxious... about *everything*."

I laughed, smiling at the thought of the anxious father. Babies? Fathers? I *was* going crazy. I had never thought about anyone being a father but my own dad before Logan. "I bet."

"Sure, you can laugh, because someday you'll be the one expecting, and you'll be calm and collected—like mothers are."

"Do you know me?" Shaking my head at him, I laughed again.

His dimple pierced. "Well, when the time comes, I think you'll have it together."

"Oh, yeah." I nodded without a hope. "And you'll be the one freaking out?" I couldn't imagine Logan in a panic. He was like a boy scout, always prepared.

"Isn't that every father's job?"

I propped my feet up on the coffee table and examined my shoes. "So, you want kids then?"

"Yeah," he said. "You?"

"Yes," I said, confident in my answer.

"Come on." He stood and held his hand out to me. "Let's go for a walk."

"A walk?"

"To Callie's." He pulled me to my feet. "We'll see how she's feeling and find out if she has your book."

Callie's house was small, but sweet. What looked like a fresh coat of Carolina blue covered the outside. The white trimmed window at the front held eight square panes. Logan rapped on the canary yellow door. His other hand tucked in mine.

Opening the door, Callie seemed to have grown. Her loose fit T-shirt draped over her protruding stomach and her cut off sweats just inched below her T-shirt. Her curly blonde hair fell to her chin in a messy bed-head sort of way. She smiled upon seeing us and her blue eyes widened when they hit our knotted hands.

"So, the rumors *are* true." She crossed her arms over her enlarged abdomen.

"Ah—"

"Rumors?" Logan squeezed my fingers. "Come on, Cal, you don't believe rumors."

"Normally, I don't believe half of what Hank Henderson says, but it looks like he was dead on this time." She sighed, tired. "Come in."

Flushed, I followed after Logan. "How are you feeling?" I asked, taking the attention off of my relationship.

"Fat." She did not hide her irritation.

"You look beautiful, Callie." I meant it. Her skin sparkled, her hair shined, her eyes luminous—Callie made me believe every old wives' tale ever told about glowing pregnant women.

"Right. You're sweet, Olivia."

"So, other than a few extra pounds, how are you feeling?" Logan pulled away from me to adjust the crooked coffee table out of her way.

Falling into a tan La-Z-Boy, she motioned for us to take the couch. "Oh, fine." She popped out the recliner. "I really don't want to bore you with my achy back and swollen ankles."

"How much longer do you have?" I asked.

"Two weeks. My mother had all six of her children early. All of them! And at least two weeks early. I was really hoping to follow in her footsteps."

"You still could," I said.

"Nope. The doctor says it looks like I'll be right at my due date, if not over. This little one is perfectly content to stay inside her mother forever! That's the only reason Paul agreed to work out of town this weekend." Sitting a littler straighter, she eyed me. "Just so you know, Olivia, because no one ever told me, when you're pregnant, you spend half your time in the bathroom. If you aren't puking then you're peeing." She held the underside of her stomach. "Ugh, I shouldn't have said pee. Excuse me." With an awkward push, she forced herself up and out of the chair and disappeared around the corner.

"She's funny." I chuckled and sat back on the couch rubbing shoulders with Logan.

"Callie's always had a good sense of humor. Paul says pregnancy has made her *feisty*."

Covering my mouth to stop the laugh trying to escape, I whispered through my fingers. "I can see that."

"I can see you two being friends."

"Yeah?"

He nodded and put an arm around me, squeezing my shoulders and pulling me, if possible, closer to his side.

"Ohhh, you two are gonna upset Lucille," Callie said, waddling back into the room.

Thinking of the older lunch lady who outweighed me by a hundred pounds or so, I cringed.

Logan laughed as if Callie were a comedian.

Plopping back into her chair, Callie raised her feet once more. "So, how do you like Rendezvous, Olivia?"

"I love it."

"That's wonderful," Her eyebrows rose and she looked to Logan. "Not many can say that. Does that mean you plan on staying a while?"

"For the summer." I suppose when September came I would have to return to school. I couldn't stay and work as Amelia's fill in forever—right?

We talked and laughed and Callie invited me to her baby shower. Logan was right. I could see Callie and I being friends.

"Oh, Cal," Logan said, "We were hoping you had a copy of *Jane Eyre*. Livy's subbing for Jamie Monday and Tuesday."

"I'm sure I do." She attempted to stand, but Logan stood and extended a hand toward her, helping her to her swollen feet.

Waddling into a back room, she called over her shoulder. "Come on back."

Through the arched doorway was another sitting room. A bookcase ran along the lower half of three of the four walls in the room. A plush chair sat in one corner covering part of it. The shelves were filled with books. It looked like heaven.

"Paul makes fun of me, they're alphabetized." She ran her finger along the book bindings, mumbling to herself.

"It's amazing." I poked Logan in the side, staring at the row of books in front of me. "And you said Rendezvous didn't have a library."

"*Jane Eyre, Jane Eyre,*" she said, ignoring us. "Ah-hah! Here it is."

"Thank you, Callie." Maybe—just maybe, I could end my subbing career without making a fool of myself.

"Sure. Stop by again. We could sit in here together. And then Paul could make fun of both of us."

"I'd like that." I couldn't care less who made fun of me. I needed to find my way back into that room!

The road was deserted and quiet on the walk home. I'd always loved the city. I couldn't believe how much Rendezvous had grown on me. And having Logan right beside me sweetened the place for sure. "I could get used to this."

"You shouldn't tease a fella."

Swinging our hands, I ignored his funny comment. "I already am used to this."

He smiled and that thump in my chest quickened when he did so. "Me too."

Somehow through all the joy and heart thumps, my stupid head conjured doubt. How could he possibly feel about me the way I felt about him? I mean chemistry—sure, we had that going for us. So much had happened to help me figure out what I wanted. I was here learning, growing, feeling—and he was here, already amazing—with me as his one and only option.

All right. The time had come. Time to get this over with. I promised Logan I would.

"Well, it's about time." Benjamin sounded irritated. "Do you have any idea how long it's been since you phoned?"

"No, I don't." I wasn't trying to argue, I just didn't know. Logic told me I'd only been in Rendezvous a couple of weeks, but my head, my heart all told me it had been longer.

"Well, let me tell you exactly—"

"Benjamin." I pumped my free fist into the air. "I don't care. I need to talk to you."

"Liv—"

"Please, just let me speak!" I paced the small length of my kitchen.

"What?"

"Don't come here this weekend or ever for that matter. Benjamin, I'm sorry. I didn't mean to hurt you, but this relationship is done. It's over."

"Explain," he said, lawyer-like.

"I don't love you. I'm sure that I never did. I need someone who will hear me out, who will respect my choices, who loves me for me."

"What are you saying?"

Dropping the phone to the counter, I smacked my hands to my head.

"Olivia," the fallen receiver said. "Where is this coming from?"

Picking the phone back up, I held it to my ear. Had I really called him a genius? "*This* has been building for a year now and I'd been choosing to ignore it." I stomped my foot. *Listen to me!* Sure I owed him an explanation, but he had to listen—he had to accept! "This whole ordeal in Rendezvous has really opened my eyes. I wasn't happy before—not like I should be. I cannot continue with this relationship. I won't. Don't come here. Don't call me." Plain. As. Day. Right?

"Honey—"

"Ben!" Smacking the receiver into the countertop, I pulled it back to my ear, my hands shaking. "Don't call me that. Breaking up is difficult enough, please don't patronize me."

"You're breaking up with me?"

"How on earth did you get into law school?" Angry tears filled my eyes. "You know exactly what's happening here. Please just accept it."

"I can't do that. At least come home and conference with Jonathon."

"This has nothing to do with him." My gaze burned a hole in Amelia's linoleum flooring. "Accept it. Move on. Goodbye, Benjamin." I punched the button on the cordless phone, held my head in my hands and cried.

Pressing my hands to my swollen eyes, I breathed in and then out. Had it really taken Amelia dropping a house in my lap for me to realize I didn't want Ben? The way he just spoke to me was no different than how he'd acted the past year—how could I have been so blind to my own heart, my own desires, to what makes me light up and what makes me ticked off? I sat with my head in my hands—pondering my own sanity

"I don't have time for this." Sitting up I shook my head. "I have work to do." I sighed, setting my sanity contemplation aside. *Jane Eyre* time.

Time passed so fast when I read. Dentist appointments… waiting in line at the grocery store… it all flew by happily when I had a book in my hands. I pulled out another kitchen chair and propped my feet up, then continued in Callie's copy of Jane Erye. *Do you think I am an automation? – a machine without feelings? and can bear to have my –*

The phone buzzed and I didn't bother looking at my caller ID. Placing my finger in Callie's book, I found my place again.

Do you think I am an automation? – a machine without feelings? and can bear to have my morsel of bread snatched –

"Honey, pick up the phone, please. I talked to your dad and he agrees, we need to talk about this... Olivia?"

Covering my ears, I adjusted in my seat. What had I just read? Scanning over the page, I found my spot.

Do you think I am an –

The shrill ring of the home phone broke through my barrier. *Argh*!

"Olivia, talk to Jonathon, we can't figure this out if you won't speak to us—"

Sliding my chair along the floor, I stomped the few steps into the kitchen and yanked the message machine cord from the wall.

Ben had one thing right. And as long as I was breaking hearts, I might as well break another. Picking up the receiver, I dialed Dad's cell.

"Hello, Daddy."

"Olivia?" He sounded surprised. He sounded sorry. Maybe he was.

"Yeah, it's me."

"How are you, honey?"

"I'm wonderful. Staying here was the right choice." I bit my lip. My father loved me. He'd always worked hard to make me happy. I hated our last few days together.

"Oh, really?" His voice turned from joy to disgruntled. "I'm sure. People just can't get enough of Rendezvous. That's why the population is up to 332."

"Dad." I hung my head, my tone solemn. "I mean it. I'm not trying to prove you wrong. I don't want to argue anymore. But I'm going to start making my own choices. Please be happy for me. Isn't that what a father wants for his kids, happiness?"

"Yes, Olivia, a father wants that. He also wants to know those choices are wise and sound and secure."

"I know that, Daddy." Clenching my fist, I kept my voice in control. He was happy to hear from me at first—I wanted him to still be. How could I get that back? "I'm just living on my own, thinking about what I want to do with my life."

He cleared his throat. "How's that going?"

"Well." My voice shook, but I kept on. "It's been enlightening. I've made some decisions."

"Yes?" His every word sounded more unhappy.

"I don't want to go into medicine. Or law. I realize I should have told you this in person, but as you know, I don't have a way home right now." I paced from the kitchen to the living room and back again. "And I thought you should know."

"How thoughtful of you," he said, his voice a high, unnatural tone.

Stop acting like a little girl. "I'll use my education. I'm just going to do something I want to do."

"Like?" His time bomb ticked in my ear, like a grandfather clock loaded with dynamite, just waiting to blow.

"Like Literature." I didn't hesitate—as long as I was digging myself a hole.

"Uh-huh." Tick. Tick. Tick.

"I know it's not what you were hoping, but it's what I love."

Tick. Tick. Tick.

"I'm going to be here all summer long. I found the silver dollar Amelia left you. I'll mail it to you." At least I thought it was her lucky silver dollar. It was the only one I'd found and it had been taped to the back of her favorite book.

Tick. Tick—BOOM! "LIVY! I don't want a silver dollar! I want you home, making sane choices."

"Stop!" Stomping my foot, I yelled into the receiver. "I don't expect you to understand this. But I would like a little support."

"Support?" He laughed.

"I don't know if that's possible for you, but I at least had to explain myself for once. Goodbye, Dad." Pushing the off button on my cordless phone, I fell to the couch. Dropping the phone to the floor, my heart beat a mile a minute. I did it. I stood up to the man. I was compliant no more—and as much as I loved my father, as much as I valued his wisdom—for the first time in my life, I believed I could do anything. I settled down to read.

September 3, 1956

Five more days until Seth and I leave for our new life. Five days as a married woman. I already wake up in the morning expecting Seth to be next to me, when he's not, I have to remind myself—days. He will be in just days. Otherwise I might end up in tears.

I told Uncle I needed a new dress for the fall dance and asked if I could get my pay-check early. He agreed. I've already given the small sum to my husband. It's not much, but I'm happy I can contribute to our new life together.

Daddy called. He actually asked about Phillip Harlem and if I was still seeing him. I haven't spoken to him in months and that's what he asks me about! I couldn't believe it, but I told him that I wasn't, that Phillip Harlem didn't interest me in the least. I could tell he was disappointed. Momma writes often, but always about home and my brothers and sisters. She'd never ask about Phillip Harlem!

Speaking of him—we saw him yesterday. Aunt and Uncle were out of town, and I felt a bit of freedom. It felt nice walking into Uncle Herb's store holding Seth's hand and not worrying if he or Aunt might see. Phillip saw though. I didn't care, let him look! Let him know I won't be even glancing his way!

Aunt and Uncle returned home today. So, it's back to sneaking around. It's not exciting anymore. I'm ready to have it done with. Five more days. Aunt made me work in her garden today, my day off. I had very different plans for this day! Uncle closed the store for some reason or another, which thrilled me of course! But here I am in their house, under their every watch. Poor Seth, he'll realize what happened when he sees the closed sign, still, I hate not explaining things myself.

It's only dinner now. Night fall will come soon and then I'll see him.

Amelia

Chapter 22

"*Wuthering Heights* holds several themes. Can anyone name one?" I scanned the classroom for hands…eye contact…anything.

Silence.

"Okay, I'll name a few. Social rankings and class distinctions, fate, prejudice, love." Like a little girl playing make-believe, I found myself in love with playing *teacher*. The literary discussions transfixed me—even if I was the only one discussing. Class hours flew by. Even my Spanish class wasn't a disaster. I wasn't shaking now. I didn't have trouble gathering my thoughts anymore. I didn't even mind the students calling me Miss Benson.

"Love?" Harvey Dowell wrinkled his nose. "It's the most miserable thing I've ever read. They all hate each other."

"There are different types of love, Harvey. And believe it or not, Catherine and Heathcliff did love one another."

"I think it's romantic." Betsy Lander, her eyes shut tight, tucked her clasped hands under her chin.

"It's sad," the girl behind her said. "They don't even marry each other. It's depressing."

"Okay, let's brainstorm different types of love. Give me some ideas." I picked up a piece of chalk and turned to the board, ready to write. The feel of chalk dust on my fingers made me smile.

"True love." Betsy's dreamy tone continued.

I scrawled her answer on the board.

"Ah, *fake* love." Harvey said with a scowl.

I laughed. "Okay, Harvey, I get what you're saying. However,

I'd like you to be more specific. For example, infatuation." I added the word to the list. "That would be what you call fake love, but it explains more." I strolled down an aisle of desks. "Infatuation is a love that's based on fantasy, something that isn't realistic. What else?"

The class discussed and I scrawled more answers on the board. I thought I would burst. Why couldn't Mr. Ice be gone the rest of the week? "Can you think of anymore?"

"Sex?" The younger boy reminded me of Roy, his grin far too big and devious.

"Sex isn't a type of love." He didn't scare me. "It falls under different love categories, like infatuation, passionate love, or romantic love. It wouldn't fall under, say, brotherly love or maternal love. There are plenty of love types that have nothing to do with sex."

Every eye was glued to my face. The room was silent—waiting for my next words. Looking out at the classroom, I saw kids, sure, teenagers, but kids nonetheless. I was the adult, the authority in this room. Pressing my lips together, I held my giddiness inside—the type I'd only experienced in my college literature classes.

"So," I scanned their faces. "What type of love would you say Catherine and Heathcliff had?"

"Infatuation?"

The rest waited for my confirmation, my expertise. "That's an excellent guess, Jessica. However, infatuation fades. Heathcliff and Catherine's affections never faded. They weren't deceived in who the other was. I would call their feelings an *obsessed* love."

Jessica raised her hand. "If they're so obsessed with each other, why did they marry other people?"

"That's a good question. For one, obsessed love isn't healthy or normal. Does anyone have another answer for that question?"

"She says that Heathcliff isn't good enough for her," Harvey said.

"That's exactly right!" I pointed at him in my excitement. "That leads into another theme from *Wuthering Heights*. Remember when I mentioned social standings?"

Gary and I took the long way home, enjoying the warm weather. The thought of substituting had made my blood pressure rise. It never occurred to me that I might be good at it. That I might love it.

Passing Callie's, I saw her on all fours, working in her garden, her belly hanging low. I slowed to a stop. "Hey, Callie."

Putting a hand on her back, she held the other up to shield her eyes from the sun. Her yellow tank top just covered the bottom of her belly and her gray shorts hung below her shirt. Neither looked like maternity clothes. She smiled when she saw me and wiped the sweat from her brow.

"Olivia, how was teaching today?"

I slid off my bike and parked it against her chain-link fence. "It was great." I couldn't stop the wide grin crossing my face.

"Really? I kind of got the idea you weren't excited the other day."

I laughed. "That's an understatement. I was that obvious, huh?"

"I read people pretty well."

"And now?" I gave her a sidelong glance.

"And now..." She held her hand out to me and I took it, helping her stand. "You look like you just won a championship game."

Maybe I was an open book. I wondered what she'd say about my feelings for Logan. "I've never even considered going into teaching."

"Now you are." She said it like it was a fact.

"Maybe...I am. I *actually* am."

She took off her dirty gloves and leaned against the fence.

"Callie, what are you doing?"

"Gardening." She blew out a heavy breath and wiped the sweat from her damp forehead.

"You shouldn't be doing that! Here, let me help."

"In those shoes?" She pointed at my feet with a dubious look.

I looked down at my heels. She had a point. Still, I couldn't watch her, almost nine months pregnant, digging holes in the ground. I took them off, tossing them to the sidewalk.

"I never wear heels, it's tennis shoes every day for me. That's one reason I love my job." She rubbed her round belly. "I can't wait until I'm full time again. I'll have the summer with the little munchkin and then I'll be back to work—hopefully getting my body back." Callie had her life all figured out.

Moving a lawn chair into the shade, I motioned for her to sit down. Rolling up my slacks, I knelt in the dirt to finish what she had started. "Callie, why are you gardening? Are you trying to kill yourself?"

"I'm trying to put myself into labor." She rolled her eyes and shook her head.

I laughed and buried another sunflower seed.

"Great, Livy, now you've got me sitting, I'll never get back up." She held up a handheld battery operated fan and blew air into her face.

I ran out of seeds quickly, I hadn't helped much. Running inside, I grabbed two bottles of water and handed one to her. "Do you know what you're having?"

"A girl." The sweetest smile filled her face. "Michelle Paula." She lay her fan down, took a swig and then rubbed her protruding abdomen.

I stayed in Callie's yard for another half an hour. Logan was right about us. We made fast friends.

Riding up to my little house, Logan sat outside waiting for me. His hair was muffled and his T-shirt hugged the contours of his abs. He held a book in his hands, reading. No one ever looked better. Rendezvous was possibly my favorite place on the planet.

Standing when he saw me, his book fell to his side in one hand. He waited for me to park my bicycle. "How did it go?"

Picking up his book, I looked at the cover. "Hmm." *Huckleberry Finn.* "I like that one."

His lips turned up and he stroked the binding. "It's a favorite of mine."

"Is it?"

"Liv?" He dropped his book to the ground. "How did it go?"

Smiling like a little girl, I said, "It went well, very well."

"I knew it." Leaning down, he hugged me.

Wrapping my arms around his middle, I squeezed back. "I *really* liked it."

"Oh, yeah?" He pulled back to look at me.

I nodded. "Logan," I said as if it were a secret. "I *loved* it."

I prattled on about my day until one of Logan's regulars showed up with engine trouble.

"You'll tell me more over dinner?"

I nodded. He actually asked to hear more about *my* day. I had never met anyone like him and I knew I never would. There are a lot of people in California and he's—well, he's like nobody else. My happy thoughts and beating heart slowed watching him walk away. Rendezvous provided zero competition—besides Lucille's granddaughter. At first that had seemed like a plus but I realized now it wasn't a help to me. I loved Logan. I wanted him. How could he *really* say the same, when I was his only option?

Chapter 23

September 7, 1956

Tomorrow. I'm packing a small bag that won't raise questions, and I'm meeting Seth at the store. He'll pick up his paycheck in the morning and then he'll drive straight here to the store, all packed up and ready to go. Tomorrow.

And today, I'm closing the gallery early. I haven't had a real customer in a week, and Seth has a gift for me.

I keep telling myself to breathe. Everything I've been waiting for is coming. Tomorrow.

Amelia

September 7, 1956- Midnight

My heart is breaking. I can't speak – and so I write.

Phillip Harlem went to my uncle. He told him he saw us. Uncle Herb didn't believe him. So, Phillip went through Seth's suitcase. Seth had brought it to work and Phillip found our marriage license. He gave it to Uncle.

I had no idea. No knowledge of the horrible events happening right under my nose. Uncle sent me to work yesterday like usual, I had no clue he knew our secret. As I planned, I left early and spent the evening with Seth. He gave me my gift, and I went home – like always. But when I snuck into the house, Uncle and Aunt were waiting for me. Uncle grabbed me, Aunt slapped me and then they locked me in their basement bedroom. Uncle screamed his explanation through the door – what he'd seen, what Phillip told him. There are no windows, no phones. All I have with me is what was on me when I arrived at their house, my purse, this journal, and my gift.

Seth has no idea. No way of knowing. He's planning on meeting me at the gallery in the morning still, and somehow, Uncle knows that as well. He's called Father and without a doubt Daddy's on his way.

I don't know what to do. How did things get turned upside down? Things couldn't be more miserable! How do I fix this?

Amelia

September 12, 1956

Irony. What a horrible word. But that's all I think when I read my last entry. I thought I couldn't be more miserable than I was that night. I didn't know what misery was. I hadn't yet comprehended the word. How I wish I were still locked in Uncle's basement. I wish they'd have beaten me and bruised me. ~~I wish~~ It doesn't matter anymore. Nothing matters.

And yet, I won't allow myself to forget what happened.

Dad came for me. He forced me into his car, despite my screams that I was a grown up, married woman. I tore at his face, his body…he tied my hands to keep me still, but that didn't shut me up. I'm not sure how long he drove, but I cried and screamed the whole way. I wish I were back in that car, tied up and sobbing. I wish I were anywhere but here.

The way Dad looked at me – he despises me. I don't care. The sight of him repulses me. He wants to know how I could have done this to him, to Mother, to our family. I begged him to be reasonable, begged him to listen to me, to realize that I love Seth and that he would too, if he'd only be reasonable. What a waste of my breath. It changed nothing. And now nothing matters.

I can't even tell you where I am. I can't tell you the name of the town or even the state. Not that it matters. I arrived here three days ago. Can it really only have been three? This house, that's all I know, dirt roads, and this dreary house with hard floors and dull walls.

And that man, of course.

There's a man living here. I don't know his name. I don't really care. Dad's here too, but I refuse to speak to him. There's no reason to.

I spent those three days in a panicked and terrified state. I screamed until my voice ran out. And then, I pounded on the door of my room until my fists bruised and swelled. And now it doesn't matter what I say, what I do, so I'm silent. I don't pound anymore.

I wouldn't eat until the second day and even then Dad forced the cup of soup down my hoarse, painful throat. Why wouldn't he just let me starve to death? How can he do this and actually care about me?

The fact is, I only know one *thing. And I'm too afraid to even write it down. If I never write it down, if I never say it out loud, maybe it won't be true. Maybe, if I never say it, time will reverse. Anywhere, but here, anything, but* that.

Amelia

September 14, 1956

I cannot deny the truth now. As much as I want to, it's impossible now. I will probably be damned for the horrible person I am.

I should be damned. So the words I haven't said or written – must be now. I can't forget. I don't deserve to forget.

The day Dad took me away, Seth found out. I don't know how – probably Philip was boasting, or he dragged it out of my aunt. Seth, my dearest Seth. Somehow, he discovered where I'd been taken. He followed after me. Of course he would. How I wish he hadn't now. He loved me more than anyone ever has or ever will. He was a Saint, and I never did deserve him. And now I'll be saying my penance to him until the day I die.

But he never made it. His car hit another and then rolled.

Dad told me without care or any sign of a heart. I wouldn't believe him. I knew he'd try to lie to me, deceive me, tear me away from Seth somehow, but I would never have believed him. He knew that though, so he showed me the paper clipping that Aunt sent. Three pictures, Seth's car, ripped apart, and high school photos of Seth and Arnie. I couldn't read the article though. The caption above the photos read: FATAL COLLISION. I didn't have time to feel my stomach roll before the bile came spilling out.

Why didn't I try harder to escape myself? Why didn't I insist we leave right after the wedding? Why him? Why couldn't it have been me?

I'm not allowed to cry for Seth, or say his name, not unless I'd like to be beaten, Dad made that rule very clear. I can't speak his name or ever go back to Ganesworth. This morning Dad told me he'd arranged for me to marry Burt, the man living here in this house. I didn't object or fight him- that's how evil I am. What would be the point anyway? Seth's gone.

My sin was committed before the lunch hour. I was married to Burt by a preacher who didn't seem to care that my answer to his meaningless question was inaudible.

Before dinner, Dad left town. Left me to my new life, my miserable, insignificant life. I can't deny the sickening truth, not with a wedding band on my finger that Seth didn't give me. Not with so much shame in my heart.

He's gone. He's truly and actually gone. And I might as well be.

Amelia

Sobbing, I sat on the couch, my head in my hands. I had been waiting for this, expecting this, but not in this way. Not in this cruel, horrid way. It's no wonder *this* Amelia never existed in my world.

Engrossed in my reading, I forgot all about my dinner plans. I jumped at Logan's knock on the door. What time was it?

I took deep breaths but there was no gaining control *now*. I opened the door. Another sob fell from my chest. There he stood—so good, so loving, so healthy and whole.

His face fell—I must have looked worse than I thought.

"Olivia?"

"Yeah, hi." I gave my best effort not to frown. "I just need a minute." I hurried to the bathroom. Oh, it was so much worse—running mascara, puffy eyes, swollen nose, the works. How long had I been crying anyway?

I dabbed my face with a wet cloth, trying to gain some control. Rubbing and dabbing and rummaging through my makeup bag, I attempted to fix my reflection. The whole time more and more tears falling. And then his reflection joined mine.

His hands rested on my shoulders. "Liv?"

I couldn't look at myself anymore. The redness, the puffiness, it wouldn't go away and now Logan stared at me as if I might break. And I just might. I spun around, only to stand face to face with his chest. Burying my face into his T-shirt, I wrapped my arms around his waist—at least he couldn't see me anymore.

"Seth died."

Wrapping his arms around me, he didn't make me look at him. He didn't say anything, only squeezed me tighter.

September 19, 1956

I haven't said his name out loud in five days.

I tried to send a letter to Seth's mother today. Neither Dad nor Burt ever said anything about letters. I owe her that much. I only met the woman once, but I felt the need to let her know how sorry I was and that I loved her son. I wanted her to know that someone else found him special and wonderful. I couldn't bring myself to tell her how I'd let him down in the end.

I made the mistake of asking Burt for a stamp. I don't have money to buy one. He insisted on seeing the letter though. I refused and then he forced it from my hands. We don't even normally talk to one another. He lets me sleep in the spare bedroom, so he isn't all animal. But when he saw the letter, he hit me. I fell to the floor, my broken lip spilling blood everywhere. He told me I was his wife and I needed to act like it. He left the letter in pieces on the ground. I crawled to the front door and was able to make it outside before vomiting.

I've been his cook and maid and I imagine that's how it will continue. I haven't any complaints really (except for forbidding my letter). What else do I have to do?

Amelia

p.s. Aunt packed my things up and sent them here. Amongst them I found the envelope that held my gifts from Seth, my drawings. Either she didn't know what they were or she has a conscience after all.

"What about her ring?" Logan asked.

"She's wearing it, remember? On her right hand, or at least she was." I gasped. "Her ring! Her ring! I have her ring." I jetted from my perch beside Logan on the couch and ran up the stairs.

I hadn't opened her box in days. Bringing it downstairs, I set it on the table next to Logan. I opened it and pulled out the thin gold band. Its luster had dulled, but it held so much more meaning for me now.

"Here." I laid it in his palm. Then I pulled the pictures from the box. Sitting back down, I held one up. "That's him."

Logan set the ring back inside the box and took the picture from my hand.

"They look right together, don't they?" I stared at the picture, a shaky breath escaping my mouth.

"They do."

I touched the corner of the photo in his hand. "I didn't even realize this was Amelia the first time I saw it."

"Really?" He sounded surprised. Of course he probably knew right away. Turning to the next picture, we looked at Seth alone. His handsome face grinned back at us. After all I'd read about him, his broad shoulders and fair hair sounded familiar to me.

"So, what does the letter say?" Logan set the pictures down and searched through the box, pulling out the letter.

"Actually, I haven't read it yet. Sounds silly, but as much as I wanted to discover—I also wanted to respect her. It's still sealed. I couldn't break into it. I'm going to have to open it now, I think. I'm not *that* strong." I sighed, tired. Laying my head back, I closed my eyes. "I just wish—I wish she could have had the life she wanted."

His eyebrows crowded together and he looked over at me, thoughtful. "I know it's awful. I know it's sad, and I hate that she lost Seth. But I knew her for years. I knew Burt. I saw them together. And though I was young when he passed—they loved each other."

Mulling over those words, I thought about my discussion in class, the different types of love. Is it possible that she ever loved Burt? In any way? Logan believed so, but I couldn't be sure.

Chapter 24

Sitting at Amelia's table, I stuffed the last bite of chicken into my mouth. We read, cooked and ate...it was late. Peering over at Logan, I didn't want him to leave—but then I never wanted him to go. How would I ever be able to return home to California, if the thought of Logan walking next door made my insides ache?

"So, did you hear, Lucille's granddaughter is in town?" I twirled my fork with my fingers, watching it spin—avoiding his eyes.

"Yeah, I know."

Of course he knew. Lucille wouldn't let either of us forget. "Have you met her yet?"

"No, but I will. Lucille's invited me over for dinner next week."

"Oh!" My head shot up and I dropped the fork to the table. "And you said yes?"

"Well," he stirred in his seat, biting his bottom lip and looking like a kid in trouble. "Yes. I mean, it's Lucille. I've known her my whole life. She didn't ask if she could set me up on a blind date. She offered dinner."

"It's fine. Of course it's fine. Why wouldn't it be fine?" I shrugged and shook my head at him, eyes wide. *Oh, this is ridiculous!* Getting up, I gathered our plates, walked into the kitchen and set them in the sink. *What was I trying to do here, anyway?*

"You're upset." He followed after me, his eyebrows knit

together.

"No!" I yelled and forced a laugh. Standing by the sink, I looked down into the basin, away from his face.

"Liv."

"No. No." I shook my head. "Not in the least." Maybe Lucille's granddaughter had the same figure as her grandmother and...a few visible warts. Baldness wouldn't hurt. An obnoxious personality would wrap her up nicely.

"It's nothing, Liv." He wrapped his arms around my waist from behind.

And I knew he meant what he said. I fought it, but the stupid jealousy seeped into my voice without permission. Forcing too much cheer I elbowed his ribs. "I know!"

Turning me around so that I faced him, he pinched my chin, forcing me to look at him. My arms hung, wilting at my side. With his hand on my cheek, he leaned in, brushing his lips to mine.

My chest heaved and a shaky breath escaped my throat. *Competition. Wasn't I just complaining that I didn't have any? That Logan had no other options.* Ugh. I wanted Logan to *choose* me, but I didn't want him to ever look at Lucille's granddaughter—or anyone else. I squeezed my eyes shut.

"All right. Come on." He dragged me behind him. "It's been two hours. Let's see what that letter says."

If he was trying to distract me—it was working. "Ah… okay."

The box and letter still sat on my coffee table. Logan lifted the lid, retrieved the envelope, and led me outside. Sitting on the concrete, our backs up against my house, he handed me the letter. Laying it in my lap, I peered up at the towering elm to the side of us.

"That's where I first saw you," I said, pointing.

A quiet laugh fell from his chest. "My dad was afraid I'd wear a hole in the side of our house with my soccer ball. I lived outside in the summers."

"Isn't it strange? If my family had visited more, we probably would've met, maybe even been friends."

"Why didn't you visit more?" He turned his head, leaning it

against the house, and looking me in the eye.

"I asked my dad that same question the last time my family came here. I was meeting cousins that I didn't recognize and uncles who couldn't get my name right. It baffled me. It was quite the opposite of my mom's family and I wanted to know why."

"What'd he say?"

"He gave me some excuse about not getting along with his dad. He said that was hard on Amelia and so it was just easier to stay away."

"That's a shame," He tucked a strand of hair behind my ear. "We would have been good friends."

Closing my eyes, I thought he might kiss me again. My lips waited—

"Ready to read?"

Opening my eyes, I sighed. Nodding, I reached for the letter and ran my finger along the lip of the envelope, I loosened the sticky edge. It unstuck easily, this wasn't the first time someone had opened it.

Dearest Amelia,

When I was a boy, my Uncle Jon was my favorite person in the world. He told me the best things in life will always take effort. It'll be in your grasp and then the world will challenge you for it. He told me that if I wanted to be happy, giving up wasn't an option. He was the best man I knew, as well as the happiest. He was smiling the day he died, so I take his word for gold. He knew how to live right.

Loving you is the easiest and best thing I've ever done. Keeping you is my challenge. But giving up isn't an option, despite what the world says. I have no doubt we can make it. Take courage in that.

Before he passed, Uncle Jon gave me a gift. His lucky silver dollar, so you see sweet Amelia, even luck is on our side.

Forever Yours,
Seth

"Luck." I puckered my lips, my eyebrows rising at the word.

Logan squeezed my hand, his forehead lined with worry wrinkles. "I don't think Uncle Jon's silver dollar..." I dropped her letter, zoning out into space.

"Liv?"

I jumped to my feet. Amelia left Dad her lucky silver dollar. It had to be the same one. Running inside, I skipped every other step up to Amelia's room. Rummaging through her books, I found the one I needed: *Pride and Prejudice.* Opening to the back, I let the heavy end page fall open on its own to the silver coin, old and worn. Running out to the stairs, I jumped down three of them, before stumbling down the rest.

"Whoa!" Logan caught me at the bottom.

"Look." I held up the silver dollar. "She left this to my dad in her will. I had no idea what it meant to her until now."

Taking the coin from my hand, he held it up to the light, looking at the front and back and the bumpy ridge around it. Amelia's lucky coin. *Seth's* lucky coin.

October 3, 1956

Rendezvous. That's what this place is called, a small, dreary town in northern Wyoming. Far from anyone or anything familiar to me. My memories of Seth feel almost like a lifetime ago. Except for the pain, the pain's only gotten worse. Still, I haven't voiced his name. Who would I say it to anyway? My... husband? Legally Burt is my spouse, but he is a stranger to me and could never be my husband as Seth once was, as short as that time may have been.

I'm thankful for this room, my own room. He never comes in here. And at night I'm free to sob into my pillow. Last night I cried so hard, so painfully, that I had to run outside to vomit. When Burt saw my red streaked face, I told him I was ill. He told me to stay in bed today.

I don't know Burt's occupation, but I do know he leaves the house for nine hours a day twice a week. He works in the shed on the days he's home. So, for nine hours today I've had this horrible place to myself, without an expectation that anything will be done when he gets home. So, I decided to leave, see what stood beyond the house and yard. I only walked a short distance. There wasn't anything to see anyway, no escape. Where would I go anyway? Would it really matter? Legally I'm bound to this place, to this man.

Maybe I am sick, because one little walk exhausted me. I was lying down when someone knocked on Burt's door. I was surprised. In all the time I've been here, longer than I was married to my Seth, I've never seen another person. No one has ever come to Burt's house before. It was the woman who lives next door, the side with the little elm. She said she thought she'd seen a woman over at Burt's and asked who I was. I haven't spoken to another person in so long. I live in silence. It felt so strange, so normal, and I hated that. The woman…

Setting the book in his lap, Logan said, "She's talking about my grandmother."

"Seriously?"

"The woman next door, the elm…My Grandma Thomas, Mom's mom, she lived in my house forever." He looked back to Amelia's journal, his finger finding the date.

Grettie Thomas, I think, she was nice enough. I just can't have "normal" in my life, it betrays Seth even more. Not to mention she wanted to know who I was. I had to say the words: "Burt's wife". I had to hold back the phlegm rising in my throat. She told me she was expecting a baby and again I thought I might be sick. I couldn't listen to her anymore. I told her I didn't feel well. She left with an offer to be of help if I needed anything. Then I went inside and cried myself to sleep.

Amelia

October 5, 1956

I think this house is making me sick. I had to run to the bathroom again this morning. Burt found me there and this time, my explanation wasn't a lie. He didn't say anything, which I assume means I'm still expected to complete my chores. The awful knot in my gut stayed the whole day through.

Grettie came by again, this time with an apple pie. She said it was to welcome me. My face must have spoken for me, because she commented on me still being ill. She laughed and actually joked about me expecting as well. I couldn't help it. I told her bluntly that that was impossible. I can't imagine being with Burt that way. Then she asked when Burt and I were married. How strange and wrong that sounded. I stood there stupidly. I couldn't tell her. I didn't know. It wasn't important to me. So, I just said "A while ago." She laughed and retorted that it was quite possible then. I was grateful Burt wasn't around. I may have gotten another smack for my stupidity.

Seth's birthday is coming. I never got the chance to give him a gift. And his gifts to me are hidden in my closet rather than out where I can see them. Burt would burn them if he ever found them. He won't though. He won't come in here.

Amelia

Setting the book down, Logan looked at me, his eyebrows creased—like when he's worried about me. "I need a drink," he said, his voice odd and slow.

"Ah, okay." I stood and stretched my legs. "What do you want?"

"Umm…" He looked different. His countenance had changed.

"You're acting weird. Are you okay?"

His forehead wrinkled like a withering prune.

I shoved his shoulder. "Come on. What's wrong?" I studied his face. What was with the sudden secretive show? What could have brought this on? My skin pricked.

He cleared his throat and stood up to face me. "Nothing's wrong. I just have a suspicion and I could be off base…but I don't think I am."

I'd never seen him act so strange, he was always forthright. "What are you talking about?" What could have happened in the last three minutes that had him so jittery? I waited for his epiphany to realize I don't deserve him, but how had *this* journal entry done that?

Taking my hand, he walked me inside and pulled me down onto the couch. He sat facing me, looking into my eyes he took his time. "What if—I'm wondering..." Putting his hand to my cheek, he rubbed his thumb over my cheekbone. "I think Seth is your grandfather."

"What?" I knew my grandfather. I didn't know him well, but I called him grandpa, I saw him—his picture clear in my head.

"She's sick. She and Burt haven't been together—he never goes into her room. You said yourself that your father's birth is soon." His eyebrows knit together.

"They're married and she's broken, she doesn't have much fight left in her. She'd give in to him. Maybe soon—" I shook my head at him, my hands tightening into fists in my lap.

"With what she's said, I really doubt it. They're more like roommates that never see each other."

Opening my fist, I rubbed my sweaty palms on my jeans. My heart beat fast—angry beats. "They have sex." I didn't love the idea of Logan and I discussing Amelia's sex life! "Remember Earl and Red? She and Seth never even got the chance to live together."

Biting his lip, he offered a sad smile.

My blood boiled again. *I am not a* silly *child!* "I realize that doesn't mean they were never together, it just seems unlikely."

"Really? It seems very likely." Again with the pathetic grin.

Was he trying to contradict everything I said?

"They were so crazy in love they married without anyone knowing about it. They planned to run away together." Running his hand though his hair, he shook his head. "I could be wrong. I just felt like I should warn you."

"Well, thanks." Not really—no thanks. "Why don't you continue?" Amelia would prove him wrong.

October 15, 1956

Grettie came over again. Burt was gone and I felt free to ask her questions. I knew she wouldn't mind, she's asked me plenty. Half of which I don't know the answer to, or at least what lie to tell her.

So, I asked her how she was feeling. She said better now that she's a few months along. I asked what was so bad before, how she felt. She told me, leaving little left for imagination.

And that's when I decided it was certain, I'm going to have a baby. At first I was terrified. A child, a baby, and here in this awful place, with Burt!

But then the shock wore off. I realized this is the greatest blessing God could have sent me. Something they CAN'T take away from me. Something I certainly don't deserve. I think I smiled for the first time in weeks. Also, for the first time since I arrived here I had a desire to speak with my mother. I borrowed a few dimes from Grettie, she was thrilled to lend them when I explained the news, and walked the few blocks into town to the only pay phone. Burt doesn't have a phone, or television set, I suppose I'm lucky for indoor plumbing. I called Mother. She was thrilled, and it was so good to hear her voice. I could hear her as she told Dad. I wouldn't speak to him and she didn't make me. I could hear his joy over the phone and that's when I knew he thought this child belonged to Burt. That would be impossible. But I also knew I couldn't say as much, or this baby would be taken from me. I can't allow that to happen. This child is my last gift from Seth.

Amelia

Logan stopped reading and stared at me, waiting for my insane, irrational reaction, I'm sure.

I didn't know how to react. Everything I knew was wrong. The facts I held fast to as a child were broken. I knew Amelia had secrets. I just didn't realize how deep those secrets ran.

Chapter 25

When Logan left I was ready. I needed to be alone. I read through Amelia's last entry and Seth's letter three more times. Searching through the box again, I examined her ring, the silver dollar, and each picture with new eyes. At two in the morning I decided my six a.m. alarm was coming all too soon. I just—I had to make sense of this. How had the idea of Seth being my grandfather never occurred to me? Seth talks about his favorite "Uncle Jon". How could I have been so blind? Reading it through the first time it never occurred to me that my father, Jonathon, was named after Seth's Uncle Jon. The second time it was like a jack hammer knocked the truth into me. And the pictures, how often had I looked at Seth and thought him familiar? He resembled my father so much it was almost ridiculous! His light hair, his broad shoulders, his smile. The pictures alone should have tipped me off.

I had come to love Amelia—and in truth, I loved Seth. But I couldn't stop my building anger. Anger for my dad, for myself, for being lied to. There was an entire half of Dad's family he knew nothing about. He may not have been able to know Seth, but surely he could have met his grandparents, aunts, uncles, perhaps cousins. He could have known his dad through them, through her.

Maybe Dad and Burt didn't get along because Burt knew my dad didn't belong to him. His existence was a reminder of another man.

After another lonely bout of tears, I gathered everything up—

the pictures, the silver dollar, the ring, the journal—and put them inside the brown box. Folding down the lid, I set it back inside my closet and went to bed.

My blaring alarm clock made it clear, three hours of sleep would have to suffice. Sitting up, my instincts kicked in, my eyes darted to the night stand for Amelia's bulging book. It wasn't there, of course. And I wouldn't be taking it out of the closet any time soon.

Teaching proved to be a good distraction. I fell into the routine of yesterday, picking up where I'd left off in each class. The more I taught, the more I could see myself doing this—forever.

My eyes drooped and I fought to stay awake as I rode Gary home. It had been another good teaching day, but emotional and physical exhaustion made my head ache and my stomach roll. I propped Gary against the house and fumbled with the door handle. Rubbing my stinging eyes, I drew Amelia's curtains closed and plopped on the couch. Kicking off my heels, I fell onto the thin cushions.

Tap, tap, tap. I lifted my head at the sound. Cracking open one eye, I peeked at my watch. My head fell back to the couch pillow. I'd been asleep for over an hour. Stretching my arms out, I rose to a sitting position. Again, another tap. *Coming*, I said in my head, but didn't move. My eyes drooped closed again, but I forced them open. *Up!* I stood, slow, sluggish, and moved my feet. Shielding my eyes from the sun, I opened the door.

A long neck bottle sat on my porch with a pink tulip inside. Picking it up, I peeked over toward Logan's. He was walking back to his house, his hands smashed into his front pockets.

"Hey!" I brought the flower to my nose and smelled its sweet-honey fragrance.

"You *are* home." He walked back to me.

"Yeah, I was resting."

Smiling, he took a hand from his pocket and put it up to my cheek. Bringing his face to mine, he kissed the corner of my mouth. "I didn't mean to keep you up so late."

"It wasn't your fault." My head spun and my knees went weak. "Thanks for the flower. Where'd you get it?" I couldn't remember a flower shop in town.

Motioning to his house, he said, "They bloomed late, just today."

I'd never noticed the array of plants he had in front of his house hiding behind the stony rock wall. But now the tulips stood tall and pretty. I looked at my own yard, dirt.

"Why didn't Amelia take care of her yard?" I was willing to be irritated with my grandmother over anything at the moment.

"She didn't want *me* taking care of it," he said. "She had a yard, for years. When I moved back I started weeding and mowing for her. She told me I had plenty of work to do. She didn't want to give me more. After that, she refused to water the grass anymore. I watered for her a couple of times, but your grandmother had a bit of a temper." He laughed at his own memory.

My eye brows rose, amused. "She gave you a tongue lashing, huh?"

"The only time she ever scolded me." He nodded.

I smiled despite my frustration with Amelia. It was as if I thought she and I would be able to talk through this trouble and until we did, I was determined to be annoyed with her.

"Wanna come in?"

"Yeah." He took my hand and I led him inside to enjoy a journal free evening.

I convinced Logan to go shopping together in Cody to buy a baby gift for Callie. Changing out of my work clothes, I headed to Logan's, excited for an evening in the city.

Opening the door, his hair still wet and shirt half buttoned, he stepped aside. "Come in." His hands fumbled over the buttons and the collar on his navy shirt. Hurrying past to the kitchen, he left a waft of cologne in his path. "Sorry, I'm running behind." He returned with keys in hand. "Ready?"

Following him out to his truck, I opened my own door. "Busy day, huh?"

"Yeah. I had a few appointments, but then Sadie's car stalled and Lucille called me to go pick her up. She knows Rendezvous about as well as you."

What did that mean? Rendezvous wasn't exactly buzzing. Really, how hard could it be to find your way around this tiny town?

"And Lucille was concerned about her."

Concerned? Concerned my—

"I'd never met her, but Lucille assured me I'd know her when I saw her."

I smiled, not making eye contact with him while thinking unholy thoughts about the lunch lady.

Looking over his shoulder, he backed out of the driveway. "Her little red Mazda RX-8 was easy to spot, Lucille was right. No one in Rendezvous has a sports car."

Peeking at his face, he looked normal. No indication of what he thought of Lucille's granddaughter. I bit my lip, wondering what Sadie looked like, when Logan picked up my hand. Our knotted fingers lay on the middle seat and the tension flowed out of me. I had never been the jealous type. I didn't want that to change—it didn't feel good, at all!

"I get to sub again," I said, changing the subject. "For Hannah this time. She's taking three days off for her son's college graduation."

"That's great." Staring out the windshield, he looked so content with the world.

"Why are you so kind?" The words came out as I thought them.

"What?" He glanced at me, his eyebrows raised at my stupid question.

"You're not just a nice guy, Logan. You are genuinely kind."

Chortling, he shook his head. "Where's this coming from?"

"You're so happy for me. I'm talking about *substituting*." Ben would have dozed off, Dad would have discouraged it, but Logan just listened—to my every word. "And Sadie," I pushed down the green monster inside me, "you don't even know her and you went and picked her up, fixed her car, saved the day."

He laughed again and brought my hand up to his lips. "Anyone who cares about you would be ecstatic for your happiness, and Sadie's car *isn't* fixed. I need to pick up a part while we're in Cody."

"I'm serious, Logan. You ... you are the best person I know." I squeezed his fingers and thought of little Logan babies filling the world—making it a better place.

He kissed my palm again. My stomach fluttered, and I was happy Logan didn't count mind reading amongst his many skills.

"Do you know what you want to get for Baby Michelle?"

"I do, actually. Not knowing much about babies myself, I thought I'd get her something that Callie and I both have a fondness for."

"A book." He nodded. "That's perfect. They'll love it. I don't know what to get them. I can't say I know much about babies either. So, diapers? It's not very personal."

"We could go in together." I liked the sound of that... *from, Logan and Liv*. "Diapers *and* books."

His dimple creased with his smile. "I'd like that."

Across from the auto parts store, we found a used bookstore. I discovered a few classics, gathering a small collection for Michelle Paula.

"Look at this." I juggled the stack of books in my arms. "Doctor Seuss, Eric Carle..." I maneuvered one out from the middle. "Look, Mother Goose." I giggled, pleased with my find.

We continued our search through the rest of the old bookstore. My favorite scent in all the world, paper and words mingled together like an aged wine. I breathed in the familiar, addictive aroma and ran my finger along a row of bindings.

Logan had gone the opposite direction, and I watched him from the corner of my eye, pretending to peruse a paperback.

His brows furrowed in study. He stared at the packed shelf in front of him. His face softened into delight and he pulled a brown hardback from the mantelpiece.

I wondered what he had found, but I didn't interrupt.

He flipped through a few of the pages. And then he looked up to find me.

I jerked my head into the unknown book I held.

"Liv, look at this." He held out the book and made his way over to me.

"*The Adventures of Tom Sawyer*. To go with your *Huckleberry Finn*?"

"Yeah. Look." He inched closer and pointed at the inside cover. "It's a UK first edition."

My eyes widened. *A first edition?* "Wow, that's fantastic." Logan in a bookstore with a first edition classic—it was like my own custom-made romance novel.

"What did you find?" He motioned to the book in my hand.

Looking down at the title in my hand, I shoved the story of Lizzie Borden back onto the shelf—yikes! "Ah, nothing yet."

"I'll find you something." He took me by the hand.

I didn't object. "I don't know what I'm looking for, how is it you do?"

He only grinned. He led me into a vacant row and looked through only half a dozen novels before pulling one out. He turned, inches from me and put the book in my hands.

The cover was a faded blue and didn't show the title. I turned the novel to its side to read the binding: *The Scarlet Pimpernel.* I glanced up at his triumphant face. "I do like this one," I said. "Have you read it?"

"No, but I know what's it about. Let's see." And then once again he scanned the book titles. "Ah-hah, here's one. My mom liked this one, too." He handed it over.

It was an aged hardback. The title was written in faded gold on the front: *Sense and Sensibility.*

"Love it," I said. "So, your mom liked this one, too?"

"Yep. I have read this one. She made me."

Again he turned to the shelf and pulled out another old hardback. *Romeo and Juliet.*

"So, I'm fairly predictable." I took one of my favorites from his hands.

Logan's large, calloused hand came up to my face, his palm cupping my chin while his fingers rounded my neck. "Well, maybe when it comes to books."

I laughed, light, nervous—waiting. He leaned in, and I held my armful of books closer, his lips soft and sweet lingering on mine.

Walmart wasn't as exciting as the bookstore. Logan and I both grabbed a few necessities and then we ventured off to find diapers. Ten minutes later, we were still staring at the purple, green, and yellow packages. So many brands and sizes.

"Okay." I clung to Logan's hand. "So, Pampers are pretty much a house hold name, right?" I looked at him for support.

His eyebrows rose in question. He knew as much about this sort of thing as I did. "Extra absorbent or leak protection?"

"Isn't that the same thing?"

He shrugged, his eyebrows raised again.

"Okay." I made a decision. "Extra absorbent Pampers it is!"

"Size?"

"Ah, small?" I shrugged.

"Perfect." He snatched a large box of diapers with the number one written on it from the bottom shelf and tossed it into our cart.

"Look at all this stuff." I rotated my head. "You should have to take a course or two before having a baby. I don't even know what all of this is."

"I think it's a hands-on class. You learn as you go."

I nodded. "It'll be fun watching Callie." Callie would be a good mom. She was organized and informed—she had everything planned out.

"It will." He took charge of the cart. "So, are we done here?"

"Yes, let's go. I'm starving. I'll buy you dinner."

We playfully argued about who'd pick up our dinner tab all the way out to the parking lot. We loaded the truck and drove the short distance to a little Japanese restaurant.

The hostess led us to a cubby at the back of the room. I followed Logan as he removed his shoes and placed them on the red mat outside our screened dining room. The hostess opened the screen door and Logan stepped up onto a flat dining area where dinner ware had already been arranged with white placemats and china. A small pot of hot tea and two miniature cups sat in the middle of the setting. Level cushions were placed across from one another to sit on. The hostess shut the door behind me—except for the waiter taking and bringing our order, we were alone.

Attempting to help Logan with his chopsticks, I formed his fingers around the long skinny sticks. Giving up, he picked up his fork. "So, what have you read from Amelia lately?"

It had been days since I'd learned who my grandfather really was. Amelia's book still sat at the bottom of my closet. I swallowed and cleared my throat before answering. "Nothing."

His eyebrows furrowed. "I know it's shocking and disconcerting, but maybe you need to read what she wrote to learn why things played out the way they did."

"I don't know."

"Liv, I understand why you're upset. I would be too. I'm just saying we both know from what we've read she's been to hell and back. Just read. Give her the benefit of the doubt. See what happens next."

Deep down I knew he was right. I knew it, but I couldn't help the feeling in my heart that she'd somehow deceived us. Forcing myself to be logical—I knew the situation wasn't that simple. I did need to read again. I would read again. I had to. Besides, I'd never left a book unfinished.

Chapter 26

With Rachel out on an errand, I twisted the office phone cord around my finger. "So, I know we always do dinner, but I wanted to do something special. You took me to Cody. I thought I could make you something really nice." I had already phoned my mother for a recipe.

"Oh, Liv." His heavy breath came through over the phone. "That sounds great. But I promised Lucille…" Logan stumbled over his apology.

I couldn't believe I had forgotten about Logan's dinner date with Lucille and Sadie. I got off the phone as quick as I could, feeling like a complete idiot. Knocking my head against the back wall, I moaned.

"Olivia?" Rachel said.

Popping my head up, I cricked my neck. "Ouch. Oh, um, hi, Rachel." I ignored her hands-on-hips stance.

"Honey, what in heaven's apple basket are you doing?"

The throbbing in my neck tweaked and I rubbed at the tender spot. "Nothing."

"Looks like you're inflicting pain on yourself, Sugar."

"Well, it wasn't exactly intentional."

"So, what exactly were you trying to accomplish, hitting your noggin against the wall?"

"Just knocking a little sense back into my head."

Laughing, she sat on the edge of my desk. "Why don't you spend the evening with me? A few of us girls are going out for a ladies' night. Maybe that's just what the doctor ordered."

I wanted to laugh, not to be unkind, but looking at my platinum blonde, petite, older friend whose eye makeup could have served three different women, made me happy. "Ladies' night, huh?" Maybe it *was* just the thing I needed to get my mind off of Logan and his dinner date.

"Yep. I'd have invited you ages ago, but you were always too *busy* to join us. Now, I know you don't have plans tonight, so what's stopping ya?"

What? How could she possibly know I would spend the evening alone and wallowing?

"Logan's going over to Lucille's, so my guess is you're free."

"How do you know that?"

Rachel rolled her eyes. "Oh, Lucille's as thrilled as an elephant in a peanut factory. And honey, I know you spend most of your days at that boy's house." She smiled as if she knew more than she let on.

"Rachel, that's an overstatement." After all, he spent plenty of time at my house. I don't know why I denied it, I was crazy about him. My own father wouldn't have defended me in court if I claimed otherwise. "Besides," my subconscious brought up old fears, "maybe it'd be good for Logan to see what else is out there. Ya know?" As much as Sadie made my nerves crawl, I still wondered if there were any competition in this town at all if I'd be the one Logan would pick. Maybe Sadie wasn't here just to annoy me. Maybe this was my opportunity.

Her face told me that she didn't agree. "What for? He's happy and so are you. Even if you don't want to admit it."

"Still," I stared into space. "Who's to say he wouldn't be happier with someone else?"

"Girl, you think too much. I can see that you're worried, despite what you say. Don't be, Lucille's granddaughter isn't that great of a catch. *You* have nothing to worry about."

She wasn't really helping. I wanted competition, but I also wanted Sadie to resemble a basset hound. How on earth had Amelia kept any kind of secret in this town?

Riding Gary up to the porch, I eyed Logan's house. I hated the awkwardness between us this afternoon. I ran inside my house, tossing off my high heels and jogging up the stairs where I slipped into some cut off shorts and a blue, sleeveless T-shirt I'd bought in Cody. It was June. There was only a week and a half of school left in the year, and the weather cooperated with the coming season. I hadn't invested in sandals yet and Amelia didn't have any. So, barefoot, I trotted over to Logan's. I would fix this mess between us.

His laugh boomed from the garage, making me smile. I rounded the corner to find him next to a red Mazda RX-8, *and* a pretty little blonde with hair down to the middle of her back. She swung it over her shoulder and flashed her teeth at Logan like a runway model. Her hand was placed firmly on her curvy hip, just below her non-existent waist. Her tan, bare legs were longer than humanly possible. Her short skirt and tight blouse left little to the imagination. *Sadie.* I couldn't have conjured up anyone worse.

No wonder Lucille had said, "You'll know her when you see her." And what the hell was Rachel talking about, 'Not that great of a catch.' I guess if you don't consider Heidi Klum that great of a catch.

I turned, praying neither of them had heard me coming. But fate, or luck, or the heavens, just weren't on my side.

"Liv," I heard Logan say. "Hey!"

"Oh, hi!" I half bellowed, turning back toward them. "You *are* here. I just came by." Ridiculous ramblings left my mouth—nowhere near Heidi Klum ramblings. "I just…needed… tulips!" My heart thudding, I bent down and pulled four pink tulips up from their happy home in ground. I held up the pink flowers, their bulbs attached, as if this were my only goal and rotated back for home.

"Tulips?" Logan said behind me, trying to keep pace with me. Reaching for my arm, he stopped my speed walk. He shook his head and pulled me back in the garage, dropping my arm the minute we entered.

I shuffled my bare feet on the cold concrete floor. "The girls are coming by later tonight for dessert and I need tulips for my centerpiece." Again, I held up the bunch in my hands, this time to show Sadie.

She nodded, eyeing the stolen flowers.

"Oh, sure," Logan said as if this were normal behavior. "Liv, this is Sadie Richards, Lucille's grandbaby."

Sadie laughed. Already they had inside jokes.

"Sadie, this is Olivia Benson, my neighbor I told you about."

Neighbor. I suppose that was a correct description.

"It's nice to meet you."

Somehow I didn't believe her. "Yessss. Okay then, I'm gonna go."

I started out the large door opening as quick as my legs would carry me without sprinting. Logan was on my tail though, and didn't allow me to shut my front door. "Hey, what are you running off for?"

"I'm not running off," I said, my defenses up. "I have things to do, you know?"

"All right. Later—"

"Later, you have a date, and I have…more things to do. So, no. No later." Again I tried to shut the door, but he shoved his foot in the doorway and stopped it. I hated this stupid jealous side of me. It was ugly. And lame. And very un-Heidi Klumish, who, for whatever reason was my sudden role model.

"What's wrong?"

"Nothing. You're my neighbor, Logan, not my boyfriend." I crossed my arms, feeling more childish by the minute. "We both have things to do, that's all."

"Your neighbor?" He braced one hand on the door, the other on the casing. "I guess I was under the impression there was a little more to it than that."

"Interesting." I pushed the door open all the way and kicked his foot out of the door jam. "Seeing how that's *just* the introduction you gave me."

"Liv, are you serious?" His mouth hinted at a grin. "You're jealous?"

Rolling my eyes, I shook my head at him. Heck yeah, I was jealous. "No. Maybe I was confused, but everything's clear now. It's fine."

Stepping in toward me, he said, "She's a stranger. Did you want me to explain our relationship rather than give her your name?"

"What happened to 'I'm not going to hide how I feel'?" I reiterated his words.

"I'm not hiding anything," he said without any signs of humor. He took a step toward me, coming into the entrance of the house. "Do you want me to go explain how I feel about you? To Sadie?"

Stomping further inside, I flung my arms up into the air. "Oh, yes, please, let's wander back over there, so you can explain something I don't even have the answer to. Let's humiliate Olivia just a little more!"

"I don't know what you want me to do." His arms slumped to his sides. "I'm sorry."

He didn't sound sorry. At least not in the gushy, mushy, sappy way that Ben always said sorry. Of course, Ben's apologies always sickened me. I would forgive him to stop the scene.

"Right." I didn't know what to do myself, not believing his apology.

Both of his hands ran up through his hair as he turned away from me and then back again. "I'm not sorry for the way that I feel about you, and I'm not sorry for the way I introduced you. It was simple and factual for someone who doesn't know either of us. I *am* sorry that I've given you so little confidence in the way that I feel."

Surprising me, I softened my glare. I did know he cared for me. Seeing Sadie in her glory next to *my* Logan, knowing Lucille's hopes had caused me to go crazy. Still, I couldn't help but wonder if Sadie lived here, if she were around long enough, would he still choose me? If he knew her, and me, and a hundred other girls in the mix, *would he still choose me*? That's what I needed to know. And not for myself, but for him. I didn't want him *settling* on me.

I would choose him. He'd made me happier than I realized I could be, but love is a funny thing. Real love isn't selfish, and I wanted *him* to be happy, as happy as he could be. How did he know that was me, when I was his only option?

My eyes watered with my thoughts and I stood quiet, not trusting my voice.

He diminished the space between us and wrapped his arms around me.

Weak, I fell into them, smelling his musky scent, and leaning against his hard chest.

"I am sorry," he said.

"Don't be." I looked up at him. "You were right. I was wrong. I overreacted. I'm sorry."

He didn't say anything, but watched me.

"We've never really discussed…this." I tapped his chest, and then mine.

His eyes softened and he smiled. "We could, we should."

"We could, but…"

"But?"

"But maybe you should go have fun with Sadie. Find out what it is you really want. Don't worry about me." I meant it. I couldn't let him settle. If it was me he wanted, perfect. But he needed a chance to find out. He deserved as much.

He stepped away from me and combed his hands through his hair again. *He's mad? Offended.* What male on earth wouldn't love permission to spend time with *that*?

"You don't think I *know* what I want?"

"Ah…I think you think you do." *Just don't settle.*

Scoffing a laugh, he threw a wave my direction. "Thanks, Liv." He stalked out the door, his fists and jaw shut tight.

Chapter 27

October 18, 1956

Grettie has decided to be my best friend. I see her daily. She's thrilled that we'll be going through the child bearing process together. Her mother has passed and she's feeling needful for another woman. I don't mind so much, except that she's a constant reminder of what a happy, normal home should be. Something I'll never know.

Her husband Frank is rarely home. In fact, I've only seen him once, of which I'm grateful for. The way he put his arm about her waist when she introduced us made my stomach turn and my heart literally hurt. She started sewing a few items of clothing for herself, for when she's large with child. She told me I could have them as she grows out of them. I don't sew, and I don't think Burt will allow me to buy anything. So, I'm trying to be grateful. I'm sure Momma will send me something.

I haven't told Burt about the baby yet. He's very much a stranger to me, and I haven't a clue how he'll take to the idea. Daddy may not know who the father is, but Burt certainly will. Burt's home so much, he sees me ill, and I have no desire to eat, though we don't eat together. Still, he's bound to notice, I'll have to say something soon. And Grettie, well she can hardly keep her mouth shut. Burt isn't around her much, but if she said something to him before me, I'd warrant another smack, I'm sure.

Amelia

October 25, 1956

Seth's birthday is today.

Burt was gone. I stayed in bed and dreamt of Seth. I saw myself telling him about our baby and how he'd pick me up and twirl me around. I saw him kiss me and tried my darndest to feel his lips on mine as I lay there. I saw a little blonde boy who looked just like his papa and played out a scene of the three of us in a very normal setting, at home, eating dinner around a little square table.

It was a very nice dream, but it made for a very rough day. I was more sick than normal. The guilt in my bosom tripled and sent me to bed with aches and pains.

It was worth it though.

Amelia

November 1, 1956

I'm pushing my luck. I still haven't told Burt. I'm not even sure how to start a conversation with him. I decided I needed help. It's just not working out on my own. I don't talk unless Grettie is around, and she does most of the talking. Still, it's as if I've forgotten how!

When I told Grettie I needed her advice she shut right up, excited for me to bare my soul I think. That wouldn't be happening though. My soul is still with him and will be – always.

When I told her that I hadn't told Burt about the baby yet, she about went into shock. I didn't know how to explain myself was the trouble though. I ended up telling her that our relationship was complicated and somewhat forced by our parents. She found that exhilarating and wanted to know if we had an arranged marriage, from our births. I think she reads too much. Guess I can't say a great deal, that's all I've done since serving my life sentence with Burt. Anyway, I told her no, that it was not an arranged marriage, but that our parents were overbearing and we ended up in an early marriage. She found that romantic, how odd. I gave her no romantic details, there's nothing romantic to tell, and I tried to be somewhat honest without divulging too much.

She wasn't much help at first. She told me to 'just tell him'. So, I told part of the truth further. I told her I didn't think he'd be happy about it. She didn't understand that. Frank's quite proud apparently. So, I just said that Burt isn't like that, he won't react that way. Which of course is fabricated, I don't know what Burt is like, but what else could I say?

She said he'd have to take it like a man, it was his husbandly responsibility. So I asked her, what if it made him mad. Her advice was to make him a nice dinner, set a nice, intimate place setting and to be honest.

What if Burt does want me to get rid of the baby? Can he do that? Not without killing me, it would murder what's left of my heart.

Amelia

I rode Gary to Farmer's still thinking about Amelia's situation. I couldn't even comprehend what she was feeling. I parked my bike out front, not bothering to lock it up anymore. I knew exactly what I needed, and I knew the exact change I needed to get it.

"Chunky Monkey?" Joe called as I headed for the back of the store.

"Yep!" I said, still focused on my goal. I had my money out before he'd tallied my total.

"How's Miss Olivia today?"

"Oh, fantastic." I rolled my eyes, not at Joe—but at my stupid self.

Joe smiled his kind grin and adjusted his orange hunting vest. His thick, salt and pepper eyebrows rising when he said, "I think that's sarcasm I hear."

Smiling, I held my hand out for my $1.07 in change.

"I heard you been teaching and doing a fine job." He dropped the coins into my hand.

My fake grin cheered to a real one. "Really? Who said that?"

"My niece Jess was in one of the classes, said it was the most fun she'd had all year in English."

"Wow." I stared past the man. *The most fun she'd had...* "Thanks, Joe. That means a lot."

"Sure thing," he said, winking.

With brownies in the oven, chunky monkey in my hand, and Amelia's journal in front of me, I decided I had just enough time for one more entry before Rachel picked me up for dinner. I'd noticed the red Mazda had disappeared from Logan's garage, but didn't know what else to say to him. There was a reason for *girl's nights.* Women needed women. What would the women in my life say at what I'd done?

Mom: *Probably a wise idea. Benjamin still has feelings for you and it hasn't been long since you broke up with him. How long have you known this Logan?*

Rose: *Are you insane? After the way you described this guy, not to mention the wispy tone that takes over your voice when you talk about him...you sent him off to some chick? What if he actually falls for her? How dense are you, Liv?*

Katie: *Who's Logan and why haven't you told me about him? Details!*

What would Amelia say? Her thoughts were actually the easiest to conjure. *You love him. Don't waste the time you have.*

Of course those were just my theories on what they'd say. I wasn't planning on asking for their advice. Not that I could ask for Amelia's. I was going with...well, not my gut. My gut was too closely connected to my heart. My heart would have me on my knees begging him to stay with me and never look at Sadie again—and possibly attacking him. No, hearts can't always be trusted. So, I suppose I went with...my head. My head still wanted him, but wanted his happiness more. That had to be the right choice. Right?

Arranging the flowers I'd stolen from Logan's yard in a vase, I placed them in the center of the table. I was setting the brownies on a cooling rack when Rachel arrived. She was giddy. She'd changed from her work clothes into black-leather pants and a white, frilly blouse I'd never seen before.

I could see Callie and Denise in her car. I grabbed my purse and chased behind her. Maybe this would be fun.

Logan's truck roared to a start. I looked up over top of Rachel's car toward him. He waved, and my stomach dropped. He drove off to Sadie and I was driving off with *Rachel.* My smile faded. Trying to put on a happy face for the girls, I climbed into the back seat, next to Callie.

"You don't look ready to party," Callie said, flicking my knee.

"I am!" I flashed my fake grin even wider. "I swear!"

Callie shook my shoulder. "Olivia, this is my fruitless party! You can't be all glum."

"I'm fine, honest. I'm great!" Cocking my head, I knit my brows together. "Ahh—what's a fruitless party?"

"It's like a bachelorette bash, only for a mom before she has her first baby," Denise called from the front seat. "This is her last fruitless night out!" Her Hawaiian shirt swayed back and forth to the country music filling the car, her long gray hair swinging to the tune.

"She'll be fine," Rachel said. "We'll cheer her."

"This is my first fruitless party. I can hardly wait." I said it with all the heart I could muster. "No need to worry over me!" I glanced over to Logan's house, my heart thudding so loud I was afraid it'd give me away.

Rachel winked back at me, giving me a don't-worry-about-a-thing thumbs up and then backed out of the drive. "Maria's meeting us there."

"Are we going to La Familia?" I had to distract myself.

"Nope," Denise said. "Maria's working though, so she'll meet us at Ruthie's in ten minutes or so."

"Ruthie's?" I asked, remembering the karaoke bar Logan had taken me to. I looked over at Callie's protruding abdomen. "Ah—"

"It's virgin Friday!" Denise bellowed before I could ask why we were taking our nine months pregnant friend to a bar.

Callie gave a "Whoot! Whoot!" from the back seat. As usual, my friend refused to be seen in maternity clothes. She hated the thought of purchasing anything outside her normal size or product line. She had gotten away with wearing Paul's baggy sweats to work, and the times I'd seen her at home, she'd clearly squeezed her way into something that she owned prior the pregnancy. Clothing that would never be the same again. Tonight, her yellow, cotton sundress touched just at her knees. What was meant to be a loose, flowing dress stretched tight against her stomach and chest.

Denise and Rachel copied Callie's "whoot", while raising their palms to the ceiling and pumping their hands in the air. Callie's smile and laughter bubbled over, and I couldn't help but join her.

"One more round!" Rachel bellowed, though the bar room was quiet, almost desolate.

The only real noise came from our table. The lull from the juke box couldn't be heard above the five of us giggling and chattering like high school kids. There were a few men seated at the bar just feet from our tall round table. They didn't seem to mind our volume level. The bartender, too, acted like Rachel's roars for more virgin margaritas were perfectly normal.

"Okay, okay, I've got one!" Callie said through snorts of laughter. "The week Joe decided to roller blade to work to get in some exercise." The women howled with laughter and it was easy to join in, though I hadn't been a witness to Joe's stunt.

"And he always wore those…those, those shorty shorts." Denise barely got the words out through fits of giggles.

Rachel knew something about everyone in town, so the stories seemed endless, and we were all crying with laughter.

"You've got dessert brewing at your house, right, Liv?" Rachel asked at the first quiet moment of the night.

"Yeah." I wiped the tears out of my eyes. "It's not much, just brownies."

"As long as it's chocolate." Callie rubbed her jutting stomach.

Rachel pointed at me, her fingers like pistols. "Let's stop at Farmer's and pick up some ice cream and hot fudge to go with. It'll take five minutes."

"Even better." Callie giggled.

We climbed into Rachel's car, this time three of us in the back seat. I couldn't remember laughing that hard—ever in my life.

Callie put a hand on my knee. "I'm glad you're feeling better." She was much too perceptive.

"Yeah, I'm great," I said, certain I sounded much more believable than a couple of hours ago.

"Good." She leaned closer to my ear. "You really have nothing to stress about, and Lucille will get over her disappointment."

Giving her a half grin, I knew that should make me feel better—should, but didn't.

Farmer's took a little longer than five minutes. Denise and Rachel argued over French Vanilla or Vanilla Bean ice cream. They raced shopping carts around the grocery store to decide the winner. The night just kept getting better.

Rachel danced her French Vanilla victory all the way out to the car. I laughed and wondered how she and Amelia had gotten along so well, but then I knew. I knew a whole other side of Amelia, a side that was suppressed, but never extinct.

Maria's excited tone broke through my train of thoughts. She was holding a bag of her own, sitting next to Rachel in the front seat. "Girls! Girls!" she said through her thick Spanish accent. "Look what I found!" She held up a package of toilet paper.

"Angel Soft?" Callie shook her head.

"Si!" Maria said, bobbing her head. "We can T.P. Mr. Levitz house!"

Bursting into a laugh, Rachel pounded the steering wheel with her fists. I couldn't imagine these grown women—myself included, toilet papering the principal's house!

While Rachel laughed, the rest of us stared at the white rolls in Maria's hand. Denise patted Maria's shoulder. "Let's save that for our next fruitless party. The ice cream's melting!"

We started back to Amelia's. Callie's head leaning against my shoulder, rubbing her stomach and rambling sweet things about her husband and baby.

Would I ever have my life as together like she did? I had learned so much in one night. How each of these women met their husbands, Rachel's long passed and Denise on her third. They all seemed to know what they wanted, what they had. And yes, there were careers, traveling and hobbies, but they all spoke of their families, their loves, first and foremost.

I had dazed off, thinking about my life and the messes I had made—and kept making, when Callie spoke up. "Were you expecting company?"

Peeking around the women in front of me, I looked out the front windshield. "Crap," I whispered, but the car was silent. Everyone heard me. "What the heck is he doing—"

"Who is it?" Maria asked.

"Benjamin."

"Ooo!" Rachel said like it was juicy gossip. "Benjamin." And then she had the nerve to giggle.

"Rachel!" I needed to gripe at someone.

"Who is Benjamin?" Maria said through her thick accent.

"Olivia's ex." Callie leaned in, cheek to cheek with me, to get a better view.

Benjamin stood on my concrete porch, watching the five of us inside the car. "Okay, wait here," I said. "I'll get rid of him."

The women looked from one to another, all anxious expressions on their faces. "You sure, kiddo? We can skedaddle if you need," Rachel said.

"Rachel, if you leave me, I'll let the air out of your tires Monday morning." I had told him not to come. My day had been lousy, the best part about it were the women sitting in this car. They were not going—he was.

Closing the car door behind me, I looked back at my new friends—eight eyes all wide and staring. It was the showdown at the end of our fruitless party. They were loving every minute.

Benjamin's smile covered his face. I took an approaching step. He took one toward me, too.

I stopped, holding up my hands like stop signs. I had a lot to learn, to figure out, but one thing I knew for certain was that I wouldn't spend another day as Benjamin's significant other.

"Livy, honey." It gushed out of him like a squeezed grape.

Crossing my arms, I made my tone as unfriendly as possible. "What are you doing here?"

"I told you I wanted to come."

"And I made it clear you shouldn't."

Like a choreographed dance move, he stepped forward and I stepped backward. Pressing his palms together, as if in prayer, he froze in his spot. "I just need you to give me a minute," he said with less certainty.

"I have company." I gestured to the car full of women who watched us.

Shoving one hand into his pocket, he held the other up to stop me. "One minute."

"One," I said.

Shaking his head, he gritted his teeth. Glancing at the car, he rolled his eyes. "Can we at least go inside?"

I crossed my arms. "No." I couldn't pretend. I couldn't even put up with him. I had for so long, never realizing how exhausting it all was. How had we stayed together so long when he left me wanting so much more? And I was nowhere near the high strung career girl who would work by his side and feed off of the buzz it gave him. No, I wasn't what Benjamin wanted either. How could he not see it? It was so clear to me now, but in his defense, it hadn't always been. How did that happen, how did I finally figure that out? I asked the question in my head, but I knew the answer. Logan. Amelia. Rendezvous.

My thoughts, my epiphanies kept going, and in that moment as I sat conversing with my head, something happened. I wasn't ready for it, I wasn't even aware until it was all together too late. On one knee, Benjamin held a small box in his palm. He was talking, but I couldn't hear the words, only static sang in my ears. My eyes half blurred, the world spun.

Chapter 28

Stumbling backwards, I caught myself on the car behind me. Rachel stepped out from the driver's side. I could see her, but again my ears only drummed, as if I'd just come back from an Aerosmith concert.

Staring at me, she spoke again and then she smacked the side of my cheek. The drumming stopped. "Kiddo, you okay?"

Facing Benjamin, he was back on his feet once more. His face turned beet red and his lips puckered. "Can we please go inside?" Steam seemed to exit from his ears.

Rachel's swat had brought the rest of my senses back—including my sanity. "Rachel, please show the girls inside. I'll be there in a minute."

Hopping from her protective stance next to me, Rachel opened Callie's door. Poking her head inside, she spoke to the girls. Each door opened, and out they came, eyes still on Ben and me. Callie studied me, trying to read my mind. She and my mother would get along great. Rachel called to them like cattle, corralling them all into my house.

With my front door safely shut, I turned back to Ben. "I asked you not to come."

"You didn't answer my question." He swooned like this was a normal, happy proposal.

Staring at him, I wasn't afraid of what he thought of me or disappointing him. "You don't believe in marriage, Benjamin."

"I get it." His smile deepened. "You're in shock. I am too, sweetie."

"Don't—don't call me that." Stepping away and around him, I started for the house.

"Olivia." The growl from his throat sounded foreign, so un-gushy, un-Ben like.

Turning back, I saw the black box clenched in his fist. "Goodbye, Ben."

"How can you do this?"

I didn't like hurting him. But sometimes the only way to heal is to hurt first. I couldn't move on and neither could he without the honest, painful truth. "I'm sorry," I said. "I don't love you, Ben."

He didn't give my words a minute's thought before responding. "This place has changed you. You're confused."

"No." I shook my head. "No, it's helped me. Everything I'm feeling, saying, it's all me. This isn't going to work. It never would have."

Taking a long stride toward me, he spoke with more fervor than I'd ever heard him use before, at least when concerning me. "How do you know? You can't know that! We will *make* it work."

I sighed. "I don't want to make it work."

"I don't believe you."

I was getting flustered again, losing the control I had briefly gained. Maybe Rachel would come slap me again. I wouldn't stop her. "It doesn't matter what you believe, it won't change my mind. And you shouldn't be with someone who stands before you and says she doesn't love you."

Closing the gap between us, he grabbed hold of my upper arms and pulled me to his chest. Forcing his mouth to mine, he kissed me. I couldn't kiss him back, his touch only made me sad. There was no feeling or passion there. Skin on skin, no love. The tears leaked out the corners of my eyes. No matter how he irritated or hurt me in the past, I couldn't enjoy watching his pain, feeling him hurt as I rejected his kiss.

Bruises formed where he squeezed my arms. "I don't believe you," he whispered.

"Yes, you do." A sob fell from my chest.

The roar from Logan's truck distracted both of us, and we

turned toward his house. He watched us out his window, but I couldn't quite read the expression on his face.

"Let go, Ben." I wiggled, but his grasp was too strong. I didn't want Logan in on this awful conversation.

Turning back to me, a light in his eyes, he didn't loosen his grip. His head bobbed from me to Logan and back again.

"Benjamin, let go!" I pulled back but couldn't rip myself away from him. "You're hurting me."

"Liv?" Logan hopped out of his car the instant the engine stopped. "You okay?" He crossed the yard over to us.

Ben released his iron clasp.

Stumbling to the side at his abrupt release, I had to find my balance. Standing straight, I rubbed my stinging arm. "Everything's fine," I said. "Benjamin was just leaving."

Scowling at Ben, Logan walked over to me. He took me by the hand, leading me to the porch step. "Did he hurt you?" Picking up my arm, he attempted to examine it closer in the dim light.

Pulling my arm away, not wanting him to see the bruise, I said, "No, just a difficult conversation."

Looking over to Ben, who was glaring back, I didn't know what the two would do to each other. I wasn't prepared for a brawl or even an argument between the two of them. Grabbing hold of Logan's hand, I intertwined my fingers with his and pulled him toward his own home. I opened the door, knowing it would be unlocked, and walked him inside.

Looking at the floor, I said, "Please." Dropping his hand, I crossed my arms and looked him in the eye. "He's going. I promise."

"You've been crying." His hand caressed my cheek.

Stepping away, I wiped at the wetness. "I'm okay."

Staring at me, I couldn't read his face like before. Standing inches apart, not touching, both of us quiet was awkward. I hated being awkward with Logan, it just wasn't right.

"I should get back."

"Sure."

Resisting the urge to stay with him, I walked back to Ben. "You need to go, now."

"I see what's happened here." His face scrunched up.

I walked past him. I didn't like hurting him, but I couldn't take anymore, either. I had almost reached my front door when his thin hand grabbed my wrist. Turning back, I could see Logan in the distance, on his porch, still watching us.

"You've got a crush on the neighbor," he said, disgusted. "Didn't waste much time, did you? Is this why you broke up with me?"

At least he admitted we'd broken up, even if he had it all wrong.

"Pretty *convenient* for him, aren't you? Your father won't support this and when your brain finally starts working straight, you'll be lucky if either of us takes you back."

Ripping my hand from his grasp, I pointed in his judgmental face. "*That* is exactly why I broke up with you." I marched inside, slamming the door behind me. My chest heaved with adrenaline and I buckled over for a moment, catching my breath.

A giggle from my kitchen bolted me upright. I'd almost forgotten about my guests. I took a couple of deep breaths and put on my best, phony, happy face.

Their plates sat empty and mine had ice cream melting all over it. The giggles came to a stop when I walked in the room.

"Hey, girls." Callie dropped her napkin on her plate. "Maybe we should give Olivia a little privacy."

My eyes softened toward my friend. A silent, 'thank you.'

"Privacy?" Maria said through her thick accent. "That boy was not very private when he knelt down on one knee."

"Now, Maria's got a point there," Rachel said. "We can't deny we all saw that happen, and I don't think any of us will rest until we hear your answer."

"Rach," Callie said through gritted teeth.

Rachel wouldn't stop, I knew that. "It's okay," I said. "Yes, Benjamin proposed, but as I've told you, I broke up with him, so of course I declined his offer."

"He's handsome." Maria winked.

"Maria!" Denise elbowed her. "She's dating Logan."

"Oh, si, that's right. Such a sweet boy. And so yummy, you

could eat off his—"

"It's really not a big deal, ladies." I lied, interrupting Maria. "I'm sorry I ruined our fruitless party with that little mess."

"Please." Callie waved her hand. "You didn't ruin anything. I'm almost ten months pregnant and I'm bushed. It's time for bed," she said, ending any discussion on the subject.

Hugging them each as they walked out the door, I watched them climb back into Rachel's car, no Benjamin in sight. Wandering back into the kitchen, I filled my sink with suds and dessert dishes. A tap on my door had me wondering what else Rachel wanted to know.

But it wasn't Rachel, or even Callie.

Logan.

"Hi," he said. "Can I come in?"

"Yeah." I moved aside and let him into my house. I motioned for him to sit on the couch. "So, how was your night?" I sat on the chair across from him, which was much farther from him than I would have liked, but things were awkward—I'd made them awkward.

"Fine," he said without feeling.

"*Fine*, okay…" I pressed my lips together. "Uh, I got to see Rachel's victory dance tonight, it's something else." I attempted to get a smile out him, lighten up the mood—something!

Yesterday he would have laughed. He would have had some story to tell me. Tonight though, his face was blank. "Why was Ben here?"

Clearing my throat, I hadn't yet thought how or if I would explain this to him. "He was making one last attempt to salvage a dead relationship," I opted for truth without giving up the "p" word.

"How's that?"

Could he read minds? How did he know I was leaving out one superb detail?

"What do you mean?" I stalled and shifted, uncrossing and recrossing my legs. I knew he'd be upset or angry or something in the not-so-happy direction.

"How was he planning to salvage?"

"Talk things out. Make promises. I think he's lost his mind."

He waited for more. "Promises?"

The truth bubbled over almost as if he'd forced it from my lips. "He proposed." My hands flared and then I crossed my arms, keeping my hands still by shoving them into my arm pits. "He doesn't even believe in marriage. It was crazy and desperate. But I made things clear."

"So, you said no?"

"Of course I said no." It irritated me that he would even ask.

"And you're sure?"

I couldn't believe what he was saying. I wanted to slap his beautiful face. Biting my lip to keep my words kind, I forced myself to speak. "Quite."

"All right, I'll let you go."

Jumping up, I followed after him. "Wait! What's with the twenty questions? What about your evening? Were you planning to share details?" Oh, I sounded pathetic. I should have stopped at the "twenty questions" remark. Nothing attracted men like needy, pitiful, and desperate.

Turning, he smiled, but it wasn't his dimple smile. "What did you want to know?" He stepped closer to me.

"Ah, how was it?"

"Fine."

"Fine as in good or fine as in fine?"

"It was just fine." He inched nearer. "You're sweet when you're jealous."

"Pa!" I sputtered. "I am not jealous."

"Ah," he said. "I see." Closing the gap between us, he pulled one of my lifeless arms up around his neck and then the other. His hands wrapped around my back and pulled me closer to him.

"So, are you planning to see Sadie again, I mean, while she's here? Because you can, if you want to. I'm just curious."

"Do I look like I'm planning on seeing her again?" He kissed my jaw line.

Ruining the perfect moment, Benjamin's word invaded my brain—*convenient*. It was my own concern put in Ben's ugly language.

I pulled back from him. "Maybe you should. No one, not even me, would blame you for playing the field a bit. Being certain of what you want. I wouldn't be upset."

Stepping away from me, he shook his head. "Is it really over with Ben?"

My face fell. How could he think—this was so ridiculous. "Yes. I can't believe you would—"

"You're telling me to see someone else and then out of the blue who shows up, but your old buddy Ben. What am I supposed to think?"

Stepping in, I pointed into his chest. "You're supposed to be smart enough to see what a dink he is! You're supposed to believe me when I tell you the first time that I don't want to be with him."

"But you still think I should see Sadie?"

"Just to make sure—"

Sweeping his hands up through his hair, he said, "Geez, Livy, I don't understand what you want."

"I want you to be happy." My voice cracked. And I wanted his arms back around me.

"Have I given you the implication that I'm not?"

"No, it's just, well, it's not like you have a lot of options here, in Rendezvous. Isn't it possible I'm *convenient*? I mean, it doesn't get more convenient than next door."

"Wow." He stepped farther away from me. "That says a lot about me."

"That's not what I meant."

The breach between us widened. He didn't look as if he would be closing it anytime soon, either. The thought of not touching him gave me actual physical pain. Wasn't I doing the right thing? Was it really so crazy? I just wanted him to be happy and sure.

Chapter 29

November 26, 1956

I did it. I told Burt. His reaction was surprising, not what I expected.

I had his table set and the delicious aroma of Momma's stroganoff filled the air when he arrived home. I read the shock on his face when he walked into the kitchen, but it was a pleasant shock. It was then, when he smiled, that I realized some women would probably find Burt attractive. He asked me what the occasion was. I told him that after living with him for months, I thought it would be nice to have a conversation. He immediately looked suspicious. He asked what was going on and I denied anything. It was an instinct. His smile left, but still he sat in his chair and waited for me to serve him his dinner. Normally, I leave the food on the stove and eat in my room. I'm not sure where he eats. I served him and pretended to do so with a happy disposition.

I decided not to waste time. I let him shovel in a few bites and then I told him that he was right, that I did have my reasons for the meal. He put down his fork and waited for me to continue. I'd hoped he'd keep eating, that my words would be secondary to the food. But he didn't, he waited and there was nothing for me to do but speak, so I did. I'm not a coward, more of a strategist. I said plain as day, as I'd practiced many times: "Burt, I'm going to have a baby."

If he'd had a fork in his hand, I think he would have dropped it. His mouth fell open and he stared at me for what seemed like a long time. When he didn't say anything right away, fear over took me and I went straight to my threats. I told him I was keeping this child and my parents planned on seeing a grandchild in few months.

His question surprised me. "Do your parents know that this baby isn't mine?" I was honest, I told him that they assumed it was and I didn't tell them differently. He was quiet again and then finally he asked if I'd seen a doctor. I told him that I hadn't. He was calm through the whole conversation. I was expecting at least another slap to the face, if not more.

Then he made the oddest request, well, more of an order than request. He told me he wanted dinner at the table again tomorrow, the two of us. He hadn't made one objection to my unborn child and so I nodded, agreeing to his edict. Then he finished his meal. Before he left the table, he told me he'd make an appointment with Dr. Ihler in the morning.

I feel so relieved. It's finally out there. I don't have to hide or fight for this child to stay with me. I can keep him. I can keep part of Seth forever.

Amelia

Reading this broke my heart for Amelia and for the relationship that she and my father ended up with. But I also wondered. How could she have let that happen? I saw her with him. I knew I couldn't account for years and years of happenings, but the woman who wrote this book, who was ready to run away to keep her baby, never hugged him in my presence. She didn't even look happy to see him in my young memories. He told me—she had told him he didn't belong here—the only home he knew and she told him he didn't belong.

Closing her book that night, I knew I would never fully know or understand her.

Callie gushed over the books Logan and I gave her. She was thrilled. Her eyes teared up and she reached across Rachel for my hand, squeezing it while she thanked me.

From across the room Lucille glared. I didn't know if she disproved of my books or just me. I made an effort to avoid her eye contact.

The small front room in Maria's home was packed full of women. I think every woman in Rendezvous had come to Callie's baby shower. I maneuvered past a few to reach Rachel once the games and gifts had come to a close.

She smiled at me and whispered, "I told Maria we should've had this shin-dig at the school. It's like breathing in a hog infested sauna."

"A little, yes." I fanned my face with my napkin.

"Neither she nor Callie thought so many would come, but it's not as if we get a new baby every day." And then in the same breath she changed subjects on me. "What'd you do to Logan, by the way? You didn't change your mind about your skinny bonehead ex, did ya?"

Taking her by the arm, I led her back to Maria's bedroom, the coat room. The chatter from the women died down and was just a muffle in the distance. "Of course I didn't change my mind about Ben. Why do you ask?"

"I saw Logan running last night. He hasn't gone on midnight runs since the year his parents died."

Twisting my hands together, I said, "I don't know why he's running."

She smiled at me. "I'm guessing you do, sweet cheeks. You're the only one who could make him upset enough to start that business again."

"Me? Maybe you're overreacting, Rachel. Running is a healthy exercise. A lot of people run." I couldn't imagine anyone getting that worked up over *me*. The guilt and worry rolled into one annoying knot in my stomach.

"Running at midnight until you can hardly breathe isn't healthy, it's—"

"Therapeutic?"

She laughed. "I was gonna say neurotic."

Crossing my arms over my turquoise blouse, I bit my lip. I didn't want to cause Logan pain. I just wanted him to be sure—to be happy.

"You wanna tell me what happened?"

"Not really." I slumped onto the coat covered bed.

Sitting beside me, she patted my knee. "Go ahead."

Of all the women I imagined speaking to about this, Rachel hadn't been one of them. Maybe because I couldn't guess what advice she'd give me. I didn't know if she would think I was wise or just throwing away the best thing I ever had.

Giving her the shortened version of my theory, I left out the part where I sort of wanted to have Logan's babies. "I just want to be fair to him. I don't want him to settle on me because it's all he's ever known."

Patient, she listened. "No one would be settling on *you*." She squeezed my cheek. "It makes me piss pot mad that you even feel that way, honey."

I waved off her compliment—Logan might be.

"I do think you're very selfless." She pursed her lips, and I wasn't sure I believed her. "But have you thought about things from his point of view? Not only are you pushing him away—"

My hand went up in protest.

"Uh—uh—uh." She forced my hand down. "Okay, pushing him to get out there then. But look at his life, at his parents. To him, they are the example of the truest love. They were all the other knew. They didn't need to try anyone else on for size. He wouldn't want their love diminished because of *that,* not for even a minute." She paused a moment and then with her tone lighter, she said, "And he had plenty of girls in high school after him. Look at him, Olivia, how could you question that?"

I never asked him—never thought about high school or Alaska…or his parents. I bit my lip. Man, I sure had a knack for making a mess.

Chapter 30

The next week crawled by. Sadie had long since gone, but Logan and I still weren't seeing each other, except for the occasional next-door-neighbor sightings. My stomach hurt and my heart raced each time I bumped into him. Twice I saw him leave for a run. I checked my watch both times, once at eleven-thirty at night, and then again at midnight. If Rachel was right, he was still upset. My heart ached but it comforted me at the same time. I didn't know what to do anymore. Our nightly routine had only been in place a month, but I missed it like air to breathe.

So, I kept myself busy and distracted. I visited Callie every day. She was ready to evict her infant child from the womb, and she joked about adoption to give Michelle a sibling.

With school out, I'd made arrangements to help with a few summer programs, but I still had to wait another week.

I'd read two dozen more entries from Amelia. She was now four months pregnant in the journal. She liked her doctor and the chance to leave the house for appointments. Her morning sickness had subsided and her energy returned. She and Grettie's friendship continued. She wrote about eating dinner with Burt. They still didn't speak much. She wasn't happy, but she wasn't miserable, either. The baby, my dad, had brightened her situation some. She felt in some way she'd have Seth back.

Day eight of no Logan, I woke up to clamminess. The humidity of the rain invaded the house. It was warm out, but the rain poured down. It hadn't rained once since I arrived in Rendezvous, but

Mother Nature was making up for that. I went to the window and looked up at the elm. Black clouds swirled above it. I looked down to the ground where Logan's green grass and my muddy yard sat. The raindrops spattered over the normally dry land.

My plans of working in the yard and taking Gary for a ride disappeared out the window. And how would I get to Callie now? Paul had an emergency in Worland and left Callie alone for the next two days. I promised him I'd look after her. I sighed and made my way back over to the bed. Throwing myself on top of the aged quilt, I picked up Amelia's journal.

January 17, 1957

I felt my Jonathon S. today. I thought I had the hiccups for a moment, but then he moved again and it was clear it was my little Jon. I told Grettie that I felt him, and she asked how I knew it was a him. *I told her that of course I didn't know. However, I'm certain it is a boy. I don't even have a girl's name picked out. She thinks hers is a boy as well, I think that Frank just wants a boy and so Grettie's adopted the idea too. She doesn't really know. Not like I do.*

Jonathon gave me those two little kicks early this morning and then I waited all day for him to kick me again. He didn't for a long time. When he did, it wasn't the best timing.

I made a roast with carrots and potatoes for Burt's dinner. As always, I set the table and was pulling our dinner out of the oven when Burt came in. He was silent. He's always silent. And why should I speak to him? But then, Jonathon nudged me so hard it almost knocked the wind right out of me. I wasn't prepared, all doubled over getting into the oven. I made a horrible grunting noise and grabbed hold of my stomach, toppling our dinner onto the oven door.

I cannot tell you my surprise when Burt rushed over. He didn't touch me, but his hands were outstretched as if he wanted to, and then he asked if I were hurt. I felt ridiculous and was angry I'd forced a reason to impede the silence. I told him the baby kicked. He didn't say anything, but snorted, irritated, and then cleaned up the mess I'd made. Still, for a small moment, he actually looked concerned about me, even the baby. I'm sure I saw it wrong, but I can't get the image out of my head. It was strange. Why on earth would Burt worry about me?

Tomorrow, Burt's gone, and I plan to put my feet up for the entire morning.

Amelia

"Jonathon S.," I said aloud. The Jonathon was after Seth's favorite uncle and the S. stood for Seth of course, she wasn't allowed to say his name, so she'd decided on S. However, my father's full name was Jonathon Burton. I suppose Burt wouldn't allow the S. Oh, Dad. I had to tell him. But when? How? How would he feel? What would he do about it? What would it change?

The ringing phone interrupted my confusing thoughts. Racing down the stairs, I picked up the receiver.

"Liv, if you broke up with Ben, why is he still living in Jared's room?" Katie's hello just screamed, *I miss you sister.*

"Hello to you too, Baby." I plopped into a kitchen chair. "Oh, I don't know why Ben's still there. Sorry. You'll have to ask Dad that one."

"It could have something to do with the golf ball size tears he was streaming when he came back from seeing you."

"He was crying?" I couldn't quite wrap my brain around that.

"Yeah, Mom told him he could stay, and Dad told him he needed him for a big case, and he perked right up like a spoiled two-year-old." I could hear her gagging. "I am so glad I can finally tell you, I do not like that guy."

"And you hid it so well, Katie." I laughed. "I'm sorry you still have to put up with Ben."

"Hey!" Her fifteen year old brain jumped to the next topic. "Mom and I are going to come see you! Maybe Dad will let us drive my birthday present—the Malibu! But there's a compartment light stuck on, so maybe he won't, but it runs fine—"

I wasn't sure she'd come up for air. "Well, my friend Logan is a mechanic. If you bring it, I'm sure he'd help you. He lives just next door."

Katie sighed. "Oh, I am so glad you have friends, Livy."

Laughing at the exasperation in her voice, I said, "Me, too."

"I was so worried you were spending everyday all alone, too stubborn to come home and face Daddy."

"I'm having way too much fun to come home now," I said it not just to assure her, but to say—*your big sister isn't as lame as you might think!* And it was true, aside from this week without Logan.

"Really? What are you doing?" She didn't try to hide the shock in her voice.

"I have a couple girlfriends. I've been to Cody a few times." As long as I was impressing her—"I've been on a few dates." Giving her a vague description of my nights out in Rendezvous seemed to appease her and then I came up with an excuse to go, before she asked for more.

The day dragged on into evening, the rain persisting into the night. Rendezvous would flood at this rate. I hadn't been out of my house once, and I'd broken Callie's heart when I told her I couldn't come by. Opening the old curtains to Amelia's big picture window, I lay on the couch and watched the rain in the dark.

Yawning, I glanced at the clock, almost eleven. I'd officially wasted away the day. A booming thunder rolled outside. Jumping, I went to the window, watching the sky. Looking over to the elm and then on to Logan's house, I spotted him. Outside! In this crazy weather! His long blue sweatpants and gray hooded sweatshirt were already soaked and sticking to his body. He was jogging—like Rachel had said, taking the road just north of our houses.

I didn't think. I didn't decide. I just *did*. Slipping into my shoes and jacket, I pulled the hood up over my head and ran after him. The rain came down fast, and the slight breeze blew it directly into my face. Turning onto the road where Logan had, the droplets pelted my side rather than my front. My fingers fumbled, finding the zipper to my jacket as I ran. I wasn't far behind him, but he couldn't hear me. The drumming of my feet sounded like rain drops.

I couldn't call his name. My voice locked in my throat. So I ran. I ran as fast as I could, but he ran so much faster than I could manage. We'd gone blocks already and he still didn't have the slightest idea that I ran behind him. My hood fell back with the wind and my drenched hair glued to my face and shoulders. My chest heaved, but I couldn't quite get my cry out. Who knew if he'd hear me in this, anyway?

He slowed. Peeking at his watch, his fingers went up to his neck, checking his pulse. So, I ran faster. I was half a block closer when I found my voice. "Logan!" I croaked with as much volume as I could.

He stopped at the sound I made.

Combing the wet strands of hair out of my face, I slowed my pace.

Turning, he saw me. "Olivia?" He shoved his hood off and ran toward me. Stopping a yard away, he blinked at the water coming down on his face. "What are you doing here?"

Yelling to be heard above the noise, I said, "Me? What are you doing? Are you trying to kill yourself? Running, at night, in the middle of this storm?" I licked the moisture from my lips.

Shortening the space between us, he said, "Why did you follow me?"

"I, I…" I didn't have an answer for that. Looking at the ground, I watched the droplets splatter. I didn't know why, my body acted, my brain hadn't taken time to think.

Then amongst the cold and wet, his hand slid under my chin. Lifting my face to meet his, he closed the gap between us. "Why are you doing this?" His hand rested from my chin to the side of my neck, warming me.

"I… I was worried about you," I said. "It's late, and cold, and if you haven't noticed, pouring!"

"No." He shook his head. "Why are you pushing me away?"

That wasn't what I wanted. That wasn't what I meant to happen. I just—I just—"Because." I wiped the wet locks from my eyes again. "Because, I love you." A cry burst from my chest.

His lips, wet and warm, all at once engrossed mine. Wrapping my arms around his waist, I kissed him back. I had missed him so much—more than I had a right to.

Pulling back, he wiped at the moisture on my face. "That makes no sense." He shook his head and droplets spattered from his wet hair. "But Livy, I—"

"Wait. Don't say it."

"So, you can love me, but I'm not allowed to—"

I pressed my finger to his mouth, attempting to keep it shut.

"Love you," he said through the pressure, and then his lips found mine again.

With my mouth on his, I said, "Wait." My whole body contradicted the word. "I won't let you settle."

He pulled his head back, but wouldn't loosen his hold around me. "You think loving *you* is settling?"

"Maybe, maybe not—"

Cupping the sides of my face, he glared at me. "Olivia, do you want to be with me?"

"This, this isn't about me or how I feel—"

"Isn't it? Because I thought your feelings were fairly relevant in this relationship."

Smiling, I shook my head. "I know how I feel. I've known for a while. I just want you to *know* for sure."

"I am capable of understanding my feelings."

He was trying not to be frustrated with me.

Raking his hand through his wet hair, he peered down at me. "I don't need to date every single woman in the state to figure that out."

Staring up at him, I wondered if he could tell the difference between the rain that pelted my face and the tears leaking from my eyes.

His thumb traced the outline of my lips. "That would be a waste of time."

A generic cell phone ring broke into our moment. Logan didn't seem to notice until the ring went on and on. He pulled it from his pocket, shielding it from the rain. I'd never seen the mobile before now.

His eyes met mine. "It's Callie."

Speed walking for home, I listened to the one-sided conversation.

"Callie," Logan said. "Callie, stop. I promise it'll be okay." He paused, and though I could hear her muffled voice, I couldn't make out what she said. "I'm on my way. Give me ten minutes." Another pause. "Well, I'm not home, but I will be soon. Ten minutes, Cal, I promise." Another pause. "She's with me. Did you call Paul?" Another pause. "Good, that's good. We'll get you there. It's all right." He hung up the phone, and we started to run.

Glancing at him, I waited for him to tell me what I already knew.

"Callie's in labor."

The ten minutes he'd promised her were close to up by the time we reached our homes. I ran for his truck, pulling the cab door open.

"Go change," he said.

"But—"

"Go." He pointed to my house.

Running inside, I stripped off the soaked clothes determined to cling to my wet body. Tripping up the stairs, I rushed to my room, forcing on my shorts and shirt from the day before. Grabbing a dry pair of shoes and a jacket from my closet, I sped back out into the storm. Barefoot, clinging to my shoes and coat, I ran for Logan's truck. I hopped inside the driver's door and scooted to the passenger seat, dripping only a little on the seat—mostly from my sopping hair. Alone in the cab, I pounded on the dash. *Come on! Let's go!* Thirty long seconds later, Logan opened his front door. Holding a large duffle bag, he ran to the truck in an easy three step jog. He tossed the bag into his small back seat and started up the vehicle.

More afraid than I'd ever been, I pictured him packing a bag and wanted to slug him. We didn't have time for arguments and if the last week had taught me anything—it was that I *hated* fighting with Logan. Still, it wasn't as if we were off on a three minute drive to the hospital. Callie was waiting. We needed to get to Cody. Cody, which was normally thirty minutes away and in this storm, I feared it would take much longer.

As if he'd read my thoughts Logan said, "You take care of her. I'll take care of the drive. We'll get there." Then he reached out and squeezed my hand. My anger diminished. I needed him—selfishly I needed him.

Pulling up to Callie's, Logan reached in the back seat for his duffle and drew out an umbrella. Together, we ran up to her front door, jumping over the gutters that had turned into rivers.

Opening the door without bothering to knock, I looked but didn't see her. "Callie?"

Coughing came from the bathroom, and I rounded the corner to see her slumped over the toilet.

"Callie!"

Logan followed after me into the small bathroom, looking more nervous than before. I put a hand on the back of her head. Running cold water over a cloth, I dabbed at the back of her neck.

"I'm okay. I'm empty now. I won't have to worry about working off that late night snack." She attempted to stand, and we helped her. "My bag is in the living room."

"I'm on it." Once she was up, Logan was gone.

Opening his red umbrella, Logan handed it to me and took my place supporting Callie.

"I got it." She promised us.

"Sure, okay." Logan didn't move from her side.

We'd been in speed mode, blood pumping, and now everything moved in slow motion. Together, we helped her onto the passenger seat, and then racing around to the opposite side, Logan helped me climb into the minor back seat. I sat behind her, my hands on her shoulders.

Exiting onto the highway, Callie's first contraction came—her first with us. She cried out, clutching her abdomen. Kneeling on the rear seat, I held my face next to hers. I counted, I breathed, I wiped the sweaty, blonde curls from her eyes. Anything and everything I'd seen in the movies, with no idea if any of it helped. Still, I did it anyway.

"It's okay, you're okay," I said in her ear after each pain. I ignored the rain and road, focusing on my friend. The contractions were closer and harder, and scared the hell out of me. Somehow I buried that fear like my life depended on it and spouted positive anecdotes.

After the longest forty-five minutes of my life, I spotted the lights of Cody, Wyoming. Distracted only for a second, I sighed with relief. Logan exited, following the hospital sign, and the tension throughout my body eased.

Squeezing my fingers and bringing all the tension back, Callie roared, "Livy!"

"I'm here, I'm here!" My cheek still connected hers. "You can do this, Callie."

Reaching out for the dashboard in front of her, Callie's knuckles turned a starch white. "You promise me—"

"I do, I promise. Everything's going to be fine. You can do this! We're almost to the hospital."

"No!" she said. "You promise me, you will never ever, ever, ever, ever have children."

Caught off guard, I looked away from her, to Logan, whose perfect vigilant eye on the road flinched. Pressing his lips together, he repressed a smile. I had no urge to smile, and it looked as if he stopped himself from laughing!

My hands rubbed up and down furiously on her shoulders. "Ah—"

"Livy! Stop that, please." My hands froze and she said, "Promise me. This is for your own good. I love you too much to—awww…" She trailed off into a small wail. Shutting her eyes until the contraction had passed, she was quiet. Once it had gone, she twisted her head to the side, glaring at me, waiting for my answer.

"Sure, Cal, whatever you want." I looked at Logan and shrugged. "Adoption's a great alternative, right?"

Nodding, she closed her eyes, the pain back again.

Between a couple of nurses, Logan, and myself, we wheeled Callie into the hospital. Her overnight bag slung over Logan's shoulder, while I raced along beside her.

"You'll need to check her in," the nurse said to me.

"She's coming with me." Callie left no room for argument.

"I'll take care of it," Logan said to me.

"Livy," Callie said as we wheeled down the white hallway. "Where's Paul?"

"He's on his way. He'll be here." I hoped and prayed I was right.

The birthing room wasn't far, and Dr. Reynolds strolled in close behind us. Callie relaxed a little with his presence.

"I hope Paul plans to make it to the party," he said.

"He better." She formed her hands into tight fists.

Rubbing Callie's shoulder, I said again, "He's on his way."

"Well, we'll try not to start without him then. And you are?" Dr. Reynolds said.

"Livy," Callie answered for me. "A close friend, she helped me get here."

Callie changed into a hospital gown, and I stood next to the head of her bed while the doctor examined her. "You're doing great, Callie." He smiled. "You're already at four centimeters."

Sighing, tears formed in the corners of her eyes. I rubbed her arm. "Four?" I asked. "And she has to get all the way to—"

"Ten," Callie said through tears. "Ten."

Dr. Reynolds smiled again, and it was starting to irritate me. Clearly, we weren't happy about this *ten* business.

"But you, you, you can help her, right? You have drugs—" I squeezed the metal railing connected to Callie's bed, looking from her to the doctor.

"Callie, are you ready for your epidural?"

"Yes, she is. She is." Turning to her, I bit my lip. "You are, right?"

"You're clearly uncomfortable."

I could have slugged him for his word choice, *uncomfortable*.

Leaving, Dr. Reynolds said he'd put the order in and see us in an hour. It was going to be a long night. And maybe I *would* be adopting.

Waiting for the anesthesiologist, we kept Logan busy. He got us ice chips, drinks, pillows. And then it was needle time. The play by play of the epidural made my stomach turn, but I didn't move. Staying in my spot, Callie leaned on me and when it was over, she truly seemed better.

Callie slept. Sitting next to her hospital bed, I lay my head against the back of the seat, resting my arm across the bed. Closing my eyes, I listened to Callie's even breathing and the tapping of rain on the window pane, dreaming of Logan and adoption.

Chapter 31

Shaking my shoulder, Logan shushed in my ear. The blinds were drawn and I blinked, adjusting my eyes to the dark room. Hours must have passed.

"Liv, wake up," he whispered in my ear.

Remembering why we were here, I jumped, waiting for Callie to do something… anything. But she lay sleeping, her chest rising and falling with even breaths.

"She's fine," he whispered. "Paul's here."

Standing close behind Logan was Paul. His hands together, he spun his wedding ring in circles, waiting for me to get out of the way so he could reach his wife. A cap covered his dark hair and his forehead wrinkled in what looked like permanent worry.

"Time for us to go."

A crazy protectiveness washed over me. They expected me to leave and I didn't want to, even if Paul had arrived. Logan tugged on my hand and I watched Callie. "Um, sure," I stood and forced a smile for Paul. "We'll be right here though... You know, if you need anything. I've kind of been her coach so—"

"Thanks, Liv." Turning away from me Paul leaned down to kiss Callie's head and took my seat beside her.

A small light streamed through the open door. Logan pulled me through but I looked back at Callie. My feet like heavy bricks, trudged along with Logan towing.

"What time is it?"

"Three in the morning," Logan said. "Come on, there's a bench over here, you can lie down."

"That's it? Ugh." I sighed, tired. "I thought for sure we'd been here half a day."

"Hopefully, Callie and Paul will have a baby by daytime."

"Yeah," I rubbed my neck. "At least she's resting now."

"Yes, and now you."

"I'm okay," I said.

"Come on, you're worn out." Pulling my hand, he forced me to follow him.

"I'm o-ahh—" My yawn interrupted my insistent *okay*.

The long cushioned seat wasn't far from Callie's room, and it did look inviting. Guiding me to the bench, Logan sat me down. He pulled an end table over and sat next to me. Stretching his feet out onto the table, he yawned. "Here." He patted his leg. "Lie down."

My heavy eyes didn't take much convincing. I stretched out my body, lying down on the thin cushion and set my head against his leg. It felt like a five star hotel compared to the wooden chair I'd just spent an hour in. We slipped into silence. My eyes closed, I waited for sleep to come. It didn't. Logan's hand stroked my still damp hair, and a chill ran through me.

"Are you cold?" he asked, his voice quiet.

"I'm fine." But I tucked my bare legs up close.

In the silence, he stroked my hair once more. The affection lulling me—everything would work out. I was close to sleep when he said, "Adoption, huh?"

My laughter came out exhausted and senseless. "Yeah, well, at that point, I would have signed away my life to make her happy."

His soft laughter shook beneath me.

Waking, my head now cushioned by Logan's duffle, I stretched out my bare legs covered by a large sweatshirt. Sitting up, my head spun. Blinking, I scanned my surroundings. Sunlight now lit the hallway. Scooping up the duffle bag and sweatshirt, I started for Callie's room, no Logan in sight. Rounding the corner, we almost collided. He held up the two cups in his hands, not to spill.

"What did I miss?"

"Nothing, you didn't miss a thing." He handed me one of the white plastic cups. "Good morning."

"How is she?"

"She's all right, just tired. The doctor came not long ago and said she's about ready to push."

"That's good."

Nodding, he sipped from his own cup. "How'd you sleep?"

"Great, I guess, the sun's up. The last thing I remember is your adoption comment. What time is it anyway?"

"Six-thirty."

"Wow, all right. Well, I'm going to find a bathroom, and then I'll be right there."

He smiled. "I don't think they need us."

"Really?" I mean, I had been her birthing partner half the night. "Sure, right."

Picking up my hand, he walked with me past Callie's room. We stopped in front of the women's bathroom. "Take my bag, freshen up a little. We'll go see Cal, and then I'll buy you breakfast."

That plan didn't sound too terrible. At least I'd get to see Callie for a minute. "What's in the bag?"

"Just a few necessities." That's when I noticed his changed, clean clothes, his curly hair somehow more organized, he even smelled like soap.

Why it surprised me that Logan was more than prepared, I'll never know. The Boy Scout. I took his bag and headed into the restroom. I couldn't shower, but he'd packed a new toothbrush, a clean T-shirt that most definitely wouldn't fit him anymore, a brush, a washcloth and soap. I washed my face and started on the mess I called my hair. In the night, it had dried and tangled. Soon a strawberry-hair nest sat in the sink. The shirt may have been too big for me, but it smelled like Logan and more than once I held it up to my face, breathing in his scent. I looked and felt one hundred percent better.

Opening the bathroom door, I found him waiting just beyond it. "Better?"

"Much," I said. "Thank you."

Walking side by side, his upper arm brushed my shoulder all the way to Callie's room. I knocked but opened the door without waiting for a reply. She didn't look bad and she wasn't crying out, but she wasn't comfortable either. The mass of pillows behind her back looked awkward and not exactly relaxing.

"Olivia," she said, happy, but tired, almost weak. "Did you think I'd have a baby by now?"

"Well, actually yes, but what do I know?"

"So did I." She sighed. "She's coming though. Soon."

"Very soon." I sat in my wooden chair next to her. "So soon that we won't stay long."

"You are staying though, right? You aren't leaving the hospital?"

Rubbing her hand, I smiled. "And miss Michelle's debut? No way. We'll be here."

Meshing his fingers with my own, Logan led me down to the cafeteria. His hand in mine steadied me. As natural and normal and as often as women around the world gave birth, I was still scared. Looking down at our fingers intertwined, I loved him more today than I had yesterday.

"What are you thinking about?" he asked.

"Adoption." I lied.

Laughing, he drew me into a tight hug.

Sitting across from one another, I picked at the scrambled eggs and bacon. Switching the eggs over to the burnt bacon and back again, I took a bite. "How much longer do you think?"

"I don't know. Paul said he'd text me."

"Oh, yeah." I pointed my fork at him. "Since when do you have a cell phone?"

"I can't have a cell phone?" He raised his eyebrows and his dimple pierced his cheek.

"Sure you *can*, but you don't."

"It's Paul's. He added a line just for me. He's *almost* as nervous as you. If Callie couldn't get a hold of him, he wanted her to be able to reach me. It's a good thing too, I guess."

"Yeah, it is."

Setting his fork down, he sat back in his chair. "Tell me what Amelia's been up to."

I had just finished telling Logan about the baby, my dad kicking Amelia and Burt rushing over in concern when a buzzing rang from his pants pocket. "Callie." I bit my lip.

Logan's answering smile said it all. Michelle was here.

"What does it say?" I bounced in my seat.

He held out the phone for me to read.

Family & Friends,

We're excited to welcome our little 6lb 12 oz baby girl into the world! Michelle Olivia!

Love, Paul & Callie.

Grinning, my eyes filled with tears that had threatened before, only now they were happy tears. I wiped them away and started to laugh. "She's here," I said. "And they named her after me."

The ride home was quiet. The last twenty-four hours replaying in my mind. Callie had a baby. And I was there. Logan's brilliance seemed endless. And I'd confessed I love him.

Resting my head against the seat of his truck, I closed my eyes, humming along with the unfamiliar country tune.

His hand snuck into mine and my eyes popped open. "Do you really think that's appropriate, when I'm determined to make you date other women?"

Laughing as if I'd told a hilarious joke, he said, "You can't make me date someone else. Besides, you've already spilled the beans, there's no going back now."

I didn't force my hand away. I was much too weak and emotional. "You don't believe in compromising?"

"Sure I do."

"All right," I said. "Let's compromise then. You give 5 other women a shot and if you decide after five that you're happy with me, then we'll call it good."

"You know, if I didn't already know that you're a little crazy, I might think you were lying about loving me."

"I'm not crazy."

His eyebrows rose, he didn't agree with me.

"I'm not," I said. "What if I'm not enough? What if you want more?"

"I don't understand why you keep saying that."

And then all of the things that I hadn't put into words came falling out. "I didn't realize I was settling until I met you. It hadn't even occurred to me that Benjamin would never *ever* be enough until you came into the picture. Had he proposed before I met you, I would have said yes. So, how do you know? How do you have any idea that I'm enough? I won't let you settle."

"People aren't the same, Olivia. I don't need the same revelation you had. Besides, you wouldn't have ended up with Ben."

"People end up with the wrong person every day, or haven't you heard the recent divorce rate?"

"Liv—"

"Go on a date."

"What time should I pick you up?"

"Logan." I moaned.

Pulling into his driveway, he turned off the truck engine. "You can't get rid of me that easy."

"I can be stubborn," I said.

"But you do love me." It wasn't a question, and I couldn't dispute it.

I got out of the truck, confused. What was I supposed to do?

Walking around to my side, he held his hand to my cheek. "And I love you."

Chapter 32

February 11, 1957

Six months. Half of an entire year. That's how long it's been since he died. Even if I were allowed I'm not sure I could say those words out loud, it's hard enough to write them. I'm thankful for Seth's child, but every move he makes within me is a reminder that he'll never know his father. We'll never be the family we so desired, there's no chance for Seth to ever come rescue us.

Sometimes I pray that Burt will die. Then at least I could tell this child about his real father. I could be the tragic widow, rather than the purchased wife I am now. Sometimes I'm tempted to tell Grettie the truth. I can see her look of pity. I would take the pity if I thought it would do any good. But it won't bring him back.

I wish I could go back to that Methodist church. It's the only religious place I've ever felt right in. Maybe it wasn't the church, maybe it was Seth. But I keep thinking I could find some comfort there. Something that would help this pain in my chest.

Amelia

February 23, 1957

Burt informed me this morning that we'd be having company for dinner. Important company he said. This on a mornings notice! Not only do I have to prepare some type of meal for these people, but I apparently will have to pretend to be the doting wife and mother to be. He could tell I wasn't happy. So I asked him if this company would be planning on staying with us. Thank the heavens above he answered no. What would I have had to act out if that were the case?

Amelia

Evening- February 23, 1957

His parents! Burt's parents came to see us. He smiled, he chatted, and he even patted my arm during dinner. It was an unnatural, nervous happiness that was obviously forced, but they didn't seem to notice. I'm not the only one pretending, his parents clearly don't know what a sham this marriage is. I stayed as quiet as possible. I only answered the few questions his mother asked. She was polite, but I could tell she didn't like me much. Half way through dinner, she made some comment about our shotgun wedding that she wasn't even informed of until after the fact. She made it clear she's bitter about not being there. I didn't say a word. Why should I console this woman? She's nothing to me. Besides! The things I could tell her about HER son! I wonder how shocked she'd be to find out just how we did come to marry.

They weren't surprised at my baby bump either, so Burt must have told them about me, about little Jonathon, but I don't know when. They seemed to have no opinion on the subject, which is fine by me. It's none of their business.

Raymond (his father) ate what would have been leftovers for three days for the two of us. His toothless grin and winks made me uncomfortable and anxious. Unless Martha (his mom) spoke to me, I kept my eyes on my plate, I didn't want to risk meeting Raymond's gaze.

We walked them to the front door together shortly after dinner. (One last façade before they left). I could see I wasn't the only one relieved at their leaving. And then Burt picked up my hand, with no one around to pretend for. He sighed as though he'd been running a marathon and thanked me. He let go of my hand and went off to bed. I suppose he was grateful I played along as well as I did. I can't say I understand his situation in the least. And the tingling feeling his pressure left on my hand irritated me for a good hour after the fact.

Amelia

March 29, 1957

I talked to Momma today. She's coming for Jonathon's birth. The doctor says he'll be here sometime in May. I'm so mixed up. I want to see Momma. I haven't seen her for so long. Since before I left for Ganesworth. But I don't know what Daddy told her about Seth or what happened to me or why I'm here now. I only know she supported him.

I'm so big and so tired these days. I want to see her, I want the help. I'm anxious for baby Jonathon, but I'm scared too. I'm not sure what I'm doing, and I don't know how Burt will react to this child once he's here. So, I need Momma.

However, this means more pretending, and not just sometimes, but all the time. Does she really think I'm happy? Does she think this is what I want? She thinks this baby is Burt's, so I know she thinks I sleep in his bed. When she comes, how will I pretend? How will I fake that?

Amelia

April 14, 1957

Grettie had her baby today. A girl, little Laurie.

I visited her, but only for a few minutes. Back at Burt's, I could not collect myself, wails spurt from my mouth as if I had no control. Burt was in his shop and when he came inside, he could hear me from my room. I'd gone there straight after Grettie's, shoved a pillow in my face hoping to drown out the noise. When he marched inside, I found I could not stop the howling. My chest heaved as if about to break at any moment. He asked what was wrong and when I didn't answer, he said, "You need to forget your old life and move on, accept what you have." I couldn't stand it, and I screamed at him. "I don't have anything." I waited for the blow, but he didn't hit me. He just said, "You're having a baby, Amelia." And then he left.

Amelia

April 30, 1957

Momma comes tomorrow. I've spent the entire day cleaning and moving my things into Burt's room. It was the unspoken fact that I'd have to move soon enough. The only words Burt ever said on the subject was that I could use the top two drawers of his dresser. So I moved my few things in there today while he was away. The two drawers he spoke of were empty.

I also spent half the morning looking for a spot for my only valuables. I can't have Seth's pictures and art work sitting in Burt's room. He'd destroy them. I think I found the place though. A few weeks back while scrubbing the floors, I found a loose board. Today while searching for a hiding spot I remembered it, and with some effort, I was able to pop it out of place. Looking in that hole, it felt as if I were cramming my real life into the dark. Who knows when it will see the light of day? It'll just die in the dark.

Amelia

July 1, 1957

My baby is five weeks old. The time since his birth has been exhausting and strange. So much pretending, and so many new realizations.

Mom came and stayed two months with us. The days were fine and nice to have the help. It was only hard when Mom asked about Burt. I wanted so much to ask her what she'd been told, if she knew about Seth, but I haven't spoken of him aloud in months, and the words wouldn't come out. The strange part is I know I've changed. I don't even feel like the same person, but she didn't seem to notice.

Jonathon's birth is one I'm not sure I can fully describe.

I've never experienced anything like it, and yet I find myself wondering and wanting to compare the experience with Grettie. How can I though? She is married to a man she loves. My pains started in the morning. Momma helped me through the day. She rubbed my back and made me put my feet up and then sometimes she'd make me walk around. Right before dinnertime she called Dr. Ihler. He came to the house as Mom suggested. I'd rather have had my baby in a hospital, but things are complicated here, there isn't one close by. And Mom had all her babies at home. Mom set up my room (her room). That's where I had him, on May 23, 1957, at eleven p.m.

Burt sat awake at the kitchen table all through my labor. I assumed to keep up the charade. Mom stayed with me and though I hoped for death at times, once that child was born, once he entered this world, the pain left and the most engrossing love, the most happy feeling I'd had since my Seth, consumed me. He was long and already fat and the most beautiful little toehead I'd ever seen. And of course, just as I'd known, he was a boy.

I was angry when Mom decided to ruin my almost perfect moment by telling me that she and the doctor would leave the <u>*three*</u> *of us alone for a while. That's when she sent Burt in. How could she know though, that I'd rather die than have that moment destroyed by him? She figures us a family. Burt did come in, he sat beside me and Mother left. He didn't say anything, and he didn't even look at Jonathon. My annoyance was boiling over. My only precious moment since Seth, and he was interrupting. So, I asked him, "Why did you wait up?" He actually said, "I am your husband." As if that title means anything when it comes to our marriage! That's when I said, "And why are you exactly? Who forced you into this? Or did you just decide that having a free cook and maid would be ideal?" He stood up and walked to the door, but before he left he shocked me, slapping me would have been less astonishing. He told me, "I'm your husband, Amelia, because I thought I was saving you. Maybe that was stupid of me though. You aren't happy. I heard about what you'd done. Just like my sister, you had no previous reputation, and then one day you ran off with the ruffian in town. My sister ended up six feet under. Because of your erratic behavior, your father was planning on admitting you into a mental institution. I couldn't blame him, it's better than dead. But something inside told me I could save you. He didn't have to lock you away. You didn't have to end up like Suzie. I could help." In the seconds he stood in the doorway, my insides screamed. I wanted him to come back, and I wanted to explain to him that my father had created some horrible reputation for Seth that wasn't real, that Seth had married me. Did Burt realize that? That HE wasn't my first husband. But I couldn't say anything, as much as my insides agonized, I couldn't pretend I hadn't heard what he'd said. My father was going to institutionalize me. And I thought Rendezvous was hell. I was wrong. Burt never forced himself on me, and he only expected me to take care of the house like most wives did. He wanted to save a misguided girl, only he didn't have the facts.*

As much as my heart broke, I couldn't help but feel thankful, too. Where would Jonathon be if I were locked up? That is why this baby's name is NOT Jonathon S. as I'd planned all along. When my mother came in immediately after Burt walked out and asked me his name, I told her it was Jonathon Burton. I know Burt heard me. It was my thank you to him, and I hope he understands that.

Amelia

"Institutionalize? I don't understand. Why would he do that?"

"I don't know," Logan said. "It seems pretty drastic."

"Yeah, well so does forcing your daughter into marriage."

"I've heard of parents back then institutionalizing their unwed, pregnant daughters, but her dad didn't even know she was pregnant then." I sighed and closed the book.

"Maybe he suspected she could be. Who knows? Great-Grandpa is officially crazy. Maybe they should have locked him away."

"Maybe so." Logan stretched his long legs out onto Amelia's

coffee table. He tilted his head onto mine. "So, when's your sister arriving?"

"Mom's bringing her in two days." I was more than anxious to see Mom and Katie—though Mom could only stay a couple of days. I promised if I could keep my sister a while, I'd find a way to get her at least half-way home.

"I'm excited to meet Katie," he said—not sounding at all excited.

I turned toward him. "But?"

"Nah, no buts." Lacing my fingers with his, he kissed my hand.

"No really, what?" Tilting my head, I looked at him.

"But I'll miss seeing you every day. It may be a long two weeks for me."

"You don't have to be a stranger."

"So, you won't need alone, sisterly, bonding time?"

Laughing, I cupped my hand around his rough, whiskered cheek. "I'm sure we'll have plenty of time for that. So, don't go anywhere, okay?"

My heart sped at the soft kiss he placed on my lips.

"Mom! Katie!" I rushed out to meet my family. Katie's Malibu rolled to a stop as I pulled Katie's door open.

She leapt from the passenger side, and we danced into a hug. "I can't believe I'm here!" she said, jumping from one foot to the other. I held her close—I hadn't realized how much I'd missed her. We were supposed to have so much time together this summer.

"Hi, honey," Mom made her way around the car and wrapped me in a warm hug. "It's so good to see you!"

"I am so glad you came, Mom." I beamed at her. "I can't wait to show you what I've done to the house. And you have to meet Rachel and Callie and—"

"Logan?"

"Yes." My smile welded on my face. "Yes, Logan too."

Taking my hand, she twirled me around. "Livy, darling, you look amazing."

"You do look different," Katie said. "Are you using a new moisturizer?"

"No, that's not it." Mom shook her head. "It's this place. It agrees with you."

A whole ten seconds in Rendezvous and my mom could see my happiness here. That's how she was—kind of like Callie. Did Jedi powers come with motherhood?

I showed Mom and Katie around the house and then helped them bring in their things.

"I had left Amelia's room alone, but with my first official visitors," I pointed at them, "I rearranged a bit and moved myself in here." Walking them past the bathroom, into my old room, I said, "You'll be in here. You have the best view." I pulled Katie to the window and pointed to my elm.

"It's a tree." She peered up at it.

"It's my favorite part of this place, Baby!"

Laughing, she shook her head at me. "I'm checking out more downstairs." With a side hug, she ran from the room.

"Same ol' Katie." I set her bag on the bed.

"Yep, not much about *that* daughter of mine has changed." Hands on hips, she stared at me. She unzipped Katie's bag. "She sure has longed for you though these past weeks."

"I'm glad she's here."

"Me too." She took my hand, squeezing.

Helping her stuff the remainder of Katie's clothes into the now vacant dresser, I pushed it shut. Katie had more clothes here than I did. "I've missed you, Mom. I wish *you* could stay longer."

"You've missed me, huh?" She glanced over at me, a questioning smile on her lips. "You seem to be doing very well."

Running into the room, Katie yelled breathless. "Livy! There's no dishwasher!" As if this was news to me.

"Sure there is." I put my arm around her. "And for the next two weeks, there'll be two of us."

I'd planned a simple dish of spaghetti for dinner—just the three of us. Mom wanted to make homemade meatballs to go with dinner. That required a trip to the market. I hadn't realized how much a part of the community I'd become in just two short months until taking my family out in Rendezvous.

"Will you be making it to the festivities?" Joe asked Mom and Katie.

"Mom has to leave us day after tomorrow, but Katie will be here. I'm looking forward to the fire engine suds."

"What festivities?" Katie stood in line behind Mom at Joe's one checkout stand. "

Next week is the anniversary of the founding of Rendezvous." Turning around, I explained all Logan had taught me to Katie. "See, Rendezvous was founded by two brothers. They ran a cattle business together in the late 1800's, early 1900's. One lived in Montana, the other in Colorado. Every year they'd take their herd to the others' land. Well, they wouldn't go all the way. They'd meet halfway—their *meeting place,* which became Rendezvous."

"Why do you know that?" Katie's face wrinkled in worry—or maybe disgust.

Gathering our things, we said our goodbyes to Joe and the few shoppers inside Farmer's.

"One more quick stop, okay?" I pulled Baby's Malibu up to Callie's house. "I need to check on my namesake."

"I still can't believe someone here named a baby after you." Katie slammed her car door shut.

"Hey," Mom said, "Olivia is a beautiful name."

"Well, sure, but they hardly know her."

"Maybe I haven't been here long," I said to Katie in my teacher-tone, "but quality time makes up for the lack of quantity. There are several people here I would call close friends."

Katie held up her hands. "Sorry, geez, Liv."

"Oh, wait until you meet Michelle, Mom." I opened the chain link gate and led them to Callie's front door.

"I can't imagine you with a baby, you're still a baby." Mom shook her head, her hands together at her heart.

"I'm not a baby, Mom." I laughed. "And besides, Callie's a few years older than me. Don't worry. I'm not ready for motherhood."

"Good, I'm not ready for grand-motherhood."

"I could so be an aunt." Katie smacked her gum. "I'd be the most fun aunt ever."

Callie answered the door with one hand, her other cradling Michelle. The baby snuggled inside a fuchsia sling wrapped around Callie's torso. The fabric clung to her body like spandex and held Michelle in place next to her mother. She probably didn't need that one arm supporting her infant, but protective nature kept it there.

"Livy." Her tired eyes widened at seeing us. She hugged my side, so as not squish the baby. The wrinkles under her eyes matched the slowness of her words. "Come in, come in."

Callie's organized home had fallen into disarray in just two short weeks. With her foot, she moved aside a baby seat and a bucket of gardening tools, leading us into her house. Michelle squawked, and I peeked inside Callie's wrap to spy her little face. "May I?"

Unraveling the long cloth, she handed me the baby. I'd grown quite attached to the little girl. I sat on a chair, not bothering to move the small pile of clothes set on its seat.

I ran my fingers through her blonde curls—so much like her mother's, her double chin on the other hand was nothing like Callie.

"Oh!" Mom crooned over my shoulder. "She's beautiful."

"She's so little." Michelle's little hand wrapped around Katie's finger.

"And she's grown." I couldn't believe how much.

Katie sat on the couch across from Callie, making herself comfortable as she always did. "So, you named her after Livy?"

Callie smiled and brushed a curl from her view. "We did. She was my angel that night."

"Here, Mom." I handed Michelle to her. Sitting on the arm of Callie's seat I asked her, "What can I do?"

"Nothing, don't be silly, you've done enough."

Glaring, I waited for a different answer.

She sighed. "Well, maybe next time you're at Joe's you could grab me some milk, something chocolate, and a Coke, but mostly just milk."

"I've changed my mind." Mom let out a sigh. "We could use one of these."

"I thought you weren't ready." I laughed, watching Mom coo over Michelle. "You're too young to be a grandmother."

"Yeah, you can forget that speech."

Shaking my head, I said, "Talk to Jared then. He's the oldest."

"I bet you and Logan beat your brother by a kid or two." Callie laughed at herself—delirious and then yawned.

I smacked her shoulder and she sat up straighter, biting her lip and at least *looking* sorry.

Katie's brow furrowed. "Logan—"

"Callie," I said through my gritted teeth. "You are hilarious. Such a kidder."

"So, Callie." Mom ignored me. "What do you think of Logan?"

"Me?" Callie looked to me to help. "Umm…" She drawled out the syllable. But then she turned to Mom. And it was like their Jedi-minds connected and she disregarded I was even in the room. "I love him. He's one of mine and Paul's closest friends."

"And Liv?"

"Oh, she's crazy about him." Callie waved away my gasp. It may have been true, but my family already thought I'd gone insane… this wouldn't help.

"I gathered," Mom said.

"Crazy? Log— You said you'd been on a few dates." Katie's red face whipped from Callie to me.

"You think I'll like him?" Mom asked, looking down at Michelle.

Callie nodded. "Oh, yeah."

"Okay!" I held up my hands. I was starting to regret our impromptu visit.

"Wait until you see her with him." Callie laughed. "She glows."

"I do not glo—hello? I'm still here." I waved my hand between the two of them.

"You glow?" Katie snorted.

"All righty then! We need to go." I took Michelle from Mom. "Mom, you've got meatballs to make."

Mom and Katie bid their goodbyes and walked out to Katie's Malibu. "Bye, baby girl," I whispered to Michelle. "You're going to have to put up with a lot from this mother of yours."

"Oh, please." Callie chuckled. "I did you a favor. She's all primed to meet him now."

I rolled my eyes. "Maybe you should leave the favors to me. I'll be by in a bit with your milk."

Giving me a side hug, we both looked down at Michelle. "Thanks, Liv. Don't forget my chocolate."

"I can't believe you didn't tell me." Katie crossed her arms in a huff as I climbed into the driver's seat.

"Come on, Baby, it's just new, okay?" I offered her a repentant smile. "Don't be mad."

Sighing, I could see I wasn't yet forgiven. "I'm dropping you two off to make meatballs. I'll be back a few minutes. I just need to get Callie's milk."

I had left Callie smiling and teasing me, and somewhere in the six minutes it took me to drop Mom and Katie off, buy milk, Ho Ho's, and cola, Callie's entire disposition had changed. Opening her front door empty handed, tears streamed down her face.

"Callie, what's wrong?" I looked passed her for Michelle. What on earth had happened?

"I don't know how to be a full time mom." Callie flapped her arms like a fish out of water.

"What? You're doing great." I rubbed her arm, kicking the door behind me closed and set her groceries on the ground.

"I don't know how I'll ever have things back in order. Paul goes to work and he comes home and has time to play and be super dad, and I can't even get the laundry done."

"But you will. It's just new."

"I don't know. I don't think so." She shook her head, wiping her hand under her running nose.

Wrapping an arm around her, I walked her back into the living room, sitting her on the couch. "Once you get back to work, you'll be on more of a schedule, it'll work out."

"I don't know if I can go back." Head in her hands, she sobbed.

"But you love your job."

"I know. I do." She wiped at her uncontrollable eyes. "But Michelle—"

"It's July." I repeated her words from a month ago. "You've got the rest of this month and almost all of August with Michelle."

"Leaving her sounds impossible." She looked down at her daughter asleep in the bouncy seat next to the couch. "I don't know what I'm going to do."

And what could I say, how on earth could I know what she should do? Next to Mom, Callie was the most together person I knew, watching her flare-up had me thinking just being an aunt would work out all right. "It'll be okay," I said with new determination. It had to be. "We'll figure this out."

Chapter 33

Laughter boomed from my house. Opening the door, I listened. "That's very good, Logan," Mom said.

Oh, no. No. No. No. Braving the kitchen, Katie sat in front of Logan, his hands kneading in a bowl.

"Olivia!" Mom's head popped up. "It's about time. You missed my meatball lesson. Logan will have to show you sometime."

"I'm not sure I'll be able to repeat the process without you." Logan rolled a meatball between his hands, and smiled at me. "Hi, Liv."

"Hey." I bit my lip. How long had he been there? "What are you doing here?"

"Olivia, don't be rude." Mom made me feel about ten years old.

"I didn't... I just meant—"

"I stopped by to say hello, Shelly invited me in for a meatball lesson." His hands were back in the bowl, but he watched me. "I hope that's okay."

Forcing a smile, I said, "Of course it is." And it was. I just wished I had been there. Logan, Mom, and Katie alone—without me...it made me nervous. Katie swooned, batting her eyes at everything Logan said and Mom had already put him to work.

"Hey, can I talk to you for a minute?" I said, looking at Logan.

Katie swiveled in her chair, watching Logan rinse off his hands and I led him into the living room. We stood next to the front window, out of the prying eyes of my baby sister. Bringing his hand up to my cheek, Logan traced the small shadow under my right eye. "Are you okay?" he asked. "I didn't realize you weren't here."

Covering his hand with mine, I brought it down and held it. "No, that's not it. It's Callie. She's kind of a mess. I've never seen her like this. She's talking about not knowing how to be a mom and never returning to work. I didn't know what to tell her. I had no idea what to say, not one comforting word came into my pea-sized brain."

"Stop." He returned his hand to my cheek and I let it be. "She'll be fine. It's a life changing adjustment."

"You're right." I bit my down on my thumbnail, mulling that over—*life changing*. "You're right. Of course you're right. You're always right."

Snickering, he wrapped his arms around my waist. "I'm going to remember you said that."

"And use it against me, I'm sure."

"Well." Mom rounded the corner to the living room. "Meatballs are in the oven and my sauce is thickening. Dinner will be ready shortly."

Pushing his chest, I knocked Logan a step away from me. Folding my arms over my chest, I bore all my teeth, grinning at her. "Smells great."

"Let's sit." Mom pursed her lips, staring at us. She wanted to *observe,* see what she could see—without me telling her a thing. I cursed her motherly Jedi skills. Well, I wouldn't let her *see* anything. I wasn't ready to *share* how I felt with the rest of my family—they already thought me a little crazy. I could maneuver my way around Mom's special, psychic gifts.

Logan sat on the couch, so I took the chair, leaving Mom and Katie to sit with Logan on the couch. Let her make of that what she would! Making sure my eyes didn't linger or even glance on Logan's chiseled chin or stout chest or chocolate eyes, I forced my gaze at Mom who happened to be speaking at the time.

"So, what do you think of what Livy's done with the place?"

"It's great. It's her and Amelia rolled into one."

"It is." Mom chuckled.

"What did you change?" Katie looked around the room.

I ran through a quick list including curtains and some décor.

"That picture's new, isn't it?" Mom stood and touched the edge of the frame with Seth's drawing. "New, but old, I don't remember it."

I coughed, choking on nothing in particular.

"Yeah," Logan said, as I continued to sputter. "I'm an art fan. That piece was mine, Olivia admired it. I gave it to her, kind of a house-warming."

Sitting back down, Mom crossed her legs. "So, what's your opinion? Everyone seems to have one. Should she sell or keep the place?"

"Mom, you are just full of questions." Gritting my teeth, I hoped she'd read my thoughts.

"I know!" She smiled, looking around. "Here I am back in this old place, it takes me back. And you, you're spending all your days and nights here. I never thought I'd see that day. I'm just wondering what someone else thinks about it. Someone who isn't you or your father." She turned to Logan, waiting for an answer.

"Well," he said, looking at Mom. "I think Olivia's the only one who can answer that question. But I do think Amelia gave it to her for a reason."

"Let me know when you figure out whatever that is," she said, giving him a playful wink.

Logan and I shared a brief knowing glance, and then Mom continued to quiz him until dinner was ready. The Logan Show continued through our meal. Mom seemed to like him. Katie, on the other hand, drooled half the night in Logan's direction.

When it came time to say goodnight, I stood back and watched Logan speak to my family. Finally, after what seemed like forever, I allowed myself a sincere smile his way. "See you," I said without making any attempts to close the gap between us.

Sensing my need for space, he returned my grin, and my heart ran a relay race.

Shutting the door behind him, Mom released an audible sigh. "Well, that was interesting."

I refused to ask what she meant, what she thought. I wouldn't give her ammunition. I might be dying to know, but it would only aid her mind reading ability. Instead, I forced a yawn and asked, "Hey, Baby, help me with the dishes?"

"What?" she said, still staring at the door. "Oh, yeah, sure."

Taking out her cell, Mom plopped onto the couch. "I'm going to go call your father."

Smirking all the way into the kitchen, I couldn't believe it. I had given nothing away. "Wash or dry?"

"Wash," she said, filling the sink with suds. "Why have you never told me about him?"

"I guess it slipped my mind."

"He's beautiful, he's amazing, and he slipped your mind? Liar."

"I'm sorry, Baby, I'd just broken up with Ben, it just seemed too fast to mention to anyone, you know? Mom does not need to realize how much I like him. Okay?"

"Really?" She rolled her eyes at me. "You're so lame, Olivia. Callie already mentioned you and Logan and kids—all in the same sentence. And you're worried I'll give something away?"

"Callie was exaggerating. Besides, I'm still not sure we should be exclusive."

Katie scoffed. "You're crazy."

Laughing, I splashed in her tub of water. "Yeah, probably."

Sitting on Amelia's bed with her legs outstretched, Mom looked around the room. The sprinkling of Katie's shower was the only noise in the quiet house. "I don't think I ever came in here before." Mom reached out, picking up a small frame with a black and white photo inside.

"She was pretty private."

Mom nodded. "So, what are your plans, my girl?"

"Well, I'm helping with summer programs now, it doesn't pay as well as the secretary job, but it's enough to get me by."

"What about after that?" She brushed a strand of hair out of my eyes.

"I want to go back to school, get my teaching degree."

"What about this place?" She didn't go into shock or awe

about my major change, surely Dad had told her though.

"I want to keep it." I laughed. "Maybe a summer home?" I didn't know anyone who would have a summer home in Rendezvous.

"What about him?" She peered at me behind a row of long lashes.

Readjusting, I brushed another non-existent hair away from my eyes. "Logan?" I knew perfectly well whom she meant. "What about him?"

"Will he follow you? I don't see him loving the idea of you being away for two years to get a degree."

"Isn't that a bit hasty?" They were the words I thought she should be saying.

Ignoring my question, she sat beside me and covered my hand with hers. "And what about you? You'll hate being away from him for so long."

Sitting up straighter, I said, "Again, jumping the gun, Mother."

"It's not hasty, Olivia, and you know it, not for the way you feel anyway. Be honest with me. I can sense your affection for him. Callie's right, you practically become a lighthouse when he's around. I've never seen you look at anyone that way."

"I-what? I didn't even look at him!"

"You're half in love with him, that's plain to see, and he's mad about you. I just think separation will be really difficult."

"Mom!"

"He's charming." She ignored my plea. "But he's sincere. He fits you. Who would've thought—here in Rendezvous? Yes, I like him, very much." Chuckling, she nodded, her auburn hair swaying with the motion.

"But it's too fast," I said, peering over at her. "Isn't it?"

"You can't control when you're going to fall in love, sweetheart."

"But you…you said." I pointed at her. "You said it was too soon."

"I did." She looked down and shook her head. "I guess I was being hasty in my judgment. I just wanted to protect you, Olivia. But I'm not always right—at least not until I've seen it with my own eyes." She winked at me.

"You should be a private detective. You should learn another language and work for the government, be their secret spy or something."

She looked at me like I spoke a foreign tongue, then threw her head back and laughed. "Oh, Livy. You crack me up." She sighed. "Just be happy. All right, honey? That's all your father and I want for you."

I raised my eyebrows in disbelief. "You sure? I don't think Dad will be satisfied until I'm a surgeon."

"He gets his mind set and it's hard for him to change it, but he can and he will. You are more important to him than your career choice. Just give him a little time." She crossed her feet. "You know, he told me once that his mother pushed him out of Rendezvous. She told him the world was a great big place, and he belonged somewhere else. At seventeen it about broke his heart, but he told me that's what drove him to get his law degree. He wanted to prove something to her. Believe me. He just wants you to be happy."

I tucked my feet up under me and lay my head back against Amelia's headboard. "And what about Ben? I think the breakup was more difficult for Dad than anyone else."

Laughing, Mom patted my cheek. "He'll heal."

"I still can't believe you saw right through my act." I laid my head on her shoulder.

"Act?"

"My act with Logan. I tried so hard to not let you see how much I like him."

Laughing, she cupped my cheek. "Oh, honey, if that was you low-key, I'm not sure I want to see you acting 'normal' with him."

Chapter 34

Mom's two day stay went much too fast, leaving just Katie and me. Katie and I went to my summer programs. We visited Rachel, Callie, and of course, Logan. We went to karaoke and visited Joe's for plenty of Chunky Monkey. I think he ordered extra just for us. We stayed up late every night. She had all kinds of things to tell me about Benjamin's stay, and a million questions about Logan.

I wore my teenage sister out. A week into her visit, she went to bed early, ten o'clock. I hadn't read an entry in Amelia's journal since Katie's arrival. With my sister in bed, I changed into my comfy sweats, poured myself a glass of homemade lemonade and set my feet on the coffee table.

July 30, 1957

I moved back into my room with little Jonathon the day Mom left. Burt didn't argue, but he's been talking to me at dinner. No more silence. He's been asking questions about my growing up and interests. I've asked him things too. He's not as bad as I thought. He's even held Jonathon a few times when I found myself occupied and the baby needed tending. He smiles at him and even talks to him. It's strange and odd, but better than I ever thought life could be here.

Amelia

With the demands of motherhood, Amelia seemed to write

less. She had one, sometimes two entries every other month. I read until late. She still spoke of Seth and her longing for him, but her tone had transformed. She was happy, not fulfilled, but happy with her son and her home and even with Burt most of the time. She still slept with my dad in the guest room and she and Burt still visited over dinner. Then the day of Dad's first birthday came.

May 23, 1958

My Jonathon is a whole year old. What a beautiful, sweet little toehead he is. We had a small gathering for his special day. I wish Mom could have come, last she saw he wasn't even crawling and now here he is walking around! In the end it was Grettie, her little Laurie, and Burt and me.

Jonathon called Burt da-da. He's called me momma many times, but we've never named Burt for him. I don't know what to call him. I suppose for our charade I should refer to him as Dad. Burt is good to little Jonathon, but it doesn't feel right to me. Jonathon had a dad, and Seth would've been the perfect father. Jonathon said this right in front of Grettie. To my shocked face she asked if that was the first time he'd said it. I only answered yes. At least it was the truth. And then Jonathon screamed it again until Burt came to him and picked him up. That night Burt read to Jonathon before bed. He's always good to the boy, but it felt different.

Amelia

Laying my head back on the couch, I wondered how the man who read to and treated my dad so well ended up without even a relationship with him.

I woke to a stream of sunlight finding its way in through a crack in the curtains. It was almost ten o'clock, and the crick in my neck was fierce. I'd fallen asleep on the couch, Amelia's journal bulging in my lap. Closing it, I set it on the coffee table. Rubbing the sore spot on my neck, I stood and stretched. Slumping into the kitchen, I poured myself a glass of orange juice and headed back to the living room. A fully dressed Katie sat in my seat, Amelia's book, *my* book, in her hands.

"Baby!" I yelped. "What are you doing?"

Rattled, the book came down from her face. She'd opened to the middle, a place I hadn't yet reached. "This is Amelia's diary."

I started toward her.

"Listen to this: *Surprisingly, I love Burt. I never would have thought such a thing was possible, but I do, I love him.* Do you believe this? What a crack up."

"Baby!" I barked a second time, and then I snatched the book from her hands.

"What? Geez, Liv."

"Sorry—I'm sorry." I stuttered an apology, all the while my head whirling over what she'd read aloud. "It's just—should you really be reading someone else's diary?"

"*You* were." She crossed her arms, peering at me, waiting for an answer.

"So, what did you say?" Logan stood on the side of the road waiting for the parade with me.

Shielding my eyes from the sun, I said, "I told her she shouldn't be reading other people's journals."

Logan's rupture of laughter startled me.

I jumped beside him. "I know, I know, hypocritical isn't it?" I nudged him with the side of my body.

"Just funny." He put an arm around me. "Where'd she run off to again?"

"Maria's selling churros, I sent her off to buy a few."

"Well if she doesn't hurry back, she'll miss one super, eight-minute parade."

Laughing, I snuggled into his side. "Wow, that lengthy huh?"

The first homemade float started down the road as Katie returned. She wasn't alone.

Flaring, my hands went to my hips. "So, you just like getting your paws into anyone new. Is that it?"

Roy smiled, though my tone was anything but friendly. I'd made my peace with Roy, that didn't mean I wanted his claws into my baby sister.

Katie's eyes went wide. "Gosh, Liv, Roy was sweet enough to give me directions."

"You're telling me you got lost?" Was that even possible in Rendezvous? We weren't on the outskirts of town. This was Main Street. "Maria's stand is a whole thirty yards away."

Glaring, Katie spoke through gritted teeth. "Can I talk with you for one minute, sis?" She marched away.

Grabbing Logan's T-shirt, I pulled his face down to mine. "You tell him!" I whispered. "You tell him, she is too young and he better back off." Letting him go, I followed after Katie.

"What's your problem?" Katie's fifteen year-old hands looked out of place on her hips.

"He is too old, Baby. And I know him, you don't." I matched her stance, using my one inch taller carriage to my advantage.

"I won't be here that long—there's nothing to freak about, Livy. Besides," she narrowed her eyes at me, "it would be a shame if Daddy found out about Amelia's diary, wouldn't it?"

I gasped. "Seriously? Blackmail?" I couldn't have Katie spilling the beans. She didn't even know all the details. This was important—sacred even. She needed to zip it.

Changing her gruffness to a pout, she held her hands together. "Come on, Liv, it's not that big of a deal. I'm out of here in a week."

Rolling my eyes, I crossed my arms over my chest. "Fine. But you stay close. No alone time, Katie."

She jumped in place.

"I'm serious. Zero privacy for the two of you."

"Yes, *Mo—om*. I get it." Kissing my cheek, she ran back to where Roy and Logan stood.

Twelve floats strolled by us, Sheriff Lane on a horse with an American flag, children dressed in pioneer clothing threw beef jerky into the crowd. Logan was right, it wasn't long. Right after, the crowd met in the park for a BBQ.

Refusing to leave Katie's side, Roy raked on my nerves. He

paraded her about, while I watched like a hawk.

"Liv. Oh, Livy…"

"Don't mind her." Logan said, waving a hand in front of my face. "She's busy scrutinizing Roy's every move."

Turning, I saw Callie next to Logan. "Uh, hi." I returned my focus to Baby.

"Why?" Callie spoke to Logan. Stepping in front of me, she crossed her arms over her pink tank top. Her cut off shorts were already buttoned. That couldn't be normal. Michelle sat in a stroller, a bonnet covering her eyes.

"He's flirting with Katie."

"Ah, I see. Liv, hon, he's harmless."

"I've heard that before." I looked around her to see my sister better.

"Olivia, stop it." She forced my chin to face her. "Say hello to your namesake. You're hurting her feelings."

It was possible I was obsessing—just a little. Their hormone-filled teenage bodies sat a good foot apart. So, I willingly turned to her. "I'm sorry, Callie." Bending down on one knee, I peeked at the baby. Lifting the bonnet off Michelle's eyes, she slept. "I'm sure to cause her all kinds of grief by ignoring her. She's asleep!"

"I'm going to find Paul." Logan kissed my cheek goodbye and I watched him go.

Sitting on the bench behind us, Callie pulled me down beside her. "So," she said. "I put in my letter of resignation."

"You did?" I jerked at the news, unable to hide my surprise.

"Yep."

"And…you're…okay?"

She turned to face me better on the bench and pulled up her big violet sunglasses so they were perched on top of her head. "Yes," she said without even a quiver in her voice. "I could go back, many do and it works, but I'd be thinking about Michelle every minute. I would drive myself crazy. And I don't want to. It would be one thing if I was dying to go back, if I felt torn, but I don't."

"You don't?" I didn't believe her. I knew how much Callie

loved her job.

"Not anymore. They aren't lying when they say a baby changes everything. I'll go back one day. Work will be waiting for me. But she won't be. She's almost a month old and already she's so much bigger, doing new things every day. I can't miss it. She'll grow whether I'm around to watch her or not."

My mouth fell open. Her perspective was so clear, so resolute, so *Callie*. The girl was back.

"Yeah." She sighed like a load of bricks had lifted from her chest. "What about you? How's your dilemma?"

"Dilemma? Me? I have none."

"Ha, ha." She mocked a laugh. "Are you still stressing over Logan settling?"

"Nah—" *Yes.* It upset him whenever I brought it up, and I was too weak to resist whenever he touched me, so, my body may not have acted like it. But my head—oh yeah, my head doubted *for him*. Worried, *for him*.

"Right." She drawled out. She wasn't buying what I was selling. "Liv, you love him, everyone knows it. Your mom saw it the minute you were in a room together."

I looked at him, standing with Paul, talking and laughing, his hands snug in his pockets. I saw our whole lives. I saw the faces of our kids, playing alongside of Callie's, but it seemed too perfect, too easy maybe. "I do love him."

"Then have faith, Olivia." She squeezed my hand. "Do you think I could quit my job and go into this crazy-not-so-Callie world of stay-at-home-mom if I didn't have faith? I have faith that my love for Michelle and my conviction to be with her is right."

I nodded. And for some reason, my uncertain face made her laugh.

Running a hand through her tousled hair, she grabbed her glasses and slid them on. "Maybe it's because you didn't know him before, but Logan's never been this happy. Ever."

August 29, 1958

Two years. Two years ago today I was married to the man

that I'll love forever. He was beautiful and kind and incredibly talented. Burt was gone all day, so I took out the drawing Seth did of the church where we were married. It's been so long since I've looked at it. It's been locked away in the floor for I don't remember how long now. Once I put Jonathon down for a nap, I laid down and closed my eyes. I tried to remember the way it felt when he touched me, when he kissed me, when he said my name. I found myself caressing my own cheek, trying to bring back the memory more clearly. It didn't work and then I cried until my eyes were puffy and swollen. That's when Jonathon woke up. I had Seth's photo out and in my madness I showed Jonathon his father's picture. He was standing in his crib and he clapped his hands for the picture, wanting to hold it. Thank goodness he doesn't say much or in his innocence, he'd tattle on me.

Maybe one day I'll show it to him for real – when I can tell him the truth and he won't forget.

Amelia

Reading more entries, with Katie sleeping in the room next door, I came to this one – the one I'd been waiting for since Katie's discovery of the book.

June 29, 1959

Surprisingly, I love Burt. I never would have thought such a thing was possible, but I do, I love him. He's very good to Jonathon. He treats me fairly and kind. He's the best friend I have. And though I can't imagine loving him romantically, he is my dearest friend, and I love him as such.

We stayed up late, talking and laughing and I couldn't help but think back to our first few days together. Life doesn't always turn out how we'd like, but I have become grateful for what we do have. And everything good we have right now is because of Burt. It's not what I wanted in life, but when I think about where I almost ended up…it could have been so much worse. I guess you just have to have faith.

Amelia

Have faith. It echoed in my mind, first Callie and now Amelia.

August 5, 1959

Burt put his arm around me yesterday. It was strange and at the same time seemed so natural. We are married after all. We were standing on the porch watching Jonathon as he dug in the mud. And then out of nowhere, Burt put an arm around my shoulders.

I was surprised but didn't shake it off. I looked up at him, and he was just smiling at Jonathon. I am happy he's happy. He deserves to be happy.

And though I'm content with this life, I cried myself to sleep that night and in my pillow repeating again and again, I'm sorry.

Amelia

August 29, 1959

3 years.

Jonathon is two years old. I know he's still a baby, but I want him to know who his real father is. I want to at least say Seth's name out loud. And the only person that he'll really matter to other than me is Jonathon. I'm going to explain myself to Burt. He's rough on the outside, but I know him. He's kind and good, he'll understand.

Amelia

September 14, 1959

Burt wants to talk tonight. I'm glad. I haven't yet had the courage to speak with him about telling Jonathon the truth. I'm putting the baby to bed early and making liver and onions, Burt's favorite.

Amelia

Later-

How didn't I know? I should have seen this coming. He gave signs. Oh, Burt.

Burt was so pleased with his dinner. Before I could speak, before I could ask about telling Jonathon, he handed me an envelope and told me to sit. We sat at the table and while he ate, I opened the sealed wrapper. It was a card. A pretty pink and gold card with words embossed on it, "Happy Anniversary". I honestly couldn't have told you the day we were married. It wasn't a joyful event for me, and though I wrote about it in this book, it wasn't a date I remembered or even thought to celebrate. I couldn't find words. It was such a surprise. So I uttered a simple thank you. Then he took my hand from across the table, and he told me that he loved me. He said he loves me and he wants to live like married people should live. He wants me to move into his room with him.

I was quiet. What could I say? How can I do what he's asking? Finally he asked what I thought. I didn't know what to say, but I had to reply and so I said that I needed some time to think about it. He said that was fair enough. He was still in a good mood – that's when I decided to ask my question. I thought the timing was good. I was very wrong. I started with telling him how grateful I was for him and for all he'd done for me and little Jonathon. That made him happy and he took my hand again. I told him that as grateful as I was, I wanted him to know I wasn't rebelling against my upbringing when I married the first time. (I couldn't say Seth's name to Burt, I just couldn't). I told him that we'd loved each other, and I want Jonathon to know who his father is. I told him despite what Daddy has told him, Jonathon's father was a fine man. He practically threw my own hand at me. I tried to explain myself. I told him Jonathon doesn't belong here, not really. He needs to know where and who he comes from. He raised his hand, and I thought he was going to hit me, but he didn't. He just said, "You mean this place isn't good enough for HIS son." He felt totally disgraced. He confesses his feelings, and I tell him Jonathon is better than what he can provide for us – his words, not mine. I didn't see it that way…or I wouldn't have asked.

I tried to apologize, but he was too offended to listen. He stormed off to his own room and though I waited up late, he never came out again.

Amelia

September 28, 1959

Things are worse than they were in the beginning. Burt won't eat with us. He won't talk to me. I've ruined everything. Not for me, who cares about me, but for Jonathon, and even for Burt. He's my dearest friend, and I'm the reason for his misery.

Amelia

October 13, 1959

I have to make this right. Maybe if I love Burt like he wants me to…Maybe he'll love Jonathon again. We could be a family, for the baby. For Burt. If I'm being honest, for me too. I may not have been happy exactly, but I was more content than I realized. And all because of Burt. I've made him unhappy and now no one is happy. Jonathon's moods range from angry to melancholy with all of the contention in our home.

So, I'm moving my things into his room today while he's out, and I'll have the table set for dinner once he returns. I will be his wife. If he senses my hesitation, he won't accept me and we'll live in this wretchedness forever. So I'll give myself to him fully and I believe it will help our family. The only person it'll hurt is me. And really, I'm happy to make Burt happy, my pain will be linked with my guilt and that cannot be helped.

Amelia

October 14, 1959

What's done is done. I can't take it back. Most of the time I wouldn't want to. I do love Burt, my dear, kind friend.

I couldn't tell you if he was surprised by my meal or not. He made no change in his demeanor. He acted as if it weren't there. So, I voiced an invitation to him to eat with us. He didn't answer until I practically begged, telling him I needed to speak with him.

And then I told him he'd misinterpreted me before, and that he didn't allow me to finish. He waited without speaking. And so I told him that I loved him, too, and I would be forever thankful for all he'd given to us. When it looked as though he would not believe me, I stood from the table, walked over to his side, and kissed him. That's when I told him I'd moved my things into his room. He was happy, but still hesitant. He asked if I was sure and so I kissed him again.

And it's okay. If I cannot make myself happy, I will focus on making those I love happy. And in order to do that, I cannot cry for my lost love anymore. I cannot wish for the life I should have had. I have to move on. As long as my sweet friend Burt is with me, I will not allow myself to wallow and cry for the husband I lost. It's not fair to him, and it won't work. I've shed my last tear.

Amelia

Chapter 35

As long as Burt is with me—the more I read, the more clear things became. She didn't tell Dad the truth to keep happiness in their home. She bottled her feelings for the sake of her family, until Burt had passed. I caught her that night, the first time she'd let herself cry for Seth, since the day she made her decision to be Burt's wife, for real.

I was more than half way through the book now. There were still entries, still time, but I found myself fretting the end. Like a mother who looks at her child and sees them all grown up, I knew this book would end, and when it did, I would mourn for Amelia all over again.

Sighing, I stretched my legs out on my bed and fanned through the remaining pages in Amelia's journal. My fan stopped short at the end, at a bulge. Opening to the back, I discovered a yellowed envelope sealed and taped to the last page. The tape was aged and yellow too, and it unstuck with my slight touch. How had I not noticed this before? The back side faced outward. Turning it around, I saw Amelia's careful scrawl – *Seth.* I knew—it was a goodbye letter to him.

I twirled the old envelope, watching Seth's name appear and then disappear, again and again. I zoned out, staring at the sealed envelope. A soft tap on my bedroom door, and the materialization of Logan brought me around.

"Hey, ready for dinner?"

"Sure. Yeah." I gave him a brief smile and then turned back to the letter in my hand. "Katie's just about ready. At least she should be. She got out of the shower an hour ago." Setting the envelope in my lap, I covered it with my hands. "You shouldn't have invited Roy. She would have been ready ages ago."

"Ah—"

"You still aren't forgiven for that." I glared at him.

Ignoring my frown, he leaned in to kiss me. "Were you reading?" He asked, eyeing the book beside me.

"I was," I said, unable to stop the melancholy in my voice. "Do you still have a free weekend?"

"Yeah." He helped me to my feet, and we started down the stairs together. "Do you want me to drive Katie halfway with you?"

"If you don't mind taking a couple more days off, I'd like you to drive all the way to California with me." I needed him. So, I practiced having faith. "I want to add an extra stop after we drop Katie off. And I'd like for you to be there."

"Yeah, of course. What kind of detour are we talking about?"

"Ganesworth." We stood at the bottom of the stairs. Wrapping my arms around him, I held him close. I had to have faith, because I couldn't do this without him. "I want to see where they met. I want to find the church. I want to give Seth this..." I held the sealed letter out for him to see. "She wrote this when she decided to truly be Burt's wife and not look back. I'm certain she was saying goodbye to him. I know it's crazy, but I want to give it to him."

Cocking his head to see my face better, his brow furrowed with worry or maybe he was deciding if I had gone mad.

"I know he's gone Logan, but he has to be buried there. I want to visit my grandfather's grave. I need to bring him Amelia's goodbye. I owe her that much."

Nodding, he held my face in his hands. "Okay."

"Thank you." I stared down at Amelia's handwriting.

"What about your family?"

"That's why I want to go all the way to L.A. It's time. I'm going to tell them. My dad deserves to know, she wanted him to know. She was so much more than what any of us thought."

I couldn't sleep. We would be leaving in a few hours, but I couldn't shut my eyes. Maybe it was the pain of watching Roy flirt with my baby sister all night—or maybe it was the fear of what I would be telling my father soon. I picked up Amelia's copy of *Pride and Prejudice*. I was halfway through the book when four-thirty came. I might as well get ready for the day. Six would be here soon enough.

When I woke Katie up at five-thirty, she growled at me. Threatening to call Roy to say goodbye to her unshowered-pajama self got the grouchy girl out of bed.

Ready as she would get, we trotted down Amelia's stairway together. "Logan!" Katie said, happy to see him.

"Oh sure, he gets a smile." I folded my arms across my chest and rolled my eyes.

"Well, he didn't wake me up!"

Walking outside, a cool breeze hit my face. It was like smelling salts, waking me up. The cool temperature wouldn't last though. I breathed in the clean air and looked around my little neighborhood, reassuring myself I would be back. I left valuable things at Amelia's, things I wanted with me next semester, my bike and the majority of my small, new wardrobe. I had this awful feeling once Dad had me home, he'd find a way to keep me there. Once away from Rendezvous, could he convince me of all my silly nonsense this summer? My brain ran on zero sleep and had me in all sorts of trouble. I did pack Amelia's journal and the silver dollar she set aside for Dad.

Jabbering from Katie about cheerleading, school and Roy lulled me to sleep in no time.

The sun was high in the sky when I opened my eyes. I'd slept for hours. I blinked as the light poured in, hurting my eyes.

We took turns driving and sleeping, and only stopped to eat when Katie's whining became unbearable. Making good time, we made it to my California home in less than twenty-four hours.

Pulling into my parent's large tri-level home, Katie flew from the vehicle, leaving the door wide open behind her. Logan stretched his arm out, reaching for my hand. "You ready?"

"Yeah." I lied. "Let's go see the parents."

Jared was the first to greet us. He reached for a brother-type hug, whispering in my ear, "Ben moved out." I squeezed him about the waist. He'd read my mind.

Dad nodded at Logan, chastisement all over his face. Thank goodness for my mother, who hugged Logan and I both hello, reassuring us she was thrilled that we were *both* there.

It was late when Jared left. We'd eaten and visited, Dad abnormally quiet. I had been building up nerves to talk to Dad. I sat with Mom and Logan on the couch when Dad announced he was off to bed.

"Oh, um, Dad, can I speak with you?"

I was hoping he'd be in a better mood. But in the morning Logan would still be here and in the fall I would still be heading to college to get a teaching degree. I couldn't wait for his mood to improve.

Sitting on the couch, he looked at me, waiting. "Just Dad." I smiled at Logan and Mom.

"Come on, Logan," Mom said. "I've got books filled with embarrassing pictures to show you anyway." She winked before guiding Logan into the kitchen.

"Dad." I sat beside him. "I need to talk to you about Amelia."

Half an hour passed and he still hadn't spoken. I held in my hands her journal and Dad's silver dollar. I did my best to reveal this truth, which to me was now a blessing, with care. I knew what a shock it would be. Starting from the beginning, I read short inserts from Amelia every now and then, ad-libbing the rest. His brows remained furrowed. I couldn't tell if he was in shock, or angry. I tried to protect her. To explain she didn't have a choice.

His hand covered his mouth as I read her words concerning him. *"...it was then I realized he thought this child belonged to Burt. That would be impossible."* When I read her speech to Burt—how she'd said Dad didn't belong there, his eyes welled with tears. She had told Dad that growing up, but he never realized what it meant until now. I brought him up to where I was in the book, what Amelia had done to make them happy—to make them a family. Standing, he turned away from me, his hands wiping furiously at his eyes. It was a lot to take in. I had taken the journey over time. I dumped it all on him at once, and it didn't feel fair.

"I know it's a lot to take in."

"I need to go to bed." He stood and waved me off with his hand.

Putting my hand on his back, I said, "Dad, can we talk about this?"

"Later. I'm going to bed."

Reaching for his hand, I placed the silver dollar in his palm. "Daddy, I know it's a lot, but—"

"A lot to take in is my daughter changing her entire life course. But secrets—"

"I wasn't trying to keep a secret from you. I was just—"

"This is…impossible. Ridiculous." He forced the silver coin back into my hand. "Goodnight, Olivia."

Setting Amelia's book on the coffee table, I hoped he'd come back and read for himself.

I went to Logan's room and found him still awake, sprawled across the bed with one of my old yearbooks in his hands. His dimple indented, he smiled and turned another page.

"Hey." I grinned at him.

"So?"

I told him how things had gone.

"He'll come around," he said.

"Yeah, I hope so. I was hoping this could bring him closer to Amelia, like it did for me."

"I'm sure it will, but the man grew up with her. He was raised by her and now everything he knew about his childhood is being challenged. Give him a break."

I hugged Logan goodnight, feeling like all would be right as long I could stay in his arms.

Shuffling off to my room, I fell into bed. With the burden off of my shoulders I fell into a restful asleep.

Despite my late night, I woke early. Going out in to the living room, I hoped and prayed to see my dad on the couch with

Amelia's book in hand. The book lay open, but it wasn't Dad who was reading, it was Mom.

Looking up to see me, her face grave, she said, "So, it's true. I couldn't believe it when your father told me last night."

"So, he talked to you? How is he?" That was a good sign. At least he wasn't in denial.

"Yes, he told me everything, well, everything you told him. You're not done?" She held up the book.

Shaking my head, I said, "Not yet. I've been taking my time."

"Liv, you didn't say anything." Her voice shook, sounding so disappointed in me.

"I know. I was waiting. I wanted to tell Dad in person. Mom, I—"

Yawning, she rubbed at the rings under her eyes. "I know, honey. But it's not just a *storybook*. This is your father's life."

"I know that!" Tears stung at my eyes. "You think I was just joy-reading like Romeo and Juliet, just another tragic love story? This is my history, too, and this book, these words were written by my flesh and blood. And she gave this to me. She knew I would find it. Don't you see? Mom, that's why she left me her house. She wanted us to know. And now I know, she lived an extraordinary life and suffered grief most of us won't ever understand." The tears that stung at my eyes now fell and I held my hand out, possessive of the book that Amelia had left to me.

Handing it over, she didn't argue.

"For Dad." I held up the silver dollar and set it on the coffee table. "It was his dad's. It's what she left to him."

Mom nodded.

"Logan and I are leaving in a couple hours."

"But—"

She didn't understand yet. But I knew she would. "We're going to Ganesworth, to visit Seth's grave. We'll be back in a day or two."

I woke Logan and within the hour we were on the road.

Chapter 36

Three hours into our seven hour drive Logan started singing road trip tunes. "All righty then! That was lovely," I said when he started on ninety-nine bottles of beer on the wall. "You've been in a car too long." Two days, twenty-six hours of driving—yeah, it could make anyone a little crazy.

"Are you asking me to stop?" He glanced over at me from the road, both his hands on the steering wheel.

"Yes, I am." Laughing, I reached over for one of his hands. "Thanks for doing this."

"Why don't you read a few entries out loud?"

So close to the end of the book now, I read short, simple entries about the births of both of my uncles as well as a few more and then came the day my dad got married.

> *...I wish Jonathon knew how grateful I am for him. We aren't close. We haven't been for years now. He's so different than Burt. There's so much of his dad in him. He's never belonged in Rendezvous. It's a good place, but Jonathon, he could do anything. He keeps his father alive for me, even when I don't allow myself to wish for such a thing.*
>
> *He's married now and I don't know when I'll see him again.*

"That's the first time in a several entries she makes reference to Seth," Logan said.

"I know. Well, she promised to be Burt's wife without looking back. I guess that's what she was doing. Gosh, it hardened her.

She changed so much."

"To an extent, but to me she wasn't hard. I don't know why, I guess she didn't have to lie to me. I was just a neighbor kid who she could be herself with."

The next entries came much later, skipping years.

August 11, 2003

My Burt is gone, he died in his sleep, peacefully. How I loved my friend and the life he generously gave to me.

Seth would have been grateful, too. Burt took care of us. He helped us when no one else would. He was a true friend. And with his passing, I feel for the first time in years allowed to long for my love. For my Seth. He's never left my heart all these years.

Amelia

August 15, 2003

She saw me. She heard me. I'm certain of it. My granddaughter, Olivia, heard me cry out for Seth. For her grandfather. Someone she'll never meet, or even know about.

I didn't hear her come in. I thought she was asleep. I was so careless. But I hadn't had his picture out in so long. So many years without his face and when I saw him the other night as I recorded Burt's passing, my heart felt like it was beating for the first time in a long time. And I couldn't wait any longer. I needed to see him again. My Seth.

What if she tells Jonathon? What if she asks me about him? I wouldn't know what to say. I've been lying for so long, I'm not sure I'm able to tell the truth.

I don't know what the girl will do. Only time will tell.

Amelia

"She wrote about me." I whispered more to myself than to Logan. "She was afraid I'd tell on her."

Logan squeezed my hand. "But you didn't."

It was strange, reading my name in Amelia's curvy scrawl.

Zoning, I watched the moving road in front of us. Sighing, I looked back down to the book. Turning the page, I saw what would be her last entry. I gasped and covered my mouth.

"What is it?" He glanced my direction and then back at the road several times. "Liv?"

"Her next entry," I said.

He waited and I began.

Dear Olivia,

I received your graduation announcement today. I must admit, I was surprised to receive it. I haven't been much of a grandmother to you. You have been a much better friend to me. You've kept my secret. I know you saw me, dear Olivia. You heard me. I know you did. But you didn't say anything, at least it seems that way. I'd like to ask you why. However, I'm certain I won't ever see you again.

Seeing that picture, in your announcement, your smiling face with eyes like your grandfather's, reminded me that I do love you, dear girl. I'm sorry to say I needed reminding, but it's true. Now, I won't have any more secrets from you, Olivia. I love you, you and your brother and your sister. And of course your father. I'm showing you by giving you my home. You'll find my treasures, my secrets. I know you will. I know this, you see, because you remind me of him. He was kind and creative and he never gave up. He fought for me until he died. And you'll search until you find my secrets. I know you will.

All my love, darling Olivia,
Your Grandmother

Wiping at the tears on my cheeks, I could hardly finish the entry out loud.

Ganesworth was small and everything seemed the same sort of brownish color. I could see why Amelia thought her life had come to an end when she first arrived. It was larger than Rendezvous, maybe I would have felt the same way about it had someone forced me there. But Rendezvous was home to me.

Holding a printed map from the internet, Logan asked, "Where to first? Gallery? Church? Cemetery?"

"Cemetery." I couldn't wait any longer. We could explore later, but first I needed to see where my grandfather lie. I needed to deliver Amelia's letter.

There were hundreds of plots. Lilacs trimmed the edges of the small cemetery and filled the air with their sweet scent. Stretching our legs, we got out of the rental car. Shaking, I reached for Logan's hand.

"I did an obituary search online," Logan said, squeezing my fingers. "But I couldn't find a Seth Garrison from Ganesworth. Apparently no one's entered it on any family history sites. So, we're going on your intuition here."

"He's here." I could feel it. He had to be. Holding tight to Amelia's letter, I walked row by row looking for Grandfather.

The small graveyard was bigger than it seemed. We split up and continued to search, but I became less confident the more stones we passed.

"Hey, you want a water bottle?" Logan asked, crossing the yard over to me.

"Sure," I didn't trust myself to speak much. Tears were close.

"We'll find him." He rubbed the nape of my neck. "Don't stress."

We searched an hour longer with little ground left, when I found a subdivision of Garrisons. "Logan!" I yelled. "Logan, over here!" This had to be it. He ran toward me and seeing the names on the stones where I stood, we both searched. Leonard, Charles, Arnold, Betsy, Grace, Lila… no Seth. Where was he?

"Check it out." Logan pointed to a stone I'd already scanned over.

"Arnold?" I shrugged.

"Cousin Arnie? Their priest."

"Ohhh!" I could have kissed Logan—I would later. "He must be close now." So, we searched, again and again, but if he was in that yard, he wasn't with his family.

"Maybe he was buried next to his home. People used to do

that years ago."

He was grasping, but I didn't have any other answers. My intuition had led me to the graveyard—without success. Logan handed me the directions, and we were off.

Seth's old home was large, with no second story and a lot of ground to cover. It was the greenest part of Ganesworth thus far. The front yard was fenced in along with the back, but it was a small fence, only reaching to my hip line. We could see the yard and the big tree within it.

"Carpe diem?" I said and Logan opened the gate. "I just want to see this tree, maybe there's a marking on it, or by it. Then we can knock."

"Excuse me?"

The call came before I reached the tree. I just need to see—

"Excuse me! What do you think you're doing? This is private property."

Turning, we saw the young man, not much older than me.

"Sorry." Logan held out a hand, but the man ignored him. "We should have knocked."

"It's my fault." I tried to smile. "I just wanted a quick look at your yard."

"The yard?"

"Yeah, crazy question." Laughing a not-so-believable laugh, I said, "Is anyone… by chance, buried there?"

"Buried?" His face scrunched. "No one's buried here."

"Do you happen to know the Garrison family who used to live here?" Logan asked.

He crossed his arms. "Yeah, I'm Joshua Garrison."

Jackpot! A nephew or cousin—someone at least who might be able to tell us where they buried Seth. Grinning, I held my hand out—not caring he had ignored Logan's.

With a long slow motion, he took my hand. "What's this all about?"

"I'm so sorry to just barge in on you. I'm Olivia, this is Logan. We've traveled quite a ways. We're looking for the gravesite of Seth Garrison. We couldn't find it with the other Garrison plots at the cemetery. Could you maybe tell us where we could find it?"

I rambled, rubbing my hands together. "He's a relative of mine."

Joshua's brow furrowed. Stepping off the grass, he climbed the steps to the front door of the house. What was he doing? Did he think I would lie about this? Opening the screen door, he looked back at us. "Must not be a very close relative. My grandfather isn't dead. You're looking for a grave that doesn't exist."

My heart raced at his words. Yet I knew he was wrong. He had to be wrong. "There…there…must be some type of misunderstanding. Maybe it's a different Seth Garrison."

"This is a small town, miss." He shook his head, pity filling his eyes at my distress. "If there were more than two, we'd know it. If you don't believe me, that's fine. Ask Grandpa." Joshua yelled inside for his grandfather.

My insides melted until they were just a numb tingling Jell-O. My feet wouldn't move. The shaking in my hands started up again as Logan pushed me forward.

"Grandpa, you have visitors," Joshua said. He must have decided to trust us, because he held the door open, inviting us inside.

Standing in the living room, we waited. Looking around the room, I stumbled back into Logan. Framed sketches hung on every wall. Seth's sketches. If I questioned before, I couldn't now. These were no doubt my grandfather's artwork.

With a slight limp, Joshua's grandpa rounded the corner and stood in the doorway. I thought of the photographs I stared at so many times in the last two months. His hair had turned gray, but it was still full. He was thicker around the middle and wrinkled in his face, but this man could have been my father twenty-five years from now. He rubbed his hands on the pant legs of his smudged jean overalls, smiling, he held out a hand.

"They say they're relatives," Joshua said.

Covering my mouth with my hand, I stared at Seth. Amelia's Seth. "I'm sorry," I whispered. Hurrying from the house, I ran out to the car. Climbing inside, I covered my face with my hands. And then I cried, like I never had in my entire life.

Opening my door, Logan folded me into his arms. "Olivia, baby, it's okay." Holding me, he kissed my head, my cheeks, my hands. "Liv, this is a miracle. You can know him, *really* know him."

Hiccupping, I tried to meet his face. "Their whole lives, Logan. They spent their whole lives separated. What happened? Why didn't he come for her? He's never even met his son—or me, or—"

"Let's find out. Let's fix that."

Sitting across from Seth at a family-size kitchen table, we made our introductions.

"So, you came from California?" Seth's bushy gray eyebrows scrunched together, confused. "And you say you're family?"

I nodded—seeing my father in his every expression. "I've been living in a small town in Wyoming though, Rendezvous." Logan winked at me, encouraging me to continue. "My grandmother left me her home there."

Offering us a weak smile, Seth said, "I'm sorry. I'm not sure what...and you're a relative?"

Swallowing, I found my failing voice. "Yes. A granddaughter, I believe. Yours..."

Staring at me, he looked bewildered. But even in his confusion, there was kindness. His eyes were soft and his expression tender. I could see the Amelia from my book sitting next to him—no grouchiness within her. Her wrinkles ones of love and joy.

"Yours and Amelia's," I said with the vision still in my mind.

His eyes widened at the sound of her name. His wrinkled hand shook as he brought it up to cover his mouth. Tears pooled in his eyes as he reached across the table to touch my face. His once strong voice now trembled. "The baby lived, then? My son didn't die with his mother?"

Taking Seth's hand in mine, I held it. It was wrinkled and shaking, but strong and large. I looked at Logan, but his brow furrowed, confused as I was. Clearing my throat, I turned back to Seth. "Yes, the baby lived, my dad. But Seth," I said, not wanting to say the words to him. But I had to. "Amelia died three months ago."

Shaking his head, he looked from me to Logan and back again.

"But her father—he showed me the death certificate."

"I'm so sorry," I said, squeezing his fingers. "It would seem as if her father was good at forgery. He tricked Amelia into believing you had died as well. He showed her a headline clipping with a picture and everything—saying you had been in an accident."

Standing, Seth held onto the row of chairs for support, retrieving a book—one of many on a shelf behind him. Flipping through it, he stopped and set the book in front of us. There it was, the newspaper clipping Amelia's father had shown her. The one she'd described. "This is not a forgery," Seth said. "I was in this accident trying to get to Amelia. It took me over a year to fully recover, but it was my cousin Arnie who died. The headline reads, *Garrison Dies in Fatal Crash.* If he didn't allow her to read the article, she would have thought it was me." Seth looked down, shaking his head. "Her father knew different though. He made certain to visit me in the hospital bed I was confined to. He told me about the baby and he told me they'd both died in childbirth. He had the papers to prove it."

"And then you remarried?" I knew it wasn't fair. He thought she'd died. He had grieved—oh, how he must have grieved.

"I did," he said without reservation. "Grace was my nurse after my accident. She took extraordinary care of me all those months in the hospital. I was a broken man. My body was mangled, but my heart and spirit in even worse shape after I heard what happened to my sweet Amelia. Grace became a good friend. A couple of years later, I realized I loved her. We married and raised five kids together. Gracie passed two years ago, next month. My heart was broken again, but Gracie wasn't here to fix it this time." Pulling out a white handkerchief, he wiped at his eyes and nose. "Thank goodness for all those grandkids. And now you, another granddaughter. And my son! My son. After all these years…What's his name, my son?"

Tears welled in my eyes. Doing my best to smile at him, I said, "Jonathon—"

"After my uncle. Oh, Amelia. She kept everything I gave her right in her heart. She's been my angel all these years."

He asked me a dozen questions and I did my best to answer

them all. Halfway through, I realized he thought my father knew of him all these years. And so, again, I was forced to explain Amelia's life—and how she came to be in Rendezvous. I was honest and forthright—if anyone deserved to know, it was Seth.

"Tell me she was happy." He cried, again wiping at his eyes with the hanky.

Stifling my own cries, I couldn't answer.

"She was happy," Logan said, his own eyes rimmed with red. "She was a blessing to our little community, and she was *happy*."

"She wrote you this." I held the envelope out to him.

"My sweet Amelia," he whispered, bringing the letter to his lips.

Evening came and we still sat talking. Seth gathered the picture albums Grace had made, and sitting with his arm around my shoulders, he pointed out each of my aunts and uncles. When the time came to go, Seth looked as reluctant for me to leave as I felt about leaving. It was so surreal.

Hugging me goodbye, he kissed my head. "I love you, dear girl."

Nodding and crying and holding him close—for myself and for Amelia, I answered him. "I love you too, Grandpa." And I did. I loved him before I met him. Amelia made sure of that.

Climbing into the car, I sat quiet. Peeking at me, Logan reached out for my hand. "Liv? Are you okay?"

"I don't know." I smiled for him. "I think so."

"I love you."

He loved me. The best person I'd ever met sat right next to me, and *he* loved me. Brushing a tear away, I looked at him.

Leaning closer to me over the emergency brake, he placed a hand on my cheek. "Come on, what are you thinking?"

Knowing what I wanted didn't make me crazy or impulsive. I had faith, and I wasn't going to let anyone stop me from living the life meant for me. Taking a deep breath, I kissed him—the most amazing person in the world. "I'm thinking we should get married."

Chapter 37

How did I obtain so many things in such a short time? I hadn't even packed everything. I was coming back after all. Still, my little Rendezvous front room looked like hoarders-ville. Boxes with lids open sat half filled. Piles of everyday items stacked in between the boxes. *Blah.* The joys of moving.

Resting her hands on her hips, Rachel asked, "Anything else you need me to do sweety-peety?"

"Aw, Rach, you've done enough. Besides, Logan will be over in an hour to help."

Walking to the door, her platinum curls bounced up and down. "Oh, I wanted to spend the time with you, anyway. I can't believe you'll be gone an entire year!"

"Yes, but only a year and then I'll have enough credits to do my student teaching—here!"

"I know. I know. It's just—I've gotten attached." She pinched my cheeks and stood on her toes to kiss my head. Laughing, she wiped the tears from her cheeks.

"Well, in two years when Jamie retires, I'll be first in line for his job—you'll have plenty of time to get sick of me." I hugged her goodbye.

Giggling, I watched her leave. But I couldn't stand around all day. I had a load of work to do and two days until Logan and I left for California again. I started classes in a week and a half and Logan his new job in just five days. Before school started, Dad and I planned a trip to Ganesworth. I couldn't wait for him to meet his dad and siblings. He'd read his mother's book, and just like me, his heart softened. It was still a shock, but Seth would win him over.

Taping up the full box in front of me, I reached for the next one, but stopped short at a knock on my door. Callie, Maria, Rachel…now who? All these visitors made it hard to get packed.

Three strangers stood in my doorway—no friends. I had never seen the two adults and small child in front of me before. "Can I help you?"

"Did Janie call you?" The woman glanced up to the man. "Janie didn't call her." Back to me. "You look confused."

"Ahh, I am. I'm sorry. Janie?" I peeked past them, searching for a *Janie*. The unfamiliar minivan in front of my house had Colorado plates.

"I told you this would be intrusive." The man looked at who I assumed to be his wife. She smiled at him, and her eyes seemed to plead. Turning to me, he said, "Well, we were told that at one point this house was on the market."

My mind spun… Janie, Janie Forester, that dreadful realtor. "It didn't stay on the market, because it was a misunderstanding. The house isn't for sale."

Peeking past me into the house, the woman said, "But you *are* moving."

My boxes were a giveaway. "Well, it's complicated. See—"

"Mama, my book." The small girl beside the woman tugged on her mother's jacket.

"Come here, Charlie." The girl's father picked her up. "We'll get your story in a minute."

The woman sighed and held a hand out to me. "We're the Sanders. I'm Audrey, this is my husband Ethan and our daughter Charlie. Ethan just got a job in the mines not far from here. We're having trouble finding a place to live though."

"Oh, um, welcome to Rendezvous. I'm Olivia."

"Would you mind if we looked around the place?" She glanced over my shoulder.

"Oh. Well…" I crossed my arms. "I don't know that it would help your situation. It's *not* for sale."

"There are two other places to rent in town." Ethan said to his wife.

"He's right, there are." Audrey looked me in the eye. "I'm just—I want the right place for Charlie. Could we just get an idea from your place?"

It's not for sale. How would looking about my place help this woman? "I suppose you could look." I mustered my best Rendezvous politeness—Rendezvousans helped each other, they didn't yell and slam doors.

"Daddy, my book." Charlie had been more patient than me—lucky for her, four-year-olds were allowed to be grumpy and demanding.

"I've got a book," I said, still in my home-town girl mode. "Would you like to look at it with me while we wait for your parents to look around?"

Pulling a book of fairy-tales from my bookshelf, I held it out to show her.

She looked skeptical. "Is there a princess?"

Nodding, I opened the cover to show her. Ethan set her back on the ground and she followed me to the couch. Setting the book on Charlie's lap, I opened to the first page. "We'll be okay," I told the Sanders.

"She has a prince," Charlie explained to me. "He lives in a castle and pretty soon he'll see her out in the woods." Charlie didn't wait for me to read, she told me the story, finishing as her parents came back down the stairs. "Mommy, Olivia's book is almost like mine." She held the book up for her mother.

Audrey nodded. "That's nice, honey." Biting her lip, she looked at me. "She loves her books."

"I can see that."

"Charlie, look at the book for another minute, okay?" Audrey said. "Olivia, if your For Sale sign were still up, we'd be making a deal about now."

"I'm sorry." I didn't know what else to say, I told them the house wasn't on the market.

"No—no, thanks for letting us look." Ethan pulled at Audrey's elbow. "Come, Charlie."

Charlie stood, but she came to me, rather than her dad. "You have a ring." She pointed to my diamond.

"I do." Squatting down, I met her, eye to eye. "I'm getting married."

"Like the princess in the book." Charlie looked back at the coffee table where she'd left my fairy-tale book. Bringing her pudgy little hands up to my face, she smiled. "You're like a princess."

A lump formed in my throat. Before I could stand, Charlie wrapped her arms around my neck.

"Charlie, come here, honey." Ethan held a hand out to her.

Smiling at me, she walked to her father, waving as he led them to the door.

My heart too big for my chest, I looked at little Charlie. I was no princess, just a girl who'd learned a lot over the course of a summer. "Ah, Audrey?" I stopped them. "Call Janie. We can work something out with the house."

Folding me into a hug, she thanked me and cried, and thanked me again.

Walking them outside, I waved goodbye to their Colorado plates driving into the distance. I couldn't believe what I had agreed to, and yet it felt right.

I still stood outside when Logan came over, boxes in hand. "Did you have company?"

"Sort of." I kissed him hello and followed him inside. "I sold Amelia's house."

"You what?" Dropping the empty boxes in his hand, he turned to stare at me.

"We won't need two homes."

Taking my hand, he said, "I guess not. Are you sure?"

"I am." I wrapped my arm about his waist. "It felt right."

"Ah—wow."

"Yeah, well I'm learning to have faith. Besides, I learned all I needed from Amelia. Knowing her, knowing Seth, that was her gift to me. Are you okay with it?"

"If you are, I am." He pulled me over to the couch. "Sit. I have something for you." Pushing me until my knees gave way,

I plopped down.

"You have given me quite enough." I held up my left hand, letting the light from the window catch my diamond.

He walked over to the stack he'd brought in. "Yeah, but this one I couldn't resist." He picked up a rectangular box from inside the large packing box. He set it in front of me.

I pulled the lid from its snug place. A brown leather bound book lay inside. "What is it?"I didn't see a title on the cover.

"You tell me. It's a journal. You know, for our children and grandchildren to read."

Gasping, I jumped up, wrapping my arms around him. As much as I loved to read others stories, it had never occurred to me to record my own. Luckily, I was marrying a brilliant man—who at times knew what I needed more than I did. Tangling my fingers into his hair, I dropped the book to the couch. Standing on tiptoes, I pulled him down to me, feeling the warmth of his breath on my skin before my lips connected to his. "Thank you, Logan."

Pulling away, he sighed. "I have more boxes to bring over. And we both have packing to do."

Nodding, I sent him on his way. But I didn't pack, not just yet.

August 24

I met Logan the summer Amelia died…

Jen Atkinson, An avid reader and writer, enjoys spending her time writing stories filled with meaning, hope, and love. Her days are busy with family, teaching special needs adults, and playing pretend with youth groups. She is the author of novels *LIKE HOME* and *KNOWING AMELIA*. Jen lives next to one of Wyoming's many mountains with her husband, Jeff, and four kids, Tim, Landon, Seth, and Sydney.

CPSIA information can be obtained
at www.ICGtesting.com
Printed in the USA
FSOW03n2135180516
20442FS